Checking

OUT

ALSO BY NICK SPALDING

Mad Love
Bricking It
Fat Chance
Blue Christmas Balls
Buzzing Easter Bunnies
Spalding's Scary Shorts

Love . . . Series

Love . . . From Both Sides
Love . . . And Sleepless Nights
Love . . . Under Different Skies
Love . . . Among the Stars

Life . . . Series

Life . . . On a High
Life . . . With No Breaks

Cornerstone Series

The Cornerstone
Wordsmith

NICK SPALDING

Checking OUT

LAKE UNION
PUBLISHING

Published by Lake Union Publishing, Seattle

www.apub.com

Amazon, the Amazon logo, and Lake Union Publishing are trademarks of Amazon.com, Inc., or its affiliates.

ISBN-13: 9781612185941
ISBN-10: 1612185940

Cover design by Lisa Horton

Printed in the United States of America

This is dedicated to everyone who lives an unpredictable life. I can't dedicate to anyone else, because they don't exist.

CONTENTS

LYRICS TO THE FOODIES SONG 'WE LOVE TO WAVE GOODBYE'

Libby the Happy Lemon sings:

It's time to go! It's time leave! It's time to say
goodbye!

Pip the Juicy Orange sings:

We're off to somewhere new, to give something
new a try!

Chewy the Cheeky Toffee sings:

We're happy and bright, we won't sleep tonight!

Smedley the Smelly Cheese sings:

And I've already packed my case!

Frank the Silly Sausage sings:

It's time to leave this all behind!

Herman the Grumpy Potato sings:

But I don't want to leave this place!

Libby, Chewy, Smedley, Pip and Frank all sing together:

Stop being so grumpy, Herman! Stop being so sad!
Leaving is a lovely thing! Going away isn't bad!
So hold out your arm, hold out your hand!
And wave along with the band!

All of The Foodies sing:

We love to wave goodbye! We love to wave
farewell!
We love to say we're going away! Because leaving
is so swell!
We love to wave goodbye! We love to say ta-ra!
We don't know where we're going to, because it
really is quite far!

CHARMED

17 MARCH

Oh my God, I don't think she's wearing any underwear.

I shield my eyes from the bright stage lights and take a second, longer look.

. . . nope.

She's *definitely* not wearing any underwear.

Sienna is sat six rows back from the stage, behind the small gathering of bored reporters and the show's producers, and she's just flashed me her bits and pieces.

Right as I'm about to start taking questions, my uninhibited girlfriend has given me a seductive wink and pulled her slinky red dress up over her thighs to reveal the fact that she's evidently forgotten to wear her knickers to this press conference.

What a *startling* revelation.

. . . now she's biting her bottom lip and her eyes have gone extremely *smoky*.

I'm completely *transfixed*.

I have no doubt that this was exactly the reaction she was after.

'Are you looking forward to getting down to it, Nathan?' a voice asks.

'Yeah, you fucking bet,' I reply in a hoarse whisper, not taking my eyes off Sienna.

'I beg your pardon?'

I look down at the skinny ginger reporter from *The Evening News* as if seeing him for the first time. 'I'm sorry . . . what did you say?'

The guy gives me a funny look. 'I said, are you looking forward to getting down to it?'

My eyes flick back to Sienna, who is now sucking her index finger. 'Getting down to what?' I say slowly, reluctantly returning my gaze to the five-foot-four junior reporter. I assume he's not actually enquiring about what I'm going to be getting up to later with the glamorous brunette sat a mere couple of metres behind him.

'The *shows*, Mr James,' he replies. 'The last tour of Foodies shows you're going to be doing?'

'Oh . . . oh yes! The tour! That's right. That's what I'm here to talk about, isn't it?' I look at Sienna again. It's a little hard to do anything else right now. The Queen could ride into the back of the theatre on a red, white and blue gryphon and I'd have trouble paying much attention.

Sienna is now sucking *two* fingers. It's the most erotic thing I think I've ever seen.

I knew I shouldn't have brought her along. She is always one hell of a distraction – in the nicest possible way, of course, but I really should be paying more attention to what's going on.

. . . *three* fingers. Three bloody fingers are in there now. I think I'd better wrap this press conference up soon, before she tries to stick her whole fist in her gob.

'So, are you looking forward to doing it?' the skinny reporter asks, exasperation clear in his voice.

When I still fail to offer a coherent response, he follows my eyeline over his shoulder to where Sienna is sitting. The second he turns to look at her, the fingers are out of her mouth and a demure expression instantly appears on her face.

'*Of course* Nathan is looking forward to the tour, *aren't you, Nathan?*'

I look to my left to see my tall, bespectacled manager, Taylor, standing up from his front-row seat in a hurry, giving me a look that screams *get your shit together.*

'Yes!' I blurt out. 'I'm very much looking forward to the tour! It should be a fantastic way for me to bow out from performing with these guys.' I stick a thumb over my shoulder at the gigantic Foodies poster pinned to the closed stage curtains behind me. A photographer standing next to the ginger reporter takes a couple of pictures as I do this. The bright flash of his camera instantly sparks off a headache.

'And you can't wait to see the brand-new stage set that Brightside Productions have designed . . . *can you, Nathan?*' Taylor adds, eyes bulging.

I stare at him for a moment, trying as hard as I can to remember the rest of the scripted responses he had me learn in preparation for this conference. 'No! I absolutely cannot *wait,*' I eventually say, faking enthusiasm for all I'm worth. 'Brightside are going to do a *fabulous* job with this Foodies tour, and . . .' I trail off. There was something else, but I can't quite remember . . .

Taylor silently mouths the word 'future' at me.

Ah yes, that was it. '. . . and I also can't wait to see what they've got in store for my characters in the future!'

My manager rolls his eyes and sits back down with a relieved grunt next to Richard and Mary Brightside, the people who have forked out an idiotic amount of cash to take my singing foodstuffs away from me.

An Asian guy who I don't recognise stands up next to Taylor. 'Hello, Mr James, I'm Sonny Duhal from *The Daily Torrent.* I know this deal to hand your creations over to Brightside Productions is going to be very lucrative, so I guess my question to you is . . . what are you going to do with all of that cash, now you're done with The Foodies?'

Ah yes. *The cash.* The great big pile of wonga I should be receiving a short time after I gallop off into the sunset. What exactly am I going to do with it?

I shrug. 'Go on holiday somewhere? Maybe get a swimming pool?' I shrug again. 'To be honest, I've not really given it much thought.'

Or maybe buy Sienna some new underwear? my brain adds silently to itself. *Possibly of the crotchless variety?*

I very deliberately don't look at my girlfriend. If I do, I'm likely to lose my train of thought again, and Taylor will be very angry with me.

Sonny Duhal seems relatively satisfied with that answer. 'Secondly, Mr James . . . will you *miss* The Foodies?' he adds.

I blink a couple of times. What an odd question to ask. 'What do you mean?'

Duhal points at the enormous poster behind me. 'Will you miss them? Not being around them any more? Not working on the albums or the shows?'

I look back at the poster again. On it, all six Foodies are posed in a variety of outlandish ways around the cartoon kitchen they inhabit. All of them look resolutely *stupid.* They also look like second-rate versions of the Teletubbies – because that's exactly what they *are.*

In a masterpiece of poor Photoshopping, I am also represented on the poster by way of a large floating head stuck rather haphazardly in the top left-hand corner. From my facial expression I appear to have lost control of at least ninety per cent of my mental faculties.

Front and centre on the poster, though, are the two most popular characters – Libby the Happy Lemon and Herman the Grumpy Potato. Their fixed expressions only get more disturbing the longer you look at them.

I'm about as sentimental towards them as Sienna is about her missing underwear.

I honestly couldn't give two shits.

I look back at the reporter. I figure I'd better lie and say something positive. 'Yeah. I invented them, didn't I? I'll miss them . . . I guess.' How *convincing*.

Sonny Duhal narrows his eyes slightly, but writes down what I've just said in his notebook anyway and sits himself back down again.

Katie from the *Daily Mail* then stands up to ask me a question. Katie has been a big advocate for The Foodies ever since they first started getting popular, so it's nice to have her here to cover the big handover and tour announcement.

'Hi, Nathan,' she says. 'My only real question for you is this: you're only thirty-three . . . what are you going to do with yourself now? Once you've done the final tour?' She grins. 'Other than go on holiday, that is. The Foodies have been your life for the past half a decade . . . what's going to fill it up now you're not going to be working on them any more?'

Wow.

Now that's a question.

One I also have no good answer to.

I scratch my head. 'I guess I'm not sure at the moment . . . I'll probably try to write some new music. For adults this time.' This puts a smile on Katie's face. Taylor's, too, for different reasons. 'I might try to get a band together, maybe do some . . . do some . . . er . . .'

Sienna is licking her lips and running her finger between her breasts.

I have no idea what the long-term future holds, but I sure as hell know what I'm going to be doing in the very short-term.

Possibly twice if I can get my breath back fast enough.

'What Nathan means to say,' Taylor remarks, getting quickly out of his seat again, 'is that he has many new projects simmering on the back burner, and we'll be sure to let you know more once he's progressed them.'

I nod dumbly. That sounds pretty good to me.

Taylor claps his hands. 'Well, folks, thank you for coming. I think that about wraps things up for today. You have all the information you need about Brightside's plans for The Foodies in the press release I gave you. And please don't forget to mention the dates of Nathan's farewell Foodies tour in your articles.' He gives them all a meaningful look. 'It's seven nights, ending the fourteenth of May right here at the Roundabout Theatre! Put that in your stories, please . . . and in your diaries if you have kids!'

Taylor really is good at all this shit, isn't he? I'm glad I hired him.

I'm also glad he's brought this press conference to an end – for two important reasons. One, the headache that the photographer's flash set off is getting worse, and two, Sienna still isn't wearing any knickers under that red Prada dress I bought her last month.

I climb down off the stage as Taylor sees the half-dozen reporters out of the theatre, chatting with a couple of them as they go. I give Katie from the *Daily Mail* a little wave and a smile. Always good to keep the tabloids onside.

Richard and Mary Brightside approach me with broad smiles on their faces. 'Thank you, Nathan,' Richard says, shaking my hand. 'We really are grateful you're putting so much into this tour.'

'Especially when you could have easily said no,' Mary adds. 'It makes the handover that much easier for the public.'

'No worries!' I tell them. I can afford to be generous with my time, because they've been very generous with their pocketbook.

'We'll be off, then,' Richard says. 'See you in a few weeks.'

'You will indeed!' I shake both their hands again and watch them disappear up the aisle.

As they leave, Sienna rises from her seat and slinks her way down to where I'm standing.

'Nicely done, handsome,' she tells me. 'I think you made them all very happy.'

I smirk at her. 'No thanks to you, miss.' I flick my eyes downwards. 'Forgot something when you got dressed, did you?'

Sienna's eyes go smoky again. 'I didn't forget anything, Nathan. It was *totally* deliberate.' She runs a hand down my arm. 'Now, why don't you take me home and make *me* very happy?'

If my life were a cartoon, steam would now be shooting out of my ears.

'For crying out loud, Sienna!' Taylor exclaims as he walks back down the theatre aisle towards us. 'He nearly fell off the stage!'

'I did not,' I protest.

'Yes, you did!' he says to me. 'And I'm not surprised, with all the blood rushing from your head to your crotch!'

My eyes go wide and I point at Sienna. 'Did you . . . did you see what she was doing?'

Sienna chuckles and places her hands daintily on Taylor's shoulder. 'Taylor knows I can be a bad girl, don't you?'

My manager rolls his eyes. 'I should never have introduced you two at the bloody bar. You've been nothing but trouble together ever since.'

She gives him a swift kiss on the cheek. 'Please. We're your two favourite clients, and we're the *perfect* couple. Young, hot, exciting' – she gives me a smouldering look – 'sexually compatible.'

I think the temperature in here just went up ten degrees.

Life with Sienna has indeed been exciting ever since Taylor introduced us at the Elysium Bar a couple of months ago – so much so that I'm surprised I haven't suffered a heart attack.

Taylor's expression reminds me that there are more important things in life than my libido. I tug an earlobe. 'It went all right in the end, didn't it? I said everything I had to, didn't I?' I ask him.

He folds his arms. 'Yeah. Just about. You gave them enough to go away and write a nice puff piece about the handover and the tour anyway' – he looks at Sienna – 'despite this one's best efforts.'

Sienna pokes her tongue out.

I look at my watch. 'Well, I think it's time we headed off,' I say, trying to keep the excitement out of my voice. 'Things to do, you know.'

Taylor shakes his head. 'All right, all right. Give me a call in a few days. We can discuss the tour a little more then.'

I give him an exasperated look. 'I've done hundreds of shows, Taylor. We don't need to chat about it.'

He winces. 'Just humour me. Brightside are throwing a lot of money into this, and I want to make sure it goes well.'

Sienna gives me a meaningful look. 'Enough talk, boys. I want to go . . . and I want to go *now*.'

Who am I to argue with a lady?

We both bid Taylor farewell and hurry arm in arm up the aisle towards the theatre exit, the car park outside and my super king-sized bed some twenty miles away . . .

'Er, Sienna! I'm not sure that's such a good idea!' I exclaim as the zipper on my jeans is slowly tugged downwards.

'Why not?'

'Because we're doing eighty in the fast lane?'

'Shh. You just concentrate on the road,' she replies as her hand snakes inwards.

'Oh boy.'

As my girlfriend goes prospecting for treasure in my boxer shorts and I feverishly try to concentrate on keeping my Porsche 911 between the white lines, my mobile phone starts to ring. I roll my eyes. I do not need yet another distraction right now.

I glance at the car display and see that it's my cousin Eliza calling. My heart plummets. 'Oh no,' I say quietly to myself.

Sienna looks horrified. 'That's not the response I was after, mister,' she says with a pout.

'No, no! It's not you!' I reply. 'I promised I'd go around to see Eliza and Callum after the press conference! I'd completely forgotten' – I briefly look down at my unzipped fly – 'in all the excitement.'

I hit the button on the steering wheel that answers the phone remotely. 'Hi, Eliza!' I say in a cheery voice.

'Afternoon, Nate,' she replies. 'How did it go, then?'

'Oh . . . you know . . . fine. All went fine. Absolutely *fine*!' Sienna's hand has made its way back into my jeans.

'Good for you. Are you still coming over? Callum's got his toy Foodies all lined up waiting for you.'

Oh shit.

'Um . . . look, I'm really sorry, Elsie,' I say, using the nickname I gave her when I was three and couldn't say her real name properly, 'but I've got a really bad headache and just need to go lie down in bed this afternoon.'

This is actually quite close to the truth. I *do* have a headache and I *am* going to lie down in bed this afternoon. I just won't be alone.

I hear a disappointed sigh at the other end of the line. It's not the first time I've heard it. 'Okay, Nate. I'll tell Callum you're not coming . . . again.'

Oof.

That smarts.

'Look, I promise I'll be over in the next few days to see you both!' I tell her in as conciliatory a tone as I can manage while cruising down the motorway with another person's hand in my pants.

'Yeah, yeah. Okay, Nathan,' Eliza replies in a flat voice. 'You do that.' I hear another sigh – followed by loud banging in the background. 'Look, I'm going to have to go. I can hear Callum slamming the oven door again. Hope your headache gets better.'

'Okay, Elsie, thanks. I'll speak to you soon.' The line goes dead before I finish. Looks like I will have some apologising to do next time

I see them both. I'll buy her a nice big, expensive bunch of flowers, and Callum a new toy or T-shirt. That should do it.

Satisfied that I can take care of that problem quite easily, I return to what's going on in my crotch.

. . . only good things. Only good things are going on in my crotch.

Then the phone rings again.

'Oh, good grief,' I say under my breath. Sienna is blocking the car's display so I can't see who's calling. I hope it isn't Eliza ringing me back to have a proper go for not coming around today. I *said* I'd make it up to her, what more does she want?

'Hello?' I say in a slightly offhand manner, answering the call.

'Nathan? Are you all right?' my mother says, worry in her voice as she immediately picks up on my irritated tone.

'Oh! Hi, Mum! Yes, yes! I'm fine, thanks!' I babble, mentally switching gears.

I'm also receiving a mild handjob while on the phone to my mother. This is not a state of affairs I am comfortable with in the *slightest*.

'How are you?' I ask Mum, slapping Sienna's hand away as I do so. This earns me another pout.

'I'm okay, son. How did your press thingy go?'

'*Quickly*, I'm pleased to say,' I reply. 'Good to get it over and done with.'

'I'm sure it was. Richard and Mary seem like nice people. I'm sure The Foodies are in good hands.'

'Yeah, I suppose they are,' I reply blandly. Frankly, once the cheque clears, I couldn't care less if they were going to baste The Foodies in hot sauce and set them on fire.

'Will I be seeing you sometime soon, son?'

'Yeah, yeah, of course! I know it's been a couple of weeks since I was around last, so I'll be over soon.'

'It's been *two months*, Nathan.'

'Bloody hell, *has it*?'

'Yes.'

I squirm in my car seat. 'Sorry, Mum. I've been very busy, and—'

'It's okay,' she interrupts. 'You just come around when you have the time.'

Oh God.

Looks like I'll be buying *two* big, expensive bunches of flowers in the next few days.

My breath is then neatly taken away by Sienna as she starts to nibble on my earlobe.

'Hmngngnm,' I mumble in response.

'What?' Mum says. 'Are you okay, Nathan?'

'Yeah! I'm great, Mum! Look . . . I have to go now, but thanks for calling. I promise I'll be around in the next few days!'

'All right, son. I hope to see you soon.' Mum sounds a little disappointed. I barely notice, what with all the earlobe nibbling that's going on.

'Okay! Great! Love you! Bye!' I blurt out, and immediately hang the phone up before my mother has a chance to answer.

Sienna takes the opportunity to quickly kiss me on the lips, before returning her attentions to my overexcited crotch.

As she starts prospecting once more, I let out a loud and happy laugh.

Could things be going much better for me right now?

I've just dumped The Foodies off on to a couple of schmucks for a very tidy profit, I have a beautiful woman's hand down my pants, I'm going eighty miles an hour towards a golden sunset in the best car on the planet and I feel free and happy for what seems like the first time in *years*.

With a self-satisfied grin that extends from horizon to horizon, I press hard on the Porsche's accelerator, eager to get home as quickly as I can so Sienna can explore my nether regions in more exquisitely pleasant detail.

A short time later, you find me naked and legs thoroughly akimbo.

Sienna is doing something to my John Thomas that makes me wonder if she can breathe through her ears.

All in all, this is turning into a *splendid* evening.

'Okay, baby,' Sienna eventually gasps in a breathy voice, moving back up my body again. 'That's enough fun for you – it's my turn for a while . . .' She gives me a playful bite on the bottom lip and arches her eyebrow speculatively, then rolls off me on to the bed.

I can't breathe through my ears, sadly, but I'm going to do the best job I can anyway.

As I lean over and start to slide my way down the bed, Sienna grabs my hair, stopping my progress briefly. 'Talk dirty to me,' she orders. '*Talk* dirty before you *get* dirty.'

I try to resist a groan. This isn't the first time she's wanted me to do this.

I find the whole thing exquisitely *embarrassing*.

I can write lyrics for children's songs about singing potatoes until the cows come home, but trying to come up with any kind of sexy talk in the bedroom that doesn't sound cheesy as all hell and back is virtually impossible for me. The last time I tried it, I told Sienna I wanted to pump her bottom.

What does that even *mean*?

Quite how I intended to do this, or what implements I was going to use to accomplish it, is entirely beyond me.

I have no idea why she wants me to have another go, but I guess I'd better give it the best of British, as she's just spent the last fifteen minutes treating my penis like royalty.

'Er . . . I want you so bad,' I say uncertainly.

Sienna's eyes light up. 'How bad, baby?'

'Oh . . . really, *really* bad. Like . . . *super* bad. I'm so hot for you right now, I can feel my balls throbbing.'

This sounds like the kind of thing I should be telling my doctor about rather than my girlfriend. Throbbing balls are not something you should ignore.

'What are you going to fucking do to me?' Sienna gasps, displaying far more aptitude for this talking dirty lark than I ever could.

'Er . . . I'm going to . . . I'm going to . . .'

Don't say pump her bottom.

'I'm going to kiss your tits!'

Okay, not great, but not too awful, either.

Sienna seems to approve as her eyes go wider. 'And what else, Nathan? What else are you going to do?'

I think for a second. 'I'm going to pound your arse!'

Yes! That's much better than the pumping of the bottom. I'm definitely warming up to this now.

Sienna moans and then tightens her grip on my hair. 'And what about my *pussy*, Nathan? What are you going to do to that?'

Good God.

But what the hell *am I* going to do with it? I can't pound it. I've used that one. Don't want to get repetitious, it's not sexy. Pumping sounds awful, and kissing sounds a little too twee.

I cast my mind back to every porno I've ever watched, and what I think is the right dirty thing to say pops into my head.

'I . . . I want to eat it!' I announce triumphantly.

Sienna writhes. 'Oh yes!' she exclaims.

'I want to eat . . . to eat your potato!' Yeah. That should really get her going!

My girlfriend gives me a rather perplexed look.

Oh no. Maybe that was the wrong thing to say? Have I gone too far here? Have I screwed it up?

I instantly feel incredibly embarrassed.

'What did you say?' Sienna asks, letting go of my hair.

'Shit. Was that not right? Wasn't that what you wanted to hear?' I sit back on my knees. 'I mean, I thought you'd like the idea of me eating your potato . . . that you'd find it sexy. Did you just want me to kiss it or something?'

Sienna sits up against the headboard, that perplexed look still on her face. 'Why do you want to eat a potato?' she asks. 'Are you hungry? I don't even *have* a potato, Nathan.'

'What? What are you talking about?'

'You just told me you want to *eat my potato*.'

'What? No, I didn't!'

'Yes, you did!'

'No, I didn't! I said I wanted to eat your potato!'

Sienna nods her head up and down hard. 'Yeah! Yeah! There you go. You said it again!' She points a wobbly finger at me. 'You think I have a potato, and you want to eat it!'

Oh dear.

I fear my girlfriend has had some kind of traumatic mental breakdown.

'I didn't say anything about potatoes, Sienna,' I explain to her very slowly. 'I was talking about eating your potato. I thought you'd think it was sexy.'

'Why would I find potatoes *sexy*?' she replies in a horrified tone of voice.

I throw my hands up. 'What are you talking about?! I don't care about potatoes! I just want to eat your potato!' I cry, pointing at her vagina.

She looks down between her legs. 'Why are you calling my fanny a *potato*?' she says with some distress. 'What's wrong with it?' She looks down, examining herself. 'Does it look like a potato?? Oh God!'

'I'm not saying "potato"!' I scream. This is becoming *very* disturbing. I point at her vagina once more. 'That's your potato! Your bloody p – p – p – potato!'

I'm so mad now, I'm stuttering.

Sienna's eyes go wide. 'Are you trying to say "pussy", Nathan?'

'Oh, *good God*! That *is* what I'm saying!' I point at the subject of our heated discussion one more time. 'That's your potato! Not a potato! Your potato! Potato! Potato!'

She shakes her head. 'No . . . you keep saying "potato" when you mean "pussy"!'

'No, I don't!'

'Yes, you do!' Sienna leans forward. 'Are you feeling okay?'

I rub my hands over my face in despair. 'Yes! I feel bloody fine! Why wouldn't I?'

As I bring my hands away, though, I notice a distinct and obvious tremor in the left one. I make a fist a couple of times, but that doesn't make it go away.

Then a blinding, massive and instant bolt of agony strikes from deep down inside my brain. 'Jesus!' I scream, my hands flying to my head.

Sienna reaches out to me, fear etched across her face. 'Nathan! Nathan! Are you okay?!'

I try to focus on her, but my eyesight has gone extremely blurry all of a sudden. Blackness starts to intrude around the edges of my watery vision, and a feeling of extreme light-headedness overcomes me.

'P – p – *pussy*!' I stutter at Sienna's blurred face. 'I want to eat your—'

And with that, I am plunged into darkness as my consciousness is switched off like a light bulb.

CEREBRODONDREGLIOMA

'It's called a cerebrodondreglioma.'
   'I'm sorry, it's called a what?'
   'A cerebrodondreglioma.'
   'A serrybobondeglioma?'
   'No. A cerebrodondreglioma.'
   'A serrydobonblogleglioma?'
   'No. Repeat after me, Mr James . . . a *cerebrodondreglioma*.'
   'A serrobebrodendoglioma?'
   'CEREBRODONDREGLIOMA.'
   'Serrebolbo . . . serrodogbonelio . . . serbolobonob . . . serrybellynoblio – *oh, for crying out loud*, I'll just call it a brain tumour, how's that?'
   'If you'd prefer.'
   My neurosurgeon, Mr Chakraborty, sits back in his plush leather seat and looks down his vastly expensive spectacles at me.
   'So, that's what caused the blackout?' I say to him. 'And the whole thing about the potato?'

He gives me a solemn nod. 'Blackouts of that nature and confusion in the speech centre are both symptoms of a tumour in the position yours occupies in your brain, Mr James, yes.'

I let out a long, deep breath. 'And you can't just get in there and *whip it out?*' I ask, already knowing the answer from the grave expression on his face.

'I'm afraid not. As you can no doubt see from your scans, the tumour is placed in a *very* difficult location, deep between the temporal and frontal lobes, and is therefore impossible to access with surgery. If we were to try, the odds are zero that you would survive.'

I look down at the various bits of paper and the MRI scans that Mr Chakraborty provided me with at the start of this happy discussion. They all look completely incomprehensible. I'm just going to have to take his word for it.

'So there's nothing you can do,' I remark, trying to keep the wobble out of my voice.

'I'm afraid not, Mr James. I'm very sorry, but this is an extremely rare tumour, one that's unfortunately inoperable.'

'But it's not . . . you know . . . the "*C*" word?'

'No. The tumour is benign.'

'I thought "benign" meant it wasn't bad?'

Chakraborty attempts a smile. He's not particularly good at it. 'In most cases it does, Mr James. As I say, unfortunately the position of your tumour means that we cannot remove it. Therefore, it will continue to grow. Very, very slowly . . . but growth *is* inevitable. It's already large enough to be affecting some of your brain and motor functions, and even a very small increase in its size will have a major effect on your brain's ability to function.'

'Meaning?'

Chakraborty's voice lowers an octave. 'Meaning that, at some stage, the tumour will cease to allow brain function on any meaningful level to continue.'

I open my mouth to respond to this, but my brain – still functioning for the moment, just about – sensing that there is no way to improve the contents of this conversation, decides that discretion is the better part of valour and freezes my vocal cords shut.

'As I say, it's a very rare and difficult type of tumour,' Chakraborty continues. 'In fact, it's a variant I've only read about in journals until now. I've never seen a case of Stryzelczyk's Syndrome before in my career.'

'I'm sorry, *what?*'

'Stryzelczyk's Syndrome. It's named after the Polish neurosurgeon who first wrote a paper on it about twenty years ago. He was a sufferer himself. I met him in Brussels at a conference shortly before his death. He was a physical and intellectual powerhouse before it. Such a tragedy to our profession.'

'Strizelik's Syndrome.'

'*Stryzelczyk's* Syndrome.'

'Strikelikik's Syndrome.'

'*STRYZELCZYK'S* Syndrome.'

'Stryclickyzik's Syndrome.'

Chakraborty looks down his glasses at me. 'Close enough, Mr James.'

I put my head in my hands. 'What about radiation?' I ask. I've seen enough movies, TV shows and features on *Sky News* to know that radiation therapy is the treatment of choice for this kind of thing.

. . . I'm fairly sure it's also what created Spider-Man, but I choose not to say this for what should be blindingly obvious reasons.

'Radiation therapy is something that could be explored,' Chakraborty hazards, 'but as I said, this type of tumour is extremely hard to treat given its location. It would probably prove to be ineffective.'

He says this like we're discussing a new toenail fungus cream that's just come out and had mixed reviews on Amazon.

It also sounds like he's paying lip service to try and make me feel better about the whole thing.

He's failing.

'And chemotherapy?' I enquire. 'What about that?'

Chakraborty's frown tells me all I need to know about that option. 'There's no evidence to suggest that chemotherapy has any effect on the kind of tumour you have. I fear it would not improve the situation even if it were an option, and may even worsen your health considerably – the side effects can be extensive. The blood–brain barrier prevents effective treatment at the depth we're talking about. As I say, it's a very difficult—'

'—tumour to reach. Yeah, I get it.' I pick up the glass of water that Mr Chakraborty's assistant provided me with at the start of this life-changing conversation. I manage to just about get it to my lips without spilling too much of it.

The next thing I say is the worst thing to come out of my mouth since that time when I was four and I tried to eat three slugs in quick succession off the patio table. I can't remember how bad they tasted going in because the taste of them coming back out was so horrific.

'How long have I got?' I ask the unflappable Mr Chakraborty.

He pauses for a second.

I wonder how many times he's had to answer this question. More than once, I'll wager. It can't be easy for him. I'd like to feel sympathy for the difficult position he finds himself in – however, I am far too full of my own fears and confusion for any of that business. All Chakraborty is to me is a complete bastard who's probably about to tell me I have three months to live.

'It's difficult to determine exact time frames, Mr James. The tumour's growth is very hard to predict. It only requires a small increase in mass to become immediately life-threatening, but it may not grow at all for some time.'

'But if I had to push you for a timescale?' I shouldn't be asking such a pessimistic question, but I am – if nothing else – the kind of person who doesn't like to stick his head in the sand.

Chakraborty looks discomfited at being pressed this way. 'There really is no way of knowing, Mr James. It could be six months away' – he pauses, swallows and continues – 'or six minutes.'

Jesus Christ. Jesus Christ on a rusty bike.

'But you say that the tumour might not grow at all?' I ask, clutching at what are probably some very thin and unattractive straws.

Chakraborty squirms. 'It is a possibility. But I'd say a very *small* possibility. Stryzelczyk's research concluded that the chances of surviving a cerebrodondreglioma in such a position and of such a size were—'

I hold up a hand. 'Please don't tell me the odds.' I may not like to bury my head in the sand, but it doesn't mean I want to leave the beach entirely.

I take another gulp of water, this time draining the glass. My mouth remains resolutely dry. I then sit back in the uncomfortable office chair and look into the middle distance. 'I'm going to drop dead . . . and I'm going to drop dead from something completely unpronounceable.' I rub a shaking hand over my face. 'How the hell am I going to explain this to my friends and family?'

'We do have counsellors who can help you with that,' Chakraborty says in a soothing voice.

I shake my head. 'No, I don't mean that. I mean how the hell am I going to *explain it to them* when I can't even say it myself? I won't get halfway through breaking the news without covering them in a thin film of spittle.'

Chakraborty smiles in the self-satisfied way of someone who hasn't just learned they have an inoperable, life-threatening tumour in their cranium. 'I'd be happy to write everything up for you in an email, Mr James. That may help them to understand.'

Oh, *lovely.*

What an extraordinarily twenty-first-century way that would be to break the news of my impending death: a forwarded email. Perhaps we should go the whole hog and he can summarise it all in a tweet, or maybe a nicely composed photo for Instagram, featuring me sobbing in the corner. Is there a Snapchat filter for '*I've just been given a death sentence, please come to my funeral*'?

Chakraborty stands up and walks around the desk. 'We will of course provide you with as much care and support as we are able to, Mr James. My assistant will be able to give you all the details of the next steps we can take.'

Aaaah . . .

Chakraborty obviously feels that his work here is done and that he'd very much like it if I and my tumour could vacate his office as swiftly as possible so he can get back to planning his next golfing holiday.

I, too, rise from my seat on unsteady legs. I then do something so unbearably *British* that I instantly hate myself. I hold out my hand.

'Thank you, Mr Chakraborty,' I tell him as he shakes it.

Yes. That's right.

I've just politely said thank you to the man who's told me I could die any second.

And look how I'm continuing to warmly shake his hand like we've just concluded a satisfying and profitable business deal, not a terminal diagnosis.

Before I came into his office today I was happy, healthy and about to embark on a new lifestyle of loafing about with a wad of cash in my back pocket – but now, thanks to this man, I have been transformed into a walking corpse who might as well not have that wad of cash because I'll be dead before I get the chance to spend it.

I let go and turn to the door. As I do, I am gripped by a sudden wave of overwhelming fear and cannot move. I feel my breath shorten as I watch Chakraborty open his office door to let me out.

Don't go out of the door, you idiot. Stay here. Everything will be all right if you just STAY HERE.

It's completely irrational, but for that briefest of moments, it also feels like the solution to my problems. If I don't walk back out into the world, then I'll be okay. If I just stay here in this cool, calm office, then I will live forever.

I can help Chakraborty plan his golfing holiday.

I can make myself a nice bed out of the couch over there in the corner.

First thing in the morning, I can greet him with a cup of tea. I will become Chakraborty's helpful mascot, ready and willing to offer support and sympathy for all those other poor buggers who have inoperable brain tumours.

Reality then reasserts itself.

I have an inoperable brain tumour that will keep getting bigger until it switches my lights off.

'Mr James? Are you okay?' Chakraborty asks from by the open door.

I take a large gulp of air. 'Yes, yes, I'm fine, thank you,' I lie heroically.

With some effort, I manage to get my legs moving and push myself towards the open doorway.

'Please sit down with Claire for a few moments. She will take you through the procedure from now on.' Chakraborty indicates to where his assistant is sat behind her small reception desk. She looks up at me with the practised smile of someone who knows how to handle the recently pre-deceased. 'I'm sure we'll see each other soon, Mr James,' Chakraborty concludes.

He doesn't wish me well, or hope that I have a good day. That would just be bloody silly, wouldn't it?

I thank him again for his time and make my way over to where Claire has prepared a whole series of leaflets for me with titles like 'Dealing with Terminal Illness', 'Coping Mechanisms' and 'So You've Recently Been Shafted by the Universe. Try Not to Let It Get You Down'.

One particularly edifying pamphlet is from something called the Heavenly Outlook Evangelical Church, which promises succour to those in need thanks to God's holy love. I don't think I'm a big enough succour to fall for that one at the moment.

I spend the next five minutes trying my hardest to pay attention to what Claire is telling me – without much success. All I want to do is leave this expensive office and drive home as fast as my overpriced sports car will take me.

'So, we'll schedule your next appointment with Mr Chakraborty in four weeks, okay, Nathan?' Claire says to me, tapping away at her computer.

'Yeah. Fine,' I reply, wondering why we're even bothering. What's he going to do? Invent some new piece of amazing technology in the next twenty-eight days that can cure me of my tumour in one fell swoop?

With worthless follow-up appointment made and useless pamphlets grasped in one dry hand, I depart the hospital with the foot-dragging weariness of one who has just received extremely bad news.

Outside, the sun has the sheer bloody audacity to have come out from behind the thick April clouds and is bathing the hospital car park in a warm spring glow that I would have absolutely loved about an hour ago, but now loathe with a passion. If ever I needed proof that the universe simply does not care about the travails of Nathan Michael James, it's this simple change in the weather.

Screw you, Nathan! Mr Sun seems to say. *You might be one tiny growth spurt away from an early grave, but I still have to keep this world going, don't I? Those plants aren't going to photosynthesise themselves! They'll all be here after you're long gone, by the way!*

Tears form at the corners of my eyes as I drag my feet back to where my car is parked. I wipe them away as I climb into the driver's seat and stare out of the windscreen at the VW camper van parked in front of me.

I've never been in a VW camper van before . . . and now there's every chance I'll never get the opportunity to do so.

I'm thirty-three years old and have only just *started* living. Until today I had a long and happy life stretching out before me, but now I may never get the chance to do fun things like go for a drive in a VW camper van.

I spend the next few minutes sat there in the car park staring out of the windscreen at the camper van until a skinny bloke with wild, straggly hair climbs into it and drives the thing away, the engine backfiring as it goes. This snaps me out of my horrified reverie.

I get the Porsche started and manage to drive out of the car park and on to the road without much fuss.

. . . which immediately leads me to my next problem.

What the hell do I do now?

What are you supposed to do when you've just been told that you have the sword of Damocles dangling over you and that your life is now quite literally hanging in the balance?

People from other cultures may have ways of dealing with such a trauma that I am not aware of. Some may take themselves off to the nearest church to pray, some may surround themselves with loved ones, some may climb the nearest mountain looking for insight. I am British, however, so I do the only thing I possibly can at a moment such as this.

I go home and put the kettle on.

The tea should probably be tasteless, but it isn't, because it's *bloody tea*, and tea makes everything better. At least for a few moments. The tumour can make me think pussies are potatoes all it likes as long as it doesn't take away my appreciation for a good cup of tea any time soon.

I sit at my kitchen table and look out past my open-plan lounge-diner and on to my exquisitely manicured back garden, which lies beyond the set of extremely expensive bifold patio doors I had installed a month ago.

Well, they were a waste of money, I think as I take another gratifying sip.

The garden – which is looking particularly marvellous right now, as the gardener came in last week – is bathed in that same irritating spring sunshine. I watch as a couple of tiny birds flit from the bird feeder to the garden fence with the precision and grace of two creatures utterly at home in the air. What a marvel of evolution they are – to be so perfectly designed as to make the process of moving between fence and bird feeder so completely effortless.

I sit up with a start. What the *hell* am I thinking? When did I start channelling David Attenborough? I've never given two shits about the birds in my garden before – beyond filling up the bird feeder occasionally because Michaela Strachan told me to do it on *Springwatch*, and nobody wants to let Michaela Strachan down, do they?

Here I am now, though, gazing out at the beauty and grace of two little brown, feathery idiots getting their fill of sunflower seed like it's the Second Coming.

Is this what I'm destined to be like now I know that my life could end at any minute? Will I spend all of my time reflecting on the world around me in purple prose, while I sip English breakfast tea at my overpriced oak kitchen table?

Will every sunset be a revelation? Every raindrop a prism through which I see the glory of the universe laid bare?

Will I try to marvel at the beauty around me as much as I possibly can before the cold spectre of Death comes to claim me as his own?

Bloody hell.

I need a proper fucking *drink*.

***

I tell you who doesn't care about my tumour – Kyleee the checkout girl in Tesco Express. Kyleee only cares for two things: the amount of letter 'E's at the end of her name and getting rid of customers as quickly as possible so she can bunk off for a smoke around the back of the shop.

I could stand here and tell Kyleee about my diagnosis. We have swapped small talk about the weather before, so the ice is already broken. There's not really that much of a leap from discussing how much it's going to drizzle today to talking about the painful inevitability of death.

I fear, however, that any woman brave enough to spell her name with no fewer than three 'E's at the end probably has no fear of the undiscovered country. Add the fact that she chain-smokes at a level unseen since the boardrooms of the 1960s and I'm pretty sure she wouldn't have much sympathy for my predicament. This is a person scared of nothing.

'Twenty-eight quid,' she says in a bored monotone as she sticks the bottle of Jack Daniel's in a carrier bag for me.

I pull out my credit card and hover it over the pay terminal, waiting for it to let me purchase my booze through the miracle of the contactless transaction.

A dark thought springs into my head as I do this.

How many more times will I get to pay for something with my contactless credit card before I die? A thousand? A hundred? *Ten*?

Will I drop dead while *using* my contactless credit card? Will it be Kyleee who witnesses my demise through her several layers of Tesco-brand make-up? Will she ring for an ambulance in the same dull monotone she employs when interacting with her customers?

'You gonna pay or what?' Kyleee says in a flat voice. 'You've gorra wave it a bit closer.'

I shake myself out of my reverie, realising that I'm standing over the contactless payment machine in silence while the queue builds up behind me and Kyleee becomes ever more impatient for her next cigarette.

I pay for the Jack Daniel's, pick the bag up from the counter and turn to leave. Then, a horrible compulsion seizes hold of me and I turn back to face Kyleee.

'Are you happy?' I ask her, for reasons that are quite beyond me.

'You what?' she replies, brow creasing and nostrils flaring.

'Are you happy, Kyleee? Are you fulfilled?'

It's very important to me to know if Kyleee is happy with her life or not.

I'm not sure whether this is a step up from worrying about how many more times I'm going to use my contactless payment card, or a step down.

'What do you mean *"fulfilled"*?' she asks, brow creasing further. Then her eyes go wide. 'Is that dirty? You wanna fill me with summink?!'

'No! No! I just mean . . . I just wanted to know . . . Do you like your life?'

Now she looks angry. 'You a perv, mate?'

'No! I just genuinely want to know if you're a happy person.'

'She doesn't look fucking happy to me,' the bloke behind me in the queue points out. 'Are you going to be long? I'm starving, and this lasagne takes thirty-five minutes at gas mark six.'

I shake my head. What in God's name am I doing?

I look between Kyleee and lasagne man with the helpless feeling that I'm coming apart at the seams.

'I'm going to die,' I tell them both in a small voice.

Lasagne man rolls his eyes. 'You're not the only one, mate. I had a couple of Hobnobs at half eleven and haven't had anything since, so get a move on, will you?'

Kyleee's expression has changed, though. 'You're going to die?' she asks, nonplussed.

'Yes,' I reply. 'I have something wrong with my head, you see.'

Kyleee looks forlorn. 'My mum died last month.'

All the wind is inexplicably sucked out of me. With one very brief conversation I've managed to transform Kyleee from a two-dimensional stereotype into a living, breathing human being with feelings. I'm not sure I'm comfortable with the change.

The look of loss on her face is heartbreaking.

Maybe that's why she's out the back smoking like a trooper half the time. Maybe that's why she speaks in that dull monotone. Maybe before her mother's death, Kyleee was just plain old *Kylie* and only changed her name as a rebellious stand against the cruelty of existence.

. . . or maybe I'm reading too much into absolutely everything at the moment and really need to go home and get fucking plastered.

'I'm sorry for your loss,' I tell her.

'Thanks,' she replies. 'And I hope you don't die.'

'Me, too, Kyleee,' I reply. 'Goodbye,' I say to both Kyleee and lasagne man, before scuttling out of the Tesco Express with my bottle of Jack Daniel's clutched in one rather shaky hand.

Back at the house, the mug that earlier contained English breakfast tea is filled with neat Jack Daniel's, and by the time I reach the bottom of it, the cold spectre of Death could be body-popping naked on my coffee table and I wouldn't care.

I haven't been this drunk for *years*.

Given that I live in a modern detached house – bought and paid for by singing anthropomorphic consumables – I can crank up the volume on my lounge stereo to its fullest extent and dance around the open-plan floor space to Kings of Leon all I bloody well like.

I then put on some Five Finger Death Punch. I have no idea who Five Finger Death Punch are, but Spotify tells me that they are an extremely angry heavy metal band – and boy does some extremely angry heavy metal sound good to me.

All I want to do right now is block out the world – let the whisky and the thrash metal consume me *completely*.

In this moment, I don't want to think about brain tumours or checkout girls or VW camper vans or MRI scans or anything else.

I just need to *escape*. If only for a short while . . .

By half past seven I'm resolutely fucked, and the only thing that'll be escaping any time soon is my lunch.

Five Finger Death Punch has ended its assault on my cochleas, and the medium-sized bottle of Jack Daniel's is empty. It's a bloody good job I didn't get the biggest one. I might be needing my stomach pumped otherwise.

The rest of the evening is spent in a drunken, exhausted stupor on the couch. I try to watch *Location, Location, Location,* but give up when I start laughing at Phil's jokes a little too hard. Phil's jokes are not meant to be *laughed* at. They are meant to be *groaned* at expansively, with much rolling of the eyes.

When I find myself wondering how many episodes of *Location, Location, Location* I'll get to watch before I die, I figure it's probably a good idea to take myself off to bed.

As my head hits the pillow, I start to go over the day's events once more, this time through the drunken haze of Tennessee sour mash whisky. I keep returning to three things: Kyleee's look of lonely sadness when telling me of her mother's death, the surreal image of Sienna holding a potato between her legs and the name of the thing that's likely to kill me.

'Serrahbrellodoglioma,' I attempt out loud to the emptiness of my bedroom.

'Serebrolodreglomia.' A bit closer, maybe?

'Cerebrolodondreglioma.' Getting there . . .

'Cerebrodondreglioma.'

There. That's it. That's what's going to kill me.

'Cerebrodondreglioma,' I repeat.

Didn't someone once say that if you can say the name of the thing that scares you, you will gain power over it?

'Cerebrodondreglioma.'

They lied.

31

LYRICS TO THE FOODIES SONG 'HAPPY ALL TOGETHER'

Herman the Grumpy Potato sings:

Being on my own, is the way I like to be,
Don't have to worry, because it's just me,
I don't need friends, I don't miss them at all,
When I'm alone, I'm having a ball.

The rest of The Foodies sing:

That's not true, Herman, being alone is bad,
You should play with us, and stop being so sad,
Having friends is awesome, sharing things is great,
There's nothing quite like having lots of mates!

Herman the Grumpy Potato sings:

I don't like to share things, I don't want to talk,
I want to be by myself, and maybe have a walk,

You don't like me anyway, it's easy to see,
Just go play together, and please leave me be.

The rest of The Foodies sing:

No, no! We love you, Herman! Come with us
and play!
Don't leave us behind here, don't just run away,
You'll see you're better off with all of us,
So come and get your love and hugs, stop making
a fuss!

All The Foodies sing:

Happy all together! We're happy all together!
A trouble shared is a trouble halved, with friends
everything is sublime!
Happy all together! We're happy all together!
Being with all the people you love, makes you
feel just fine!

THREE WOMEN

2 April

Nathan's one-man self-pity party ended when I eventually fell asleep at about ten thirty. Nathan's hangover party began when I woke up at eight.

You know the old maxim that when you have a bad hangover you just want to die? It still holds true, even when you are *actually going to die.*

As I spend a constructive ten minutes talking to God on the porcelain telephone, my head thumping harder than a Berlin techno festival, I manage to briefly forget all about my impending doom. I always thought that people got drunk to forget the terrible things that have happened to them, but now I realise that it's the hangover they're really aiming for. It's a little hard to bemoan the fact you've lost your job or that your wife has been cheating on you when you're hugging a toilet bowl and trying to violently retch up your own kidneys.

When the dry heaves finally pass and I can get to my feet again, I make my way down into the kitchen, where some rather wonderful things await me: three ibuprofen, a pint of cold water and another pint of freshly brewed black coffee.

I sit down again at my expensive oak kitchen table and stare once more out of the bifold patio doors as I sip my coffee. This time, however, I do not enter into another overblown appreciation of nature, given that my brain is comprehensively incapable of doing so. About all it can muster at the moment is *garden green, sky blue, vomit taste still in mouth, drink more coffee.*

It takes my brain a good ten minutes before the coffee stimulates it into any kind of coherent thought. When it does, however, I instantly wish I could just get good and drunk once more and forget everything again.

The full horror of yesterday's diagnosis hits me.

. . . swiftly followed by the hideous realisation that I now have to start telling *other people about it.*

I can't just keep it to myself, can I? At some point I'm going to have to let the cat out of the bag, just so people aren't surprised when I drop dead right in front of them. That would just be *rude.*

There are three people I definitely have to tell *today.* Sienna certainly deserves to know why I kept comparing her vagina to a root vegetable, and my cousin Eliza would kill me before the tumour has a chance to if I don't let her know as quickly as possible.

But before either of them, I *have* to tell my mother . . . and that is going to be *awful.*

Right now, she's probably pottering around in the aesthetically pleasing junkyard she calls a back garden with no idea that her youngest child is facing an early grave.

My heart heaves.

I can't do it. I can't do that to her.

It's taken her a good nine years to recover from my father's death from cirrhosis – how the hell is she going to take the idea that her son is likely to die very soon as well?

You don't have a choice, my conscience reminds me. *This thing isn't going away.*

No, it's not.

I blink back the sudden and unwanted tears that have sprouted at the corners of my eyes and rise slowly from the kitchen table, knowing that I have a horrible job to do today – three times over.

Trying to shake off the feeling of overwhelming dread, I head upstairs to get dressed.

I elect for something slobby and comfortable, because I quite frankly *deserve* slobby and comfortable today. Normally I wear what any self-respecting musician would adorn himself with on a day-to-day basis: fashionable ripped jeans, a rock band T-shirt and a black leather jacket – with my shaggy hair at least combed into some kind of submission. Today, though, I feel about as creative as a large sack of horse manure, so the tracksuit bottoms and hoodie feel entirely appropriate, as does the wild tangle I've left my hair in.

I end up listening to Radio 4 on the drive to Mum's house. I'd normally be shuffling through my enormous iPod music collection, but for some reason I'm finding a report on new efforts to provide arable irrigation to Sudanese farmers extremely soothing this morning.

I pull up outside Mum's expansive cottage just as Kate Adie is wishing me a good day, which is very nice of her.

As I ring the doorbell and step back, I take a deep breath, thinking about how I'm going to do this.

I've decided that it's best to just get the news out as quickly as possible. As soon as Mum opens the door, I'm going to give her a kiss, lead her into the kitchen and tell her. Then we'll have some time together so she can let it sink in and I won't have to—

The door is thrown open with a bang, startling me out of my train of thought.

My mother, hair unkempt and a wild look in her eyes, sees me standing there, grabs my arm and pulls me into the cottage before I so much as have a chance to say hello and give her a peck on the cheek.

'Mum? What the hell's going on?' I enquire in confused fashion as she slams the door behind us.

She gives me a look that is part incredulity, part towering rage. 'Nathan! Thank God you're here! They've stolen my Botti!'

'Pardon?'

'They've stolen my Botti, Nathan! My Botti!'

I resist the urge to stare at my mother's posterior. It wouldn't be right. 'What on earth are you on about?'

'My Botti! The statue Giuseppe Botti made especially for me when I was in Venice last year!'

Aaah . . .

Now I'm starting to understand.

'You mean the angel with the hard-on?'

She gives me a withering look. 'The seraphim does *not* have a *hard-on*, Nathan. He is sculpted in the Renaissance style, where the male genitalia is presented in a very specific way to denote a certain level of inherent sexuality.'

'Yes. It's got a boner, Mum.'

'No! Stop it!' My mother pauses, remembers that her son has finally come to visit her and stands up on tiptoes to plant a kiss on my cheek. 'It's such a nice surprise to see you! How are you today?'

Oh God. Here it is. The moment I've been dreading. 'Mum, I've got something I need to tell you and—'

'I can see him up the tree!' Mum shrieks, looking past me down the hallway, through the kitchen and out into the garden beyond. 'He's climbing up Horace the Oak!'

Without another word, my parental unit barrels past me down the hallway, leaving me standing with my mouth agape. It appears I'm going to get nowhere until I've resolved this current and latest act of internecine warfare between her and the long-suffering next-door neighbours.

I pursue my mother through the rear kitchen door and out into the single most ridiculous back garden you've ever been in.

My mother has been a sculptor all of her adult life and has always been good enough at it to make a decent living. What she is not good at, however, is knowing when to *stop*. Her back garden has, over the years, become a dumping ground for every piece of sculptural work that she's been either unable or unwilling to sell. And she's not one for obeying the classics when it comes to the type of statues she makes. Anything and everything is fair game as far as she's concerned.

If you can imagine a large and rather overgrown garden strewn with stone statuary, featuring everything from naked men embracing on a clamshell to an uncannily good depiction of Vladimir Putin eating a watermelon, then you're starting to get a good idea of what we're dealing with here.

If the garden stopped at just the statues it wouldn't be too bad, but my mother is the type of person who thinks that the lily should be gilded as much as possible – preferably with fairy lights and solar-powered music boxes that play Beethoven's 'Ode to Joy'.

You're probably feeling a great deal of sympathy for Mum's neighbours right about now. I can't say that I blame you. But she is my mother, so I'm going to have to climb up the oak tree at the bottom of the garden in pursuit of Mr Billingswade before he can steal the sexually aroused angel that has, up until now, taken pride of place on a five-foot pedestal, leering at him over the garden fence.

'You give that back, Alan Billingswade!' Mum roars as she pokes a finger up at him.

For a man who must be in his sixties, Alan Billingswade is doing very well to shimmy his way along the lowest and thickest branch of the oak tree with the undoubtedly heavy small stone statue under one arm.

A stepladder is propped up against the branch where it overhangs his garden. I can't see her thanks to the fence, but I know damn well that Gloria Billingswade will be standing at the bottom of that ladder, willing her husband on. After all, she's the one who's taken the greatest exception to the horny angel – which probably says as much about their sex life as it does her aversion to pornographic stone effigies.

'Alan, please give it back,' I entreat at the shimmying pensioner as I arrive at the base of the old tree.

'No, Nathan! We've had it up to here with this! Your mother is completely unreasonable!'

'Hah! I'm not unreasonable in the slightest!' Mum argues. 'You're just unable to appreciate good art when you see it!'

Alan's face crumples. 'It's an angel with its willy out!'

'It's a commentary on human sexuality and religious belief!' Mum counters.

'It's disgusting!' I hear Gloria cry from over the fence.

'You're a prude, Gloria Billingswade!' Mum roars.

'And you're a bloody maniac, Tamsin James!' Alan exclaims in his wife's defence. He wobbles rather precariously on the branch as he does so. I'd better step in and resolve this latest battle of Wilberforce Row before it ends in hospitalisation.

'Alan, if you just hand the statue over,' I say, 'I will make sure it's placed somewhere out of your lovely wife's eyeline.'

'Filth!' Gloria can be heard exclaiming over the larchlap.

Alan Billingswade appears to think about it for a moment. 'All right,' he eventually says. 'If you promise we don't have to look at it.'

'We promise . . . don't we, Mum?' I give my mother a look. '*Don't we, Mum?*'

'Yes, yes,' she intones, flapping her hands dismissively.

'Ask about the bloody Beethoven!' Gloria snaps at her husband.

I grimace.

'There's nothing wrong with a little classical music in the great outdoors!' Mum shrieks, in a manner suggesting that this is not the first time these two women have come to blows on this subject.

'There is at *three in the bloody morning*!' Gloria roars.

'Look! Everyone! Can we just settle one thing at a time, please?!' I shout, trying to end this secondary argument before it can get properly started.

'Yes, please,' Alan agrees quickly. I can't say I blame him. Every moment that passes makes his position on that branch look more precarious. He is a man in his pensionable years, after all. I doubt his body is up to sitting in a tree holding a heavy stone statue for more than a few minutes.

'Here, Alan, let me take that thing,' I tell him. As I do, I step up on to the small wooden bench that sits at the bottom of Horace the Oak (a name I gave the grand old tree when I was six) and hoist myself up on to the lowest thick branch that juts out from the trunk. Bracing myself, I hold out both hands. Alan shuffles back a bit to let me take the statue.

As he hands it over, we both momentarily lose our balance as the weight of the statue is transferred. Our combined grip slips, and the stone angel clips the side of the tree trunk.

Mum lets out an audible gasp as the penis snaps off.

Oh dear.

'My Botti!' she cries in horror.

'My back!' Alan Billingswade exclaims in pain.

From somewhere unidentifiable in the undergrowth of Horace the Oak, Beethoven's Ninth Symphony roars into life. The timing is exquisite.

'Turn that bloody music off!' Gloria Billingswade shrieks.

'Call me an ambulance!' her husband wails, clutching at his back with one hand.

'You snapped off my penis!' Mum roars at poor old Alan. She has managed to retrieve the broken member from where it came to rest in

41

the compost pile behind Horace's hoary old trunk and is now pointing it vociferously at Alan Billingswade.

I am probably at least half responsible for the instant emasculation of the little cherubic bugger, but Mum has her sights set only on her next-door neighbour, given that I am her son and can therefore do no wrong.

I take a deep breath and ponder how I'm going to defuse this rather idiotic situation before it gets any worse. Compared to handling this, breaking the news of my brain tumour to my mother will be a piece of bloody cake.

I climb out of the tree, plonk the damaged angel statue on the ground and return to help Alan down. This takes a good ten minutes, as he moans in pain with even the slightest movement. Once he is back in his garden and being helped up the path by his red-faced wife, I climb back over to the other side to find my mother disconsolately trying to push the penis back on to the statue.

Now the immediate crisis is over, it's probably time to broach the subject of my diagnosis, before anything else has a chance to interrupt.

'I just need to mix up some epoxy adhesive in the studio and I should be able to stick it back on okay.'

'Mum?'

'I might have to put some filler in the cracks, but it should still look decent once it's repaired.'

Mum gets up and starts back towards the house. Her studio is in the converted garage off to the right-hand side and it's this she makes a beeline for, stone penis clasped in hand.

'Mum!' I call after her in hopes of getting her to pay attention, but once my mother's mind is set on something, it's very hard to get her off track.

With a sigh, I take off after her, catching up as she moves to the back of the studio to rummage around in a collection of plastic boxes on shelves along the back wall. I move past her latest half-finished creation, which appears to be a porpoise playing a banjo. The porpoise should probably be happy that it's developed enough advanced motor skills to play a banjo, but it inexplicably looks decidedly worried about the entire venture instead. This is probably Mum making some kind of profound comment about Darwinian evolution, but I don't have the inclination to ask her about it now.

'Mum?' I begin again as I move hurriedly past banjo porpoise.

'Now where did I put that epoxy?' she mutters, placing the petrified willy down next to her.

'Mum?' I repeat a little louder.

'Was it with the resin? Or did I put it next to the plaster?'

'Mum?' I try again.

'Oh bother. Perhaps I didn't order any more from the stonemasons. I'll have to—'

'Mum! I've got something I need to tell you!' I have to shout, otherwise I'll never cut through all this business about epoxy and resin.

Mum looks startled. I rarely speak this loudly around her.

She gives me a worried look. My mother knows me very well and can instantly tell something is wrong. Maybe it's the fact that I can feel tears pricking the corners of my eyes.

'Let's go in the house,' I say, putting my arm around her shoulder. 'I'll make you a cup of tea and we can have a chat.'

'Okay, son,' she replies. All the anger and passion have gone from her voice. Thoughts of broken penises have been forgotten.

On shaky legs, I escort my mother back into the cottage and put the kettle on. Once I've brewed us both a cup, I lean against the kitchen counter, take the deepest breath I think I've ever taken and begin to tell my sorry, sorry tale to the one person in the world I would rather keep in the dark more than any other.

'Nonsense.'

'I'm sorry, *what?*'

'A load of nonsense.'

My mouth hangs open. I had expected tears and much gnashing of teeth. I didn't expect flat-out *denial*.

'Mum. It's not *nonsense*. Mr Chakraborty was quite clear about what I have.'

And *I've* been as clear as I possibly can in relaying the information to my mother over the last fifteen minutes. I'm quite proud of the fact that my voice didn't waver once.

Not that my detailed and level-headed explanation appears to have done much good.

'You're not going to die!' Mum exclaims.

'I kind of am,' I argue.

'No, you're not! You said it yourself . . . he doesn't know if the tumour is going to grow any more. You could be *fine*.'

'Mum,' I say softly, 'the odds of the tumour not growing any more are very, very slim. The odds of surviving are even worse.'

'Well . . . you *will*!' Mum insists, before lapsing into a tight silence.

'I won't, you know,' I reply in a quiet, miserable voice.

Mum's eyes narrow. 'Now, look here, Nathan James. I had nearly thirty years of your father's defeatism, I won't have it from you as well!'

My father was a writer – an unsuccessful one, commercially speaking – and as such was prone to bouts of deep depression on a monotonously regular basis. When he wasn't writing he was miserable because he couldn't think of any good ideas, but when he *was* writing he was *also* miserable because he thought the story he was working on was terrible. It was like living with an ambulatory rain cloud duct-taped to a typewriter. He was always searching for the 'great novel' – that one defining story which would catapult him into the ranks of the bestseller.

Sadly, all the cigarettes and cheap brandy he consumed while waiting for that great novel to come along got the better of him before he'd actually written it.

I wearily give my neck a rub. 'This isn't the same thing, Mum. I'm not being a defeatist – I'm just accepting reality.'

Mum shakes her head. 'No. You're being like your father. He could never look on the bright side of things. Like father, like son.'

I open my mouth to argue with her, but judging from the expression on her face, it probably wouldn't be a good idea. Mum appears to have convinced herself that I'm not as sick as I think I am and won't hear any argument from me – instead deciding that I suffer from some kind of hereditary negativity passed down by my father.

I should stop her thinking like this, but right now I just don't have the strength.

'Okay, Mum,' I say to her, placing a hand over hers. 'We'll just see what happens, eh?'

'Yes, we will,' she replies firmly. 'You'll have a good, long life, my son, believe me. You've done so much with it already with The Foodies, and now you've handed them over, I know there's so much more to come from you.'

I groan.

Ah yes. The ruddy *Foodies*. A bunch of dancing, talking foodstuffs. I could have been a rock star or a celebrated session musician or an Oscar-winning film composer. Instead I created ambulatory fruit and veg with the ability to sing loudly at small people about such edifying topics as going to the toilet, taking a happy trip to the seaside and being nice to animals.

I didn't even set out to create The Foodies. I was just asked to write a song for a children's show about tackling climate change, and it escalated from there.

I blame Taylor. He's the one who played 'The Sun Makes Us Shine' to the head of a record company specialising in children's music. From that moment on, I was stuck on a path that I've literally only just managed to jump off.

Don't get me wrong, I'm not complaining. I own a nice house and car thanks to Libby the Happy Lemon and her consumable friends, but when I was at the London College of Music, I had slightly grander ambitions for my career than educating the children of today via the means of melodic fruit.

'The Foodies aren't really that great, Mum. In fact, they're a bit shit, when you get right down to it. I didn't accomplish much by creating them.'

Mum looks horrified. 'They are *not* shit, Nathan! You should be proud of them!'

'I'm proud of the cash they've made me,' I reply flippantly. 'I just don't want them turning up at my funeral.'

'Stop talking like that!' Mum exclaims with irritation – and then instantly looks horrified. 'I'm so sorry, son. This must all be so hard for you. You don't need me snapping at you like that.'

I give her a morose look. 'Can I . . . can I have a hug, Mum?' I ask, trying very hard not to let my voice crack.

'Of course you can!' she replies, and gets up from the kitchen table.

Mum then embraces me in the fiercest hug I can remember ever getting from her. It's a hug full of warmth and love – but I can also feel her shaking ever so slightly against me.

When we part, I can see the underlying fear in her eyes. It's exactly the same fear I see in mine when I look in the mirror.

***

Two hours later, I find myself in another kitchen telling somebody else I love about my diagnosis over a rapidly cooling cup of coffee. This one is no easier. In fact, in some ways it's far harder. Eliza is in a fragile emotional state at the moment, and I'm about to add to her troubles.

'Oh my God,' she says in a voice barely above a whisper when I've finished speaking. 'I don't . . . I can't . . .' She looks at me, eyes wide with shock and sadness.

I take Eliza's hand, much the same way I did with Mum's. 'It's okay, Elsie.'

'And your surgeon was certain? There's no chance he's wrong about it? Or that the tumour won't be quite as bad as he says?'

I shake my head. 'No. He sounded very sure. This Strzlylikik bloke did a huge amount of research into the disease when he discovered he had it. That's why I know how bad it's likely to be.' I give Eliza a plaintive look. 'Nobody gets out of this one alive, kid.'

Eliza looks heavenwards. 'Oh fucking shit.'

'Yep.'

'Fucking hell!' she exclaims angrily, slapping her hand down on her kitchen table as she does so. 'Ow.' She winces, looking at her reddened palm.

Kitchens always seem to be the place where both good and bad news are generally imparted, have you ever noticed that? Must be something to do with being in such close proximity to the teabags.

'I'm so sorry to do this to you,' I tell her.

She looks confused. 'What the hell have you done to *me*, Nate? You're the one with the tumour!'

'I just meant . . . because of how things are for you . . . what with Bryan leaving and everything.'

Eliza gives me a look of disgust. 'Don't be so silly, Nate! I threw that cheating piece of shit out myself. He didn't *leave*. And none of that should affect you being able to tell me about something like *this*! You're my *family*, for fuck's sake, and a far better man than that twat ever was!'

Eliza has always had a large and obvious temper on her at the best of times, but she can hardly be blamed for carrying around a great deal of barely supressed fury at the moment, given that her husband has been having an affair with their son's support teacher for the past few months.

'How did your mum take the news?' Eliza asks.

My face screws up. 'Not well. She refuses to believe I could die.'

Eliza nods. 'I'm not surprised, Nate. She's the same as Dad. Neither of them take bad news well. Like brother, like sister.'

I rub my eyes. 'I know. I just hope I can get it through to her properly, before . . . before I . . .' I just can't bring myself to say it. 'How's Callum doing?' I ask, changing the subject for all I'm worth.

Eliza grimaces. 'He's not good. The split has been hard on him . . . and we were just starting to make some real progress. Children on the spectrum don't deal well with change, so losing both his father at home and his favourite teacher at school is affecting him horribly.'

'Oh no. That's . . . that's awful,' I say, before falling into an uncomfortable silence. These are things I should probably know about, but I haven't been around much recently, thanks to work . . . and Sienna.

'So, what are you going to do?' Eliza asks me, changing the subject back to my problems.

. . . which is the million-dollar question, isn't it?

I am hideously reminded of last month's press conference when Katie from the *Daily Mail* asked me what I was going to do with my life after I'd handed over The Foodies to Brightside. I didn't have an answer for her then, and I sure as hell don't have an answer for Eliza now, either. Of course, the difference is I had plenty of time to play with back then – but now I have virtually *none*.

'I don't know, Elsie,' I reply in a small voice, before looking at her forlornly. 'I'm completely lost.'

She puts an arm around me. 'Oh, I wish I could help you, Nate. I really do.'

'Yep. Me too,' I reply, giving her a half-hearted smile.

Eliza thinks long and hard for a moment. 'You definitely need something to keep you occupied,' she says. 'I know it's hard, but if you don't keep your mind busy, you'll drive yourself crazy.'

'What do you suggest? Some kind of hobby? Maybe knitting?'

She slaps my shoulder. 'Don't be an idiot. I mean . . . you can't just sit around, Nate. You can't just sit around and wait for . . .'

She trails off, not wanting to say it.

'. . . the spectre of Death to start body-popping naked on my coffee table?'

'What?'

I shake my head ruefully. 'Never mind.'

Eliza's phone starts to ring. She gives me a kiss on the cheek, gets up and goes to retrieve it from the hallway. As she answers the call, I look down at my left hand and slowly clench it into a fist. I remember how it shook that night at home with Sienna, which further reminds me of how my mother's whole body shook with fear as I hugged her earlier today.

What do I do now? What do I possibly fill my life with now that I know it could end at any moment?

You haven't done much with it up until now, dickhead, I hear a horrible little voice in my head say. *Why should anything change?*

Eliza comes back into the kitchen, a distressed look on her face. 'I'm so sorry, Nate. I have to go to the school. Callum's . . . Callum's playing up again.'

'Oh no. Do you want me to come along with you?'

She gives me a doubtful look. 'No. That's okay. Probably best I handle it on my own.'

I'm not quite sure how I should take that, to be honest.

'I promise we'll talk again soon, though,' she adds. 'Feel free to stay and finish your coffee. Just lock the place up when you're done.'

Eliza gives me a swift hug and a kiss on the cheek, before disappearing up the hallway and out of her house, slamming the front door with a loud bang.

I sit there for a moment in silence, staring down the hall at the front door.

Strangely, I feel a little bit hurt that Eliza has just run off like that in the middle of our conversation. It's quite a ridiculous thing to feel, but I can't help myself.

. . . people's lives do go on, though, don't they?

Just because mine is likely to come to an end very soon, it doesn't mean that anybody else's is.

What a *horrible* thing to realise.

***

Sienna's swish apartment is in the centre of the marina just outside town and is the type of place that only catwalk models and utter wankers would live in.

As I approach her front door, I can hear pop music blaring out of the apartment at a decibel level that must be *delightful* for the neighbours. Sienna is twenty-five and beautiful, so can probably get away with this kind of stuff better than the rest of us.

I have to knock on the door so loud it makes my hand hurt before she answers it.

'Hey, sexy!' she exclaims when she sees me standing there.

Sienna is wearing a tiny crop top and a pair of equally tiny white knickers. Neither of these are going to help me break the news of my terminal diagnosis to her. It's very hard to be serious and forlorn when you're stupid horny.

Sienna grabs me by the hand and pulls me into the apartment. I can see and hear MTV blaring out of her fifty-five-inch flat-screen TV as she drags me into the living room.

'Dance with me!' she orders, before beginning a strange process of sticking her limbs out at random angles in time to the music.

Sienna is many things. Many *sexy* things.

What she is not is a good dancer.

It's like watching a stick insect get electrocuted.

'I need to talk to you about something, Sienna!' I shout over Ed Sheeran's latest catchy number. 'It's important!'

'But I'm dancing!' she complains, thrusting both arms out. It looks more like she's directing air traffic than having a boogie.

'Please, Sienna! Can you mute that bloody TV?! I have something I need to tell you!' I wail, wincing at the volume she's got the UK Top 40 playing at.

Sienna pouts. It's something she's very good at. 'But I *really* want to see who's at number one.'

I rub my eyes. 'Just . . . just turn it off for a few moments.'

She rolls her eyes, but does as I've asked, throwing the remote control back down on to the couch with a huff once the sound has been muted. 'What is it?' she asks sullenly, slumping on to her sofa and folding her arms.

I come to sit down next to her. 'You know I went to the neurosurgeon yesterday?'

'Did you?'

I grit my teeth. 'Yes, Sienna. I told you about it, remember? Along with the other three appointments I've had in the past couple of weeks?' Sienna looks doubtful. I look dismayed. 'After what happened the other night around my house? The potato thing and the blackout I had? I wanted to find out what was causing it?'

Sienna cocks her head. 'Oh yeah, I suppose I remember . . . you went to see someone yesterday, then?'

'*Yes*, Sienna.'

'So what did they say?' she asks. I can see that she's only half paying attention to me. She keeps looking sideways at the TV.

I close my eyes briefly and take a deep breath. 'I'm afraid it's bad news.'

'Is it?' Sienna is now barely listening and continues to sneak looks at the television.

I choose to soldier on regardless. 'Yes. I have . . . I have a brain tumour. It's very big, and might well kill me at some point in the near future.'

'Yes! Woohoo!' Sienna bursts out in excitement.

'What?!' I snap in disbelief.

Sienna clenches her fists in triumph. 'Sean Paul is at number one! Nevaeh is in the video for this song, Nathan! Oh, I'm so *pleased* for her! She worked so hard to lose that extra stone!'

And with that Sienna is back on her feet. The volume goes back up on the TV and she starts to dance around like a thing possessed. The stick insect is getting a good four hundred volts put through it.

Quite clearly news of my impending doom is less important than watching a middle-aged man cavort around with a bunch of semi-clad girls in an empty swimming pool.

I sit and watch in thunderstruck silence as Sienna gyrates around in front of me in her very small pants.

I should probably be feeling incredibly upset at her complete and total lack of interest in my news, but to be honest, I knew what kind of girl she was when I started dating her. She's the kind of girl that sticks three fingers in her mouth in public and can breathe through her ears. This tends to forgive a lot of sins – up to and including having the attention span of a stunned mayfly.

'I think I'm going to leave you to it,' I shout at her as I stand up. Today has been an exceptionally draining day. I just don't have the strength to keep this conversation up any longer. With any luck, I'll be able to catch Sienna in a less excitable moment at some point in the next few days and tell her then. Either that or I'll make a pop video about my incipient demise and rap about it to her from a disused septic tank. That might get her attention.

Sienna watches me turn to leave. 'Are you going?' she shouts after me over Sean Paul's middle-aged wittering.

I yawn. 'Yeah. It's been a long day.'

Sienna pouts again and turns the volume back down. 'But don't you want to stay and play with me?' she says, once Mr Paul is again silenced.

'Um. I'm not sure, Sienna. I'm not really feeling . . .'

She takes off her crop top in one swift and well-practised movement. My penis – hitherto completely uninvolved in proceedings – wakes up and starts metaphorically poking me in the ribs.

This is *completely* inappropriate. Today was supposed to be about breaking the worst news I've ever had to the people I care about most, not getting a shag.

The tiny pants have now come off as well.

I look down at my crotch. 'You are a stupendous idiot,' I tell my penis, who chooses to completely ignore me and instead directs my body back towards the naked twenty-five-year-old model standing in front of me.

Later that evening over Thai food, I eventually managed to tell Sienna about the tumour.

Her response?

She looked sad for about four seconds, before asking if I thought Channel 5 might want to do a documentary about it.

For some strange reason, I actually preferred this response to Mum's or Eliza's. It was easier to deal with.

Things are very *simple* when I'm with Sienna.

She's self-involved, I'm self-absorbed and the sex is *tremendous*. Anything complicated like emotion or empathy is almost entirely absent. Any effort I make to keep her happy is purely sexual or comes directly from my wallet.

You see?

Simple.

My *whole life* was simple until yesterday. Now it's become so hideously and irrevocably complicated in every other way, it's nice that at least one thing hasn't changed.

Sienna is Sienna.

All of my other relationships will be changed forever by the news of my diagnosis. I'm never going to be treated the same by anyone.

The fact that Sienna seems not to care that much should hurt – she is my girlfriend, after all – but instead all I feel is a great sense of *relief*. It's almost as if the tumour doesn't *actually exist* when I'm around her. If she doesn't care about it, then why should I?

As long as Sienna keeps being herself, then I have something from my old life to cling on to.

My. Old. Life.

I talk about it like it was something that disappeared a decade ago . . . rather than just yesterday.

Good grief.

ANGER MISMANAGEMENT

22 APRIL

'Jesus Christ on a fucking bike with a fucking cherry on top on fucking fire!!'

Welcome to the latter stages of a tantrum.

There have been a lot of these recently.

This one is about a coffee machine.

'You stupid fucking machine! You stupid, stupid bastard coffee fucking machine! Why did I even buy you?? Why, God, why???'

Two days ago, I shouted at a cat. For no reason whatsoever.

The day before that I ranted down the phone at the DVLA because I've had my driving licence revoked. It transpires they don't like people with dangerous brain tumours driving around, just in case they drop dead at the wheel. The unreasonable bastards. From now on I'll be taking bloody cabs everywhere, and have already angrily downloaded the Uber app on to my phone.

A couple of days prior to that I screamed at my manager, Taylor, for giving Brightside Productions a terrible photo of me for their show posters. I look like I've just suffered a drive-by lobotomy.

And my poor iPhone was sent to Apple heaven against my bedroom wall a fortnight ago when my mother rang me for the third time in less than an hour.

You see, Sienna and I were enjoying an alcohol-fuelled evening of fun and games, which had made me completely forget about my new diagnosis for the first time since being told about it . . . and then my phone rang as I was pouring vodka between Sienna's pert breasts. The second I saw that it was Mum, I knew she'd be ringing to see how I was doing, which instantly reminded me about the death sentence hanging over my head.

I ignored that call, and the second. By the time the third came through, I lost my temper completely and threw the iPhone as hard as I could, shattering the screen into a thousand pieces, against the dark-grey granite feature wall that looked fabulous in the magazine, but rather stupid in reality.

This was completely irrational and *totally* uncalled for, but I just wanted to have some fun with my girlfriend and not face all the questions about how I was doing . . . *again*. Even from my dear, sainted mother.

I should be grateful for her care and attention, but all I actually feel is *angry*. Stupendously, hugely, violently *angry*.

'Three hundred fucking quid! That's how much I spent on you, you noisy silver cunt! And you've never worked properly once!'

Needless to say, none of these things actually warranted such fury on my part – with the possible exception of having my driving licence taken away. I'm just going through a period of emotional turmoil thanks to the tumour that is manifesting itself in completely irrational moments of blind rage.

One of the ever-so-helpful leaflets I got from Mr Chakraborty's office detailed the stages of grief people go through when they receive a diagnosis like mine. You're supposed to start with a period of denial, before the anger phase comes along. I appear to have transferred the denial stage to my mother and have skipped directly to the towering rage portion of the festivities.

'I might only have minutes to live, you bean-chewing bastard! Just give me a fucking decent cup of coffee! Just once in your stupid, pointless life!'

There are actual, proper tears of rage and frustration in my eyes as I pick the coffee machine up, wrench it from the plug socket, carry it over to the bifold patio doors and chuck the fucking thing across the garden with all of my strength.

'And stay out there!' I rage at the now undoubtedly broken machine as it comes to rest. 'Stay out there and think about what you've fucking done to me!'

All it's done is fail to produce a cup of coffee that doesn't have grounds floating in it, but I'm really shouting at something else right now, aren't I? Something that's squatting in the middle of my brain, biding its time.

As I stand there, seething at three hundred quid's worth of broken De'Longhi, my brand-new iPhone starts to ring. I yank it out of my jeans pocket.

'What?!' I bellow down the line.

'Jesus Christ!!' Taylor screams in terror from the opposite end.

I take a few deep breaths, trying to calm myself down a bit. 'What do you want, Taylor?' I snap at him.

'I just called to see how you were doing . . . I take it not very well?'

'Been better, to be honest with you!' I exclaim, staring daggers at the coffee machine.

'Yes, well, that's why I'm calling. I may know someone who can help you with your . . . your current mood.'

'Who?' I grunt.

'He's a self-help guru. Specialises in anger management. He's helped a lot of people with their personal problems. I asked around, and lots of people recommended him.'

I groan. 'A *self-help* guru?'

'Yes. Cleethorpes has a great reputation for helping people in a similar position to yours.'

'Mad as fuck at a coffee machine, you mean? And did you say his name was *Cleethorpes*?'

'I did.'

'First name or second name?'

Taylor is silent for a moment. 'I don't know, to be honest. Everyone just calls him Cleethorpes.'

'That's the most ridiculous name I've ever heard,' I snap.

'Maybe, but I still think he can do you some good. So much so that I've already given him your email. He's going to contact you this morning to arrange a meeting.'

'Taylor!' I whine.

There's a pause on the other end for a moment. 'I'm worried about you, Nathan . . . we all are. You nearly bit my head off the other day about that headshot.'

'Yes! Because I look like I've *just been shot in the head*!'

'You see? You're not doing well, Nathan! I'm really worried about you!'

The scared tone in Taylor's voice knocks the rage out of me . . . for the moment, at least. He really doesn't deserve this tongue-lashing. Nor did the cat, the DVLA guy or the coffee machine. This is something I have to get some kind of control over before it consumes me.

'All right . . . all right, I'm sorry,' I tell him, trying to keep my voice calm. 'I probably do need some help with this.'

'Yes, yes, you do,' Taylor replies with relief. 'And Cleethorpes might be able to give it.'

'He's emailing me this morning, you say?'

'Yep.'

'Okay. I'll give it a go, I suppose.' I glare at the coffee machine. 'It's either that or I start beating up the toaster.'

The email from this person called Cleethorpes comes through about half an hour after I get off the phone with Taylor. It is as abrupt as its grammar is poor.

Nathan.

I am, Cleethorpes. Meet me, in town. 12pm. Outside, Primark.

Cleethorpes

Do you see how many commas he's employed there? *Three*, that's how many. Three, where none were actually *needed*.

Surely the sign of a diseased mind, don't you think?

And why does he want to meet me in the *centre of town*? I had visions of the bloke coming here or me going to his place. How in hell is he going to improve my state of mind slap-bang in the middle of town on a Saturday afternoon? Surely that is quite literally the *worst* place on earth to achieve any kind of mental equilibrium? I haven't been into the town centre on a Saturday afternoon for *ten years*. Being surrounded by thousands of irritated, tired shoppers and their unholy offspring ranks right up there with root canal surgery for my favourite things to do.

Still, I quite like that toaster. It's always provided me with a decent slice of toast and the occasional hot crumpet. I'd hate for it to join the coffee machine out by the Japanese maple tree, or my old iPhone in the bin under my bedside cabinet. I'd best go and meet this strangely monikered individual to see if he can do anything about this non-stop anger and frustration.

I climb out of the cab and make my way along to Primark at midday. I scan the crowd, looking for someone who's likely to be called Cleethorpes. In my head, all self-help gurus are dressed like hippies, so I'm on the lookout for a tall, lanky man with a wispy beard – wearing flip-flops, a kaftan and round sunglasses with red lenses in them.

No one fitting that description is immediately evident.

'Nathan James!' a voice booms out from behind me.

Oh Lord.

Here we go, then.

I turn slowly – ever so *slowly* – to find myself confronted with . . .

Not a hippie, it turns out. Not even remotely close to a hippie.

If you placed a hippie on one side of a scale, then this person would be diametrically opposite.

Cleethorpes, it turns out, is a chartered accountant. Or at least he *looks* like one.

He's also not tall and skinny. He's a black guy of about five foot three and has a very stocky build.

The blue pinstriped suit he's wearing is so tight that it's a wonder he can breathe. On the lapels are various badges, each of which depicts a cartoon series from the 1980s. The *Thundercats* one is particularly excellent, featuring a rampant Lion-O holding aloft his mighty Sword of Omens. I'm not so sure about the *Chip 'n' Dale: Rescue Rangers* one, though. I always felt there was something entirely untrustworthy about those two little sods, but could never quite put my finger on why.

There's no shirt to go with the suit. Under the tightly buttoned jacket I can see a black T-shirt. The '80s cartoon theme continues, as it's a *He-Man and the Masters of the Universe* T-shirt. I can just see He-Man and Battle Cat poking out from behind the suit's lapels, as if attempting escape from their Cleethorpian confines.

And wait for it, boys and girls, wait for it . . .

He's wearing a small blue pork-pie hat.

Cleethorpes, it transpires, is Bob Hoskins – if he had chosen a career in chartered accountancy.

The little man is carrying one of those blue IKEA bags in one hand, tied up tightly so I can't see what's inside.

'Er . . . are you Cleethorpes?' I say.

The small man drops the bag at his side and opens his arms expansively. 'Well, of course I am! Who else could I possibly be?'

There's every chance this is some kind of complicated existential question I'm being asked here, but I'm not going to fall for it. 'I'm Nathan,' I state matter-of-factly.

'Well, *of course* you are!' Cleethorpes exclaims happily. Cleethorpes sounds like he comes from . . . well, *Cleethorpes*. His broad northern accent sounds almost exotic to me, living as I do amongst a plethora of flat-vowelled southerners.

Now the initial introductions are out of the way, it's time we addressed the elephant in the room – or in this particular case, the elephant in the middle of a busy shopping precinct.

Why exactly is Cleethorpes called *Cleethorpes*? Just how does a fully grown man, in what looks to be his early forties, get saddled with such an odd moniker?

'So, why is your name Cleethorpes?' I ask bluntly.

This is quite rude, I'm sure you'll agree. I wouldn't normally be so uncouth as to launch into an interrogation of someone's name having only just met them, but these are rather exceptional circumstances. I have been summoned to a place I detest by a person I have never met before and I'm angry as fuck at everything, so I'm not feeling particularly inclined towards politeness.

If Cleethorpes is offended by my rudeness, he doesn't show it. In fact, he beams at me happily. 'It is a very interesting story, Nathan. But one that would take me a long time to explain. The short answer is I was found as a baby at Cleethorpes railway station.'

I'm slightly stunned by this revelation, but not one hundred per cent surprised. 'And somebody decided to name you Cleethorpes in honour of where you were found?' I surmise.

'Exactly! My adoptive parents, Eileen and Trevor Oldham, were quite the amusing couple. I have a huge love for them.'

'I bet. So, hang on . . . your full name is Cleethorpes Oldham?'

'No, no! That would sound silly, wouldn't it?'

'Well, I guess it does sound a bit like a train route, yes.'

'Indeed! As I say, I am named after where I was discovered as a baby . . . and very proud I am of the name, too!'

'I'm confused.'

'It's quite simple, Nathan. My name is Cleethorpes Railway Station.'

'Your full name is Cleethorpes Railway Station?'

I start to look around, trying to see where the hidden cameras are.

'Indeed! Or just Cleethorpes Station for short.'

'Okay.' I ponder this for a moment. 'Good job you weren't born at the local tip, I suppose. Cleethorpes Refuse Facility doesn't sound quite as noble.'

Cleethorpes smiles and nods in agreement. 'Are you ready to begin, Nathan?' he then asks me.

'I literally have no idea, given that I don't know what we're doing here.'

'We are here to help you deal with your current anger issues, of course!'

I look around at the throng of shoppers passing us by. 'I'm not sure how bringing me here is going to do that.'

Cleethorpes smiles. 'Trust me, Nathan. This is the *perfect* place.'

'If you say so,' I respond in a very dubious tone. 'What exactly do you think you can do for me?'

The little man looks around. 'Anger is a thing that lives and grows in isolation, Nathan. The reason we are here, amongst all these people, is that I firmly believe that all the negative feelings you have inside right now can only be exorcised when they are exposed to the world in a cathartic experience.'

'What do you mean by that?' The man is speaking in riddles.

Cleethorpes smiles and crouches down to untie the IKEA bag. 'What I mean, Nathan, is that for you to release the anger you have about your illness, you must display those feelings in front of your fellow man in a clear and concise manner.'

I shake my head. 'Nope. Still as clear as mud, I'm afraid.'

'You must let go of your inhibitions, embrace the inner rage and release it in a glorious cathartic gesture that will make your heart sing!'

Complete nonsense. 'What?' I snap.

Cleethorpes produces a large yellow foam bat from the IKEA bag. 'This, Nathan. I mean this.'

Cleethorpes then hits me over the head with the yellow bat. It's quite clearly a toy, given that it makes a high-pitched squeak as it comes into sharp contact with my forehead.

'Ow! Fuck about!' I wail – understandably given the circumstances. 'What did you do that for??'

'I am helping to release your pent-up rage, Nathan! In front of all these people, where the catharsis will have the most impact!'

'And you think you can do that by twatting me with a squeaky bat?!'

Cleethorpes nods gleefully. 'Yes!' he exclaims, and whacks me on the head again.

'Stop it! Stop hitting me, you bloody maniac!'

'It is *cathartic*, Nathan!'

'It's fucking *certifiable*!'

Cleethorpes leans in. 'Are you *angry*, Nathan?'

'Of course I'm bloody angry! You keep hitting me with a squeaky bat!'

As you might expect, the sight of one small man in a pork-pie hat hitting another over the head with a bright-yellow foam bat is something that is likely to be noticed. As such, people are starting to stare at us both.

'But is it *me* you are actually angry with?' Cleethorpes asks.

'Well, nobody else is hitting me over the head with a fucking bat, are they?!' I rage.

'And what do you want to do about it?'

'Get away from you as quickly as possible!'

'Really? Is that what you really want to do, Nathan?' Cleethorpes kneels down and produces another foam bat from the IKEA bag. 'Or is there something *else* you'd like to do?' He throws the bat to me.

Yes, Cleethorpes. There is something else I'd like to do, actually – you small, weirdly named maniac.

Without giving him a verbal answer, I smack Cleethorpes right on the pork-pie hat with the bat as hard as I can. Such is the ferocity of the blow that the high-pitched squeak is accompanied by a low, hollow boom, indicating that the bat isn't solid all the way through. This effort startles Cleethorpes only for the briefest of moments, before he laughs out loud and thrusts his arms out triumphantly. 'Yes, Nathan! That's exactly it!'

SMACK. SQUEAK.

Cleethorpes' bat connects with the top of my head once again.

To be fair, the blows aren't painful. It's a little hard to do any real damage with a spongy foam bat – but *by Christ* that doesn't stop it being *extremely irritating*.

I respond in kind.

WHACK. SQUEAK. *FLOOM.*

This only makes Cleethorpes laugh even louder, so I hit him again. He doesn't even try to dodge the blow. It's like the world's easiest whack-a-mole machine.

We now have a crowd surrounding us, most of whom have got their mobile phones out and are recording proceedings, because that's what we now all do in the twenty-first century. If Armageddon ever does strike, it will definitely happen in portrait mode rather than landscape.

I'm far past caring about the onlookers. Cleethorpes has worked up an unholy rage within me that cannot be quelled by anything other than repeatedly battering that fucking pork-pie hat until it is unrecognisable.

Cleethorpes has stopped fighting back and is just taking the repeated blows to the top of his head with a good grace that is equal parts admirable and quite disturbing. This only makes me want to hit him even more, so I continue to do so, with even harder and more rapid blows. My assault on Cleethorpes' head is also accompanied by some rather horrific and frenzied swearing that punctuates each and every strike.

SMACK. SQUEAK. *FLOOM.*

'Aha ha! That is it, Nathan! Express your rage!'

'Fuck you!'

WHACK. SQUEAK. *BOOM.*

'Let it all out!'

'Go fuck yourself!'

BLAT. SQUEAK. *FLOOM.*

'Be at one with your inner feelings!'

'You arsehole!'

SMACK. SQUEAK. *BOOM.*

'Allow yourself to be in the moment!'

'Go to fucking hell!'

'Now, Nathan!' Cleethorpes exclaims, holding out his hands to stop me. 'Tell me what you're angry about. Tell me why you feel this way!'

I stare at the little man for a second, the foam bat held aloft and ready to hit him again. 'Because it's so fucking *unfair!*' I scream at him.

'What is?'

'All of it!' I rage, waving my arms. 'I'm only thirty-three! Thirty-*fucking*-three! This shouldn't be happening to me! It's *not bloody fair!*'

Cleethorpes stares at me intently. 'And what can you do about that?'

'Nothing!' I look desperately to the sky. 'There's *nothing* I can do!' I look back down at him, the anger draining from my body in an instant. 'I'm *lost*, Cleethorpes. Totally lost.' I throw my hands up. 'I had it all figured out! My life . . . my future . . . it was all looking so fucking *good*. But now? What the hell am I supposed to do *now?*'

He looks at me with sympathy. 'I understand, my friend. I truly do. You feel trapped. You feel adrift. You think your life has lost its meaning now everything has changed so much. That is why you feel such anger.' He smiles at me again. 'But you will find peace, Nathan. You will find meaning again. You *will* find a way to relieve these feelings of frustration and helplessness.'

I shrug my shoulders disconsolately. 'Really? How?'

Cleethorpes points at me. 'That is up to *you* to find out for yourself, my friend. You alone must choose the path you want to walk down. You alone must find your purpose in all of this.'

Aaaarggh!

What kind of bloody advice is *that?!*

I am once again enraged.

WHACK. SQUEAK. *FLOOM.*

'What the hell is going on here?' I hear a voice say from behind me.

'What does it fucking look like?!' I scream, and hit Cleethorpes over the head one more time – before turning around to see two police officers standing behind me.

Oh my God, I'm going to jail. I'm in so much fucking trouble. Why did I get out of bastard bed this morning? Aaaarggh!!

I immediately stop my rabid assault on the person of Cleethorpes. In a panic, I throw the bat away. It describes a rather awkward arc in the air, before hitting a nearby tree with a characteristic squeak and ricocheting off through the door into Primark and into a massive pile of women's knickers, never to be seen again.

'Muuurrrgghh,' I exclaim in horror.

I have only ever been in trouble with the law once in my life, and that was twelve years ago, when I got caught larking about on top of a bus shelter, holding a frozen chicken. I would explain how that set of circumstances came about, but I'm deathly afraid I'm about to get carted off by the local constabulary, so I don't have the time right now.

The police officers – both of whom look big and burly enough to come first and second in a biggest and burliest police officer competition – look at me the same way that two grizzly bears might regard a lost Japanese tourist. I can already feel the cuffs going on. Here I am, assaulting another human being in front of hundreds of phone-clutching witnesses.

The burliest of the two burly policemen looks past me at Cleethorpes, and his stern expression softens. 'Oh, it's you,' he says with a sigh. 'Charing Cross, isn't it?'

'Cleethorpes!' Cleethorpes says with a beaming smile.

'Right, *Cleethorpes*.' The copper pulls out his pocket notebook and skims through a few pages. 'Yep. I knew it,' he says, stabbing a finger at a particular page. 'I've had to warn you about this kind of thing a few times, haven't I? The last time was a couple of months ago, wasn't it?'

Cleethorpes continues to smile. 'Yes indeed, sir.'

'I had to stop you from being repeatedly kicked in the arse by a teenage goth outside the Carphone Warehouse, didn't I?'

'You did!' Cleethorpes replies. 'Her name was Araminta.' The little man looks at me. 'The poor girl was struggling with the end of a long-term relationship.'

'And you thought the best way to make her feel better about it was to have her kick you in the bottom?' I respond.

Cleethorpes gives me a reproachful look. 'The session was very valuable to her state of well-being.'

'Was it?' I reply with extreme doubt.

'Well, you can't keep doing this, Colchester,' the large copper says.

'Cleethorpes,' I correct, instantly wishing I hadn't.

The copper gives me a look of deep disdain and then continues to talk to Cleethorpes. 'You can't just turn up on a busy street and let other people beat you up. It's causing a disturbance. I don't want to have to arrest you and your friend here for a public order offence.'

'But this is how I work,' Cleethorpes says in a sad voice. The little man now looks quite dejected. The change from happy-go-lucky masochist to down-in-the-mouth depressive is so fast it very nearly gives me whiplash.

The copper folds his arms. 'Well, you're just going to have to work somewhere a little more private, Chelmsford.'

Cleethorpes' shoulders slump. 'But these cathartic moments must take place where others can see them! Otherwise they mean nothing! There *must* be an audience!'

This is probably a good time for me to say something constructive, before I get arrested for assault and Cleethorpes gets hauled away for psychiatric evaluation.

I place a hand on his shoulder. 'Why don't we pop back to mine for a nice cup of tea?' I suggest to him. 'If you like, we can go out in the garden and I can slam your plums into my bifold patio doors. We could invite the neighbours around to watch.'

'Why don't you take your friend's advice, Chepstow?' says the copper. 'I think a nice cup of tea somewhere far away from here would be a *very good idea.*'

Cleethorpes still looks unhappy about the whole thing, but nods his head and picks up the IKEA bag.

'A cup of tea would be lovely, Nathan. Thank you,' Cleethorpes says with a grateful expression.

I pat him on the shoulder, give the two coppers one last apologetic look and begin to move us both away.

By the time we get back to my house, Cleethorpes looks about as happy as the people of Cleethorpes generally do in the middle of January. All the passion, brightness and animation is gone from his face, and even the blue of his tight-fitting pinstriped suit seems duller.

I feel at this stage that it's somehow my duty to help the poor guy out of his malaise.

Let's hope Cleethorpes enjoys English breakfast tea while looking out through expensive bifold patio doors at a manicured garden full of mating birds, as that's the only view I have to offer him – unless he wants to go and stare at the canvas of the Maldives I've got hung up in the downstairs toilet.

'Thank you, Nathan,' he says, as I plonk said cup of tea down in front of him.

I regard his solemn expression for a moment, wondering how I'm going to make him feel better. Then it hits me.

'I think you've really helped me, Cleethorpes,' I tell him.

'Do you?'

'Yes! You've helped me release a lot of anger and resentment about my condition today.'

'I have?'

'Yes. I feel like a weight has been lifted from my shoulders and that I am better able to cope with things.'

'Really?'

He's not sure I'm telling him the truth. And who can blame him?

'Oh yes! I think I can face the world now . . . all thanks to you,' I say with a smile.

He gives me a shy look. 'If you think today has helped, would you like to book in for another session?'

Oh crap.

'*Another* session?' I reply, cursing myself inwardly. My cleverness is backfiring. In trying to cheer the little sod up, I've painted myself into a corner.

How do I respond? If I say no, I'll probably make him miserable again, but if I say yes, what will I be volunteering myself for? Will I find myself slapping Cleethorpes across the face in the ready meals aisle at Iceland? Or perhaps rubbing a Brillo pad across his forehead beside the blueberry muffins in Starbucks?

My brain freezes in an agony of indecision. 'Well, Cleethorpes . . . I think that you have . . . have done me a lot of good today . . .' I trail off, desperately thinking of a way to word my refusal for more 'treatment' without sending him crashing again. 'And I'm sure that you have probably done enough today for me to carry on with life . . . um . . .'

Okay, okay. This is good. We're getting somewhere here.

'Your technique is very . . . *unique* . . . but I must say it has definitely worked . . . and I can see how more would be of help . . .'

What? Wait a minute! That's not right! Don't say things like that! Get out of it! Get out of it *now*!

Cleethorpes, for his part in this conversation, is just sat sipping his tea and regarding me with a careful expression. This only serves to discombobulate me even further.

'. . . but maybe I've gained enough from today to see me through for the time being . . .'

Better! Yes, yes! Much better!

'. . . so if we could leave it a few weeks and maybe arrange another session for next month?'

What?! What are you saying, you bloody fool! You're not telling him no! Say no! Say NO!

Cleethorpes continues to merely look at me, but that smile is starting to creep back on to his face.

'. . . do you think you'd be available next month?' I ask.

Please say no.

'Yes, of course!'

Oh, *for crying out loud.*

'Excellent!'

Idiot!

Cleethorpes' face darkens slightly. 'I will have to think of a place where the police will not disturb us, though.'

'Maybe we should do it in the evening? Fewer foot patrols then.'

STOP MAKING HELPFUL SUGGESTIONS, YOU CRETIN.

'A good idea, Nathan!' He claps me on the shoulder. 'I will let you know when I am free.'

'Great stuff. Looking forward to it,' I say in a voice that sounds like a deflating balloon.

Cleethorpes stretches out his arm. From under the blue jacket sleeve an *Inspector Gadget* watch appears, which he peers at intently. 'But now I'm afraid I must go,' the little man tells me.

'Oh no, really?'

There is something deeply wrong with me, isn't there?

Some common sense then reasserts itself in my head, and I actually manage to say something sensible. 'Let me show you out.'

I lead Cleethorpes out of the kitchen and across the hallway to the front door. 'Thank you for the tea, Nathan,' he says. 'And thank you for telling me how much my session has helped you.'

'Not a problem,' I reply, grasping hold of the door handle.

'I am so glad that we have started to deal with your feelings of anger.'

'I do feel a lot less angry.'

This is the truth. I now just feel comprehensively awkward.

Still, at least my towering rage has been dampened – for the time being, at least. With any luck, nothing will spark it off again any time soon.

I pull open the front door.

Standing there is Sienna with an excited expression on her face.

'Nathan! Nathan! I have to speak to you!' she squeals, before noticing I'm with someone. 'Hello. Who are you?'

The little man bows floridly. 'Delighted to meet you, young lady. I am Cleethorpes!'

Sienna looks him up and down for a second, then leans closer to me with one hand by her mouth. 'Is he your drug dealer?' she whispers. There's a hopeful tone to her voice I suppose I should be disturbed by.

I roll my eyes. Sienna's not normally one for a bit of casual racism, but dangle the prospect of scoring some drugs in her face and she reverts to stereotype in the blink of an eye.

'No!' I reply, not meeting Cleethorpes' expression. 'He's my new . . . self-help guru.' Saying it out loud sounds extremely silly.

'Er . . . I must be going, Nathan,' Cleethorpes says, moving round Sienna and giving her the widest berth possible.

I say goodbye and watch Cleethorpes walk down my driveway, before returning my attention to my excited girlfriend once he has disappeared from sight.

'Sienna. What . . . what are you doing here?' I ask.

She gives me a look of such unbridled glee I start to fear for her sanity. '*Cosmopolitan*, Nathan!'

'What?'

'*Cosmopolitan*!'

A few minutes later, we're stood in my kitchen – me with my arms folded and looking suspicious, her talking animatedly and bouncing around like a jack-in-the-box.

'So, what are you on about, Sienna? Why are you so excited?'

'Well . . . I saw Nevaeh a couple of days ago. You remember her, she's my friend from the Sean Paul video?'

'Which one?'

'The girl in the really small bikini that gives him a lap dance?'

'Yeah, that doesn't really narrow it down much.'

Sienna flaps her hands. 'It doesn't matter. The important thing is that her boyfriend is a guy called Jordan, and he works for *Cosmopolitan*. So when I told her all about your tumour, she told Jordan, who called me, and—'

'You did what?!'

You know all that anger I thought Cleethorpes had leeched out of me? It's back in an instant.

'I told her about your tumour. That was okay, wasn't it?'

I'm incredulous. 'Telling complete bloody strangers about the fact I'm going to die? A hugely personal and private matter?' I facepalm. 'Yeah . . . why would I have a problem with that, eh?'

Sienna laughs. 'I knew you wouldn't mind!'

Oh, for fuck's sake.

'Anyway,' she continues, completely oblivious. 'Nevaeh spoke to Jordan, who said he would be really interested in doing a story about us!'

'Us? What do you mean "*us*"? And what kind of story?'

Sienna rolls her eyes. 'How you're coping with your brain tumour, *silly*. Jordan says there's a lot of human interest, as you're well known for creating those Foodie things.' Sienna grins at me almost maniacally. 'He says they can get us a *two-page* picture spread! Two pages in *Cosmo*, Nathan!' Her eyes light up. 'I'll be in *Cosmo*!'

I am *dumbfounded*. I knew Sienna was prone to being shallow – but this? 'So basically, you've told complete strangers that I'm dying, to help you with your career?'

She contrives to look hurt. 'No. No . . . of course not, baby. But the story could help, you know? Other people like you?' She bites her lip seductively. 'And it would be a nice thing to do for me, too. After all, you'd love to be fucking a *Cosmo* model, wouldn't you?'

Jesus Christ. How can anyone be so *self-centred*?

I stupidly thought that Sienna not caring about my diagnosis was a good thing – that if she doesn't care, then I don't have to, either.

I was utterly *wrong*.

Silently counting to ten, I take a long and deep breath, before fixing my eyes squarely on my very soon-to-be ex-girlfriend. I have made an important decision. Probably the first wise one for quite a long time. 'Get out.'

Sienna's face crumples. 'What?'

'Get out of my house, Sienna. Get out of my house, and make sure you never come back here again.'

'What? You're throwing me *out*?'

'Yes. That's precisely what I'm doing.'

Sienna now looks like she wants to murder me. 'Fuck you, Nathan! I try to do something *nice* for you, to help you get your story out there—'

'Get my *story out there*?' I spit. 'Make your CV look better, you mean!'

Her hands go to her hips. 'And why shouldn't I do that? Why can't you do that for me? I do *so much for you*, Nathan!' she snarls. 'You're so fucking *selfish*!'

'*I'm* selfish??'

'Yes! The most selfish man I've ever met! You only ever think about yourself!' She grabs her tits. 'This is all I am to you!'

'No, it's not!' I blanche. Sienna might be getting uncomfortably close to an unwanted truth here . . .

'Yes, it is! I let you do what you want to me, whenever you want! And I don't want much in return!' She clenches her fists. 'All I want is a two-page spread in *Cosmopolitan*!' She thrusts a finger above her head. 'If you'd agreed, I was going to let you put it in my arse tonight, Nathan!'

'*Cosmopolitan*?' I reply in confusion. I have no particular desire to insert periodicals into another human being's rectum. I have no idea where she's got that idea from.

She looks at me in disgust. 'You hateful *idiot*!' she screams.

Christ. I'd better wrap this up before I get attacked by eight stone of enraged model. 'Seriously, Sienna, get the rosy royal fuck out of my house,' I tell her.

She goes to say something else, but I hold a hand out. 'No. Don't talk. There's simply nothing you can say to make me change my mind. We're *over*, Sienna. *Finished*. You could offer to let me insert an entire branch of WHSmith up there and it wouldn't make any difference. I am tired, and I now have a pounding headache thanks to you . . . so, pretty please, leave this house, and my life, *right now*.'

Sienna stares at me in horror for a few moments, before turning in a massive huff and storming out of the kitchen.

As she stamps into the hallway, she turns to me with an expression of pure loathing. 'I hope that tumour *does* kill you!'

Well, that's charming, isn't it? Although entirely to be expected, I suppose.

I point towards my still-open front door without saying a word. Sienna gives me the finger and storms out, not looking back.

I slam the front door with a gratifying amount of force and take a step back, my heart racing.

'Fuck about,' I exclaim in a hurried breath, to no one in particular.

A feeling of overwhelming remorse then courses through me. What the hell have I *done*? I've just thrown out the only good thing in my life!

Good?! another part of my brain screams at me. *She was fucking awful, you idiot! She didn't care about you at all!*

Yes, but that doesn't matter to me!

. . . or at least it didn't until I found out I had this stupid tumour!

In a fit of anger I punch the front door, leaving a dent in the wood. 'Ow! For fuck's sake!' I wail, clutching my throbbing hand.

How many more things will this bloody tumour take away from me?

I've lost my happiness, my hope, my future, my Porsche 911 and now my bloody girlfriend!

How much more am I going to *lose*?

I think back on what I said to Cleethorpes outside Primark. He told me I had to find something to replace all the things I've had to lose thanks to this bloody tumour . . . but what? What the hell can I possibly do with my life now there's probably so little of it left?

'Jesus Christ,' I moan, still to no one in particular.

It takes me a good few moments to calm myself down, but when I eventually do, I make my way back through to the kitchen to grab some painkillers for my hand.

It's probably a good job I did agree to more sessions with Cleethorpes.

When I see him next I might ask him if he minds holding up a picture of Sienna while I batter him over the head repeatedly – or I might stick him in a red Prada dress and a wig just to go the whole hog . . .

Good grief.

I started the day enraged at a malfunctioning coffee machine and have ended it picturing a small, stocky man in drag. At this rate, I'm likely to go stark staring crazy before the tumour has a chance to kill me off.

LYRICS TO THE FOODIES SONG 'I'M A POORLY PANTS'

Herman the Grumpy Potato sings:

Oh no, oh no, I'm a poorly pants. My tummy is
so sore, and my head is full of ants.

The rest of The Foodies sing:

Oh no, oh no, he's a poorly pants. He's not feeling
well, and he's far too ill to dance.

Herman the Grumpy Potato sings:

Life is so hard when you're feeling rather sick,
You can't get out of bed, your nose is really thick,
The best thing to do is sleep until it ends,
If you go out of the house, you might sneeze on
all your friends.

(Sneezes on friends)

The rest of The Foodies sing:

Oh, that's so horrible, Herman! You are so gross!
We're all covered in snot, and we've probably
caught a dose!
You should go to bed, before you start to cry,
We all know you're ill, but you're not going to die!

Herman the Grumpy Potato sings:

Oh no, oh no, I'm a poorly pants. My head is
thumping hard, I haven't got a chance.

The rest of The Foodies sing:

Oh no, oh no, he's a poorly pants. It won't stop
him moaning, though, we might run off to
France.

(The Foodies all put on berets and strings of
onions and dance around Herman again)

The Foodies all sing together:

Oh no, oh no, don't be a poorly pants. Just listen
to what we sing, listen to our chants!
Oh no, oh no, don't be a poorly pants. Make
sure you wash your hands, so you'll all stand
a chance!

SHOW'S OVER, FOLKS

14 MAY

'So, Callum. Are you looking forward to seeing The Foodies today?'

Stony silence.

'Ahem. Mummy says you like Libby the Happy Lemon the most.'

Continued stony silence.

'I've managed to get you both seats right at the front, so you'll be able to see everything.'

More stony silence, accompanied by a piercing glare that suggests contempt on levels hitherto unexperienced by humankind.

'Callum, say something to Nate,' Eliza tells him. When the little boy buries his head in her leg, she gives me an apologetic look. 'He really is looking forward to the show, Nate. He's been talking about it all day.'

I raise an eyebrow. As far as I can tell, the kid looks about as happy as someone about to go in for a colonoscopy, but I guess I have to take his mother's word for it. 'Okay,' I reply, very unsure.

She gives me a hesitant smile. 'He just doesn't know you all that well, and he's not good with stra' – she just about manages to stop herself from saying it – 'with people when he's out and about.'

That smarts. Callum and Eliza are family, yet he thinks of me as a *stranger*?

Eliza gives me a sympathetic look. 'How are you doing? After the break-up with Sienna, I mean.'

I wave a hand. 'Oh, fine. Good riddance to bad rubbish and all that.' I'm not entirely sure I believe what I'm saying, but it sounds about right. 'She was no good for me.'

Eliza's face clouds. 'No. She definitely wasn't.' The sympathetic look then returns. 'And what about . . . you know?'

'Oh . . . er, fine, I guess. Not troubling me too much.' This is not in any way reflective of the truth, but I don't particularly feel the need to burden Eliza with even more of my problems right about now.

'Good,' she replies, with a half-hearted smile. She knows I'm not being completely honest with her. She always does.

One of the Roundabout Theatre's stagehands appears at the fire exit door to the green room. 'Nate, we need you inside,' he tells me.

'We'll go and get into our seats,' Eliza says. 'Give me a kiss for good luck.' She leans forward and plants a kiss on my cheek, before looking down at her thunderous offspring. 'Want to give Nate a kiss, too, Callum?'

There's more chance of Callum kissing Freddy Krueger than me, I'd wager. 'I'll see you both backstage after the show, then?' I say, not attempting to meet Callum's gaze again.

'Yeah. See you later. Have a good show,' Eliza replies. With another apologetic look, she turns and leads the little boy away, leaving me to wonder exactly what I've done to incur such an intense dislike from someone in my extended family.

Speaking of disliking something, welcome to my nightmare backstage, fifteen minutes later.

Actually, I don't just *dislike* The Foodies . . . I actively *hate* The Foodies.

I mean, just look at them, would you?

No, seriously, I mean it – *look at them*. Over there, across from me in the other wing of the theatre, crammed together backstage like particularly fat sardines as we wait for the curtain to go up on what will be my last ever show. A bunch of brightly coloured idiots that I thought up in a lunch break one day while I was trying my hardest to write something of value about climate change to educate our children.

Needless to say, this singularly failed to materialise. It's very hard to rhyme anything with 'biodiversity'.

Instead of composing a thoughtful, life-changing song about how we can all make the world a better place, I ended up throwing together a quick and upbeat ditty about how the sun gives us our food. If I'd have known it would go on to become something of a national phenomenon I would have tried a little harder.

I certainly would have chosen some slightly more worthy foodstuffs for inclusion in the ensemble, that's for sure.

Smedley the Smelly Cheese and Frank the Silly Sausage are quite literally only in there because I'd had a sausage-and-cheese toastie for lunch. If I had a more mature palate, they would have been Billy the Bourgeois Brioche and Penelope the Pretentious Pancetta.

Libby and Pip are fine, I guess. They're fruit. How wrong can you really go with fruit? Parents love fruit, kids love fruit. Everybody loves fruit.

Chewy the Cheeky Toffee is in the group just because I'm a big *Star Wars* fan and I always go for the toffee pennies in the Quality Street. He's a bit incongruous when compared to the others, I suppose. You can argue that the other five are all part of a balanced diet, but I don't think anyone's sung the praises of toffee's nutritional value since Werther's were original.

And then there's Herman.

Herman the Grumpy Potato.

While I didn't think it was right to have a proper villain as part of a children's singing ensemble, I did want a character in there that could cause some low-level friction between the anthropomorphic little twats. Herman seemed perfect for that role.

When I was a small boy, Mum used to feed me at least three jacket potatoes a week. This was a period in her life when she was obsessed with growing her own vegetables. Sadly, she was terrible at it. Potatoes were the only thing she could manage to grow with any real success. Everything else just rotted or refused to grow at all in the first place. The potatoes had no such problems, though. In fact, it quickly became clear that while Mum was a hopeless grower of vegetables in general, she was a *master* of the home-grown potato – hence my heavy, starch-based diet throughout my formative years.

I grew to loathe the sight and smell of a baked potato. It didn't matter how many different toppings she forked on top of the bloody thing, underneath it was still a sodding potato.

Luckily, Mum grew out of her allotment phase within the space of a year or two, and I got to eat different kinds of food again, but to this day I cannot stand the sight of a cooked potato. When the local Spudulike shut down, I had a fucking party.

Herman, then, represents my childhood loathing and is the perfect foil for the rest of the gang. He's grumpy all the time, because wouldn't you be if you were a talking potato?

The guy currently attempting to squeeze his rather round posterior into the Herman the Grumpy Potato costume across the way from me looks more forlorn than enraged. Let's hope he's a good actor. Herman requires a certain degree of barely supressed fury to be captured properly in live action.

I heave a sigh as I slip the guitar from its case, wishing I was anywhere but here right now.

'Here' is the Roundabout Theatre, just outside the city centre. This is the seventh and final night of my last Foodies tour of the country – a fact I am *delighted* about. A week of touring Foodies shows is bad enough when you're feeling hale and hearty, but when you're nursing a problem like mine, it's made a thousand times *worse*. I've been suffering from this bastard headache the entire tour. I can't wait to get finished with it so I don't have to stand onstage in front of bright theatre lighting any more.

I should have probably cancelled my appearances after I found out about the tumour. Brightside could have easily started using the session musicians that will be replacing me after this tour anyway, but then after what happened with Sienna, I figured I could probably use something constructive to occupy myself with. The joys of travelling across the country, staying in different hotels and playing my music live seemed liked a good distraction.

It's a choice I'm coming to wholeheartedly *regret*.

What I'm not regretting is the decision to extricate Sienna from my life. Since the break-up, I've spent a great deal of time mulling over my relationship with her and why I was with her in the first place. When I ask myself the question 'why did I date a woman like that?' the answers I come up with are universally unpleasant – and provide an insight into my state of mind that turns my stomach a little when I think about it too much.

After all, how shallow does someone have to be to want nothing more from a relationship than perky boobs and an even perkier bottom? What does it say about me that I viewed my relationship with Sienna much like the one I had with my Porsche?

Okay, she was quite clearly even worse with her attitude towards me – that was proved with the whole *Cosmopolitan* thing – but I didn't exactly care about her much, either, when you get right down to it.

Aaaargh!

This bloody tumour is forcing me into a degree of self-reflection I am extremely uncomfortable with.

I pinch the bridge of my nose tightly for a second, forcing myself back into the here and now and away from such unproductive thoughts. I look out into the darkened auditorium at the gathered ranks of overexcited small people and swallow heavily. Even Callum looks animated now. I can see him jiggling around on his seat next to his tired-looking mother.

I'm not normally nervous before doing these shows, but tonight is a different story. You see, that tremor I first felt on the night I blacked out has come back.

It's almost imperceptible, but it's definitely there. I noticed it as I was taking a shower after last night's show. My denial kicked in and I put it down to tiredness at the time, but when I woke up with it this morning I knew it was tumour-related.

I've spent the rest of the day convinced that I'm about to drop dead any second.

That's what this kind of disease does to you – it takes any small ailment you may be suffering from and blows it out of all proportion. It also sends your stress levels rocketing – hence the thumping headache that came on at about 4 p.m., which has only been tamed by four co-codamol and a double JD and Coke at the theatre bar.

So, while I am nervous, I'm also high as hell on over-the-counter drugs and alcohol.

It's an unpleasant combination. I don't know how rock stars do it. If I had to go onstage feeling like this every night, I think I'd throw in the towel and get a job as an accountant.

'Curtains up in one minute, Mr James,' says a stagehand from behind me.

'Thanks very much,' I reply, taking a deep breath.

What I resolutely *don't do* is hold my left hand out in front of me to see if the tremor is still there. That way lies madness. Right now, the hand is gripping the neck of my guitar and it feels perfectly normal. Let's just hope it stays that way once I walk onstage, sit on my seat and strum the C major open chord that begins the first song of the show.

To take my mind off needless self-reflection, the tremor and the headache, I look back across the stage at The Foodies once more, who are now lined up and ready to rock and roll. I feel an instant pang of pity for the poor buggers underneath those costumes. I feel hot in my Foodies T-shirt and jeans. I can only imagine what it's like to have to parade around a stage under those searing lights for an hour in that get-up.

I'm ashamed to say I have made no attempt whatsoever to get to know this latest group of actors who are bringing my characters to life. I know that they are all new recruits to The Foodies experience, hired by Brightside Productions. I couldn't even tell you their names or pick any of them out of a line-up after a week of performances. I've tended to keep myself to myself, thanks to the tumour – preferring splendid isolation to interacting with those around me. They probably all think I'm a right bastard.

Usually, this would bother me no end, but I have a tremor and a headache to worry about, so my social graces have gone out of the window somewhat. It's a little hard to make nice with your work colleagues when you're afraid you might shuffle off this mortal coil at any moment.

Even in the big padded suits, you can tell which of The Foodies are enthusiastic about this debacle from the extremely limited body language on offer. Smedley, Pip and Chewy are standing alert and ready to go, while Frank appears to be sending a last-minute text. How he can see through the gauze window in the front of his sausage head to do this is beyond me, but he appears to be coping fine.

There's something going on between Libby and Herman, though. Libby is grasping Herman by the arm and is leaning in close. This isn't easy, as both costumes are very rotund. It looks like she might well be saying something important to him. Herman, for his part, is trying to turn away from her and look back at Frank, who is completely oblivious to all of this, as he's still texting. Libby takes hold of Herman's foamy head and turns it back to her, so she can carry on talking to him. It doesn't seem like Herman's happy with what he's being told in the slightest. He keeps on trying to gesture towards Frank the Silly Sausage, but Libby is stopping him at every attempt.

If you've never witnessed a heated discussion between two human beings dressed in overblown fancy dress costumes, I can safely report that it does look exactly as ridiculous as you'd imagine. It's rather like looking at two people at a Weight Watchers meeting having a meltdown about pizza toppings.

Some sort of accord looks to have been struck, though, as Herman now bobs his giant brown foam head up and down a couple of times in agreement with something Libby has obviously just said. It looks like whatever issue the two Foodies have, it has at least been put on hold for the next hour or so.

And with that, The Foodies theme begins to play in the auditorium. The gathered ranks of phlegmy children all start to scream excitedly.

This is my fault. This is something I have wrought upon the world, God help me.

I hate the theme tune with a *passion*, having heard it about seventeen million times. I invented The Foodies on a lunch break, and I invented their simple three-chord monstrosity of a theme tune while having a luxurious poo. There was a bird outside having a nice sing-song and it sounded rather pleasant, so I stole the melody and made it the basis of the song.

Now I wish I could find that bird and squeeze him until his eyeballs pop.

The Foodies theme winds to a grateful close after about a minute. The curtains open to reveal an expensively designed set that looks like a large country kitchen has somehow inexplicably mated with a bouncy castle. That cooker may look delightfully squashy and soft, but the chances of whipping up a nice chicken hotpot in it are zero. Brightside really have forked out a lot for this new set, though. It puts the old cardboard one completely in the shade.

I wander onstage by myself and take up my position. Looking out at the audience, I see the usual reaction to my appearance. The parents all look confused and the kids look disappointed (including Callum). It says on all the posters that the creator of The Foodies is part of this tour, but nobody paid their twenty pounds to watch a bloke in a cheap T-shirt sat on a stool. They want to see jobbing actors in bulbous fancy dress costumes and won't be happy until they do so.

Let's not keep them waiting.

I hold my breath as I sit the guitar in my lap and place my fingers on the strings. There's a moment – a fleeting, tiny moment – when I think I feel the tremor in my left hand return, but it disappears as soon as I strum downwards with my right hand and hear the C major open ring out clear and divine through the theatre's PA system.

At this point, muscle memory takes over and my tremor worries are gone. I guess there is a chance I could drop off my stool at any minute and send all these kids into therapy for the next fifteen years, but until that happens, I will do what I've always done when I'm playing my guitar – enjoy the hell out of every moment.

I glance over to see that The Foodies are making their way onstage, accompanied by a roar of appreciation from everyone in the audience under the age of ten. Everybody else other than Eliza is looking at me with intense hatred, given that I am the reason why they have to suffer through this shit for the next sixty minutes.

Five of The Foodies look happy to be there. They dance around the stage like things possessed, waving at the children like maniacs. The sixth member of the troupe looks decidedly less happy. In fact, Herman looks like somebody has just shot his dog. He lopes on to the stage with his head bowed, not even trying to acknowledge the audience.

Something definitely isn't right here.

While Herman is meant to be the Foodie with something of an attitude problem, he is not meant to be a miserable bastard. He gets grumpy with his fellow Foodies for what he perceives to be their rather childish ways, but he generally does so in an animated and upbeat fashion.

The portrayal of Herman being played out in front of me this evening appears to be more downbeat than a Radiohead album.

As both I and the musicians backstage start to play the opening bars of 'Come on, Give Us a Hug', Herman stumbles into place alongside his compatriots with about as much enthusiasm as a real potato.

. . . actually, no, I tell a lie, I saw a strangely shaped Maris Piper in Asda once that looked enthusiastically out at me from its cellophane bag, so even that's not an accurate comparison.

While the rest of my creations are on the money with their performances, Herman is barely doing anything. He's just swaying back and forth a bit. It's like watching a potato-based episode of *The Walking Dead*.

Having seen our awful live show more times than I care to count now, I know when things are not going according to plan. I therefore know something is most definitely wrong when Libby dances her way closer to Herman and gives him a swift poke in his brown potato arse. She then stares at him for a second. This seems to snap Herman out of his miserable reverie, as he starts to dance with a bit more animation, finally getting back on track with the rest of the performers.

I give Herman one more suspicious look before fully concentrating on my guitar playing. The chorus of 'Come on, Give Us a Hug' contains a rather complicated transition between C minor and E minor that I always struggle with a bit. I'll just have to hope that whatever problem Herman is dealing with is taken care of.

Everything goes quite well for the next forty-five minutes. There are no mishaps, no major issues, and my hand stays resolutely solid as I play my way through the set list, while my characters strut and fret their way across the boards, their previously recorded vocals belting out of the theatre's loudspeakers.

Then, we reach a song that I regret writing to this day.

'I'm a Poorly Pants' is the single most irritating piece of music ever conceived by man. The catchy – yet soul-destroying – five-note harmony worms its way into my brain every time I hear it.

You know how awful it is when you develop an earworm and spend weeks singing or humming it to yourself? Now imagine that *you wrote the bloody thing in the first place.* Can you imagine the self-loathing? The knowledge that you, and you alone, are responsible for the musical madness currently threatening to take away your sanity?

About the only thing 'Poorly Pants' has going for it is that it's mercifully brief. I have no doubt this comes as as much of a relief to the rest of the cast as it does to me, as the level of physical activity required on their part to realise the themes of the song through interpretive dance is extremely high.

Herman has to herk and jerk around the place, sneezing his tuberous head off, while the rest of them have to dance around him, trying to avoid his germ-laden spittle.

. . . I really know how to create fine art, don't I?

We're a good thirty seconds into the song when a small calamity strikes. While doing his sneezing impression, the guy in the Herman suit stumbles forward and crashes into Frank the Silly Sausage, who in turn staggers into the inflatable refrigerator, before bouncing back off it and tumbling to the floor.

Now, in and of itself, this isn't much of an issue. People falling over in those idiotic costumes happens every now and again, and the children all get a kick out of it, so no real harm done. However, on this particular occasion, Frank doesn't just jump to his feet and carry on with the performance as if nothing has happened. No, Frank, it appears, is decidedly *unhappy* about being pushed over by Herman. I can tell this because I then hear – loud and clear over the sound of my guitar and the rest of the orchestra – Frank shout, 'You did that on purpose!' to Herman as he dances past him.

I look out into the auditorium to see if anybody else has picked up on it, but the kids are too hyped up on E-numbers and overexcitement to notice and the adults couldn't give two fucks.

The song continues. We reach the chorus once again where the rest of The Foodies run circles around poorly Herman, this time wearing hastily donned berets and strings of onions. I keep a close eye on Frank to see if any retaliation will be forthcoming for the perceived attack upon his sausagey person. Sure enough, as he circles around Herman, Frank sticks out a leg, deliberately tripping the potato up.

Now, I should be disgusted by this unprofessional turn of events, given that I am the de facto leader of this little troupe, but I've had to watch this show so many times now that any deviation from the accepted narrative is a positive *godsend*. I shuffle myself around a bit on the stool to await further developments.

Herman does not fall over, thanks to the fact that Libby holds out her hands as she goes past him to offer her support. She also gives Frank an angry look. At least, I assume it's an angry look. She could just be constipated for all I know. The giant lemon head doesn't let me actually see her expression, so I'm well and truly in the realms of guesswork here.

Herman's next action is far easier to read and understand, though, given that he charges straight at Frank, sending them both tumbling to the stage floor in a tangle of arms, legs and moulded foam rubber.

This wakes up the adults in the audience. I hear an audible gasp rise from everyone over the age of ten, alongside the giggles of two hundred children – who enjoy a bit of casual violence as much as the next person.

While I and the invisible orchestra backstage gamely try to play through the rest of the chorus, the actual Foodies themselves are now caught in an impromptu fight that has little or nothing to do with being a poorly pants.

Herman is slapping at Frank's head with his big, foamy potato gloves. Given that Frank's face is frozen in a permanent smile, it makes it look like he's a severe masochist who just loves getting a hard palming across the forehead. Frank is also holding up his arms protectively. I can hear him screaming for somebody to get Herman off.

Herman, as far as I can tell, is sobbing loudly into his costume.

Pip, Chewy and Smedley are still trying to dance happily around both of them, as if seeing a potato physically assault a sausage is the most natural and wonderful thing in the world, but Libby is not such a happy lemon right now, as she's trying to break the two of them up, without much success.

Over all of this is the heady combination of my irritating five-note harmony and the happy, delighted sounds of singing coming from the pre-recorded vocal backing track.

'Don't be a poorly pants!'

THWACK.

'Just listen to what we sing!'

SCREAM.

'Listen to our chants!'

SOB.

I look over to both wings to see if anybody is going to actually come onstage and break this shit up, but I'm greeted with a series of faces frozen in horror.

Given no one else is doing anything, I figure *I'd* better do something, before all the little darlings below me in the auditorium are sent home this evening traumatised by having to watch a supermarket version of *Fight Club*.

Still playing my guitar as I walk across the stage (ever the professional), I reach the warring twosome and proceed to gently kick them in the ribs to make them stop. As I do this, I maintain a cheery smile on my face so as not to scare the children.

Through gritted teeth I demand an end to this charade.

'Stop it, you idiots!' I hiss at them both.

Libby looks up at me. 'I'm so sorry, Mr James!' I hear her muffled voice say.

'Just get them to stop!' I repeat, giving Herman another boot to the midsection.

'Why did you leave?!' Herman sobs at Frank, ignoring me completely.

'This, Hamish! This is why I left!' Frank screams. 'You can't control your mood swings!'

'He *is* Herman the Grumpy Potato, you know,' I point out. While this may be factually accurate, perhaps now is not the *best time* to be reminding them of such.

Frank looks up at me . . . well, sort of, anyway. 'Yes! I knew it would be the perfect part for him!' he wails.

'Yes! Yes!' Herman squeals. 'You said that, didn't you? Right before you walked out of the fucking door!'

'Oi! Less of that!' I shout, kicking Herman hard enough this time to knock him off Frank completely. I don't mind a little light violence in front of the children, but swearing is a no-no.

I hear the orchestra start to wind up 'Poorly Pants' and accompany them on the guitar, exhibiting the grinning rictus of a man who knows that this show has ten minutes left to run. It's ten minutes that won't feature Herman the Grumpy Potato, as he has now stormed offstage in a tuberous huff.

'Oh God,' Libby says from next to me.

'God can't help us,' I reply. 'I don't think intervention in sausage-versus-potato warfare has ever been his thing.'

'Don't worry, Mr James. I'll get us through the rest of the show,' Libby says.

Good. At least someone around here has some common sense. 'Thanks. Get Frank up and we'll battle through the rest of it without Herman.'

'Hamish.'

'Whatever.'

I walk back across the stage as the first few chords of 'We Love to Wave Goodbye' start to play. This should be good. How the hell are The Foodies going to convince Herman that he shouldn't stubbornly refuse to leave and come home with them when he has already resolutely fucked off?

I decide it's best if I just concentrate on my part of the show for the remaining song instead of worrying about what the others are doing. There's not much I can do about Herman and his relationship problems now.

Luckily for me, the woman inside the Libby costume seems to have the qualities of someone who knows how to rescue a situation from impending disaster, and rallies the rest of The Foodies for the last two numbers. Okay, there's nothing she can do about the giant potato-sized hole in the show's climax, but at least we haven't had to call the whole thing off early. There may be a few refund requests coming in at the end of the night, but not as many as we would have had if the last thing everyone in the audience saw was two fully grown men dressed in foam rubber costumes belting each other to the accompaniment of a song about having the sniffles.

'We Love to Wave Goodbye' finally segues into the last song of the night: 'Happy All Together' – a tune about being friends and getting on with one another. This makes a lot of the parents in the audience laugh their arses off at the obvious irony, so at least we've managed to give them something to smile about.

Finally, the curtain comes down on what will be remembered as easily the most eventful night of this seven-night theatrical run. I spy Callum clapping and whooping like a madman down in the front row right before the curtain closes completely.

The second it has, I turn to my cast members with a scowl on my face. 'Right, what in fuckery was all that about, please?'

'I'm sorry, Mr James,' Libby repeats. 'This has been a very bad time for Hamish and Jonathan.'

'Jonathan?'

Frank the Silly Sausage holds up a meaty hand. 'That's me.'

'They've had relationship problems and—'

I hold up a hand. 'Can I just stop you there? It's very hard to have a serious conversation with someone dressed as a grinning lemon.'

'Oh . . . oh yes, of course.' Libby reaches up and gently flips up the entire top third of her costume, revealing a woman in her late twenties.

'As I was saying, Hamish and Jonathan have recently split up, and I think the wounds are still fresh, so that's why Hamish was the way he was tonight.' She gives me an imploring look. 'He's a lovely man usually, Mr James. *Honestly.*'

Libby the Happy Lemon is hot, red-faced and sweaty, and her blonde hair is plastered to the side of her cheek and forehead. There's also something of a disconcerting smell emanating from the bright-yellow costume she's wearing.

She's also very pretty, in a sweaty kind of way.

Libby breathes heavily and wafts a yellow foam hand in her face. 'Excuse me, Mr James, but do you mind if I go and get out of my costume? It's incredibly hot in here.'

'Um, yeah, of course,' I reply.

Libby gives me a bright smile, turns and walks away in the direction of the large changing rooms off to the left-hand side of the stage. The remaining cast members go with her, leaving me standing alone onstage, the sound of muffled movement coming from the departing crowd beyond the curtain.

I lift my left hand up to my face and regard it gravely. It's shaking ever so slightly.

'Oh, fuck off,' I tell it under my breath, before shuffling offstage towards my dressing room.

As this is my last ever night doing a Foodies show, a party has been laid on in the green room backstage by the theatre's owners.

Taylor and the Brightsides asked me if I wanted them to come along, but I immediately told them no, because I didn't want much of a fuss made. I've been comprehensively dreading this occasion, and having them there would have made it ten times worse.

When I arrive in the rather tatty green room, a few crew members are milling around a couple of tables full of snack foods and drinks. A sign saying 'Best of Luck, Nathan!' is hung haphazardly on a wall at the back of the room.

It all looks a bit forlorn, to be honest with you. I walk over with a forced smile and engage a few of the crew in light conversation. Most of them seem quite nervous about talking to me. Eliza should turn up with Callum pretty soon, so at least I'll have two people I know to talk to.

Eventually, a group of chatting actors make their way from the doors to their respective changing rooms and out into the drab green room.

The two female members of the cast who play Libby and Pip emerge first. Pip is a middle-aged woman who I just know is in desperate need of a cigarette the second I lay eyes on her. Libby is with her, a rather concerned and tired look on her face.

'Hi!' I say to them both as they walk across the floor to where I'm standing. Libby looks pleased to see me. Pip is searching through her pockets for a lighter.

'Hello, Mr James,' Libby says again, with a cheeky half-smile, her green eyes twinkling in the room's light. 'Are you pleased it's all over?'

I laugh. 'Yeah, I guess so.'

'All right,' Pip says in a broad east London accent. She seems less impressed with my presence. This may be because I am not a white cylinder containing tobacco. She looks at Libby. 'I'm just popping out for a ciggy,' she tells her before looking at me again. 'Nice to meet you, Mr James.'

Pip then shuffles off to the fire exit at the rear of the green room, letting in the cold air as she goes through it, lighter held aloft and cigarette screwed in one corner of her mouth.

I turn back to Libby.

. . . no, her name is not Libby, *you bellend. Find out what it really is before you actually start calling her* Libby.

'Please, call me Nathan,' I say, trying to sound cool. 'What's your name?'

'Alison. My name's Alison. Though my friends call me Allie.'

'It's nice to meet you, Alison,' I tell her.

She smiles. 'You too . . .'

From somewhere in the men's changing rooms over Alison's shoulder there is a thump and a loud, rather high-pitched exclamation of pain that makes me wince.

I notice that the majority of the theatre crew have now started to exit the green room. They obviously have an idea of what's about to happen.

'Do you think I should go and do something?' I ask Alison, keeping a wary eye on the men's changing room.

She shakes her head. 'No. I'd let Joel handle it. He's been keeping them at arm's length the whole tour.'

'Who?'

'The guy inside Chewy.'

'Ahh.'

I've noticed that Chewy towers appropriately over everyone else in the group. Maybe Alison is right. I should leave it to someone who knows the situation well and not go blundering in myself.

'So, what happened between Herman and Frank?' I ask.

'Hamish has . . . some *issues*. Has had for a long time,' Alison explains. 'Jonathan told me it all started when he got fired from a lucrative mascot job in London last year.'

'Really?'

'Yeah. He was playing Baa Baa Bad Sheep from that stupid video game when he got into a fight with someone at a convention for no good reason,' Alison explains. 'It lost him and Jonathan a *huge* amount of money. Things only got worse from there. Jonathan just reached the point last week where he couldn't cope any more and broke off the engagement.'

'Ouch. He could have picked a better time to do it.'

'You're right . . . and that's half the problem. Putting them both onstage together after something like that was always going to be a recipe for disaster.'

I'm about to agree with her when Hamish, Jonathan and Joel all appear from the men's changing room, banging the door open loudly as they come through. None of them look like happy campers.

'You're a maniac, Hamish!' the one I assume to be Jonathan exclaims.

'And you're a *bastard*, Jonathan!' Hamish responds.

'Can the two of you just calm down!' Joel interjects.

I'd calm down if Joel told me to. He's an *enormous* guy, with the kind of physique I could only dream about having.

'No! I will not calm down! This has been a—' Hamish spots me standing by Alison. 'Oh God!' he exclaims, hand going to his mouth. It appears Hamish has forgotten about the party and my august presence in the green room tonight.

I figure I'd better say something to make him and everyone else feel more at ease.

'Thank you all for your hard work over the past two weeks,' I tell them. 'I know The Foodies will be in good hands after I've left.'

Given what transpired onstage tonight, this is something of a fib, but I figure there's no point in making things worse.

Hamish looks distraught. 'Are you going to fire me?' he asks, fear etched across his face.

'What?' I blurt out.

'Don't be surprised if he does! It wouldn't be the first time!' Jonathan opines, storming away from Hamish to grab himself a bottle of water.

Hamish actually starts to cry.

He's quite a heavyset lad, with a face that's already flushed from all the excitement, so I'm afraid to say he rather reminds me of a squalling newborn baby. '*Please*, Mr James! It won't happen again! I've never done anything like that before!'

'Ha!' exclaims Jonathan in a derisory fashion.

Hamish looks daggers at him. 'That was entirely *different*, Jonathan! I was provoked!'

'Ha!' Jonathan cries again, taking a swig of water.

'I'm not firing anybody!' I shout, trying to head this off before it comes to fisticuffs again. This earns me a look of pathetic gratitude from Hamish.

'You see?' Joel says to Hamish in a deep, rumbling voice. 'I told you he'd be an okay guy.'

I don't quite know how to take that.

'Well, it was lovely to meet you, Mr James,' Hamish remarks, still red of face and snotty of nose, 'and in other circumstances I'd like to stay and chat a little longer, but I really need to leave now.' He shoots Jonathan another look of hatred. 'I need some time alone.'

Jonathan rolls his eyes and Hamish storms off through the exit, nearly knocking Pip over as she makes her way back inside. 'What's his fucking problem now?' she says as she watches him go.

'The usual, Sophie. It's Hamish being *Hamish* again,' Jonathan replies in a huffy voice. He then looks at me apologetically. 'I'm leaving as well, I'm afraid. I need a decent night's sleep for once. Goodbye, Mr James. Best of luck to you for the future,' he says as he passes me, before heading through the exit as well.

Joel sighs. 'I'd better go after them before they get into another fight in the car park. It was nice working with you, Mr James.'

I watch him leave as well, feeling a little put out. I didn't want much of a party to celebrate leaving The Foodies, but something that lasted more than *five minutes* would have been nice. It seems Hamish and Jonathan's ongoing relationship difficulties have taken precedence over me tonight, though. The crew has been scared away, and now the cast members are leaving, too.

'Er . . . I'd best go and help Joel,' Sophie says. 'We don't want a repeat of what happened in the car park in Leamington Spa.' She gives me an awkward look. '. . . if that's okay with you, Mr James?'

'What? Oh, oh yes, that's fine,' I reply, a little despondently. What else am I supposed to do? She hardly knows me. I can't exactly order her to stay here and commemorate my passing, can I?

. . . *ugh*. That's an unfortunate turn of phrase, given the circumstances.

'Thanks!' Sophie looks at Alison. 'You coming, sweetheart?'

Alison looks at Sophie for a moment, then looks back at me thoughtfully. 'I think . . . I think I'm going to stay and chat with Mr James for a little while.'

Well, that's very nice of her, isn't it?

'Okay, hun,' Sophie replies, before giving me a sheepish look and scuttling out of the exit door to find out what shenanigans are going on outside with her castmates.

When she's gone, an awkward silence descends. Alison and I are now the only two people left in the green room.

She points over at the sign on the wall. 'Nice of them to do that,' she says, breaking the tension.

'Yes,' I reply, scratching my nose. 'I guess so.'

'Will you miss doing these shows?'

'Hmmm. Probably not, no. If Hamish and Jonathan are going to go another round onstage sometime soon, I think I'm better off a long way away from it.'

Alison chuckles. 'Fair enough.'

At that moment, the main door to the green room bangs open and a very harassed Eliza appears, dragging what appears to be an ambulatory storm cloud.

On a second, closer inspection, the cloud turns out to be Callum, who now looks angry enough to kill. Eliza hauls him over to where Alison and I are stood.

'Sorry, Nate! I meant to get back here sooner, but Callum . . . Callum got into an *altercation* with another boy in the entrance lobby,' she tells me with a pained expression. 'The kid bumped into him on the way out and Callum really doesn't like to be touched, so he . . . he got a little *punchy*.'

'Oh dear,' I reply, looking down at the tiny ball of barely supressed rage on the end of her arm.

I wonder if Cleethorpes does a children's discount.

Eliza looks at Alison. 'Hello,' she says in as cheerful a voice as she can muster.

'Oh . . . er, this is my cousin Eliza,' I say to Alison, remembering my manners. 'And this is Alison, Eliza. She played Libby the Happy Lemon.'

Alison smiles. 'Pleased to meet you.'

'Likewise.'

I look down at the beetroot-red face of my cousin's only child. 'And this is Callum.'

Before Alison can say anything to him, Callum grunts and starts to shake his head back and forth rather violently.

Eliza's pained expression grows even darker. 'I might have to take him home. It'll be ages before I can get him calmed down.'

As if to underline this, Callum starts to try and yank himself away from his mother as hard as he possibly can, growling as he does so. If we don't do something soon, the kid is likely to hurt himself – or more likely someone else.

'Hey, Callum!' Alison says in a bright voice. 'Did you enjoy seeing The Foodies tonight?' As she says this, she drops down to his eye level. 'I'm Libby the Happy Lemon,' she tells the boy, waving her arms from side to side.

Callum goes from incandescent fury to deep suspicion in a nanosecond. He looks at Alison gravely. 'You're not Libby,' he says. 'Libby is big and yellow and fat.'

Which is a pretty accurate description, when you get right down to it.

Alison's eyes go wide. 'That's the suit I wear, but I am Libby the Happy Lemon, Callum. No doubt about it!'

To prove this, Alison stands upright and starts to twirl around on the spot, doing the same dance Libby has to do during 'Come on, Give Us a Hug'.

Unbelievably, Callum starts to *giggle*. His towering rage has completely disappeared. 'Libby! Libby!' he cries with excitement, before giggling again.

Alison holds out a hand. 'Want to dance with me, Callum?'

He cries with delight and runs forward to take Alison's hand. Together, they start to dance around the empty green room, Alison singing my irritating song and Callum laughing like a tiny drain. There's something quite captivating about all of this, for some reason. Maybe because Alison's singing voice makes my stupid song actually sound . . . I don't know . . . *good*? Or maybe it's the way she's transformed Callum so swiftly with a few simple song lyrics and a dance.

'Bloody hell,' Eliza remarks. 'Can I take her home with me?'

'She certainly has a way with kids,' I reply, watching on with amazement.

Alison continues to twirl around the green room with Callum for a few minutes more, before coming back over to us, a broad smile on her face.

Eliza's smile is decidedly grateful. 'Thank you so much,' she says to Alison.

'My pleasure,' Alison replies as Callum goes back to his mother to take her hand again. He's now quite placid, but he is gazing up at Alison with an adoring expression on his face.

'Did you enjoy that?' Eliza asks him, eliciting a dramatic nod of the head. 'And you know who wrote that song, don't you?' she says to him.

This time he shakes his head slowly, still looking at Alison affectionately.

'Nate wrote it. He wrote that song. Isn't that *wonderful?*'

Affection is instantly replaced with loathing as Callum turns his attention to me.

'Er, maybe you should take him home while he's still in a good mood?' I suggest to Eliza, resisting the temptation to step back a bit.

Eliza gives me a worried look. 'Maybe I should.' She once again looks down at her tempestuous offspring. 'Say goodbye to Alison and Nate, Callum. It's time to go home.'

Callum instantly breaks free of her again and goes to hug Alison around the legs. He completely ignores me.

'Thank you for tonight, both of you,' Eliza says. 'It really has been good for him.' She holds out her hand. 'Come on, Callum. Home time.'

The boy is extremely reluctant to leave Alison, but eventually does so after she's bent down and given him another hug.

We share a few goodbyes (Callum continues to ignore me, of course), and my cousin and her son leave the green room, him skipping as he does so and her looking a little less anxious than when she came in.

'Wow,' I say. 'I thought he was going to kick off spectacularly.' I look at Alison. 'Thank you for that.'

She smiles. 'Not a problem. One thing this job teaches you is how to make a kid happy.'

'Well, you certainly made my cousin very happy.'

'Glad I could help.' Alison looks around the empty green room. 'Well, I guess it's time I made a move.'

'Er, yes. I guess it is,' I say slowly. For some reason, I've all of a sudden become extremely reluctant to say goodbye to her.

Alison holds out a hand. 'It really was nice working with you, Nathan.'

I take her hand. It feels rather warm and lovely. 'You too, Alison.'

We continue to shake hands. I don't want it to stop.

Apparently, neither does she.

The handshake goes on for another few seconds, before we both look in each other's eyes and simultaneously burst out laughing. Alison is the one who eventually breaks her grip. 'Well, goodbye then, Nathan.'

'Yeah. Goodbye, Alison,' I reply and start to back away from her. This I do with reluctance.

Still smiling, she turns and heads towards the fire exit. I turn as well, heading back in the direction of my dressing room down the corridor.

'Nathan!' I hear Alison say from behind me. I turn back and see her coming over to me. From her jeans pocket she has produced a pen. As she sweeps past one of the tables full of half-eaten food, she gathers up a napkin. On it, she writes something down and thrusts it out towards me when she's done.

'This is my phone number. If you'd like to go out with me for a drink sometime, give me a call.'

I gulp, and blink a few times.

'Wow,' I say, a little taken aback. A broad smile blooms across my face as I take the napkin and look at the digits she's written down on it. I look back up at Alison's expectant and slightly nervous face. 'I . . . I'll do that.' I nod a couple of times. 'Yeah. I'll definitely do that.'

Alison beams. 'Great! Well, I'll hear from you soon, then!' She lets out a small laugh of what I guess is probably relief and backs away from me again, not turning away until she's reached the exit.

I watch her disappear from sight with a dumbfounded grin on my face. What the hell just happened?

A pretty girl just asked you out on a date and you said yes, the voice in my head informs me. It sounds as shocked as I am.

With a rather strange, floaty feeling in my head and in my feet, I leave the green room and walk back along the corridor to my dressing room.

When I close my left hand around the dressing room doorknob, I notice that the tremor from earlier has returned in force. That pleasant floaty sensation is instantly quashed.

What are you doing, *Nathan?* a voice in my head demands. *Why are you agreeing to go out on a* date? *You're* going to die. *You lost Sienna thanks to the tumour, remember? Your days of having a woman in your life are OVER.*

I feel the breath catch in my throat as the horror and fear of it all crashes in on me again.

For a while there I'd forgotten what was happening to me. When I was with Alison, the tumour took a brief back seat – but now it's returned with a vengeance, thanks to that slight tremor.

What the *hell* was I thinking?! I *can't* go out on a date with Alison. I don't get to do things like date any more!

Suddenly, I feel incredibly sick. I throw open the dressing room door and just about make it to the en-suite bathroom before heaving up the contents of my stomach into the toilet.

After the worst is over, I sit back against the wall, breathing hard and thinking about the last hour of my life.

I won't call Alison, of course.

She might feel a little let down about it when I don't get in touch, but that's surely better than watching me drop dead at her feet, right?

I make it back to my house about an hour later. The short delay is caused by finding a twenty-four-hour off-licence to buy the largest bottle of whisky I can get my hands on. The Uber driver gave me a long look when I got back into the cab, which I gamely ignored. Oh, to still have my Porsche on the road . . .

As I start to drift off to sleep later that night in a drunken stupor, the single image that keeps returning to me is of Alison dancing around the green room with Callum. She managed to bond more with that kid in five seconds than I have in five years.

What I wouldn't give to be in a parallel universe where I was fit and healthy so I could go out on that date with her. I'm sure it would have been great fun – and maybe the start of something good in my life.

If nothing else, she could have taught me how to put a smile on Callum's face when he looks at me, instead of that permanent scowl.

But you'd still be with Sienna if you didn't have the tumour, my internal consciousness reminds me. *Someone like Alison wouldn't have got a look in.*

Oh God.

Here we go with the unpleasant self-reflection again . . .

It's true, though. There's no denying it.

Without the diagnosis, I *would* still be with Sienna in a gloriously shallow relationship that was devoid of any real emotional attachment.

And I'd be *delighted* to have that again, if it meant I was *healthy*. Without a doubt.

After all, I was more than happy with my carefree girlfriend and my carefree life!

. . . wasn't I?

Wasn't I?

COMMUNING WITH NATURE

12 JUNE

'Get up, Nathan.'

   'No.'

   'Come on, get up.'

   'I can't.'

   'Yes, you can. Get out of bed, it smells in here.'

   'Leave me alone.'

This is a conversation any teenager will instantly recognise. It usually occurs on a Wednesday in the middle of summer at about 11.15 a.m.

The parental unit of choice will be standing over the recalcitrant teen, urging them to get out of bed and embrace the day, while the teen will resist all attempts to make them do so by holding the duvet over their head in pure adolescent stubbornness.

It's a conversation I remember having many times when I was fourteen.

It's probably not one I should be having with my mother at the age of thirty-three.

I should never have given her a bloody key.

And yet I did, so here she stands with her hands on her hips, staring down at me as I refuse to leave the safe and happy confines of my super king-sized bed. I have all I need here – Netflix, Just Eat, and an en-suite bathroom. Why should I ever feel the need to go anywhere else?

It's been a month since the last Foodies show and the night I said yes to a date with a pretty girl, knowing full well that I have a death sentence hanging over me.

The one-two punch of splitting up with Sienna and meeting Alison have thrown my sorry state of affairs into sharp relief. I've been forced to have a good, long look at myself – and the realisation that I haven't exactly been living the most worthwhile of lives has thrown me for a large and unpleasant loop.

I've been cruising along, making money hand over fist, having some truly memorable sex and generally gadding about the place like I owned it – but at what cost?

I have, if I'm being completely honest about it, been a *bit of a dick*. It's a crying shame that it took a terminal diagnosis for me to realise it. It's also a crying shame that I'll probably be robbed of the chance to be less of a dick in the future thanks to my vastly shortened lifespan.

My despair over all of this was so intense that taking to my bed was literally the only thing I could do.

What followed was a month of self-pity, self-loathing, self-analysis and self-abuse. The fourth option was the only enjoyable one out of the lot.

In a strange way, I have been content in this lazy, miserable fug. Life is easy when all you have to worry about is how many episodes of *House of Cards* you have left, whether the local Chinese will deliver at

10 p.m. and how many Kleenex are left in the box. There have even been times when I've forgotten about my bloody tumour. Those forty-three seconds were some of the best of my life.

But now, here is my evil mother to ruin it all.

'This is ridiculous, Nathan. You can't just lie in bed for the rest of your life.'

'Yes, I can. I might only have a few minutes left, so it's fine.'

Mum lets out an exasperated gasp. 'Oh, for God's sake. Is this how you're going to behave from now on? Completely incapable of having any kind of life because you're permanently worried it's about to end?'

'Yes.'

'You don't know how long you've got! You don't know you're going to die!'

'Yes, I do! We all die! We all must face death alone! Everything slides into entropy!'

Mum looks baffled by this. 'What are you on about?'

'I've been doing a lot of reading,' I explain defiantly. It's never, *ever* a good idea to google information about death – it leads you down a rabbit hole of cod philosophy and overwrought moralising that gets you nowhere.

'Well, it's time you got up and started doing something constructive with your time, my son,' Mum tells me in no uncertain terms.

'I don't want to,' I say with a Sienna-sized pout. I yank the duvet back over my head, channelling my inner fourteen-year-old, pubescent idiot.

'Not so fast!' Mum exclaims, yanking the duvet back down again. 'You're going to get up and you're going to do something about your state of mind, Nathan. Whether you have months, years or decades left, it's not going to help if you just wallow in bed like this the entire time!' She points a firm finger at me. 'Don't be like your father!'

'What do you suggest I do exactly?' I ask in a sullen voice.

Mum sits on the end of the bed. 'There's a place I've found that might be able to help you.'

'Is it an off-licence?'

Mum rolls her eyes. 'No, Nathan. It's a commune.'

'A what?'

'A commune. Down in the West Country. I heard about it from one of my clients – that architect chappy Donald who commissioned me to make those gargoyles for him. You remember?'

'The ones with the tits?'

Mum grinds her teeth. 'Yes . . . the gargoyles had breasts. He was trying to provoke a reaction in his visitors.'

My eyes narrow. It seems to me that statuary is at least ninety per cent about sex in some way or another. There seems to be an obsession with carving out figures in rock with their bits and pieces on display for the world to see. This probably says something profound about the human race, but I'm not sure what. 'Yeah. I bet he was,' I say.

She waves a hand. 'Anyway. I bumped into him the other day and got talking about you.'

'Mum!' I exclaim, horrified. What is it with people I'm close to speaking to complete strangers about this bloody tumour?

'Relax, Nathan! I didn't tell him about your diagnosis, just that you've been feeling down recently.'

'Hmmph. That's an understatement.'

'Yes . . . well, Donald told me that when his wife left him, he fell into a similar depression, but that he visited this commune for a few days and it really helped him. The off-grid, back-to-nature lifestyle helped him gain a bit of perspective.'

I give Mum a very suspicious look. 'Really?' I run a hand through my hair. 'Well . . . it doesn't sound like something that'd do me much good. I haven't lost a wife, I've lost a life.'

'Just try it, Nathan!' Mum snaps with exasperation. 'Anything has got to be better than this!'

I'm slightly taken aback by her tone of voice. To see her riled up like this is extremely disconcerting.

'The commune is called the Light Havens,' she continues. 'Donald gave me their contact details. I want you to give them a call.'

'Yes, yes, I will!' I reply quickly, not wanting to hear that authoritative tone of voice again.

'Good. Now, I'm going downstairs to make a cup of tea. I expect you to join me after you've got dressed' – she sniffs the air – 'and had a *long* shower.'

And with that, my mother rises from the bed and exits the bedroom, leaving me alone with my thoughts.

Given that my thoughts are largely unpleasant and full of holes, I choose to ignore them and finally rise from my disgusting bed like a zombie emerging from its grave.

I clamber into the shower to wash off the grime of more days than I care to mention. After about five minutes I do indeed feel a little more human . . . and a little more alive. Mum is probably right – I can't just wallow in misery for the time I have left, no matter how much a part of me would love to do so. I have no idea whether this commune can actually do me any good, but anything's got to be better that my current lifestyle. Give it another few days and I will have exhausted Netflix, and then where will I be? Watching daytime terrestrial television, that's where. It would only take about three episodes of *Loose Women* or *Homes Under the Hammer* before I'd be trying to suffocate myself with the duvet.

***

I've never considered myself to be much of an environmentalist.

I watch every David Attenborough documentary that comes on the TV and make tutting noises whenever there's a story on the news about fracking, but that's about as far as it goes. To tell the truth, it's one of those issues that always bores me rigid. Eliza made me go and see that movie *An Inconvenient Truth* when it got a rerun at the local art-house cinema. The only real inconvenience for me was that it stopped me sitting at home playing my guitar all evening.

It therefore feels unbelievable to me that I'm actually seriously considering a visit to an environmentally friendly commune on the edges of Exmoor National Park.

The Light Havens – which sounds like a name directly lifted from a Tolkien novel – is run by a chap called Martin Sizemore. I have a chat on the phone with him later that afternoon about a visit.

It transpires that Martin and his community are more than happy to invite strangers into their lives for as long as they want to stay. He's very keen to promote their off-grid way of living. He thinks it's a fantastic way for people feeling stressed or miserable to find a measure of happiness again. And the more people he can spread that philosophy to, the better.

The people of the Light Havens have left their modern lives behind for something more simple and down to earth. They've sacrificed their iPads for well-thumbed books and their overpriced M&S quinoa salads for a cabbage patch in the garden. This is either very admirable or spell-bindingly crazy, depending on your perspective. I tend to have a love-hate relationship with most modern technology myself, but quinoa makes me gag, so I'm on the fence.

Martin comes across as a sane and lucid individual during our phone call, so I guess I'm prepared to pop down to his patch of land in Devon to see if this off-grid philosophy can help me out. It won't cure my tumour, but it may help lift my spirits and change my perspective on a few things. If nothing else, a change of scenery will do me some good. I can't wallow in my Netflix wank palace any more. My mother won't allow it.

As I jump on the train down to the south-west the next morning, I have images of Richard Briers in *The Good Life* circulating around my head. My parents used to love that show and would often sit me down in front of repeats when I was a child. While I never quite understood the allure of Felicity Kendall's bottom, I did giggle at a lot of the jokes – my high-pitched child's laughter in perfect accompaniment to my father's loud, baritone guffawing.

Being a city boy, I of course believe that the whole of the south-west is served by three dirt roads and is permanently chock-a-block with caravans and tractors, so the idea of letting the train take the strain feels like a sensible one. I don't actually have a lot of choice in the matter these days, of course. The Porsche is now permanently parked on my driveway, thanks to the DVLA driving ban.

Being carried through England's green and pleasant land with the sun shining down is most definitely one good way of improving your state of mind. I'm not even that perturbed when we get held up for twenty minutes in Taunton because a driver is late for his shift. I do have to put my headphones in and listen to some music to drown out the copious amounts of tutting when the announcement is made over the tannoy, however.

I can see why the Light Havens is named as such when I arrive in the taxi from the train station. The cabbie gave me a funny look when I told him the address that Martin had provided, but I ignored him, safe in the knowledge that a taxi driver will give you a funny look when you tell him your destination about nine times out of ten, wherever you are in the world.

We're somewhere about half an hour north-east of Barnstaple, on the edges of the national park – and boy is it a beautiful part of the world. The coast is a scant ten-minute walk away, and yet here we are, surrounded by sun-dappled oaks and beeches in a rather lovely wood-land setting. A small smile creeps across my face for the first time in weeks as the taxi turns on to a gravel track that leads away from the B road we've been on for the past few miles.

A little further along, the track widens into a makeshift car park, with a gate at the other end preventing further access up the road. Standing by the gate is Richard Briers.

Okay, okay, it's not *actually* Richard Briers, but it is a man in his late forties wearing a sensible beige cardigan and with a haircut twenty years out of date, so you can forgive me the comparison. It's rather nice to be confronted by a person who looks so comfortingly *normal*.

'Good morning!' he says as the taxi driver pulls up.

'And to you!' I reply, jumping out of the cab with a spring in my step, brought on from a combination of good weather, attractive scenery, two recently downed painkillers and the sight of a sensible beige cardigan. I pay the taxi driver, who gives me and Martin another strange look, before he turns around in the car park and hightails it out of there.

Martin ignores this and holds out his hand to me, which I shake enthusiastically. 'Lovely part of the world you've chosen to set up shop in,' I remark, looking up at the sunlight slanting through the trees.

'It is, isn't it?' Martin replies. 'And thank you so much for coming along, Nathan. I'm really hoping our community will be able to help you.'

'Actually, I think it might be having an effect already,' I say with a grin, basking in the warm sunlight.

Martin bids me follow him past the closed gate, and we ascend the gravel track together, chatting about the nice weather and the train service to Barnstaple as we go. Within the space of five minutes we have rounded a bend and come in sight of the Light Havens.

It is, on the face of it, quite idyllic. The commune sits in a large, open forest glade, surrounded by tall and proud pine trees. There are, from what I can see, seven small dwellings dotted around the glade, forming a very loose circle. All of them are surrounded by their own vegetable patches, ramshackle greenhouses and other rustic accoutrements. A couple are square(ish) and apparently constructed from wattle and daub, one coloured red and the other pale blue. A further two are log cabins, but each constructed of a different wood. Two more are built of a strange combination of haystacks and old tyres, and the final house – the grandest and largest of them all – is a mishmash of all three approaches to construction. Every building has an air of quiet permanence about it that I find quite lovely. In a world of cookie-cutter Bovis Homes buildings that look flimsy enough to fall over at any minute, this bespoke, 'earthy' style of construction is very refreshing.

'Rather wonderful, isn't it?' Martin says, noting my approving expression.

'Yes. It really is,' I reply. 'It's so *peaceful*.'

'I know. We were very careful when we were looking for land to buy fifteen years ago,' Martin explains. 'It took us six months to find this location. You can't hear any traffic from here, and we're nowhere near a plane route. It's just the birds and us.'

And they're not even *noisy* birds. Wonderful stuff.

I notice a light on in the log cabin closest to where we're standing. 'You have electricity?' I say.

Martin chuckles. 'Oh yes. We're off the grid and self-sufficient, but that doesn't mean we don't have a few of the twenty-first century's home comforts!'

I want to point out that electricity was also one of the *nineteenth century's* home comforts, but I like this man and don't want to offend him. At least not deliberately.

'Where does the power come from?'

Martin points to the house roofs. 'Solar panels on every one.'

'They must have been expensive.'

'Actually, we received a grant from the council and sponsorship from the solar panel company. They didn't cost us much in the end.'

I'm very impressed by how well planned and organised this commune is. Martin and his friends have clearly done things the right way from day one and are reaping the benefits.

I say as much.

Martin smiles again. 'Thank you, Nathan! It has been going well. We're even hoping to expand the place in the coming months. If you look past Frannie and Bork's house to your left, you'll see that the land we own stretches on much further back. There's room there for at least another six houses. The more we build and show that our community can grow sustainably, the more attention we get from local businesses and the media.'

This all sounds *very* admirable. I'm even more impressed than I was a few minutes ago. I'm not even going to bring up the fact that Martin's just told me he lives with a person called Bork – that's how much I want to stay on this bloke's good side. There's something ever so *noble* about him and his project. I'm sure the cardigan has something to do with it.

'Shall we go to my house?' Martin suggests. 'The other members of the community would like to meet you, and I had them gather there for your arrival. It's what we like to do for all of our guests from the outside world.'

Hmmm. That feels ever so slightly uncomfortable.

I'm somewhat reminded of those old nature documentaries from the 1950s when the white man was greeted by the local natives in their biggest hut. They would usually give him some kind of food as a gift, normally made from something quite disgusting like mealworms or peacock vomit. I always thought that they did this quite deliberately, having hidden all the home-made chocolate and fruit salad somewhere out the back.

Martin makes off towards the biggest house, which I rightly assumed was his. Instead of just being square or circular, this place is a very rough 'L' shape and is built into the side of a small hillock. It's the only house that has two levels – probably because the hillock props the foundations up enough to allow a second storey to be built. The roof is of course thatched. The solar panels Martin pointed out look quite incongruous against such an old-fashioned building material. The walls are a mainly white wattle and daub, with one retaining wall at the back made of car tyres.

As we enter the property through a hand-carved oak front door, I am immediately surprised by the space inside. Martin obviously likes the open-plan feel, as I can see his lounge area off to the left and the kitchen to the right. The kitchen has all the appliances you'd expect it to have, which would be surprising were it not for the solar panels on the roof. There are a couple of rooms at the far end of the open space and an ornate wooden spiral staircase at its centre, but other than that, I'm standing in a large, open room that somehow contrives to feel cosy, despite its size.

Standing and sitting around a handmade oak table in the kitchen area (if Martin isn't a carpenter by trade, I'd be amazed) are several people, all dressed in a manner that those who attend Glastonbury Festival will immediately recognise as the height of fashion. A couple of the younger women are holding babies, and most of the men have unkempt beards. One woman, who is auburn-haired and about forty-five or so, is busy making tea beside the kitchen sink. When she sees us enter, she smiles broadly and comes over to greet us.

'Hello, Nathan!' the woman says. 'Welcome to the Light Havens. I'm Celeste, Martin's wife.' She holds out a hand for me to shake, which I do happily.

Celeste has possibly the most *magnificently* large breasts I have ever seen. I know that pointing this out makes me sound like a gigantic misogynist, for which I apologise, but by crikey they are *whoppers*. The light-grey T-shirt she's wearing does little to disguise their ampleness. She's not wearing a bra, either.

I heroically manage to look her square in the eye as I shake her hand, though. This is a woman who has dedicated her life to environmentally friendly, sustainable living. The last thing she needs is a wasteful city boy like me staring at her tits instead of her compost heap.

'Thanks for having me,' I reply. 'You really do have a lovely place here.'

'Thank you, Nathan, that's most kind,' she says, with a pleased expression on her face. 'Allow me to introduce the rest of our extended family.'

Celeste and Martin take me over to where I shake hands with the eleven other people that make up the community of the Light Havens. Bork is from Norway, so the name is not as strange as it first sounded. I am rather taken aback when I am presented with a small girl called Peggy, who is a big fan of The Foodies and is clutching a Libby the Happy Lemon soft toy. Peggy and Callum would get along well, I think. I feel a pang of regret in my chest for a moment, as this reminds me of Alison, but I brush the feeling away as swiftly as I can. This has been a good day so far, and I don't want to let anything spoil it.

All in all, the folks of the Light Havens seem a laid-back, happy bunch. Okay, they're a little oddball, but that's to be expected, given their counterculture way of life. They are all unfailingly good-natured and welcoming, which is the most important thing.

So much so that the next couple of hours of my life are some of the nicest I've ever had. Being taken around the commune to see all of its off-grid delights is a very pleasant experience. The lovely weather helps. There's nothing quite like eating a gigantic home-grown strawberry with the sun shining down on you while somebody with a big smile on their face brings you a cup of tea.

Apparently, a barbecue is being held later, where I've been promised at least one pint of Martin's home-brewed beer. Celeste has told me that I'm invited to stay in their guest bedroom for as long as I'd like – an offer I'm seriously contemplating, as not even my bifold patio doors can compete with gigantic, juicy strawberries and a complete lack of traffic noise.

By the time the clock hits six, my knowledge of how the Light Havens functions is complete. It really is a marvel of off-grid living. Okay, they haven't quite cut ties with the outside world completely – Martin still makes regular visits to the supermarket in his clapped-out old Volvo estate, and the Wi-Fi signal is surprisingly good for such a rural location – but in terms of their carbon footprint and their impact on the environment, they really are doing a fantastic job. When I get home, I'm definitely going to stop using the dishwasher as much and use the half flush on the toilet a bit more.

Martin sparks up the home-made brick barbecue outside the front of his house as the sun starts to go down. The community all gather on a collection of old deck chairs and patio furniture to enjoy the food, Martin's beer and the fortunate life they're living. I should probably resent them for their happiness, but I'm too stuffed with cheeseburger and strong beer to put any real effort into it.

This is easily the best mood I've been in for months. Mum (and Donald) were right – this place really is good for the soul. My spirits have lifted considerably.

The evening takes a very interesting turn at about 9 p.m., after the children have all been packed off to bed, when Bork produces a tobacco pouch from his back pocket and starts to roll what is quite obviously a spliff.

Being a musician, I am no stranger to the delights of marijuana. In fact, some of my most memorable nights as a young, struggling muso were spent comprehensively boxed on Afghanistan's finest export. While I've traded cannabis for alcohol as I've got older, I am not averse to the odd nostalgic smoke, should the opportunity present itself. And it has presented itself right now in the shape of a giant Norseman with a big, bushy beard.

Everyone in the commune seems quite comfortable with the idea of a little class B entertainment, something I am not surprised about at all. Marijuana has always gone hand in hand with the people of the counterculture – and the Light Havens is no exception.

I watch as Bork lights the spliff, takes a couple of long drags and passes it to Martin.

Don't let the sensible cardigan fool you – Martin is quite happy to partake of a little weed. He inhales a heroic amount of the sweet-smelling smoke, before passing the spliff to his wife, who does much the same thing.

Then she looks at me. 'Would you like some, Nathan?' she says, her head wreathed with smoke that lingers in the still summer air.

'Er, yes. I would, actually,' I say with a grin, taking the joint from her hands and sucking in a great lungful of THC.

This really is quite, quite *splendid*. What a great idea it was to come here.

Things are starting to cool down by 10 p.m., so Martin suggests we withdraw into the big, comfortable living room, where beanbags (what else?) are strewn around the floor in a haphazard fashion. I quite like a beanbag. There's one in my loft that I keep meaning to get down so I can sit in it while I play video games. There's something quite relaxing about having your bottom hugged by thousands of tiny polystyrene balls that I can't quite put my finger on.

I get the distinct impression that this kind of late-night gathering is a regular occurrence here, and I feel very fortunate to be included.

'Nathan?' Celeste says as I drop myself into one of the beanbags.

'Yes?' I reply, a dreamy sense of well-being overcoming me as I settle back into the bag.

'I have a guitar somewhere . . . Would you mind giving us a song? I'm okay on it, but I have a feeling you might be able to do a better job than me!'

Okay, so this now is officially the best night I've had in *years*, not just since the tumour came along. 'Of course!'

Celeste goes to the back of the room and retrieves an old and rather battered acoustic guitar from the corner. She hands it to me and I spend a couple of moments tuning it. Surprisingly, given how old the guitar is, it's not too badly out of tune, and in no time at all I am strumming through a couple of chords, wondering what I should play.

'Okay then, I'll start playing . . . Let's see if you guys know the words,' I tell them all.

Given the cannabis now flowing through my system, it should come as no surprise that I pick a bit of Led Zeppelin. I don't go for the ultimate cliché of 'Stairway to Heaven', but do start playing 'Dazed and Confused', knowing full well that it'll go down a treat with this lot.

And indeed it does! My song choice is much appreciated. As it is when I follow up with 'Wild Horses' by The Rolling Stones and 'Behind Blue Eyes' by The Who.

Bork rolls another spliff. By the time I've taken three good lungfuls, I have to stop playing as my fingers don't want to work the fretboard properly any more.

I think I may have discovered the cure for my brain tumour. At least, I think I've discovered the cure for *caring* about my brain tumour – which is nearly as good.

'So,' Martin says, leaning back into his beanbag, 'I hope your visit here is helping your sense of well-being, Nathan. It's what we're here for.'

I nod at him in a languid fashion. 'It is. It really is.' I think for a moment. 'I'm no clearer on what the hell I'm supposed to do with my life, but I don't seem to care that much about it at the moment . . . which is fine by me.'

Martin frowns a little. 'Life not going the way you planned it?'

I sigh. 'Not at all. I thought I had it all figured out, but now . . .' I trail off, not really knowing what else to add.

Celeste shuffles her beanbag a little closer to me. 'What changed?' she asks.

I heave another sigh. I might as well explain to these lovely people why I am here, even if it brings the mood down a little.

I give Martin, Celeste and the rest of the commune the short version of my tragic recent life history. By the time I'm done, everyone has a sympathetic look in their eyes that makes me feel uncomfortable, even through the cannabis fug.

'That's so sad, Nathan,' Celeste says, resting a hand on my leg. 'So sad that you feel that way about yourself after such a horrible discovery.'

I nod again. 'Yeah. I guess it is, isn't it?' I take another drag on the joint that's just been handed to me. 'I wish I had time to set things straight a bit, but I don't think I'm going to get it.'

Martin leans forward. 'And what would you do, if you did have the time?'

I shrug. 'I have no idea.'

He gives me a speculative look. 'And that might be your problem. You're so worried that you have no time left, you've not even considered the idea that you might have *plenty of time* left.'

My eyes widen. He's right. I hadn't considered that *at all*.

Martin smiles, seeing my reaction. 'So, I'll ask you again, Nathan – what would you do if you did have the time?'

I lean back and stare at the ceiling. Thoughts, feelings and fears all bob around in my head for a few moments, adrift on a sea of marijuana smoke.

What would I do?

What would I do if I wasn't going to die?

Then it hits me. My head drops back down to regard Martin. 'Something worthwhile,' I say purposefully. 'I want to do something *worthwhile*.'

Martin nods. 'To leave your mark on the world?'

'Yes! Yes! That's it!'

'What like?' Celeste asks, face afire with curiosity.

'Er . . .' That's stumped me. It's all very well having a cannabis-based epiphany about a need to do something of worth with what's left of my life, but I still have no idea what that something is.

'I don't know,' I reply, then bang a fist down on the thigh that Celeste isn't touching. 'I don't know!' I repeat, with frustration.

Martin holds out his hands. 'Hey, chill out, Nathan. You don't need to have every answer straight away, my friend. Just be happy you've discovered the first one here with us tonight, yeah?'

This is possibly the most Zen thing I've ever heard anyone say, but then I am now high as a kite, so my judgement is somewhat impaired.

I take yet another drag on the joint. 'Yeah. You're right, Martin. You're so, so right. Thank you . . . Thank you all.' I give everyone a smile that I think is warm and friendly, but is in fact the grin of someone who's just had a frontal lobotomy with a blunt spoon. I really have had far too much cannabis this evening. 'This is such a great place,' I tell them all. 'Such a great, great place.'

'It's lovely to have you here,' Celeste says, squeezing my thigh gently as she does.

'It's lovely to be here,' I reply.

'Good,' she says, tightening the squeeze a little.

'We all think you fit in here really well,' Martin adds, to the general positive acknowledgement of the rest of the room. 'Now you've shared your story with us.'

'Thank you, I think I do, too,' I say.

'It's lovely to share ourselves with you,' Celeste says, which is an odd way of phrasing things, but I like the sentiment just the same.

'I like sharing myself with you as well,' I drowsily reply.

'Great!' Martin exclaims in a happy voice, taking another drag on the spliff.

And then, I'm asleep.

The beanbag is too comfortable, the cannabis is too strong and the open-plan living room is too cosy for anything else to happen at this point. I should feel dreadfully embarrassed at falling asleep in a room full of people I've never met before, but I don't, such is the way they've welcomed me into their lives and such is the strength of the cannabis I'm smoking.

In my drugged, sleepy haze, I feel a hand on my leg again, which feels *extremely* pleasant. I think Celeste may have taken a *real* liking to me today. I open my eyes to see that those wonderfully large mammaries are now within inches of my face. Celeste is leaning over me with both hands now on my thighs.

'Is this okay, Nathan?' she says, hands sliding up even further.

Of course, it *shouldn't* be okay. Not in the slightest. Another man's wife is quite clearly attempting to seduce me while I'm in a vulnerable state – and in front of several other people to boot. I should be jumping out of the beanbag with an embarrassed cry, horrified at the whole idea. But I'm not. Because, hey – I'm single, lonely and living moment to moment these days. If Martin isn't bothered at the idea of his wife feeling me up, then I'm not going to be concerned about it, either. The combination of marijuana and beer has lowered my inhibitions to levels that are virtually non-existent, so why shouldn't I let Celeste have a little fun with me?

'Yeah, carry on . . .' I mumble.

Celeste smiles. 'You really want to share yourself?' she says with a seductive smile that makes my penis twitch.

'I do,' I reply, flapping a hand around. 'Go for it.'

My eyes close again as I feel her start to knead my crotch.

Her other hand continues to squeeze my left thigh, while her other hand squeezes the right.

. . . squeezes the right.

. . . her *other* hand.

One hand is massaging my cock, one hand is squeezing my left thigh and one is squeezing my right thigh.

Things do not add up here, my friend. They do not add up *at all*.

Unless Celeste has somehow morphed into the human form of the multi-limbed Hindu elephant god Ganesh, events have taken a decidedly odd turn.

Sadly, I'm so religiously off my tits on cannabis that my brain is functioning at about fifteen per cent of its normal capacity, so it is slow on the uptake, to say the least. A thought process that should take less than a second to assert itself instead requires a full half minute to break through the drug-induced fug.

When it does manage to break through, though, it is *most* insistent.

Somebody else is feeling you up, you idiot!

I open my eyes to find that Celeste has been joined by . . .

No, not Frannie.

No, not Martin, either, though I'm sure that's where you were thinking this was heading, weren't you? However, Martin is still sat back in his beanbag near the fireplace, watching proceedings with *great* interest.

No, it's Bork, folks.

I'm being felt up by Celeste and six foot three inches of prime, grade-A Scandiwegian beefcake. And he's *leering* at me. So is Celeste – but that's kind of all right given her gender and the size of her mammaries.

Oh, and there's *caressing* going on, too. In point of fact, it's Celeste who's being the aggressive one. Bork's hands are actually quite gentle, which is surprising, given his size.

If I was bisexual, then this would all be just about the best thing *ever*, but I'm not, so *it's* not – no matter how gentle his hands are.

A confusing welter of emotions fills my head. On the one hand, I'm naturally shocked and horrified that I'm being felt up by a bloke, but on the other hand, Celeste is still kneading my penis for all she's worth and that is a very pleasant sensation in and of itself, no matter what else is going on at the periphery.

And let's not forget that I'm still drunk and high, so there's also a small part of my brain that's just hoping I go with it, because fuck it

— We're probably going to be dead soon, so what's the harm in seeing what a little Scandinavian man love is like? We might end up enjoying it.

The small crowd is certainly enjoying things. In fact, over Bork's shoulder I can see three of the other commune members crawling all over each other, removing clothing as they go. I do hope these beanbags are wipe clean.

It's at this point that Bork's hand starts to snake up to my crotch to join Celeste's. The part of my brain that might be up for a little experimentation is still there, but is now being drowned out by the sober part of me that has just caught up with proceedings and is starting to make its feelings known in no uncertain terms.

'Er, could you stop, please?' I say in a timid voice.

Bork smiles. 'It is fine, Nathan.'

'Yes,' agrees Celeste in a soothing voice, giving mini-Nathan another squeeze. 'It's all going to be all right.' When somebody tells you everything is going to be all right in a soothing voice, it usually means it's time to run for the hills.

'No, thank you,' I say, watching Bork's hand cover Celeste's, adding to the squeeze. I'm in real trouble now. Judging from the size of Bork's plate-like hand, if I say or do the wrong thing right now, he could quite easily make my day end very badly by tightening his grip over Celeste's hand and my rapidly shrinking appendage.

Then Celeste moves her hand away completely and it's time to take some fucking action.

'I said no, thank you!' I scream, as if I've just been approached for the fourth time on the high street to answer a questionnaire and not because a blond Scandinavian alpha male is about to give me a handjob.

Needless to say, Bork pays no attention to this. He's now concentrating on the job and isn't going to be stopped by such a plaintive request.

'Oh my God!' I wail, trying to squeeze my legs together. Sadly, I'm still sat in a fucking beanbag. Have you tried squeezing your legs together while sat in a beanbag? It's impossible. So is pulling yourself away from an unwanted handjob.

Nevertheless, I give it a good go.

I try to pull myself from Bork's unwanted attentions by pushing back with my hands and feet as hard as I can. However, I can barely gain any purchase on the floor thanks to the way I'm flopped back in the beanbag, so all I end up doing is thrashing about like an upended turtle.

'I think he's enjoying that, Bork,' says Martin, completely misinterpreting my reaction. 'Look how excited he is.' Martin's tone of voice has taken a dark turn – one implying that nipple clamps and water sports are going to be in my immediate future if I don't do something drastic in the next desperate few seconds.

There are only two accepted ways of getting yourself out of a beanbag.

One is to roll sideways – usually with a loud and sustained grunting noise – until you are able to fall off the beanbag and bring yourself upright. This option is not open to me as I have Bork on one side and Celeste on the other, both with a knee on the beanbag, effectively blocking my escape.

The only other way to get out of a beanbag is the far more *theatrical* option, usually only open to those in the blossom of youth and vitality: rolling backwards off the bugger in an awkward roly-poly.

When's the last time you did a roly-poly?

For me, I think it was about twenty years ago. Therefore, I am royally out of practice.

My first attempt is pathetic (drunk and stoned, remember). I can barely do more than buck my hips upwards and lean my head back. This just makes it look like I'm presenting myself.

Here, Bork! Here are my genitals for your appraisal! See how eager I am to have you examine them more closely!

Bork's eyes widen enthusiastically, as do Celeste's. She must be hoping to pick at the leftovers later.

If my first roly-poly effort was pathetic, the second overcompensates *massively*. With a loud and sustained grunt, I push down hard on to the floor with my legs and simultaneously throw myself backwards with such force I will have a painful neck for the next week or so.

Celeste and Bork may well need medical attention themselves, given that as I throw myself backwards, both of my knees connect with the undersides of their chins in a move reminiscent of the final round in a game of *Street Fighter II*. I believe the correct button combination is down, sweep left, up, circle button, square button.

Bork's mouth is open, so there's an audible and dreadful clunk as his bottom teeth meet the top.

Still, at least he remains conscious. Celeste is knocked completely spark out.

None of this damage is readily apparent to me, as I'm still trying to negotiate my way through the complicated late stages of the roly-poly. With a strangled cry, I go arse over tit about as gracefully as a newborn calf. Given the amount of pressure this instantly causes to my digestive system, I also let out an enormous fart. In any other circumstance this would be a source of supreme humiliation, but I've just knocked a Scandinavian's teeth out and rendered a large-breasted woman unconscious, so in this situation it barely registers.

While I'm busy doing my impression of Olga Korbut after a heavy blow to the skull, Martin and the rest of the weird communal sex brigade are responding to the grievous injuries that I have wrought. Bork is helped to his feet by his life partner, Frannie, blood gushing down his chin. Martin is trying his best to rouse Celeste from her enforced slumber. Sadly, while he's an accomplished carpenter, he's definitely not an accomplished physician, as he's trying to do this by poking her in the bottom.

I manage to struggle to my knees and survey the grizzly scene in front of me.

'Oh God, I'm so sorry!' I cry, hands held out.

Martin looks at me with instant loathing. Even though he'd have happily condoned my unwanted seduction by Bork, he quite clearly feels that I am the one in the wrong here. 'Why did you do that?!' he screams. He's now trying to get Celeste to wake up by actively pushing down on her bottom, as if he's trying to create one giant buttock. Amazingly, the technique appears to be working, as I can see her head start to move.

I point a tremulous finger at Bork. 'He was trying to do things to me!' I exclaim, mounting my defence. 'He wanted to play with my bits and pieces!'

'Of forb bad's wab ooh 'onted!' Bork remarks, holding his bloody jaw closed.

'No! I never said that!' I snap.

'But you said you were happy to share yourself with us!' Martin rages.

I look aghast. 'Yes! My guitar playing and delightful conversation skills . . . not my willy! Jesus!'

Martin looks aghast. 'You call your penis Jesus?'

'What? No! Don't be idiotic!'

Martin clambers to his feet over the body of his still-prostrate wife, who is now making some rather odd gurgling noises. 'I think you should leave, Nathan!'

'What?'

'I think it would be best if you were to *leave now!*'

I glance at my watch. It's twenty past eleven. 'But it's really late!'

''Usss 'o!' Bork demands, now nursing his broken mouth with a moistened tea towel.

'But . . . but what about helping me feel better about myself?' I entreat. 'What about helping me find answers?'

Martin puts his hands on his hips and narrows his eyes. 'Find somebody else! I don't feel like I'd want to help someone who wants to kill my wife and friends!'

'But they were trying to give me a handjob!'

On the surface of it, this sounds like an incredibly ungrateful thing to say. The promise of a handjob should never result in the committal of GBH.

'They were trying to welcome you into our community!' Martin insists. 'We're very free with our bodies here!'

I roll my eyes. 'Yeah? Well, I'm not!'

Bork now steps forward and begins to loom. Even with the bloodied chin and look of extreme hurt on his face, he's very good at it.

I start to back away towards the front door. As I go, I point that finger at Martin again. 'You know, I thought you lot were really cool! I thought this place was great! And then you turn out to be a bunch of sex pests!'

Martin shakes his head vociferously. 'We are NOT sex pests! We are a happy commune of people with no inhibitions!'

'Hah!' I retort. 'That's what they all say!'

This comment makes zero sense. So much so that for a split second the commune's collective anger at me is overtaken by confusion. Then Celeste's head rises from the floor and I get a good look at her face. It resembles a bucket of smashed crabs.

It's time I left.

Like a small child freed from the clutches of the wicked witch in her gingerbread cottage, I flee into the night. Unlike the child – who will probably get caught again once it gets lost in the forest and trips over a tree stump – I am blessed with an iPhone, which has built-in GPS, so I manage to make my way back to the road without too much trouble.

When the same taxi driver who dropped me off arrives to pick me up a quarter of an hour later, he gives me that look again. This time I entirely understand why.

'Yes. They are a bunch of weirdos, aren't they?' I say to him as I clamber into the back seat.

He snorts. 'Yep. Famous around here, they are. We call them the Pervy Pixies, on account of the fact they live up in the woods and . . . you know . . .'

'Yes. I do *know*. Now, would you kindly get me out of here, please? I now have to try to find a hotel room at midnight down in Barnstaple.'

'I know a place,' the driver tells me.

'Are there any Scandinavians there?'

'I don't think so.'

'Carry on, then.'

The taxi takes off down the pitch-black road, carrying me away from what has amounted to an extremely unsuccessful attempt to find my happy place.

Bork had no trouble finding it, mind you – but that was the bloody problem.

An involuntary shiver runs down my spine as the taxi carries me back to civilisation, and the promise of what will probably be a luke-warm shower and a lumpy bed, knowing my luck.

When I eventually get home tomorrow, the first thing I'm going to do is go up into the loft, drag out that bloody beanbag and take it straight to the tip. Either that or I'm going to create a brand-new martial art based around it. If I can poleaxe a giant Scandinavian acci-dentally with one, think what damage I could do if I actually *meant it*.

LYRICS TO THE FOODIES SONG 'DREAM TIME IS THE BEST TIME'

All of The Foodies sing:

Sleepy time has come! Night night time is here!
We're all off to bed now, and dream time is so near!
Our pillows are so soft, and our sheets are so clean,
Off to sleep in no time at all, for the best dreams
you've ever seen!

Libby the Happy Lemon sings:

We've all been up so long, our eyes are feeling tired,
It's been a busy day, but our energy has expired,
It's time to go to bed, and we're happy the time
has come,
It's time to fall asleep, and have some dreamy fun . . .

All of The Foodies sing:

Dream time is the best time, it's when we're in
our beds,
We go on fun adventures, all inside our heads,
We always love to fall asleep, to jump into a
dream,
The best ones are when we get to eat sweets and
fresh ice cream!

Libby the Happy Lemon sings:

Dreams can be funny things, they can make you
really giggle,
But they can be a bit scary, they can make you
shake and jiggle,
Just remember dreams aren't real, nothing bad
can get you,
You'll wake up safe in bed, and Mummy is there
to hug you!

All of The Foodies sing:

Dream time is the best time, when we can be
anything we want,
A sailor on the high seas, an adventurer on a jaunt,
Nothing bad can get us, because we are so brave,
We'll wake up in the morning, and tomorrow
we'll do it all again!

LIBBY THE HAPPY LEMON

13 June

The taxi driver takes me to a small bed and breakfast just outside Barnstaple. This is run by a man who thankfully appears to suffer from insomnia, but less thankfully, is a cantankerous old bastard with a permanent look of barely concealed disgust on his face that he's probably been honing for decades.

Still, the shower is boiling hot, so we'll take it as win on a night fraught with losses.

I won't be smoking any marijuana again for a very long time, let me assure you of that. I feel absolutely *terrible* as I crawl into the tiny single bed that Captain Hospitality has provided me with for the princely sum of £130. My brain is fuzzy, my stomach feels like there's a bowling ball in it and, despite the hot shower, my skin is cold and clammy as I pull the duvet up to my chin.

Drugs really are *bad*, it appears. It just took me well into my thirties to realise it.

It's also taken me quite a while to properly understand what's going on in my head these days. I may have had to avoid a decidedly unwanted threesome to do it, but my little cannabis-fuelled chat with

Martin and his gang of perverts has at least provided me with some sense of direction for the first time in months.

I may have only a short time to live, and in that time I have to do something worthwhile.

Carpe diem, as someone in a toga once said.

I fall asleep trying to cling on to that idea and resolutely trying to forget the gentle caress of Bork's meaty hand.

I'm not normally the kind of person who dreams a lot. I guess I'm just not that imaginative. But tonight? Oh boy, tonight is *very* different. If cannabis doesn't agree with me when I'm awake, then it positively *despises* me when I'm asleep. I drop into the kind of surrealist nightmare that might keep me up at night for weeks to come.

It begins with me lying naked on a beanbag. Thankfully there's no sign of Bork, but there is the spectre of Gloria Billingswade hanging over a forty-foot-high garden fence, looking down on me with the fires of hell boiling in her eyes.

'DISGUSTING,' she says, voice booming with demonic malice, as she points one gnarled and crooked finger at my penis – which is erect and now made of stone. Gloria's hair, usually held in a haphazard bun, is now a writhing coil of snakes. Her eyes are jet black.

In my nightmares, I am guilty of a little cliché, I have to admit.

Suddenly, my mother is standing in front of me, blocking me from Demon Billingswade. She's holding the guitar from Martin's commune out in front her and is attempting to bat the enormous, gnarled hand away from my penis. Every time the guitar comes into contact with the knuckle, it makes a SQUEAK *FLOOM* noise.

'Get away from my son!' Mum shouts. 'He has to get up for school soon and his father is dead!'

Hearing this news, I instantly burst into tears.

As I do, my stone penis snaps off. I pick it out of my lap to hold up to my mother, the tears still streaming down my face. 'Fix it, Mum!' I wail at her.

She looks back at me. 'Don't be silly, Nathan! It's just a commentary on human sexuality . . . isn't that right, Bork?'

Bork is now standing on my left, looking down. The entire lower half of his jaw is missing. He reaches down to take the stone penis out of my hands. I scream . . .

. . . and am suddenly on an enormous stage in front of an audience of children all dressed in Victorian clothing. I am thankfully not naked any more, but am dismayed to find I am dressed as Libby the Happy Lemon. Standing beside me is Sienna, wearing her red Prada dress and with her fist stuck entirely in her gob.

'Sing that song!' one of the Victorian children screams at me.

'Which one?' I shout back.

'You know the one, Nathan!' every child says in perfect, Wyndham-like unison. 'The one we all love!'

For some reason, this fills me with absolute horror . . . but the show must go on. Even though playing their favourite song will probably result in my death, I have to do what the children tell me, don't I?

I strum the strings on the guitar, making it scream like a butchered pig. This seems to please the children, as they all start to laugh uncontrollably.

. . . yes, this is fucking *horrific*, isn't it?

The song that I'm playing is apparently 'We Love to Wave Goodbye'. I start to open my mouth to sing the first verse, but am struck dumb with the realisation that I've forgotten the words.

'I've forgotten the words!' I cry out to my disconcerting audience.

'Sing!' they cry together. 'Sing, Nathan!'

'Mfnmfnmn!' Sienna says, fist still jammed right in there.

'I can't! I can't! My fingers don't work!'

I hold up my hand and my fingers have now turned to stone. My hand starts to shake. One by one my fingers drop off. The children laugh so hard there's a danger they might rupture their vocal chords.

Again, the scene abruptly changes with no warning. Now I'm in Mr Chakraborty's office. He's not there with me, though. Instead of seeing the good surgeon sat behind his desk, I instead get to look at Herman the Grumpy Potato. Not some jobbing actor *dressed* as Herman the Grumpy Potato, but Herman himself, if such a thing were possible.

This nightmare version of Herman is *awful*. His brown skin is dirty and cracked, with thick black hairs sprouting from various places. His eyes are tiny little black holes of nastiness and his mouth is a slit running right across his potato body about a third of the way down from the top. When he opens this mouth, I can see the white flesh inside, pulsating.

'Hello, Nathan,' Herman says in a clipped, upper-class accent. 'How are you today?'

'I'm dying,' I reply.

Herman contrives to look surprised. His little piggy eyes widen. I'm afraid if I look into them for too long I might see infinity staring back at me. 'Oh? And why are you dying, Nathan?'

'Because you're killing me,' I say in an accusing voice.

Now Herman tries an innocent expression on for size. It isn't convincing. 'Me? I'm not doing *anything*, Nathan! I'm just a grumpy potato!'

'Bullshit! You're an allegorical representation of the brain tumour I've got in my head!'

Herman looks angry. He knows I've got him bang to rights on that one. 'Oh yes? And what are you going to do about it?' he sneers.

I stand up. 'I'm going to kill you!' I screech, and try to climb over the table. I look back, however, to see that I'm being held back by Bork and Sienna, who have hold of my feet.

Herman laughs. 'There's nothing you can do to kill me! I'm inside you, Nathan! I'm aaaaaaaaalways going to be there!'

I slump back into the chair, defeated. He's right. There's nothing I can do.

Then I see my mother come to stand at my side. 'He can do something, you stupid potato,' she tells Herman. 'He can keep living.'

Herman laughs again. 'No! He'll die! He'll die and I'll win!'

'No, you won't,' another voice says from my other side. I turn to see Alison standing there. She's now wearing the Libby costume. I (of course) am naked once more. She looks down at me. 'Isn't that right, Nathan? We can't let horrible old Herman *win*, can we? We can't let him tell us what to do. We have to stop him!'

I shake my head. 'But I don't know how to, Libby. I just don't.'

She leans down. 'It's easy, Nathan. You just have to do something *worthwhile*. Nasty old Herman goes away if you do that!'

'But what?' I implore. 'What, Libby?'

She abruptly stands up straight again. 'I don't know, Nathan. But you'd better do it soon, before you miss your chance.'

'I did miss my chance with you, though, Alison!' I wail. 'I didn't call you!'

Alison shakes her head. 'Well, that was a silly thing to do, wasn't it?'

I nod. 'Yes, it was.'

'But I'm still here, Nathan,' Alison whispers. 'So come and find me. Don't miss your chance.'

I feel Mum's hand on my shoulder. 'Don't *miss*, Nathan. It's not too late. And remember to keep playing until you can't play any more!'

One more scene change.

Now I'm at home, standing at my open bifold patio doors and looking out into the expertly manicured garden. Herman is running towards me. His mouth is wide open in a snarl of rage and I can see that he now has teeth. Each one of them is made of a sharpened plectrum.

As he rushes headlong at me, no doubt to chew me up inside that awful mouth, I look down to find that I'm holding yet another guitar. This one is the black custom Les Paul I use in the studio – the absolute best guitar ever made and one I love as if it were my firstborn.

'Fuck you, Herman,' I say in a low voice. 'I'll start playing . . . Let's see if you know the words.' I strum downwards with the kind of ferocity that Pete Townshend would have been proud of, windmilling my arm around for all I'm worth.

A strident electric chord rings out loud and true across the garden, and Herman explodes into a million gooey, half-baked pieces.

I instantly wake in my tiny single bed with a scream. My heart is racing and my skin is soaked with cold sweat.

'Jesus Christ!' I exclaim.

The door to the room opens. Standing there is Captain Hospitality. 'Not quite,' he says with disgust. 'But if you want breakfast, you've only got ten minutes to get downstairs.'

'Okay!' I blurt out. I should be highly offended at this gross intrusion of my privacy, but I'm too terrified to notice.

The Captain leaves again, slamming the door as he goes. I take a long, ragged breath in the silence of the small bedroom. That was easily the worst dream I've ever had – partly because it was terrifying and partly because it was so grossly laced with heavy-handed symbolism that the whole thing almost descended into parody.

If I'm forced to confront my own personal demons in a nightmarish hellscape of my own devising, I'd prefer it be done with a little more *nuance*.

I take another hot shower straight away – breakfast will just have to wait until I'm on the train headed back east. I can't go through the rest of the day covered in my own night sweat.

As I pull on my Adidas trainers, I start to go back over some of the elements of the nightmare, even as they start to fade. My subconscious was quite clearly working overtime, so I guess I'd better pay it some attention. The one thing I can remember with great clarity is Alison's face, as well as her telling me to do something worthwhile and not to miss my chance. I'm pretty sure I know what I was trying to tell myself with that little exchange, but I'm not sure if it's advice I should act on or not.

From my inside jacket pocket I pull out a rather battered and frayed napkin with a faded phone number written on it. For some reason, I just couldn't throw it away after that night at the Roundabout Theatre – and now I'm extremely glad I didn't.

I pull my phone out of my jeans pocket and punch Alison's number into it.

My finger hovers over the 'Dial' button.

It continues to hover for a few moments.

Cramp sets in at around the forty-second mark.

The door to the bedroom bangs open again, revealing my congenial host, who contrives to look even more annoyed at me than the last time we crossed paths. 'Nearly checking-out time!' he snaps, pointing down the hallway.

Yes, mate. I know it is. That's the bloody problem . . .

I save Alison's number in my phone and stuff it and the napkin back into my pocket. I then rise from the bed that I am eternally glad I will never be sleeping in again, provide the Captain with the best approximation of a smile I can muster and walk past him down the hallway, trying my level best to forget about the fleshy texture of Herman's mouth coming to gobble me up.

I manage a little sleep on the train journey home, which is just as well, as we're a good half an hour delayed, so the trip takes well over three hours. There aren't many better ways to pass the time in a train carriage than having a much-needed doze. Luckily, my brief sleep is devoid of further nightmares. I guess my subconscious has decided that the waking world holds enough terrors – what with all the signal delays and leaves on the track – and has decided to give me a break while I'm napping.

I get back home in the afternoon and set about the important business of doing bugger all for the rest of the day. This includes a little light cleaning, a little light masturbation and a little light drinking. In that order.

By the time I've eaten a Domino's pizza and had a very deep and relaxing bath, it's early evening and I'm plonked down in front of the TV for a bit of Netflix.

I'm halfway through an episode of *House of Cards* when my eyes flick over to my mobile phone on the coffee table. I have successfully managed to avoid thinking about Alison's phone number for the best part of the day, but now my mind has rather inevitably wandered back to the issue. Not even Frank Underwood's latest machinations can prevent me from sitting up straight and gathering the phone off the table for another round of thumb hovering.

The horrible dream I suffered through resurfaces in my mind. Again I remember Alison telling me not to miss my chance and my mother telling me to play until I can't play any more.

I'm sat there in something of a daze, thinking about all of this, when the phone starts to ring.

'Jesus Christ!' I scream, my heart skipping a few beats.

It's Eliza. Eliza's calling me.

. . . which, other than the near heart attack, is very probably a good thing. I could do with some advice.

'Elsie,' I say, replying to the call. 'Good timing. I need a chat.'

'Oh. Oh good,' she responds, a bit taken aback. 'I haven't heard from you in ages, so kind of figured the last thing you wanted to do was chat.'

I wince as I hear the obvious hurt in her voice. 'Yeah. Sorry. I've . . . I've not been in a good place recently.'

'Okay. I understand, Nate.' She pauses for a moment. 'But please don't shut me out. I want to be there for you, but I can't do that if you don't talk to me.'

'I know, I know. And I'm sorry. I've felt totally lost recently and have just wanted to shut everything out. Things have changed in my head a bit now, though. I'll be better from now on, I promise.'

'Has something happened, then?'

'Oh yes,' I say, rolling my eyes.

I then go on to explain what happened at the commune, including the minor revelation I had and my dash into the night following Celeste and Bork's attempted seduction.

'Oh God, Nate!' Eliza screams with laughter. It's a nice sound to hear. 'That's awful!'

'Pretty much,' I reply ruefully.

It takes her a few moments to get herself under control, but when she does, she asks the sixty-four-thousand-dollar question: 'So, what are you going to do now you've had this realisation?'

'Still not sure . . . about doing something worthwhile, anyway. But that's not really what I need your advice about . . .'

'Oh? And what is?'

I then tell Eliza about my dream – leaving out most of the gory details and concentrating on Alison's part in it.

'So, what do you think?' I ask her when I'm done.

Eliza is quiet for a moment. 'Hmmm. You obviously like her. And who can blame you? She was *fabulous* with Callum.' Another brief pause. 'I say go for it. Carpe diem, and all that.'

'That's exactly what I thought,' I reply, with a smile on my face. My cousin and I have always been on a similar wavelength.

'But if you do go out with her, you *have* to be up front about your tumour, Nate. You have to let her know about it,' Eliza tells me in a firm voice.

'I will, I will,' I reply. 'That's even if I get that far.'

'Good. Trust me, you don't want to keep big secrets like that from someone – even someone you only just met. Secrets kill relationships, Nate. Never forget that.'

Which reminds me . . .

'How are things with you and Bryan?'

'Terrible. He's not paying up for Callum's care again, the rancid little shit.'

I swallow hard. 'I wish you'd let me help you out, Elsie. Please let me give you some money to h—'

'No, Nate!' she snaps. 'I don't want your money! Callum is Bryan's responsibility, and he'll bloody well do his duty as his father!'

'Okay, okay!' I should never have said that. Eliza is not the type to take charity from anyone – never has been. If I'm bad at asking for emotional support, then she's *terrible* at asking for it financially. 'I'm sorry, Elsie. I won't ask again.'

'Good. You've got enough on your mind anyway, cuz. I can handle my problems just fine.' She pauses again. I can hear her taking a deep breath. 'Now, why don't you put the phone down on me and give Alison a call?'

I take a deep breath. 'Okay, Elsie.'

'Good luck, Nate. Let me know how it goes.'

I tell her I will and end the call, my left hand shaking a little. Whether it's from the tumour or just nerves I have no idea.

I stare at the phone for a moment longer, thinking back on both the nightmare and the conversation I've just had with my cousin.

Fuck it.

I don't know how many chords I have left in me, so let's play this one and hope it isn't a bum note.

I press 'Dial', and my heart rate rockets again as the phone starts to ring.

'Hello?' Alison says. I almost drop the phone. I wasn't actually expecting her to answer that quickly. In fact, I'm not entirely sure I was expecting her to answer *at all.* 'Hello?' she repeats when I don't respond immediately.

'Hi! Hi, Alison! It's me. It's Nathan.'

'Oh, hello.' Well, the flat tone of her voice is *extremely* encouraging. When you call a girl out of the blue, the first thing you want to hear is a combination of defensive indifference and mild irritation.

'Er . . . how are you?' I continue, now convinced this was a terrible and stupid idea.

'I'm fine. How are you?'

'Er . . . yeah. Not too bad. Not too bad at all.'

I pause.

I continue to pause.

'What can I do for you, Nathan?' Alison says, obviously not a big fan of being on the receiving end of such an epic hiatus in conversation.

'Well . . . er . . . I just wondered if you still fancied getting that drink sometime?'

'You want to do that?' The indifference is gone, replaced by a fair amount of disbelief. The irritation is still clear and present, though.

'Yes! Of course. Why wouldn't I?'

'I just figured that because I hadn't heard from you, and that it's been weeks, you probably weren't interested.'

'Oh! I'm so sorry, Alison. I've been' – *a moping, antisocial arsehole?* – 'really busy with work. I just haven't had the time to do anything socially, and I didn't want to arrange something with you and then cancel it.'

'Oh . . . all right. I understand.' I wince a little to myself as I hear the change of tone in her voice to one that's much warmer. I don't like telling lies like this, even if they are white ones, but there's no way I'm broaching the subject of my health before I've even had the chance to buy the woman a glass of wine, despite what Eliza says. 'I guess we could still get together, then. When are you free?' Alison asks.

'Any time! I'm pretty much free any time!' I blurt like a sixteen-year-old. 'You just tell me when you'd like to meet up and I'll be there with knobs on!'

Smooth, Nathan. Real smooth.

Happily, this makes her chuckle. 'Okay. Well, how about Sunday evening?'

'Fine with me! We could go to—' I stop myself. I'm about to offer to take her to the poshest watering hole I know, the Elysium Bar. But that's Sienna's favourite hang-out, too, and I hardly think bumping into her will help my date with Allie go smoothly. '. . . I mean, where would you like to go?' I say.

'Do you know a pub called the Shining Star? It's in the centre of town.'

'I do.'

'Great. I can get there for about 7 p.m., if that's good with you?'

'Yeah! That's fine.'

'Okay. I'll see you then.'

'Fantastic! I'm really looking forward to it!' I'm sounding far, far too enthusiastic here, but I can't help myself. This is the first bit of good news I've had in what feels like a couple of decades, so I'm making the most of it.

We exchange goodbyes and I put the phone back on to the coffee table with a trembling hand.

Well, that's that, then. I have committed to seeing Alison on an actual, real date.

I should be disgusted with myself, given that I'm consigning her to a meeting with one of the walking dead, but all I feel instead is nervous excitement.

It probably won't actually lead to anything – and even if it did, then I'd make sure it didn't go *too* far. I would be very honest with Alison about my health, just like Eliza told me to be.

Honest to God.

***

The Shining Star is a lot bigger than I remember. I haven't been here in a few years, but I was *sure* it was smaller than this.

My memory must have been playing tricks on me, however, as the bar extends right down one wall and the seating area is so vast it must cost a fortune in commercial rental. It's also bloody cold in here. They must have the air con ramped right up. The place is surprisingly empty for a Sunday night in midsummer. From where I'm sat in a booth along the opposite wall to the bar, I can see only about half a dozen people arranged haphazardly around the pub. The couple sat closest to me is enjoying an evening meal. I have to look away from their plates, as they're both tucking into gigantic, fluffy jacket potatoes.

Anyway, how am I dressed?

Looking okay, do you think?

The black FCUK jeans have come out of the wardrobe for the first time in a year, and I don't even recall buying this Ben Sherman shirt. Still, the light blue goes quite well with the black, and it's definitely more appropriate apparel for a first date than the leather jacket/T-shirt combo I usually roll in. Okay, I'm not sure if the brown Adidas trainers were such a good idea. They do clash a bit, but my grey ones are still encrusted with West Country commune mud, and for a man with a healthy bank balance, I am surprisingly bereft of decent footwear.

I fiddle with the collar of my shirt a little as I wait for Alison to arrive. I probably should have just stood outside – that's what I'd normally do, but for some reason I thought it a better idea to come in and take a seat. I must be more nervous than I thought.

The nerves really start to jangle when I see Alison come through the pub door. She's a little hard to miss, given that she's wearing a bright-yellow jumper. This seems like an odd choice of clothing for a few reasons. Firstly, it's quite a warm evening outside. She must be *roasting*. Second, it's not particularly flattering, as it's quite billowy and large. Third – and this is the most important reason – it makes her look like Libby the Happy Lemon. I don't know about you, but if my day job was to prance around in a bright-yellow fancy dress costume, then I'd be avoiding any street clothes that look similar like the bloody plague.

Maybe Alison only took the part of Libby *because* of the yellow suit. Maybe she is just a big fan of the colour yellow and can't get enough of it. This doesn't bode well for me if we did start seeing each other. Yellow generally tends to set off a headache if I have to look at it too long.

I wave. She sees me and comes over.

'Hello,' Alison says with a smile as she sits down on the other side of the large booth. Almost instantly, a blond-haired waiter appears at the table, making me jump. I guess he must have been hovering just outside my field of vision, waiting to take my order all this time. Still, you can't fault the level of service, I suppose.

'What can I get you both?' he says, before Alison has had chance to get her bum on the seat. 'The special today is jacket potato . . . in a red wine jus.'

'Er . . . we just want drinks, actually,' I tell him. 'I'll have a Jack Daniel's and Coke.'

'And I'll have a limoncello,' Alison adds.

'One Jack Daniel's and Coke and one limoncello,' the tall, blond waiter repeats. 'Are you sure you wouldn't like to both look at the menu, though? The jacket potatoes are very good!'

'No,' I say in an irritated voice. 'Just the drinks, please.'

The waiter smiles and disappears, leaving me alone with my date.

'So, how are you?' I ask her.

'I've put on weight,' she replies.

'Pardon?' I say, slightly shocked. This is a bit *personal*, isn't it? I was expecting to enter into a little small talk while we wait for our drinks, not a discussion about weight gain.

'I said, I've put on weight,' Alison repeats. 'Look.' She then lifts up her yellow jumper to show me her belly. Or rather, she shows me the pale-yellow T-shirt she's got on underneath the jumper. And indeed, Alison is correct – she does appear to have put on weight. Quite *a lot*, in fact. The yellow jumper was hiding it, but there's now a decided paunch to her stomach that I don't remember being there before. Her face is a lot more round as well.

Quite why she felt the need to broach the topic with me within ten seconds of meeting I don't know.

'And how are you?' she asks me, pulling the jumper back down again. 'Still having issues with your hands?'

'What?'

'You said your hands were shaking while you were playing the songs onstage the other night.'

'Did I?'

'Yes! Don't you remember?'

No. No, I bloody *don't* remember. I don't remember Alison being so blunt, either. It's like I'm having a conversation with a mate I've known for years, not a woman I've met once before in my entire life.

This is actually quite unpleasant. I should have ignored Eliza's advice and not made that bloody phone call.

'Here are your drinks!'

I let out a cry of surprise. That waiter can move like a fucking *ninja*. He puts my JD and Coke in front of me and what looks like a pint of limoncello in front of Alison.

'Mmmmm. My favourite!' she exclaims. Alison then picks up the pint glass and starts glugging the limoncello down.

'She loves lemons!' the waiter shouts with delight.

The couple eating jacket potatoes look around at us. 'And we love jacket potatoes!' they cry in unison, stabbing their forks into the pulpy white potato flesh sat on their plates.

Alison drains the entire pint glass and wipes her mouth. 'Lemons make me happy!' she says, and smiles. All her teeth are sharpened plectrums.

So, when did you work out this was a dream?

Was it the yellow jumper? Or maybe the jacket potatoes?

I think I probably realised deep down when the waiter just appeared out of thin air, though you know what it's like when you're having a nightmare – it sometimes takes a while to cotton on.

The waiter – who is of course now our best friend Bork – shoves a silver platter under my nose. On it is Herman the Grumpy Potato, lying on a bed of lettuce. He's giving me the finger.

'Eat him, Nathan!' Alison demands. She is now a bloated monstrosity. It's like someone has come along with a bicycle pump and inflated her to five times her normal size. Alison has become Libby the Happy Lemon right in front of my eyes. 'Eat Herman up like a *good little boy*!' she snarls.

I look back down at Herman, who has plunged both hands into his chest and is starting to pull in opposite directions. I can see his skin starting to rip. Steam begins to pump out from his flesh in a massive plume that heads straight towards my face . . .

'Aaaarggh!' I scream as I wake in my lounge. The TV is still on Netflix and the credits to *House of Cards* are playing to the darkened room, sending flickering white light up the walls. 'Fuck about!' I exclaim, sitting bolt upright. My mouth feels as dry as the Sahara and my head is pounding.

It takes me a few moments to wake up properly. Even then I stagger a little as I go out into the kitchen to open the medical drawer and grab some prescription drugs.

As I stand by the sink, glugging water, I keep a firm grip on the countertop, just in case my legs go out from under me.

What the hell has caused this? Is it still the cannabis in my system? Or is it something more insidious? Is this a new symptom of the tumour's progress?

I've certainly never suffered from nightmares like this before, so I guess it might be.

Within five minutes, I've returned to some semblance of normality. *Physically*, at least. Mercifully, the worst aspects of the nightmare are already fading and I'm just left with an odd sense of disconnection.

I'm also feeling partly relieved.

Why?

Well, that felt like a first date going badly wrong, even before all the weird stuff started to happen, so I'm quite glad that none of it was real. I don't know how Sunday night is actually going to pan out, but it won't happen in a gigantic, cold, empty pub and it won't involve a woman in a disgusting yellow jumper and a magic waiter.

I slope off to bed, the headache thankfully getting less painful with every step. As I pass my wardrobe, I open it slowly. On one hanger is a blue Ben Sherman shirt. I will not be wearing it Sunday evening, you can bet your life on that. I'm also going to make sure I stand outside and wait for Alison to arrive – and woe betide any tall, blond waiters who may be working that evening.

Of course, there aren't any actual waiters at the Shining Star, given that it's a pub.

It's also *tiny*. Comfortingly tiny.

I pop my head in quickly when I arrive, just to see if Alison had got there before me. She hasn't, but it gives me a chance to see that the dream version of the pub bears little to no relation to its real-world equivalent.

There are no booths, no dining tables and definitely no jacket potatoes on the menu. It is, however, *achingly* trendy. There's artwork on the walls from some of the more talented artists in the local area. There are more wine bottles used for display purposes than to actually hold alcohol, and the overuse of chrome and steel in the pub's decoration is quite eye-watering – especially when it's juxtaposed with old, varnished oak beams and equally varnished wooden furniture. Somebody more pretentious than me would probably say it's a fascinating exercise in incongruous textualisation. I just think it looks like someone's dropped a scrapheap on an antiques shop and given it a polish.

Despite the rough sleep I've had, I feel quite good about myself today. It's probably the nervous energy about tonight, but I've been full of vim and vigour all day.

Instead of that blue shirt, I've elected to go with a plain black T-shirt and blue jeans. I have an urge to keep things simple tonight.

When Alison arrives, she is resolutely *not* wearing a bright-yellow jumper. Neither has she piled on about three stone in weight. In fact, she looks *gorgeous*. She's a pretty girl anyway, but when your last memories of her are either plastered with sweat or in the confines of a nightmare, then the comparison just makes her seem all the more beautiful.

She is also wearing blue jeans and a black top. I hope nobody thinks we're brother and sister.

'Hello,' she says as she walks up to me.

'Hi, Alison.' I give her an awkward kiss on the cheek.

'Please, call me Allie . . . and thanks for waiting for me out here. I've had a thing about walking into pubs on my own ever since I saw *An American Werewolf in London.*'

I get the reference as I *love* that movie. Things have got off to a great start.

We both go into the Shining Star and order drinks at the bar, swapping small talk while the barman serves us. I have a small moment when I spot a bottle of limoncello behind the optics, but breathe a sigh of relief when Allie orders a glass of Chardonnay.

We find a table and sit down. While the pub is not as empty as its dream version, it's also not heaving, so we're able to hold a decent conversation with each other. Allie obviously knows how to pick a pub for a first date.

I think I'm coming across quite relaxed and casual, but that's clearly not the case, as about half an hour into the evening, Allie says, 'Are you okay, Nathan? You seem a bit on edge.'

'Do I?'

'Yes. You keep glancing around as if something's about to leap out at you.'

Oh dear. Is that what I've been doing? I have to confess that I'm having a hard time shaking the memory of the pop-up waiter and the rest of last night's nightmare. I probably *have* been looking around a lot, subconsciously reliving the dream in my head. The question now is, do I tell Allie about it? Or do I make something up?

'Sorry. This will sound really silly, but I had the worst dream last night about this pub,' I tell her, electing for the truth. I then go on to describe some aspects of the dream – missing out her weight gain and any mention of Herman the Grumpy Potato.

Allie smiles. 'You should have said something! We could have gone somewhere else.' In theatrical fashion, she puts both her hands over mine and looks me square in the eye. 'Don't worry, Nathan! I'll protect you from the evil blond waiter!'

I give her a wry smile. 'Thanks very much.'

'I had a nightmare when I was a kid that I've never been able to shake,' Allie says. 'It was when I was about eight years old. I used to dream about these little hairy balls of fur with eyes that I called the Pibble Nibbles.'

'The *Pibble Nibbles?*' I say with huge amusement.

Allie's face flames red. 'Yes. The Pibble Nibbles. You may laugh, but I tell you, things like that are *terrifying* to a small child. I used to dream that they came out from underneath my bed and suffocated me.'

'Blimey. That's dark.'

Allie takes a sip of her Chardonnay. 'Yep. See what I mean? Since then, I've always had an aversion to having anything small, round and hairy on my face.'

She had to say that just as I was taking a swig of beer, didn't she? I manage not to cover her with spray, but it's a close-run thing.

Rather than look embarrassed at the innuendo she's just come out with, Allie throws her head back and laughs.

I wipe my mouth. 'You timed that on purpose,' I say, grinning despite myself.

'Yep!' Allie says triumphantly.

'And the Pibble Nibbles?'

'Oh, they were real,' she says with a shudder. 'My mum had to come in and comfort me in the middle of the night way too many times.'

'Oh, that sucks,' I say, with heartfelt pity.

While the conversation topic hasn't been a pleasant one, I do think the discussion about nightmares has broken the first-date ice quite well. It always takes a while to move past the polite chit-chat and on to something a bit more meaningful. I don't think you really know whether you're getting on well with someone until you start talking about personal things. If a date ends and all you've done is chat about the weather and your last MOT, then chances are you're on to a bit of a loser.

But if you're both laughing your heads off about stupid nightmares and testicle gags only half an hour in, then things are probably going quite well.

In fact, they continue to go well for another hour or so, and I learn quite a lot about Allie in that time. She's been a struggling actress for the past seven years since she left drama school and is still waiting for that elusive big break to come along. Until then, jobs like playing Libby the Happy Lemon have kept her going financially. Her contract runs for another few months, but the amount of show runs she's getting is patchy, so she's auditioning for other roles in the meantime as well. It all sounds like a lot of hard, stressful work that takes a huge amount of dedication to stick with.

In some ways, Allie reminds me of myself before The Foodies took off. I'm a musician and she's an actress, but there are many parallels to our careers that give me a good insight into the way she thinks. She sounds like she has the same enthusiasm for treading the boards that I had – and still have – for music. If *I* can make a success of myself, then I'm one hundred per cent positive she can, too.

Other things I learn about her include that she also enjoys an evening in front of Netflix, thinks politics is a necessary evil, once got caught streaking down Old Brompton Road and has never been in a serious, long-term relationship before.

I've had more decent conversation in one evening with Allie than I had with Sienna throughout our entire relationship.

It's definitely been nice to hear all about somebody else's life for once, instead of constantly worrying about my own. Allie is a very expressive person – all smiles, big hand gestures and wide eyes when she talks. It's incredibly hard not to get caught up in her enthusiasm for life. By the time she's finished, I'm grinning from ear to ear.

In the back of my mind, Eliza's words about being straight with Allie over my diagnosis are trying to make themselves heard, but I'm doing a very good job of ignoring them. I'm having a fantastic time right now, and mentioning the tumour would no doubt ruin things. It's just lucky I have an alcoholic drink in front of me to drown out the small feeling of guilt I'm having over that decision. There will hopefully be plenty of other occasions for me to get around to confessing my little secret, but tonight is not that time.

The two of us make our way through a few more beers and glasses of wine before Allie says she has to leave. 'Sorry. I'd really like to stay a little longer, but I've got an audition up in the city tomorrow afternoon and have to get a good night's sleep.'

I wave a hand. 'No, no. Don't worry. I could probably do with calling it a day as well. I want to spend a little time in the studio tomorrow working on a new song.'

'For The Foodies?' Allie says with a grin.

I roll my eyes. 'No. My days of Foodies songwriting are thankfully behind me. I'm trying something a bit different.'

What I'm not telling her is that I'll probably strum a few chords on the guitar before my mind wanders off to worry about my tumour and I'll get nothing else done that day. That's the way my 'recording sessions' have gone in recent weeks.

***

Outside, the weather has cooled off considerably – so much so that I would offer Allie my coat, if I'd actually worn one. 'Do you want to share a taxi?' I ask her.

'Yeah, okay.'

I look up the street. There's no sign of a taxi rank, as the whole area was pedestrianised a few years ago, so we begin to walk past the shops towards the nearest one. I feel a bit sick as we go past Primark, but it passes quickly. I very much doubt Allie will want to hit me over the head with a squeaky foam bat any time soon.

The walk to the taxi rank takes longer that I was expecting, which is no bad thing, as it means I get to spend a little extra time with a woman I will most definitely be asking out on a second date. By the time we reach the empty taxi rank, we're having a very light-hearted chat about Libby the Happy Lemon. 'I could kill you, you know,' she says, trying not to laugh. 'That suit is the most uncomfortable, hot and ugly thing I've ever had to wear!'

'Sorry! It seemed like a good idea at the time.'

'Well, next time, if you could invent a children's character that exclusively wears Chanel and Prada that would be lovely.'

I think for a moment. 'Deidre the Designer Doughnut?'

'Perfect!'

Allie collapses into three-glasses-of-Chardonnay giggles.

'Well, you might not like playing Libby, but you do a bloody good job of it,' I tell her. 'What you did with Callum after that show was *incredible*. I've never seen the kid happier.'

Allie smiles, her eyes a little glassy. 'Thank you, Nathan. That's a lovely thing to say.' Her hand lightly touches my arm. 'It means a lot to hear that from you – the guy who created The Foodies.'

I don't know how to respond to that. What exactly does she mean? She's the one who was good with Callum, not me!

My eyes then go wide as a taxi turns up at the rank. Would you believe it's bright yellow?

'Look!' I say, pointing. 'Libby's come to get us!'

Allie sees the taxi and laughs even harder. She then steps forward off the kerb and opens the taxi door.

From it spill thousands of small, black, furry balls, each with its own set of googly eyes, and tiny, pipe-cleaner-thin arms and legs. 'Look, Nathan! It's the Pibble Nibbles!' Allie shouts with delight. She goes off into another gale of maniacal laughter.

The Pibble Nibbles start to climb up Allie's body, towards her head.

'No! No! Leave her alone!' I shout as they congregate on her face, some of them entering her wide-open mouth.

'Oh, they don't mean any harm!' cries Herman the Grumpy Potato from where he's sat in the back of the taxi. 'They just want to have fun! Just like me, Nathan! Just like me!'

Herman snarls, jumps out of the taxi and heads straight towards me with that dreadful mouth opening wide. As he closes in on me I can see Allie now completely covered with Pibble Nibbles. Her laughter has turned to choking.

I throw my arms up as Herman reaches me, staring into those black eyes as they focus on me with laser-like intensity . . .

'Aaarrrgghh! Bastard!' I bellow into my pitch-black bedroom, sitting bolt upright as I do.

I slam my hands down on the duvet in frustration. 'Fuck you, Herman! Fuck you, you stupid potato!'

It takes a second for my head to clear enough to get a handle on what's just happened, trying to separate what's real from what's not.

The date with Alison *did* happen and we *did* have a lovely time. But we did *not* have to walk all the way to the taxi rank – it was right outside the pub. She doesn't live anywhere near me, so we didn't share a taxi, either. And she sure as hell didn't climb into one that was bright yellow – or containing a psychopathic potato, for that matter.

I did ask her if she'd like to see me again, though . . . and she said *yes*.

I cling on to that happy fact as I clamber slowly out of bed and make my way into the bathroom for a much-needed piss. The vision of the Pibble Nibbles suffocating my date will stay with me for a few days, I know that. Why did she have to tell me that bloody story?

I climb back into bed almost fearfully. This can't go on. It really can't. These vivid nightmares are going to be the death of me if I'm not careful.

Tomorrow, I'm going to arrange a visit to Mr Chakraborty to see if this type of thing is a symptom of my condition or not. I may also ask for some sleeping pills while I'm at it.

On my next date with Allie, I'm going to make sure that I don't bring this latest dream up with her. Nothing is more likely to kill a burgeoning romance than continued conversations about things like the Pibble Nibbles or Herman the Dream Demon Potato.

. . . unless we were both goths. Then I suppose it would be fine.

I eventually fall asleep, resolving to get up in the morning and write a thrash metal song about killer jacket potatoes. I'm going to call it 'Raining Spuds'.

I'm sure it'll be a *massive* hit.

BETTER THAN THE ALTERNATIVE

7 July

Oh my God, I think she's actually going to eat it.

I screw my face up in horrified disgust, unwilling to accept what my eyes are showing me.

. . . yep.

She's *definitely* going to eat it.

Allie is sat across the table from me, about to pop a honey-glazed dead cricket into her mouth, and I think I'm dying inside a little.

'Ew! Ew! Don't do it!' I plead, physically pushing myself away from the table.

Allie goes bug-eyed with delight at my revulsion and ever so slowly pops the cricket into her mouth, biting down on it slowly so I can hear the crunching.

'Aaaargh!' I wail, feeling my kangaroo fillet steak and sweet potato chips threatening to make a triumphant return to the outside world.

Allie swallows the edible insect, still with that look of delight on her face, and starts to laugh her head off at my reaction.

I knew coming to this restaurant was going to be a bad idea. I mean, what good can come from dining in a place called Control, Alt, Del-Eat?

Eating dead insects, that's what. That's what you get when you come to a restaurant that prides itself on its 'alternative approach to high-class cuisine'.

I enjoy a meal out as much as the next person, but when Allie suggested this achingly trendy eatery for our fourth date, I knew I should have suggested we go to Nando's instead.

But this has been the dynamic of my ever-so-brief relationship with Allie so far. She is doing an extremely good job of pushing me outside my comfort zone, whether I like it or not.

Our second date was to an art-house cinema that she suggested to watch a subtitled French thriller – which unbelievably kept me rapt for its entire two-hour running time.

I picked the third date – a nice, sedate lunchtime trip to a country pub. Less than two hours into it, however, Allie had me wading through an icy stream half a mile away, looking for dragonflies in the sunlight filtering in through the trees. Ten minutes after, we were both swimming in the same icy stream in just our underwear.

It was the most fun I've had in *months*.

But I'm not having much fun now, as Allie has just reached for another bloody cricket . . .

'Oh God. Why on earth did you order those?' I ask her, trying not to gag as she pops another one in her mouth. 'I thought you loved little insects. I still have chilblains on my toes to prove it.'

'But I *do* love little insects, Nathan. Especially tasty ones covered in honey!' To underline this, the second cricket goes in and gets munched up. 'Om nom nom nom nom nom!' she exclaims with pure pleasure after it's swallowed.

'You're gross,' I point out, accurately.

She then offers me the toothiest grin I've ever seen. The teeth are covered in crunched-up cricket. 'Would you like to give me a big kiss right now, Nathan?' she asks in as innocent a voice as she can muster.

I make the sign of the cross with both index fingers. 'Get thee behind me, Satan,' I mutter.

This sends her off into a loud gale of laughter. I eventually have to join in with it, as Allie has a knack for comedy that is rather hard to resist.

Unfortunately, the laughing sparks off the headache I've been keeping at bay all evening. I pull out a couple of co-codamol to take while Allie helps herself to a third – and hopefully final – honey-glazed fried cricket.

As she watches me take the pills, a frown crosses her face. 'Are you okay?' she asks.

I wave a hand. 'Oh yeah, just a bit of a headache. Nothing to worry about.'

Okay, okay, I *still* haven't told her about the tumour.

We've been having too much fun and I don't want to put a dampener on things. I just have to pick the right moment, and I don't think that is sat in the middle of Control, Alt, Del-Eat on either side of a plate of dead insects. It wasn't right to tell her about it on our first date, and it still doesn't feel right to do it on our fourth. I'll know when the time is right.

. . . trust me.

Allie sits up. 'Are you sure? We could leave if you want to?'

I shake my head. This hurts quite a lot. 'No, no. It's fine. We've still got drinks, and despite having to watch you eat fried crickets, I'm still having a great time.' I force out a smile as I say this.

'Okay, if you're sure.' She pauses and gives me a closer look. 'I did think you looked a little peaky, even before I started eating the insects.'

'Oh really? I guess I haven't been sleeping much at the moment.'

. . . which is true. Sleep has been a long time coming in recent weeks. Even when it does arrive, the nightmares have been horrific. 'Guess I'm just a bit tired,' I tell Allie, yawning as I do so.

It transpires that the nightmares *are* in fact a symptom of the tumour, according to Mr Chakraborty – or at least he tells me that he wouldn't be surprised if they were. I am learning that in the field of brain tumour research and treatment, there is a lot of *woolliness*. There's as much conjecture and guesswork as there are hard facts. Not surprising, I suppose, given how complicated the human brain actually is.

Did you know that your brain has over eighty-six billion neurons in it? How exactly is that possible? How is it possible for something the size of a small side of ham to contain eighty-six billion of anything? And for that matter, do you even know what a neuron *is*? It sounds like the kind of torpedo that Captain Kirk would fire at the Klingons, but it is in fact a cell in the brain that is *electrically excitable* and can transmit information faster than a supercomputer in a wind tunnel.

I'm learning a lot about the human brain as mine continues to destroy itself. Know thine enemy, and all that.

Anyway, there is an extremely good chance that the nightmares I've been having are caused by Herman the Grumpy Tumour's assault on my cerebral cortex, and I haven't found a decent way of combatting them yet.

Allie gives me a concerned look. 'Any reason you're not sleeping?' she asks.

Yes, Allie. I have a killer brain tumour that I don't want to tell you about because I'm loving the sound of your laughter and don't want to stop hearing it.

I shrug. 'Not sure. Maybe it's because I can't think of any good songs to write and it's stressing me out a bit.' This at least is half-true.

I haven't been able to come up with a decent tune or lyric since the diagnosis.

Allie's look of open sympathy makes me squirm inside a little. 'Aww. That sucks.' An idea then seems to occur to her. 'Have you thought about trying a herbal remedy?'

'Herbs?' I say, attempting to keep any derision out of my voice.

'Yeah. Herbs can be very beneficial, you know.'

I chuckle. 'If I'm making a shepherd's pie, possibly.'

Allie makes a face. 'I'm serious, Nathan. If you take the right ones, they can do you a lot of good. I've used them before when I wasn't getting any acting work and felt stressed out. They really calmed me down.' She holds up a finger. 'Camomile can be your best friend, if you let it.'

I chuckle at this. I've never tried to be best friends with a herb before.

Allie brings out her mobile phone. 'I know someone who specialises in it. I'm sure she'd be able to help you with your disturbed sleep.'

'Really?' I reply, unsure.

'Yep. Belinda is a lovely woman and a well-respected herbalist. She runs the bookshop my mum works in. They've been friends for decades. The herbalism is something she does on the side,' Allie says. 'Her concoctions have got me through some tough times, I can tell you that. I can send you in her direction, if you'd like?'

The fact that her name is Belinda is probably a good start. If Allie had said her name was Tinkerbell Foxwings – or something similar – I would have run a mile. But surely anyone with such a stout, sensible name like *Belinda* can't be all that weird, can she?

I'm aware that this train of thought is what got me into trouble with Martin and his commune of sex maniacs, but I'm willing to risk that this was an isolated case, such is my desire for a decent night's kip – and to make Allie happy, of course.

'All right,' I agree with a smile. 'I'll give it a go. What have I got to lose?'

'Great,' Allie says. 'I'll get her to give you a call.' She picks up another cricket. 'Now, why don't you gaze at me lovingly for a while as I consume this tasty cricket?'

I roll my eyes. 'You're insane,' I remark, face scrunching up again.

'Insane for tasty crickets!' she exclaims, and gobbles the damn thing down.

It says a lot about Allie that I've had more fun watching her eat dead insects in front of me than I ever did doing *anything* with Sienna.

It probably also says something about the way I've changed since the diagnosis as well – but I'm too grossed out right now to think about that, given that Allie is now picking bits of the last cricket out of her teeth with one of its remaining legs.

***

Four days later and I'm sitting at my kitchen table waiting for Allie's friend Belinda and her herbs to arrive. I've already spoken to her on the phone to arrange this appointment. She asked me a few questions about my general state of health, which I answered – avoiding all mention of the tumour and just concentrating on the sleepless nights and nightmares. There's no real point in telling her about Herman the Grumpy Cerebrodondreglioma, as I'm fairly sure you could chuck an entire forest of lavender at the thing and it wouldn't make a blind bit of difference.

Belinda told me she definitely has something that can help me with the insomnia, though. This is just as well, as I'm still sleeping worse than a second-string character in a *Nightmare on Elm Street* movie.

Allie is at an audition this morning for a coffee commercial in the city so will miss seeing Belinda, but she's coming over later this afternoon for a look around my home studio. I've promised to show her a few chords on the guitar, as she thinks being able to play a musical instrument will look good on her CV.

Deep down, we both know this is one giant excuse to jump into bed with each other for the first time, but these are the little rituals you have to go through when you're in the first blushes of a new romance. You can't just invite someone over for a shag. It's just not the done thing, is it?

Before all of that, though, I have to meet with Belinda.

Ding-dong.

And there she is, right on time.

I walk out into the hallway and open the front door. It reveals a woman who is as stout and sensible as her name and her voice. She's wearing an awful lot of wool, and wool is always stout and sensible. There's a bit of tweed in there as well. Belinda looks like someone who's more likely to sell me shortbread than herbal remedies.

'Good morning!' she says, proffering a stout hand for me to shake. In the other is a wicker basket that I assume contains everything I need to get a decent eight hours.

'Hello, Belinda,' I reply. 'Please come in.'

I take the herbalist through to the kitchen, where she plonks her basket down on the table.

'Would you like some tea?' I ask her.

'Just a cup of hot water, thank you,' she replies. This sounds like an odd request, but it's one I can fulfil quite easily.

When her hot water and my tea are made, I return to the table. She takes a small, home-made teabag out of the basket and pops it in the hot water. I instantly get a whiff of lemongrass and camomile. Belinda obviously likes to make her own tea. By the smell of things, she does a good job.

'So, thank you for coming today,' I say.

She smiles. 'My pleasure. Such a shame to miss Alison. Lovely girl. But I'm hoping we'll find something this morning to help you with your problem.'

'So do I. What exactly do we do?'

'I'll get you to answer a few questions, then I'll put together a remedy solution that I think will help you. It'll be something you can pop into a cup of hot water like I've just done with my tea.'

'Okay.' Certainly sounds simple enough.

We spend the next twenty minutes or so discussing my insomnia and night terrors. Once again I don't mention the tumour, because I very much doubt there's anything in Belinda's basket that'll help me with that. Besides, if I can't bring myself to tell the new lady in my life about it, a herbalist I've only met once stands no chance.

Belinda nods several times during the conversation, indicating that she's heard of this kind of thing before. She then takes several minutes to rummage around in her basket and writes a copious amount of notes on her crisp A4 notepad. I give her some space by making more tea and hot water.

Eventually, she places twelve neat little packets of see-through material in front of me. Inside each is a collection of dried and fresh herbs. The smell they give off is rather delightful, it has to be said.

'Okay, Nathan, this should get you started,' she tells me. 'Each of these bags contains a mixture of ingredients I believe will help you with your problem.'

'What's in them?'

'Camomile, passion flower, valerian and Siberian ginseng.'

'Sounds . . . *herby*.'

Belinda can't help but smile a little at that. 'Yes, it does. You should steep each bag in a cup of hot water for five minutes before drinking, about half an hour before bedtime.'

'Okay.'

'However, I'd like you to drink some now, just to check whether it's a taste you like or not. There's no point in prescribing you a solution that you'll hate to drink!'

'Fair enough.'

Belinda picks up a bag of the home-made herbal tea and places it in the cup of hot water I've provided for her. It seems my need for herbal tea is greater than hers right now.

We chat about my bifold patio doors and well-manicured garden while the tea steeps. Everyone loves my bifold patio doors and well-manicured garden. They are a universal constant.

'Please try the tea now, Nathan,' Belinda suggests.

I do so, and I have to say I'm pleasantly surprised. It tastes quite sweet and fresh. I was expecting some kind of bitter, twiggy weirdness, but this is actually very nice.

'Excellent,' Belinda says when I tell her this. 'Then please make sure you drink the rest over the next couple of weeks. I'll give you a call to see if the remedy is having any effect. If not, we can always try something else.'

'Sounds like a good plan.' I reach into my back pocket for my wallet. 'What do I owe you for this?'

Belinda holds up a hand. 'I don't charge until I know my remedies have worked.'

'Well, I hope to be paying you some money very soon, then!' I say with a smile.

'I'm sure you will,' Belinda glances at my kitchen clock. 'I must be going now, Nathan. I have another two appointments to keep today.'

'Oh, okay. Sure.'

I show Belinda to the door, thanking her again for her time.

'Do give Alison my love, won't you?' she asks me at the door.

'Of course,' I reply.

We shake hands again and I watch her walk back to her car. It's a Volvo. What else would it be? Once she's gone, I return to my funny herbal tea and drain the rest of it, smacking my lips as I do. Who'd have thought such a strange collection of herbs could taste so nice? Belinda really does know her onions. And her garlic, her basil and her rosemary as well, I'm sure.

After lunch and while waiting for Allie to arrive, I've entered a state of calm well-being that can only be put down to the herbs Belinda has provided me with. When I greet Allie at the door, I do so with a content smile on my face. I'm still a little nervous at the prospect of consummating our relationship, but the bag of herbs has definitely taken the edge off. If they do for my sleep patterns what they've done for my levels of daytime calmness, I'm on to a winner here.

'Hey,' I say to Allie as she comes in.

'You look like you're in a good mood,' she replies.

'Just happy to see you, I guess.'

Allie sniffs the air and then smiles. 'I take it Belinda has been?'

'She has indeed.'

'And?'

'You know, you might be on to something with this herbal stuff. I haven't felt this relaxed in *ages*.'

She chuckles. 'Told you so.'

'Thank you for putting me in touch with her,' I say, and on impulse I wrap my arms around her in a grateful hug.

'My pleasure,' Allie says, and plants a kiss on my lips. I return it with about a thousand per cent interest. 'Easy there, fella,' she says with a wicked smile. 'I want to see that studio of yours, remember? You promised to let me have a go on your guitar.'

I take her by the hand. 'Well, *Mademoiselle*, shall we go through, then?'

She giggles. 'Yes, let's.'

When I bought this house three years ago, I did it purely for the large double garage. I probably paid a good ten per cent more than I should have for the place, but the size, shape and position of the garage were perfect for conversion into a studio. Six months and forty grand later, I had that studio, and it has served me very well ever since.

I lead Allie back past the wide front hall and through the door that connects the studio to the house.

'Wow,' she says as we enter. This is the reaction I like to get from my guests when they see it for the first time. It is a constant source of pride for me.

'You have a lot of instruments,' she says, noting the rack of guitars on the wall. There's a couple of banjos and a mandolin up there as well. I'm not all that great on either, but they look nice and are always fun to play when you've had a few.

'I do. Too many, probably. When I see a guitar I like, I have to buy it.'

'The grey, pointy foam on all the walls – that's for soundproofing?'

'That's right.'

'What's all of that?' she asks, pointing to the console of equipment in the far corner.

'That's the stuff I use to record on. I basically set up the microphones where I need them, flick a few switches and lay down whatever comes into my head.'

'Cool! Have you written anything good lately?'

I shrug. 'Not recently.'

'Can I hear any of it?'

Oh dear. That would be a *terrible* idea. What music I have managed to make in the past few months has been either morose, suicidal or downright terrifying. I don't think five minutes of crushing death metal would put Allie in a romantic mood – unless I've misjudged her character completely.

'I think I'd rather play you something live!' I tell her.

She claps her hands together. 'That'd be great!'

'And you get to accompany me,' I say, waggling my eyebrows.

'I do?'

'Yeah. I'm going to show you a couple of chords you can play along with me. Here, sit down on this stool.'

I carry two of my four chrome and black leather stools over from the side of the studio and put one down in front of her. She sits on it, an excited expression on her face.

I go over to the guitar rack and pick out a suitable one for her. It's a light and breezy hollow Fender Telecaster that I bought for stage appearances. It should suit her fine. I grab my black Les Paul from its customary place at the front of the row.

'Wow. That's a nice one,' Allie says as I put the guitar strap over my head.

I pat the Les Paul affectionately. 'It is, isn't it? It's a 1958 custom model, signed by the man himself.'

'Is it worth much?'

I gulp. 'A fair bit, yes. You could probably get yourself a decent sports car for what this guitar would cost these days.'

'Blimey.'

'Yep.' Talking about things like this tends to make me uncomfortable, so I move the conversation on. 'Right, then,' I say as I hand her the Fender and sit down. 'Let's see if I can teach you a thing or two.'

Alison nods.

'First off, this is how you hold a guitar properly . . .'

I've never thought of teaching the guitar to anyone before, but on the strength of the next half an hour with Allie, it feels like something I could very much enjoy doing in the future. It probably helps that she's a quick study. I'm sure my enjoyment levels would be tempered if I had to teach someone who took longer than thirty minutes to learn the C, G and F chords.

'Would you like to try and play a song with me?'

Her eyes go wide. 'Really? I only know how to do three things, and they're quite difficult.'

I smile. 'It's fine. We'll do something simple. Just follow me.'

I think for a moment about which songs use a simple C, G and F structure, then begin to play the opening C of 'Danny Boy'. '*Oh, Danny boy, the pipes, the pipes are calling,*' I sing in my best cod Irish accent, making Allie giggle.

A thought then occurs to me. If Allie thinks me singing in an Irish accent is funny, just wait until she hears my chipmunk voice. She's proved to me that she can be funny – what with the dead insect eating and everything – and now it's my turn to show her I can be just as amusing if I'm given half a chance.

I lean the guitar against the wall and get up.

'What are you doing?' Allie asks.

I hold out my hands. 'Wait there. You're going to love this!'

I go over to the bank of recording equipment and pick up one of the Bluetooth tie microphones I bought a few months ago. I clip this to my T-shirt and play with the sound panel for a few moments. There's a brief and quiet whine of feedback as the mic hooks up with the studio's PA system. I then play with another few buttons on the panel, making sure everything is set up right.

Smiling like the Cheshire cat, I return to my stool, pick up the Les Paul and start to play again.

Then I start to sing.

'*Oh, Danny boy, the pipes, the pipes are calling . . .*'

Allie collapses into a helpless fit of the giggles. My voice, put through one of the most expensive home voice-modulating systems on the market, comes through the speakers in a high, sing-song chipmunk voice that makes me sound like I've just swallowed a truckload of helium.

I continue to knock out a few more lines of 'Danny Boy' like this, until I can't sing any more for laughing.

'Stop! Please stop!' Allie cries, her face covered in tears.

I flick the 'Off' button on the tie mic and try to compose myself.

'Right, then, that's enough of that,' I say. 'Let's do this a little more sensibly, shall we?'

Allie nods. She's managed to regain her composure and is holding the Telecaster firmly in her hands, waiting for me to tell her what to do.

I slowly play C, then F, then C, then G, nodding as I do to get her to join in. She does so, and manages to keep time with me very well.

I start to sing again, this time in my normal voice, safe in the knowledge that all this effort is without doubt going to get me laid later. There are a few stereotypes about guitar players that I'd like to get away from, but the ability to woo members of the opposite gender out of their underwear with a few well-chosen chords is not one of them.

'*Oh, Danny boy, the pipes, the pipes are calling, from glen to glen, and down the mountain thide . . .*'

Mountain thide?

'*The summer's gone, and all the rotheth falling . . .*'

Rotheth?

'*Oh Danny boy, oh Danny boy, I love you tho . . .*'

Tho?

What the hell's going on here?

Allie has a confused look on her face and I can see why. I appear to have developed a lisp out of nowhere. I try to carry on singing, hoping it'll will pass.

'*Oh, Danny boy, the pipeth, the pipeth are callumg, from glen doo gren, and down the mounthin thide . . .*'

Oh shit, it's getting worse!

'Nathan? Are you okay?' Allie says with concern, leaning forward to touch my knee.

'I don'th know!' I reply, panic starting to set in. Is this a new symptom? Has Herman given me a big, fat tongue?? Will I never be able to speak properly again? Am I having some kind of stroke? Am I about to keel over dead right here and—

Stop it! Stop thinking like that!

'My tongueth gone fat,' I say.

'Sorry?'

'I thaid my tongueth gone fat, and I can'th thpeak properly.'

Allie's eyes widen. 'Oh God! Your face!'

171

'Whath abouth ith?'

'You've gone all red and blotchy!'

How the hell does a tumour make your skin go red and blotchy?

'I don'th think I'm very well,' I tell Allie, rising from the stool slowly. My Les Paul, something I usually treat like a baby, clatters to the floor, feedback whining through the wall-mounted studio speakers.

'Oh my God, your lips are swelling up!' Allie cries, panic entering her voice now.

I touch my face with a shaking hand. It feels hot to the touch and yes, Allie's right, when I give my bottom lip a squeeze, it feels about three times bigger than it normally does.

Mr Chakraborty never told me about any of these bloody symptoms, did he? If I'd have known that the tumour would cause a reaction like this, I would have worn a paper bag over my head for the last few months.

Then, another thought occurs – one that in equal parts makes me feel instantly better and also about a thousand times *worse*. This isn't the tumour. This is *something else*. I'm obviously having some kind of reaction to something – but to what?

Then the answer hits me square between the puffy eyes – the bloody herbal tea Belinda made me. It's that, isn't it?

I look at Allie. 'I think I'm having an allerthic reacthun do tha tea that's thuppothed to help me thleep.'

Allie looks understandably confused. I sound like Sylvester the Cat after a heavy concussion. Instead of trying to explain again, I grab her hand and pull her back out of the studio across the hall and into the kitchen, where I rush over to the kitchen table and grab one of the carefully prepared teabags that Belinda left.

'Allerthic reacthun,' I repeat, waggling the bag.

'Oh Christ!' Allie exclaims, realising what's going on for the first time. 'I'm so sorry, Nathan!'

I look at her aghast. 'Ith noth your faulthhhh, Alithon!' I try to reassure her.

'But I suggested you see Belinda!'

I shake my head. 'You weren'th to know!'

I hurry over to the mirror I've got hanging up above the toaster and gasp when I see what damage the herbs are doing to my poor face. It looks like Sloth from *The Goonies* has mated with a sentient tomato and the resultant offspring has been pumped full to bursting with helium.

As I gaze in horror at my grizzly visage, I start to feel a deep and awful itching sensation spread across my chest. The reaction is obviously getting worse. I scratch my chest right where the itching is at its most awful, getting relief for a few moments.

I also manage to accidentally switch the Bluetooth tie microphone back on in the process.

'I think ith would probably be a gooth idea to go tho hothpital,' I say, spitting all over the mirror, before turning back to Allie with an imploring look on my puffed-up face. From across the hall I can hear my garbled words coming out of the studio's PA system in a high-pitched chipmunk voice as I say them. It sounds like the Chip 'n' Dale: Rescue Rangers have been pepper sprayed. I look down to see if I can turn the mic off again, but my vision is now blurry and my hands are shaking too much to do so.

'Pleath take me to accthident and emergenthy,' I implore Allie.

She nods frantically. 'Yeah. I think that's a good idea.' Allie pulls out her car keys, her hand shaking. 'Let's get going.'

Fabulous. What was supposed to be a slow and effective guitar-based seduction has instead turned into an early-afternoon rush to A & E. The rest of the day promises to be filled with panic, discomfort, injections and distinct nausea.

. . . but first, though, there will be shitting.

Lots and lots of *shitting*.

Did you know that explosive diarrhoea can be a symptom of an allergic reaction to Siberian ginseng and valerian? No, neither did I, until I was almost completely through the front door of my house.

'Oh Jethuth!' I cry, as my bowels start to churn like a fucking butter factory.

'*Oh Jethuth!*' the electronically altered version of my voice screams out of the studio at the same time.

'What's wrong?' Allie exclaims, her hand squeezing my arm.

I look at her with horror. 'I think I'm abouth to thit mythelf.'

'Pardon?' she replies, wiping her face.

'I thaid I think I'm abouth to thit – never mindth!'

And with that, I'm turning tail back into the house and running across the hallway to the downstairs toilet. I'd rather go upstairs, away from Allie, but my need is too great and the motion of stair climbing would probably just hasten the onslaught before I reached the bowl.

I claw open the toilet door, rush inside and slam it behind me in about a nanosecond. One *picosecond* later I am sat on the toilet and the world instantly becomes a dark and dreadful place.

'Oh fuck!' I wail, as the universe falls out of my bottom.

From outside, I can hear my cries of anguish repeated across the whole downstairs floor of the house via my studio's speakers. The sound is slightly delayed now, thanks to the closed toilet door and the limits of Bluetooth technology. Not just that, either – the mic is also picking up my bottomly egress extremely clearly.

I've never heard the sound of explosive diarrhoea cranked up electronically to a high-pitched chipmunk whine before.

I can only imagine it's what listening to a Justin Bieber album is like.

'Are you okay, Nathan?' Allie shouts, wisely keeping well away from the toilet door.

'Noth really!' I tell her, frantically trying to find the 'Off' switch on the mic.

'*Noth really!*' the chipmunk version of me repeats, the delay from the Bluetooth mic getting even more pronounced as the signal gets worse.

I fail to find the switch, so Allie gets another chorus of Bieber's greatest hits to enjoy from the hallway.

'Pleath turn that offth!' I wail.

'*Pleath turn that offth!*'

'Oh Godth!'

'*Oh Godth!*'

'I'll go and turn it off!' Allie shrieks, and I hear her run over to the studio. As she does I offload once more, sending another blast of high-pitched shitting noise into her ears as she hurries in.

'Oh God! How do I switch it off?' I hear her cry.

'Jutht turn it offth at the wall thocket!'

'*Jutht turn it offth at the wall thocket!*'

'Oh thut up!'

'*Oh thut up!*'

'Sorry? What was that?'

'Pull the thucking plug outh!'

'*Pull the thucking plug outh!*'

'The big black one or the small white one?'

'Both! Pull them both outh!'

'*Both! Pull them both outh!*'

There is a vast screech of feedback as Allie finally yanks the plugs from the wall. That is not the best way to treat expensive audio equipment, but I couldn't care less if she set fucking fire to it at the moment.

'Thank you!' I cry plaintively, this time with no high-pitched echo.

'I'll just go wait in the kitchen while you . . . while you finish up,' Allie says, trying to keep the horror out of her voice. 'I really am so sorry about this!'

'It'th okay,' I say, a little disheartened. I think the worst of the diarrhoea is over now, but the damage to my love life is well and truly done.

If having to hear me shit in chipmunk stereo isn't enough to put Allie off, then the fact my face currently looks like a red bell pepper surely will.

Ten minutes later and I'm *very slowly* making my way back into the kitchen. 'I'm really thorry abouth thith,' I tell her.

She shakes her head. 'No, no. It's *me* who should be sorry!' She takes my hand. 'Let's just get you to the hospital now. I'm worried about you.'

'Thank 'oo,' I say with gratitude. This really is a very lovely person. It's a real shame I'll never get to have sex with her now.

Allie helps me out to her car. As I'm climbing into the passenger seat, I feel my bowels rumble. For a moment I'm terrified I'm going to really put the kibosh on things by soiling myself all over her upholstery, but thankfully the unpleasant sensation passes as quickly as it comes. It seems I'm going to be spared any aftershocks for the time being.

The ride to the hospital is uncomfortable, as you might imagine. I may have to ask the doctor for some cooling Preparation H.

When we get there, I'm prepared for a long wait, but given that it's a weekday afternoon and my face still looks like an overinflated balloon sculpture, I am taken in to see a doctor quite swiftly. Allie accompanies me, holding my hand as the good doctor pokes and prods me for a few minutes.

Isn't that *marvellous*? Isn't *Allie* marvellous? She's just been deafened by the sound of me crapping out my own internal organs, and she's *still* happy to hold my hand.

I could almost cry.

'Yes, you're definitely having a reaction to the herbal tea, Mr James,' the doctor says. 'I don't see any obstruction of your airway, which is a very good sign. I think the best thing we can do is give you some strong antihistamine and send you home for some rest. The worst of the symptoms should fade over the next few hours.'

'Thankth, Doctor.'

'Are you currently having any other health problems I should know about?'

Oh Christ.

I didn't know he'd ask that . . .

What the hell do I say?

I should be honest with him. After all, having a brain tumour is no small matter. Any treatments he prescribes could have a knock-on effect. It's one thing to keep a herbalist and your new girlfriend in the dark – it's quite another to do so with a doctor.

But Allie is standing right beside me! I can't say anything! She won't be holding my hand for much longer if I tell her how sick I am right now, will she?!

For a moment, I'm frozen solid, not knowing which way to go with it.

'No. I'm quite fine otherwithe,' I eventually lie.

One of the doctor's eyebrows shoots up Spock-like, picking up on my hesitation. 'Are you sure?'

I can't help but flick a quick glance at Allie.

'Yeth, I'm thure.'

'Positive? No other illnesses, problems or *transmissions* I should know about?'

Oh well, that's subtle, isn't it? I know damn well what he's thinking. He believes I've got some sort of sexually transmitted disease that I'm trying to keep from my girlfriend. It would explain the shifty expression on my face and my hesitation before answering. He's probably been here many times before when treating a cheating spouse with their significant other standing by and watching.

I daren't look at Allie, just in case she's thinking the exact same thing.

'I'm feeling a litthle ligh'-headedth,' I say. I don't feel anything of the sort, but I need to change the subject quickly. 'I think I might jutht lie down for a momenth.'

'Of course, Mr James.'

As I lie back, I do look at Allie's expression – and yep, she looks suspicious. The groan I let out as my head hits the pillow is partially faked and partially genuine. Here I was thinking that explosive diarrhoea was going to put paid to my burgeoning romance, but it might end up just being an innocuous, routine question from a physician that does it for me instead.

A little later, we're back in Allie's car and driving back to my place. She's been very quiet the entire journey.

By the time we pull into my driveway and she applies the hand-brake, the atmosphere is almost palpable.

'Are you okay?' I ask her, noting that my voice is already starting to return to normal. The antihistamine is obviously kicking in.

Her head cocks to one side. 'I'm not sure.'

'Why's that?'

'When the doctor asked you about your health, you didn't seem to be telling him the truth. Is there something you're not telling me, either?'

Well, there it is. Allie is a smart cookie. There was no way she was going to let this one go.

I still can't be honest with her, though. Not even now. It's just too . . . too damn *awful*.

How on earth do you tell someone you're falling in love with them, but that you won't be around long enough to fall all that far?

I elect for the coward's way out of the conversation.

Taking Allie's hand, I look her square in the eyes. 'Look. I really, really like you Allie – and there are things about me I wish I could tell you right now. But . . . I just can't at the moment.'

She sniffs. 'I don't like people keeping secrets from me, Nathan.'

I'm losing her. Totally and completely losing her. Actual tears start to sprout at the corners of my eyes. This is so unfair! 'Please, Alithon,' *Damn it.* 'I'm not keeping secrets from you. There's nothing bad in my patht I should be telling you about. I'm not thecretly married or any-thing.' Is this going to work? Is she going to believe anything I say? 'I don't have any venereal ditheatheth, either,' I add, making sure I get that one cleared up. 'There are things about me that I can't talk about . . . at least not yet. But none of them are bad.'

LIAR.

'Please, can you just let me have a little time? Let us get to know each other better?' I sound quite pathetic.

I can see Allie struggle with it for a few moments, her eyes grave and her lips pursed. 'I guess . . . I guess I can do that.' She bites her lower lip for a second. 'I like you, too, Nathan. I really do. You're kind and funny, and I love being with you.'

'Even when I'm suffering a huge allergic reaction?'

'That wasn't your fault.' She pauses thoughtfully for a moment. 'But I also want to be with someone I can *trust* – who doesn't keep things from me,' she continues. 'The fact there are things you say you can't talk to me about is a little worrying . . .'

'I know! And I'm sorry! But I won't keep them from you for long. I promise I won't!'

Allie nods her head. 'Okay, Nathan. I can give you a little time.' She shakes her head. 'I mean, there are a lot of things you don't know about me, either . . .'

I smile. 'And I hope I get the chance to find out what they are.'

'All right,' she says, slapping a decisive hand down on to her leg. 'Let's get out of this car and get you back inside.' Then her eyes narrow. 'But first, you can give me a kiss. It's the least I deserve after today.' Her face clouds. 'I'm never going to be able to watch *Alvin and the Chipmunks* again.'

I lean forward and plant a big smacker on her lips. Given that my own are still nearly twice the size they normally are, the suction this causes would be enough to give a Dyson a run for its money.

Back in the house, the first thing I do is grab the rest of the bloody teabags and throw them in the waste disposal. Then I make us both a coffee. I'm not drinking tea again for the foreseeable bloody future. I then order Chinese food. We eat it out in the garden as the last of the summer sun bathes us in its warmth. I can tell Allie has relaxed again, as she spends a good ten minutes taking the piss out of how much I spent on my bifold patio doors. Before I knew about the tumour, I might have been a bit offended by this, but not any more.

I think I'm starting to change.

And yes, there is some sex later that evening, thankfully. It is a far more delicate and slow-paced affair than I was hoping for, and we have to stop a couple of times so I can have a scratch, but it's still the best sex I think I've ever had. Nothing I did with Sienna comes close.

I am falling so comprehensively for this girl that it is quite, quite scary.

After it's over and we're lying in the legendary post-coital bliss, my mind returns to the conversation in the car from earlier and me telling Allie that there's nothing wrong with me.

I instantly feel quite awful.

I shouldn't be *doing this*. I shouldn't be leading her up the garden path in this way. It's just *not fair*.

In the morning, I'll tell her the truth.

. . . I honestly will.

. . . without a doubt.

LIAR.

LYRICS TO THE FOODIES SONG 'GIVING IS THE GREATEST'

Chewy the Cheeky Toffee sings:

I love getting presents! I love getting toys!

Frank the Silly Sausage sings:

There's nothing quite like presents, for all girls
and boys!

Pip the Juicy Orange sings:

I love Christmas and birthdays!

Smedley the Smelly Cheese sings:

They always make me smile!

Herman the Grumpy Potato sings:

Getting new toys is the best thing by a mile!

Libby the Happy Lemon sings:

Hang on, guys! That's not right! You can't think
that way!
Getting toys is very nice, but there's one thing I
must say,
Receiving gifts feels very good, but there's one
thing even more fun,
Giving presents to those you love, and giving to
anyone,
You'll make them smile, you'll make them laugh,
they'll really feel their worth,
And the way that'll make you feel is the best
thing on the earth!

All of The Foodies sing:

Giving is the greatest! Giving is the greatest!
Have you heard the news? Have you heard the
latest?
Giving is the greatest! Giving is the greatest!
It's the best thing in the world, we really can't
overstate this!

FOR THE LOVE OF DONKEYS

28 July

Now that, my friends, is a bloody great big pile of cash – metaphorically speaking.

I sit on my couch with the remittance advice from Brightside Productions open in front of me, my eyes wide. I knew this money would be coming along, but I didn't quite compute just how much cash it would be, when everything was taken into account from the handover.

Seventy-three thousand pounds of fine British money.

. . . and this is only the first instalment.

I stare at the remittance for a few moments, trying to decide what my feelings are about it.

In another life, on a parallel world, I would be a-whooping and a-hollering with joy right now. Just think of all the lovely things I could buy with all this disposable income. A new sports car! A yacht! Four Rolex watches! Several round-the-world cruises! A boob job for Sienna!

But back here in *this* world, I am not a-whopping and a-hollering. In fact, I can barely register a smile.

Because it's all just so damn *inconsequential*, isn't it? When you don't have much time to spare, what does it matter how much money you have? Material possessions become entirely irrelevant when your life hangs resolutely in the balance.

This new-found perspective has forced me to think long and hard about myself and the relationship I've had with money and success.

It forces me into the clear and undeniable conclusion that I have largely *wasted* my life up until this point.

And I have been a very, very wasteful person.

I live alone in a huge new modern house that I tend to rattle around in most of the time.

I have no one who relies on me financially – Mum is independently well off from her statue making and I can't persuade Eliza to take any cash for her or Callum, so I only have myself to worry about.

Until recently, I drove a rather stupid car that cost more than most people earn in five years. My bifold patio doors were hideously pricey, because I just had to have the brushed gunmetal-grey aluminium, and most of my furniture is bespoke – which is to say it was all ridiculously overpriced. I spend money every month on an expensive gardener to come over and prune my Japanese maple tree, when I could probably get out there and do it myself.

The amount of cash I paid out to keep Sienna happy before we split doesn't even bear thinking about. That silly red Prada dress was four figures, for starters.

I have been blessed by good fortune thanks to The Foodies – and have largely wasted that fortune on inconsequential rubbish.

Somewhere in my vast open-plan kitchen, there is a three-hundred-pound juicing machine in a cupboard that I used once to make a smoothie that resembled brown sludge and tasted like I'd already drunk it once. It has languished in that cupboard ever since.

The showerhead in my en-suite cost four hundred pounds. Why? I have no idea.

I have a pair of ripped jeans in my wardrobe that look like they should have been thrown out decades ago, but I paid two hundred pounds for them *this year*.

My bed sheets are imported Egyptian cotton that cost a grand.

Yes, a fucking *grand*.

Don't you just hate me right now?

. . . welcome to the club.

I could go on with this litany of wastefulness for hours if I wanted to. Looking back on the past five years since The Foodies royalty cheques started coming in, I've burned my way through tens if not hundreds of thousands of pounds – not saving one bloody penny of it for a rainy day, I might add. All that money bought stuff I neither need nor even want that much. Such is the attitude of one with a healthy and constant influx of money and all the time in the world to spend it.

What a total waste.

I crumple the remittance advice into my curled fist and thump the arm of the couch. What the hell have I been doing all this time? What the hell kind of person have I been? And more importantly, what the hell do I do to make up for it?

I sit there for a moment, letting my mind drift through a sea of self-loathing and frustration, close to drowning in both.

But then, in the distance, I metaphorically spot an island . . .

I think back to both my anger management session with Cleethorpes and my cannabis-infused revelation at the Light Havens – about how I've felt like I've lost all purpose in my life and need to find something to fill it back up again. My new relationship with Allie has kept me quite busy, but it's not solved that central problem, has it?

Maybe now, though, I've found something that can.

I uncrumple the remittance advice again and give it a good, hard look.

If I want to leave any kind of mark on the world – if I want to be remembered for doing something *worthwhile* – then maybe the key to that is in my hands *right now*. Instead of wasting all my cash on frivolous junk, why don't I find someone who actually needs it and give it to them?

. . . but how to do this?

How does Nathan James start giving back a little?

As I sit in my lounge on my three-thousand-pound white leather couch (which is extremely uncomfortable, if I'm being honest about it), a plan starts to form in my mind.

First, I will give a sizeable amount of money away to charity.

That will be a good start, but doesn't really feel like it'll be *enough*. It doesn't take much effort these days to fill in an online form on the WWF website and give your credit card details.

No, I must do something a little more proactive to prove my worth. I need something to get me out of bed in the morning with a sense of bloody *purpose*. I have to get off my arse and actually get *involved* with a project that'll benefit from my soft-earned cash.

This leads to a constructive twenty minutes on Google researching local good causes. Thankfully (but perhaps unsurprisingly in this day and age) there's a website for that.

GivingLocal.com is a veritable treasure trove of advertisements from various people and organisations looking for a little financial aid from those able to offer it.

Not that I'd describe *all* of the adverts I read as *good causes*, necessarily. I'm fairly sure that Barry needing a new engine for his 1973 Ford Capri does not qualify, for instance. Neither does Helena and her dog turd company. Helena wants money to assist her in her new venture, which involves the recycling of dog excrement. In a lengthy and slightly rambling advert, she describes how she's invented a new technology for turning dog shit into glue. She assures the reader that it would revolutionise the world and that people would be clamouring for her 'Pooperglue' in no time at all. This strikes me as being an unlikely proposition, for several reasons. I very much doubt that anyone will be clamouring to get anywhere near her if she spends all her time accumulating dog shit. Also, I'm no canine expert, but I'm fairly sure that their waste material does not contain any intrinsically glue-like properties. And lastly – and this is the most important issue as far as I'm concerned – Helena is quite clearly as mad as a box of frogs on methamphetamine.

Thankfully, though, the majority of the adverts are more sane and reasonable. In fact, there are so many that I end up feeling comprehensively *guilty* that I don't have even more money to spread around.

Being an inveterate animal lover, I find one appeal really stands out from the rest.

A rural donkey sanctuary about fifteen miles away from my house is in desperate need of money to help maintain it.

In an extremely heartfelt and personal appeal, the lady who runs it – the remarkably named Winnifred Sperlingford – details how the sanctuary has become more and more difficult to run following the death of her husband nine years ago. This immediately creates a painful parallel in my mind with my own mother, who lost my father at exactly the same time.

Both the house Winnifred lives in and the buildings in the grounds of the sanctuary are becoming extremely dilapidated. Unless something can be done about them soon, the sanctuary will be closed down. And then what will happen to all of those donkeys, eh?

Nothing good, that's what.

There are almost tears in my eyes as I finish reading the online appeal. How could I possibly ignore this one?

I manage to get ahold of myself by the time I call Winnifred Sperlingford some five minutes later to arrange a time to visit.

She sounds both amazed and delighted that someone has finally taken an interest. She's not had one single person go and see her in the three months since she placed the appeal.

I intend to change that by visiting the donkey sanctuary that very afternoon!

Winnifred sounds delighted by this. I put the phone down on a very happy donkey sanctuary owner.

As I call for a taxi and pour myself a cup of tea, I feel a new-found sense of purpose – a feeling of personal fulfilment and drive that I've been missing for *so bloody long*.

This is *it*. This is the thing I need. This is my new path in life. This is the thing that keeps Nathan James in the game, for as long as he has left!

The cabbie drops me off at the end of a long driveway leading away from the road. A rather battered sign nailed to the gatepost tells me that this place is called 'Winnifred Sperlingford's Sanctuary for Donkeys in Need of Homing' – which is about as grand a title for a donkey sanctuary as you can come up with, short of sticking the words 'royal' and 'by appointment' in there somewhere.

Winnifred Sperlingford may be wanting for money since her husband's death, but she sure as hell isn't wanting for *space*. As I walk up the driveway, I can see that on either side of me are large fenced-in and rather unkempt fields, which terminate far in the distance at several patches of woodland surrounding the whole estate. I can't help thinking that if she sold off some of this land, she wouldn't need any assistance from the likes of me, but then I spot a few reasons why she probably hasn't done this. Standing in a variety of random positions around the fields is a selection of donkeys, most of whom look relatively happy to be there.

All of them certainly look quite elderly, that's for sure. I pass one close on the left-hand side who peers at me from between the fence posts as if studying some strange new life form. Its muzzle is almost completely grey, as is most of its head. If this donkey were a human being, it would almost certainly be Phillip Schofield.

Phillip Schofield Donkey continues to watch as I walk up to the house. It only loses sight of me as I finally crest the deceptively steep driveway and emerge on to a large, open area of gravel that leads to what was once an impressive old manor house of considerable size.

Parked to one side of the sizeable double front doors is a battered old green Land Rover. In the rear windscreen is a sticker that reads 'Love a Donkey & Love Yourself!' I'm not entirely sure how I should take that, to be honest with you. It conjures up images in my warped little brain that are quite disturbing.

Close to the building, I can see how much of it has gone to the dogs over the years. I can only imagine how much money it must cost to keep this kind of house in a good state of repair. It's certainly more than Winnifred has been able to afford recently, of that there is no doubt. Everywhere I look there are signs of decay. The mortar is crumbling from the walls. The ancient drainpipes are rusting into oblivion. The paint is chipped and peeling. It really is a bit of a sorry sight.

Still, I'm here to see donkeys, not make comments on the upkeep of a property, so I briskly walk over to the impressive front doors and give the bell pull a tug.

A sonorous chime rings out from the interior of the house. I have to wait a few moments before the door is opened by a tall, frail and painfully thin old woman with a mane of long grey hair. She is of course wearing wellington boots and an ancient brown Burberry jacket, because it's the law in places like this.

'Hello there, are you Nathan?' she says with a smile.

'Yes. And you must be Winnifred,' I reply, extending a hand.

She takes my hand in a papery, thin one of her own and gives it a surprisingly strong shake. 'Do come through, won't you?' she says. 'I'm just about to feed the herd and would appreciate a little help, if that's okay?'

'Of course – please lead the way,' I reply with an ingratiating smile.

Given that this woman looks like she could snap like a twig at any moment, I'm expecting a slow and unsteady amble through the confines of the house, but Winnifred instead takes off at a rate of knots I am scarcely able to believe. In fact, I have to hurry just to keep up with her.

Internally, the house has suffered from much of the same neglect as its exterior, save for one area off to the left-hand side comprising a neat and tidy kitchen attached to a sprawling reception room. Both are well maintained and look quite comfortable. This must be the area of the house poor Winnifred lives in on a day-to-day basis.

Speaking of whom, my host has now reached the back door, which she quickly unlocks and goes through, turning back briefly to see what's keeping me. 'Are you all right?' she asks, apparently wondering how I've managed to fall behind.

'Yes, fine, thanks,' I reply, just a little bit out of breath. I join her at the back door as she turns around again and strides off towards a large barn situated about forty feet away.

Outside, I can see the extent of the house's land laid out in its entirety. It really is a huge plot, consisting of more fields, more trees and, of course, more donkeys. There must be a good forty or fifty of the buggers milling about.

The large majority of them are now making a beeline towards the barn, having seen Winnifred appear from the back door of the house. None give me a second look, having rightly dismissed me as a pointless interloper into their Winnifred-led existence.

I follow the old woman over to the barn and join her inside. The smell of old hay and donkey parts is rather overpowering. Looking up, I can see that the barn's roof has quite a few holes in it and the timbers are looking decidedly rotten in several places.

The donkeys have congregated at a long gate separating the barn's back entrance from the fields beyond. All are looking as keen as mustard for their feed.

'Could you help me lay out some hay for them, Nathan?' Winnifred asks me. 'It's stored at the back.'

'Of course,' I say, trying very hard not to hold my nose as we walk towards an area of the barn brimming with hay. The donkeys watch me from behind the gate. It's quite disconcerting to have so many sets of large equine eyes staring at me in such a way. I know donkeys are herbivores, but the hungry gazes fixed on me at the moment could convince me otherwise.

I feel as if I should learn more about the setup here, given that I might well be contributing money to it at some point, so as Winnifred starts to tug a bale of hay back through the barn and towards the donkeys, I ask her what I presume is a suitable question. 'How long have you been running the place?'

'Thirty-six years,' Winnifred replies, dumping the bale of hay just outside the barn.

Blimey. That's a lot of donkeys.

'It must be very time-consuming,' I suggest as I place my own hay bale alongside hers. This is met with some approving snorts and whinnies from the gathered throng just beyond the gate. 'And expensive,' I add, giving the donkeys a sideways look.

Winnifred gives me a small smile. 'Yes. It's my life's work, really. They're such lovely creatures.' She gives them a much fonder look than I did, before returning for another hay bale.

We spend the next few minutes lining up more bales, before Winnifred makes her way over to the gate. 'You may want to stand back a little,' she tells me as she unlatches it. 'Come on, you lot! In you come!' Winnifred exclaims, opening the gate and walking it backwards to allow her charges entry.

I do indeed step back, very briskly, as a multitude of hungry donkeys trot gamely into the barn, going straight to the hay bales with considerable gusto. It's quite the scene to behold. A bunch of hee-hawing, farting half horses with their muzzles buried in a pile of hay is not something you see – or smell – every day.

I'm starting to feel a little nauseous, so I make my way towards where Winnifred is standing, giving the feeding donkeys as wide a berth as possible.

I join her at the open gate. 'They certainly seem to know their routine,' I remark.

'Yes. Very intelligent animals, donkeys,' she replies.

'Where do you find them all?'

'Various places. Some come to me from farms that can't look after them any more. Others come from seaside attractions or petting zoos. Most have been either neglected or mistreated in one way or another.' Winnifred points at one particularly large donkey to the left-hand side of the crowd. On its back I can see long, jagged lines. 'Take Henry over there. He was beaten by his owners for years. The RSPCA rescued him from a camp of travellers and brought him here about six months ago.' She then nods towards a smaller, grey donkey with ragged ears standing next to Henry. 'People used to put their cigarettes out on poor Beatrice's ears to get her to do what they wanted. She was nearly starved to death before she got here.'

Well, that's horrible, isn't it? Up until this moment I just looked at the donkeys as one smelly, hairy mass. I'd not even considered that they'd have individual stories to tell. But now that Winnifred has pointed out poor old Henry and Beatrice, I can only imagine what the rest of them might have been through. I'm sure they all have similar tales of donkey woe.

How depressing.

This isn't just a place for old donkeys to hang out. It's a place for them to be *safe*.

'Oh no!' Winnifred exclaims, startling me out of my thoughts.

'What's the matter?'

The old woman is staring out into the field at a large bush about twenty yards away. 'He's at it again.'

I look over to where she is indicating, but all I can see is the bush. 'Pardon me?'

'Every day this happens. He's such a little bugger, he is. Always wants to do things differently. Always stubborn!'

Hmmm.

Up until now, I'd thought Winnifred was fully in control of her faculties, but it appears that she may be a bit mental. I don't quite know how to otherwise explain her attitude towards the bush she's staring at intently.

To me it looks like quite an ordinary bush. Quite large, but otherwise indistinguishable from all the others dotted around the place. It certainly doesn't look *stubborn*. Unless she's on about the roots. They can be quite stubborn sometimes. That holly bush I had to dig out of Mum's garden last summer was a right bastard to get out of the ground, and I only—

Wait a second. There's something *behind* the bush!

Winnifred isn't bonkers after all.

'Is there . . . is there a donkey behind that bush?' I remark, peering over.

'Yes, there is. And he's playing silly buggers.' Winnifred looks at me. 'Would you mind coming over and helping me with him? He can be a little bit of a handful.'

Gulp.

That sounds ominous.

Winnifred starts to move across the field towards the bush. As I follow her with some trepidation, I start to conjure pictures in my head of an evil-looking large black donkey with boiling red eyes and fangs.

This is ridiculous, but I'm prone to an overactive imagination at the best of times and am currently quite far out of my comfort zone. My knowledge of donkeys is extremely limited, so I have no idea what kind of snorting, stamping horror I am about to encounter.

'They brought him to me when he was still a foal,' Winnifred says as she slowly approaches the bush. 'Even then he was hard to handle.'

Oh *God*. This is starting to sound like a donkey version of *The Omen*.

Through the bush I can see movement. I grind to a halt, not wanting to get any closer. Winnifred, however, moves around to the side of the bush and puts her hands on her hips, regarding the concealed donkey with a look of exasperation. 'Now, what do you think you're doing, young man?' she says to the donkey. 'It's feeding time. You need to come and eat.'

There is no response from the donkey. Winnifred moves forward and holds out a hand. 'Now, come on. Stop being such a silly billy,' she says in a commanding voice.

Then she moves back out from behind the bush. She is accompanied by a tiny orange donkey.

Yes, I said *orange* and I meant it.

The tumour has not started replacing the word 'brown' with the word 'orange'. This is indeed an *orange* donkey.

'That's . . . that's an orange donkey,' I remark, rather unnecessarily.

Winnifred chuckles. 'Yes. He's got a rather unique hair pigmentation, hasn't he?'

The orange donkey gives me a look. It's slightly cross-eyed.

I'm looking at an orange, cross-eyed donkey.

. . . at least I *think* I am. If the tumour can give me epically realistic nightmares, can it also conjure up strange and bizarre daytime hallucinations of the brightly coloured equine variety?

'I'm sorry,' I say to Winnifred. 'I have a bit of a problem with my brain, so I'm not sure whether I'm actually looking at a very small, cross-eyed orange donkey or not. Can you clear that up for me, please?'

Winnifred laughs again. 'You are, Nathan. This here is Pipsqueak. Pipsqueak the Donkey.' She pats the donkey on the head. 'Say hello to Nathan, Pipsqueak.'

Pipsqueak looks up at me with an expression of such instant love and adoration that I'm slightly taken aback.

'*Heee-horrrgghhh,*' Pipsqueak says loudly by way of greeting.

'Pleased to meet you, Pipsqueak,' I respond, moving forward to give the tiny orange donkey a pat. He responds by moving towards me and nuzzling my hand affectionately.

Winnifred looks delighted. 'I think he likes you!'

I smile back. 'I think you're right!'

'I'm very surprised. Pipsqueak is a contrary little bugger at the best of times,' Winnifred explains. 'He once bit the postman.'

Pipsqueak shows no signs of biting me, I'm pleased to say.

He is pushing into me rather a lot, though. I'm forced to take a step back, such is the small donkey's insistence on getting even closer. He really is being *very* affectionate.

'You're very lucky, Nathan!' Winnifred remarks with happiness. 'The reason why I got Pipsqueak in the first place was because the farmer who owned him couldn't put up with his mood swings.'

'Mood swings?' I reply, giving Pipsqueak another pat. 'Do donkeys have *mood swings?*'

'This one appears to, right from when he was born. He's full of character, but can be happy as a clam one minute and mad as hell the next.'

I look down at Pipsqueak, who has an expression of ecstasy on his little, cross-eyed donkey face, given that I am now tickling him behind one flapping ear. 'Winnifred, are you trying to tell me that this donkey has *borderline personality disorder?*'

I knew someone at university who suffered from that very thing. Lovely girl, she was, when you caught her on the upswing. Not so much on the downturn, though. She once stabbed her boyfriend with a cotton bud. You wouldn't think something as inoffensive as a cotton bud would cause much damage. You'd be wrong.

Winnifred looks a bit confused. 'Well, I'm not sure I know what that means, but he's a character, and no mistake.'

I find it hard to believe that this little thing has the mental capacity to suffer from such a serious complaint.

I mean, just look at that face of contentment, will you? If I handed over an apple or a small tangerine right now, Pipsqueak might reach a level of donkey bliss hitherto unseen in the species.

'I think I have an apple in my pocket somewhere . . .' Winnifred says, and goes rummaging around in her jacket.

I give Pipsqueak a smile. 'Oh boy. Your day is about to go into the top five, Pippers.'

Pipsqueak nuzzles my hand again. He knows what's coming. You can tell.

'Oh, I don't seem to have an apple,' Winnifred says. 'I've only got this old pear.'

'I'm sure that'll do,' I answer, plucking it out of her hand. It's a donkey after all. I'm sure an apple or a pear is much the same thing.

With a shit-eating grin on my face, I proffer the pear to Pipsqueak, who sniffs it before taking a large bite.

'There you go,' I say to the little donkey, feeling that we've bonded so well that there's every chance he'll want to come home with me.

I'm picturing the tiny orange donkey cavorting happily around my back garden when Pipsqueak emits a low and rumbling snort.

His ears have flattened. His eyes have gone what I can only describe as 'flinty'.

'Oh dear,' I remark. 'I don't think he likes pears.'

Winnifred then does something that marks a severe turn for the worse in my day.

She steps *backwards*.

'Ah . . . I think maybe it'd be a good idea just to leave him alone now,' she comments in a wavering voice.

I slowly turn my head from her, back down to my cross-eyed little friend – whose eyes are now *no longer crossed.*

I blink a couple of times in disbelief. Instead of having a good-natured and slightly befuddled expression, Pipsqueak now looks like the donkey equivalent of Gordon Ramsay after eating a turd sandwich. He looks pissed as all hell.

'Oh dear,' I say in a small voice. 'This probably isn't going to end well, is it?'

I, too, take a step away from the donkey, hands coming up in front of my face defensively. 'Now, Pipsqueak, please don't be angry. I didn't know you don't like pears,' I say, in an attempt to mollify him.

Pipsqueak takes a step forward. The ears have gone even flatter. The eyes are now gimlets of pure hate. I can see the thick hair on the back of his neck standing on end.

My bottom starts to pipsqueak.

'Perhaps we can get you a nice apple?' I suggest, moving back a little faster. 'Or a small tangerine?'

These words fall on deaf, flat donkey ears.

Pipsqueak moves ever closer.

'Please don't hurt me, Pipsqueak,' I plead. 'I have a tumour.'

Okay, bringing in the disease is a low thing to do, but I don't know how else to appeal to the donkey's better nature at this point. Perhaps knowledge of my sickness will bring out a little donkey compassion in the irate little orange horror?

Nope.

He's colder than Norway.

Pipsqueak then lets out a noise that I can only describe as *'Herrrrgggggguumorrrrggggg'*. It's less a donkey-like *hee-haw* and more a sound heralding the arrival of the elder gods and the oncoming apocalypse.

'Haaargggmmuurggghhhhooorrrrggghhhh.'

Oh my . . . I fear dread Cthulhu and his minions are about to crack through the earth's crust to consume me.

'Erm . . . Nathan?' Winnifred says.

'Yes, Winnifred?'

'You might want to run away now.'

'Pardon?'

'*Run* . . . run away.'

'From a tiny orange donkey?'

She nods her head violently. 'Yes. That might be an *extremely* good idea.'

'Okay, well, you're the expert here, I suppose,' I reply, turning on my heels and fixing my eyes on the safety and security of the barn. If I can get back and shut the gate, then maybe I can—

Aaaarggh!

The little fucker's just bitten me on the arse! Instant, bright pain radiates up from my left buttock.

And with that, I'm off. I may not be the sharpest tool in the shed, but even I know that when a farmyard animal has started taking chunks out of your behind, it's best to get the fuck out of Dodge as fast as possible.

I start to sprint away from Pipsqueak as fast as my legs will carry me.

Looking back, I can see that the donkey is chasing after me at a speed that is uncomfortably fast. Even more uncomfortable is the fact that Winnifred is nearly alongside him and both are catching me up at a rate of knots.

I'm not sure how I'm ever going to recover from the humiliation of not being able to outrun a manic depressive, tiny orange donkey and Mary Berry's less well-off sister.

I'm going to blame it on the shoes I'm wearing. These Adidas trainers really aren't the right kind of footwear for a tactical retreat from an angry donkey across a lush summer-green field. They simply don't have the grip.

'Pipsqueak! You stop chasing poor Nathan!' Winnifred yells. 'He's come here to help us!'

Pipsqueak unfortunately cares nothing for my potential beneficence. I am the human who dared to feed him a disgusting pear, and payback must therefore be sought upon my person.

I look back again as we close in on the barn to see that even poor Winnifred is now unable to keep up the chase. She slows to a halt and holds her chest, breathing heavily.

Excellent. The old girl is going to have a fatal heart attack now, thus leaving me at the mercy of Pipsqueak and his donkey brethren.

I double my pace as I desperately try to reach the safety and security of the barn. If I can just get the gate shut again before Pipsqueak reaches me, I'll be okay!

Now, let's pause for a second to consider physics. Or, more exactly – and most pertinently to my current situation – the physics of *friction*.

Friction, as we all know, is the force acting on an object as a result of its interaction with another object.

In this case, the first object is my Adidas trainer and the second object is the grass below my feet. Bring the sole of an Adidas trainer together with a patch of fresh, slippery grass and only one result will be forthcoming. You don't need to be Professor Brian Cox to work out what it is.

My left leg goes out from under me as I run past the open gate.

I don't immediately fall to the ground, though. Instead, my momentum carries me another good ten feet towards the rest of the feeding donkeys in a tangle of arms and legs. Eventually, gravity asserts its supreme authority and I crash to the ground, sliding across the grass like I'm stealing first base.

'Fuck about!' I wail as I go over, instantly regretting my choice to wear the six-hundred-pound leather jacket I bought in London last Christmas. Getting these grass stains out is going to be a dry-cleaning nightmare.

These are concerns that will have to wait, however, as I have a far more important problem that I'm going to have to deal with in the next few seconds – namely, an enraged orange donkey catching up to my prone form with the intent to do evil things to it.

I scramble to my feet, hoping against hope that I still have time to get away.

Hope deserts me.

Pipsqueak jumps on my back.

Yes, I know Pipsqueak is a *donkey* and not a *monkey*.

I'm well aware that a donkey – especially a tiny orange one – shouldn't have the ability to jump on the back of a fully grown human being, but that is nevertheless what Pipsqueak has just done, so we're all just going to have to accept it and move on. There will be time for detailed analysis of how Pipsqueak has managed to overcome the deficiencies of donkey anatomy to accomplish this feat at a later date, but for now, I have a donkey on my back and must do something about it as fast as possible.

What I choose to do is scream.

'*Aaaaaarrggghh!* No! No! Pipsqueak! Please don't eat me!'

Any second now, I expect to feel donkey teeth close around the back of my neck as Pipsqueak tears my head off.

Instead, I feel something *prodding* me in the back. This, as I'm about to discover, is *oh so much worse* than having my head ripped off.

I'm not being savaged, but there is every chance I'm about to be sexually assaulted.

Pipsqueak's mood has quite obviously changed in a split second from murderous intent to something decidedly more *amorous*.

I'm being molested by a hairy orange creature with a personality disorder. Now I know what it feels like to be a woman locked in a room with Donald Trump.

Why is there never a beanbag around when you need one?

'No, Pipsqueak! Stop doing that!' I wail, fearing it will have no appreciable effect. Pipsqueak may be a tiny donkey, but he's also quite heavy, so I am forced back on to the ground, where the donkey is ready, willing and able to have its wicked way with me.

Maybe it's the leather coat.

I should have bought a fake one for forty pounds from H&M and had done with it.

And if the grass stains are going to be hard to get out, I can only imagine how bad it will be to remove the stains potentially left by my new donkey 'friend'.

I can now hear Pipsqueak grunting in my ear.

This is quite comprehensively awful by every measure possible.

If Herman the Grumpy Tumour has any kind of pity in his cold, brain-hugging soul, he will kill me right here and now before Pipsqueak has a chance to build up any kind of *rhythm*.

'Please, Pipsqueak! There's hay over there. Why don't you go eat some hay?'

My pitiful cries for mercy continue to fall on deaf ears. My fate here is sealed. I am the plaything of a tiny orange donkey. It's probably best I just accept my new lot in life as quickly as possible.

'Get off him, Pipsqueak!' I hear Winnifred angrily shout.

I crane my head around past Pipsqueak's vibrating muzzle to see that the old lady has not in fact died of a heart attack, but has instead caught us up and is intending to put a stop to this awful scene as swiftly as she possibly can. This seems to involve hitting the horny donkey across the back with a long stick she's found somewhere.

I'm not normally one for advocating violence against animals of any kind, but I'm willing to put my morals aside in this instance, given that my shirt has now been pulled out of my waistband and I can feel donkey penis against my skin.

'Get it off!' I scream with renewed vigour. 'It's so wet . . . and I can feel it *pulsing*!'

Winnifred belts Pipsqueak a couple of times with the stick.

Thankfully . . . gloriously . . . *mercifully*, this seems to do the trick. Pipsqueak jumps off my back with a loud and angry snort.

I continue to thrash around for a second before realising that my ordeal is over. 'Oh God,' I moan into the grass. 'Oh dear, sweet God in heaven.'

'Are you okay, Nathan?' Winnifred asks me, bending down.

'Yes,' I lie. 'As long as I'm not pregnant, I'm sure I'll be fine.'

I rise unsteadily to my feet, keeping a watchful eye on Pipsqueak as I do. It appears that now he has had his way with me, the donkey has completely lost interest. He joins his friends at the hay bales for a feed.

Charming.

Find 'em, fuck 'em and *feed*, it seems.

'I'm so, so sorry about this,' Winnifred says, trying to brush the grass away from my now ruined leather jacket. 'They really are lovely animals for the most part. Pipsqueak isn't like the rest of them at all.'

'Really? Do the others take you out for a nice meal first?'

'Pardon me?'

I shake my head. 'Never mind.' I give Pipsqueak another uneasy look. 'Would you mind if we went back to the house so I can clean up a bit?'

'Of course! Of course! The donkeys will be fine for the minute.'

I'm sure they will. I don't know what passes for good donkey conversation in these parts, but I'm confident the sexual subjugation of an innocent human being will be right up there.

'I'll show you where the bathroom is,' Winnifred finishes, holding one hand out towards the house.

Luckily, the route back won't take us too close to the feeding donkeys. I don't want to take any chances that Pipsqueak might want to engage in a second booty call upon my person, or that his mates might get any ideas and try to join in.

About ten minutes later, I'm sat with a cup of hot, sweet tea in Winnifred's front room. The jacket is going in the bin, but the rest of my clothes are salvageable. Whether my pride is or not is another thing, though.

Winnifred sits down on the couch beside me rather tentatively. Her expression is one of combined concern and deep regret. 'I am sorry about Pipsqueak, Nathan. I had hoped that you'd see the donkeys in their best light, and that you'd be willing to . . . well, you know . . .'

Winnifred leaves the sentence hanging, but I know what she's hinting at.

She probably feels that any desire I had to give her some cash to help with the upkeep of the sanctuary has well and truly disappeared, given that one of her little bastards has assaulted me in broad daylight – but, in actual fact, I think I'm mature enough to see past that and acknowledge that what she's doing here is a very worthwhile thing.

'I'm happy to help, Winnifred, I really am,' I tell her, thinking back to the large and painful-looking marks across Henry's back. 'What you're doing here is fantastic, and I want to make sure you can carry on doing it. How much do you think you might need?'

Winnifred looks down a little shyly. 'I'd need about twenty thousand pounds, I'm afraid. That would give me enough to spruce the place up, reroof the barn and pay for more feed during the winter. And I'd like to open the sanctuary to the public to make a little money, too, but I need money up front to do that.'

I place a hand over hers. 'Done. I will write you a cheque as soon as I get home.'

This essentially means that I'm just about to give an old lady twenty grand for the privilege of getting nearly rogered by an insane orange donkey.

My life is complete.

Winnifred looks at me in delighted shock. 'Thank you, Nathan! Oh, thank you so much!'

I return the smile. 'It's my absolute pleasure.'

And it really, really *is*.

I feel a warm glow in my heart and an absolute sense of *rightness* about what I've done here today. This was definitely a worthwhile thing to do. Even with the donkey sex.

Back out at the front of the grand old house, I wave goodbye to a rather tearful Winnifred and walk back down the bumpy track towards the main road, where a taxi is waiting for me.

As I do, I see that the donkeys have finished eating and have gone back to milling around the place with not a care in the world.

I reach the main entrance and see Pipsqueak standing just off to one side behind the fence, looking at me as I pass.

Yeah, go on, beautiful, his eyes seem to be saying. *You go get that cash and come back. And next time . . . wear something pretty and see-through for me.*

I'd like to say I didn't start running at this point, but I'd be lying through my teeth.

I have seen and experienced things today that I shall never forget for as short as I live.

Nevertheless, I'm going to try my bloody *hardest* to forget – largely through the consumption of strong alcohol and by way of several expensive therapy sessions, all of which will hopefully combat my newly developed and intense fear of donkeys.

And pears.

And large bushes.

. . . but mostly donkeys.

INSIDE OW

27 AUGUST

'Oh, go on. Please.'

   'No.'

   'Please.'

   'I said no.'

   'Pleeeeeeeeeeease.'

   'Eliza . . . no. I'm not doing it.'

   'But the children will love it.'

   'I'm sure they will, but I don't do children's parties.'

   'Why not?'

   'Because the place will be filled with *children*.'

   'Ugh! You're being unreasonable.'

   'And you've taken leave of your senses.'

   'You should do it for me, Nate. I'm your *cousin*. I'm family.'

   'Oh, that's cold, Elsie.'

   'Callum would love it. You know how much he loves The Foodies. I'm sure it'd make him very happy to have you play at his birthday.'

   'You think?'

'*Yes*, Nate! He'd love you to play a few songs, I'm sure. And they've told me the party will be good for his socialisation with other children, so I could do with your help.'

'Eh, I don't know, Eliza, I'm really not sure—'

'You owe me.'

'What the hell do I owe you for?'

'That time you forgot your mum's birthday because you were stoned in Amsterdam and I bought all those presents for her!'

'That was *twelve* years ago!'

'Yes. And now I'm calling in the favour, Nathan.'

'*Damn it.*'

So, I'm doing a children's party.

Callum's sixth birthday party, to be exact. It promises to be a heaving mass of small, intensely annoying children full of party food and fizzy drink.

It will now also be featuring the vocal and musical stylings of Nathan James – because I was stupid enough to get off my tits on the Continent when I was a young man and forgot to buy my mother a birthday present.

Also – and it pains me to admit this – I could probably do more to help my cousin with Callum, rather than just trying to throw cash at her. This party will give me the chance to redress the balance a little, even if it's something I could personally do without, given that the timing could honestly be better.

The headaches are getting worse – *much* worse, if I'm being truthful about it. At the same time, the nightmares have faded away, but in all honesty I'd much rather have sleepless nights than thumping headaches nearly every day. I'm going through co-codamol like they're going out of fashion. This means I'm constipated half the time and am therefore also suffering from haemorrhoids.

Oh, happy day.

Visits to Mr Chakraborty haven't helped at all. He just ended up prescribing me *even more* powerful painkillers – which I probably could have got from my regular GP anyway.

Given that my tumour isn't the kind that will respond to treatment, I get the distinct impression that the surgeon is doing no more than paying me lip service by giving me the occasional scrip for hard drugs. He makes an effort in the conversations we have and certainly isn't shy about sticking me through the MRI machine to check the tumour's progress, but other than that, I think he's highly embarrassed to have me anywhere near him – as if my untreatableness is somehow an affront to both his profession and his personal skill.

I'm clutching the latest MRI results in one hand as I have the conversation with Eliza about the bloody children's party.

They show that the tumour has increased in size slightly over the past few weeks, which probably explains the increased headaches. Chakraborty expressed surprise that my speech centre hasn't been more affected by the continued growth. I couldn't quite tell whether it was happy surprise at the apparent slower pace of my deterioration or irritation that his diagnosis hasn't been as accurate as he would have liked. It's been over four months since he told me about the tumour taking up residence in the darkest recesses of my brain and I'm sure he thinks that I should have shuffled off to join the choir invisible by now.

Fortunately, the headaches tend to come and go within a period of a few hours, so they're not crippling me all of the time, but for that period, I just want the world to *end*.

I'm able to keep my health problems a secret from Allie for the time being. I've only been struck down with a tumour migraine once when I've been with her. I put that one down to staring at my iPad for too long in the dark the night before. A lame excuse, but it appeared to do the trick. Each and every time I have to lie to her, I feel a little bit worse inside, but I'm still completely unable to be truthful, knowing that it'll kill our relationship off if I am. I'm a selfish, stupid man, but I'm also a man who is quite clearly *in love*, and men in love do very stupid things sometimes.

I crumple the MRI results in one hand and return my attention to the information about the party that Eliza is trying to impart to me.

'. . . and we've probably got a clown coming as well. I'm not so sure about it, but Bryan thinks it'll be fun for Callum. The catering's being done by that company I told you about last year. And your mum said she'd come along to help me set everything up, before she goes off to her hair appointment, which I'm very grateful for.'

'Great,' I reply with a smile.

'We're hoping that the weather's going to be good enough to not have to use the gazebo,' Eliza continues, 'but we'll put it up anyway, just in case. You should be able to set your stuff up under it if you need to, Nate.'

'Mnmnm.'

'Nate? Are you listening to a thing I'm saying?'

'What? Yes, of course I am. I've just got a bit of a headache.'

'Oh. I see.' Eliza doesn't mean for her voice to suddenly be filled with cold fear, but it is anyway.

'It's okay, Elsie,' I reply. 'It's not too bad at all.'

'Okay, good. Has it been bad recently, though?'

My hand tightens on the phone a little. 'Oh . . . could be better, could be worse. Having Allie around has been good for me. She definitely takes my mind off it.'

'Have you told her yet?' The chilliness in Eliza's voice is still there, but for very different reasons now.

I roll my eyes. 'No. Not yet. And *please* don't have another go at me about it. You know why I haven't said anything yet, and you know I'll tell her sooner or later.'

'You'd *better*. It's not fair on her, Nate. She deserves to know.'

'And she will, I promise. Very, very soon. Just let me do it at the right time and in the right place.'

'Okay. Well, I'm going to invite her along to the party as well. God knows I'll need someone to drink wine in the kitchen with when it all gets too much for me, and she's so bloody good with Callum it makes me feel like an inadequate mother.'

I chuckle at this. Ever since Allie's first meeting with Callum, he's absolutely *adored* her.

The prospect of my new girlfriend being at the party makes me feel better about performing at it. Let's just hope she's actually happy to come along.

'Can I not spend the entire time doing Foodies songs, though?' I ask plaintively. 'Maybe a couple here and there – but otherwise, can I play something else?'

'Good grief, man, you'd think those songs hadn't made you a small fortune over the years.'

'The bloke who invented urinal cakes has made a fortune over the years, too, but it doesn't mean he wants to be anywhere near one.' It's a very poor analogy, but the headache has started to get worse, and I'd really like to get off the phone so I can go and down four co-codamol.

'All right! Play what you like!' Eliza snaps. 'As long as it's suitable for small children.'

'No Slayer or Public Enemy, gotcha,' I reply. 'I guess I'll see you at about 2 p.m. on Sunday, then?'

'You will.' She pauses for a moment. 'And think about telling Alison the *truth*, Nate,' Eliza says, her voice soft. 'It's the right thing to do now and you know it.'

My eyes close. 'I will, Elsie. I promise.'

I put the phone down on Eliza with that familiar ball of guilt in my stomach and go to find the aforementioned painkillers.

The right time to tell Allie *will* come – but I'm pretty sure it won't be in the middle of a hectic children's party. Revealing a dark and terrible truth to someone you love probably shouldn't be done to the accompaniment of loud screaming and vast amounts of ice cream consumption.

It's a good job the gazebo is up, as the day of the party is overcast and a little drizzly.

Unfortunately, it means I have to set my equipment up underneath the bloody thing, which isn't easy, given that I have to trail wires from the small Marshall amplifier across the garden and situate the stool on the grass in such a way that it doesn't instantly bury itself halfway up the second I sit down on it. I haven't brought my Les Paul with me today, given that I don't want it within a thousand miles of these sticky children. Instead I have brought the lightweight Telecaster Alison played back on Chipmunk Day. It's probably the cheapest guitar I own – if it gets half a chocolate eclair wedged between its strings, then so be it.

As I'm playing with the amp's dials to tune out the feedback, I notice the clown arriving. He comes in a small van bearing the name 'Mr Chippy' down one side, which he parks on Eliza's driveway in a decidedly haphazard fashion. Emerging from the van is the grumpiest man I've ever seen in my life. The sour expression on his face is thrown into sharp relief by the bright white-and-red-striped onesie he's wearing. I hope the make-up he's carrying in that box will do a good job of covering up his scowl.

Eliza has requested that we do a small routine together, with me on the guitar and him doing whatever clowny things she's paying him for. I've chosen to play the song 'Take Me Out to the Ball Game', as it's the only one I know that sounds even vaguely appropriate to accompany a clown act. Although from looking at Mr Chippy as he disappears inside the house, 'Tears of a Clown' by Smokey Robinson might be a more appropriate choice.

I turn my attention back to the task of setting up my amp, playing once more with the dials on the front – one of which of course goes up to eleven.

'What are you doing?'

'Aaargh!' I wail in shock. I thought I was completely alone in the garden.

I turn around to see Callum staring up at me. The usual look of miniature derision is on his face, but it's mixed with a fair degree of curiosity, which makes a nice change, I suppose. He's wearing the Foodies T-shirt I gave him for Christmas.

'Oh, hi, Callum,' I say in a cheery voice.

'My mummy's inside. With your mummy and Allie,' the boy informs me. He walks over to my amp, where he starts to twiddle the volume knob.

'Er . . . could you not do that, please?' I ask.

Callum ignores me and continues to twiddle. There's an air of absolute concentration about him now. I appear to have been completely forgotten about.

I feel exquisitely awkward. I have no idea what to say or do. Callum can be a miniature time bomb, and I've never taken the time to work out what the disarm code is.

'Seriously, could you not do that, Callum? It'll break off in your hand eventually and then I'll – oh look, it's broken off in your hand.'

He holds the volume knob up to me, daring me to take it from him. I feel that this is yet another downturn in what is already a rather strained relationship.

'Callum! Callum!' I hear Eliza cry from inside the house. The boy drops the volume knob into my hand and immediately starts to closely examine my thumb for no adequately explored reason.

Eliza pops her head out from the patio doors leading to her kitchen, sees Callum and me, rolls her eyes and comes over.

'Sorry, Nate,' she says as she reaches us. 'Callum is like a small ninja. One minute he's there, the next he's gone. He loves to fiddle with things he probably shouldn't.'

She bends down and takes the boy by his hand. Callum immediately starts to scream. His attention was still firmly fixed on my thumb, and he quite clearly does not appreciate having that examination ended prematurely.

Eliza winces. 'Sorry. I'll take him away. He's having trouble today. What with Bryan being in the house and everything with the party, it's been a bit much for him. I'm not sure this whole thing was such a good idea to be honest . . .'

'Don't worry, Elsie. It's perfectly okay,' I tell her, hiding the volume control knob in my hand. 'He wasn't doing anything wrong.'

I can see the strain etched across Eliza's face. It can't be nice to have her shithead ex-husband here today, and if Callum's having a bad time as well, it must make things even harder for her.

Callum is now looking back towards the house, pointing and screaming as he does so. It's quite ear-shattering, so I have to confess I breathe a sigh of relief when his mother takes him away. For a moment, I'm afraid the screaming is going to spark off another one of my headaches, but the sensation passes. I turn back to the amplifier, hoping that the volume control knob is just a push-on affair, otherwise I'll be taking a trip to Tesco to buy some superglue.

Happily, it pops back on with no apparent long-term damage done. I start to retune the guitar, hoping to achieve a nice, clear, crisp sound for the party.

When that's done after about ten minutes, I pop the guitar down on its stand and saunter over to the house, looking for a drink.

'All set up?' Mum says as she sees me walk in. She bustles past me with a massive plate of small, child-friendly sandwiches, placing it on a table just inside the house that is fairly heaving with all sorts of disgusting children's food.

'Yep,' I tell her. 'Ready to slightly rock and roll. Where's Allie?'

'She's up in Callum's room with Eliza, helping him calm down a bit.'

'Okay, that's cool.'

Mum gives me a long look. 'How are you doing today, son? You look a little peaky.'

I open my mouth to tell my mother the truth – that I feel like five pounds of shit in a ten-pound bag – but then swiftly think again. 'I'm fine, Mum. A little tired, but otherwise doing okay.'

Mum smiles. 'Good! You see? Maybe things aren't as bad as you thought they were! I'm sure you're on the road to recovery.'

I groan inwardly. Mum still won't come to terms with what's happening to me.

She gives me a meaningful look. 'Your cousin tells me you still haven't let Allie know about your condition. Even if it isn't as bad as you think it is, you probably should let her know about it.'

I roll my eyes. 'Yes, Mum. Don't worry. I will. I just need to do it at the right time.'

'Okay, son. Fair enough,' she replies with a smile. Mum doesn't seem as concerned as Eliza is about my reluctance to be honest with Allie about the tumour, but then she doesn't really accept how bad my diagnosis is, so why would she?

'Did you have a chance to look at the draft will I sent you?' I ask her. I could really do without getting into this right now, but it's vital I get the damn thing sorted out before I die. Mum will be the main recipient, so she needs to see it. I'm also hoping that reading it will convince her of the seriousness of the situation.

She waves a dismissive hand. 'Not yet, Nathan.'

I rub my hand over my face. 'Could you, please? It's important.'

'All right, I will!' she says, sounding a little cross. 'I think you're being overdramatic about the whole thing, though.'

'*Overdramatic?*'

'Yes.'

I'm so stunned by this pronouncement, I don't know how to respond. My mother's denial is starting to become a big problem, one I need to solve before I'm in a box and it's too late to do anything about it.

I'm about to say as much to her, but we're then interrupted by the arrival of Eliza, Allie and Callum coming down from upstairs. The boy looks a lot more chilled out than he did earlier, I'm pleased to say. Talking to Mum about the realities of my condition will just have to wait.

'Hiya,' I say to Allie as she comes over, letting Callum stay with Eliza and Mum.

'Hello, stranger. You all done out there?' she asks me.

'Pretty much. The acoustics in the garden are a little flat, but it should sound okay once – *Jesus Christ!*'

It's a completely involuntary bit of blaspheming, but totally unavoidable given what's just walked into the room.

I've never been particularly scared of clowns. That might change after today.

Whether he realises it or not, Mr Chippy is a pure distillation of every horror movie clown you've ever hidden behind a cushion to avoid. The big red hobnail boots are clunky and worn, the white-and-red-striped onesie is crumpled, the multicoloured rainbow ruff around his neck is eye-watering and the two enormous puffs of ginger hair on each side of his head look wiry and coarse.

And then we come to the make-up. You may remember that Mr Chippy looked to be a grumpy fellow before putting his make-up on. Imagine that same grumpiness, only it's now covered in a thick layer of greasy white paint; a blood-red smile that extends almost from ear to ear; a pair of thick black arching eyebrows that look like two slugs have been nailed to his forehead; and a bulbous red nose that looks like

– and yes, I'm going to use the word as an analogy here because it's so fucking *perfect* – a tumour.

'Urgh,' Allie says quietly from beside me.

'Oh my . . .' Mum mumbles, unable to say much else. I doubt even she would want to craft a statue that resembled this nightmare in clown shoes.

Eliza tries to affect a happy demeanour. Somebody should give her a bloody Oscar, because I couldn't look happy with that thing coming towards me if you held a water pistol full of acid to my head.

'Hello, Toby! Everything okay, is it?' she asks him.

'It will be when you show me where I'm supposed to be doing this show,' he says to her curtly. I've never heard such a snippy, uptight voice in all my life.

Eliza swallows down a suitable response and indicates towards the garden through the double doors. 'It's right out there, Toby. The gazebo is to your left. Nathan's set up his guitar in there already. You got the email with our plan for the show, didn't you?'

I step forward, expecting to be introduced so we can go over how we're going to work together today, but Chippy gives me a look of thin disgust and stomps off through the door before I get so much as a chance to say hello.

Eliza gives me an apologetic look. 'Sorry about that. Toby isn't . . . isn't having a good time of it at the moment. Something to do with his tax returns.'

'Where did you *find him*?' I ask.

'He's Bryan's uncle,' Eliza says, trying to keep the disdain out of her voice.

'Aaaah,' I respond. Now things become a little clearer.

'He's a chartered surveyor,' Eliza continues. 'Just does the clown thing for parties at the weekends. He's doing this one for free – which suits Bryan just *fine*, as you might imagine.'

'Why is he so *angry*?' Mum asks.

Eliza shrugs. 'I think he's lost a lot of money in the last couple of days. And also, I guess it's because he's a chartered surveyor that dresses up as a clown at weekends?'

'Well, let's just hope he cheers up a bit once the kids get here,' I remark. 'I doubt they'll have much sympathy for his problems with HMRC.'

Our discussion about Mr Chippy and his outlook on the world is interrupted by his nephew, Bryan, as he comes into the room from the hallway. 'They're here!' he cries, as if he's just seen the zombie horde turn up on the doorstep. 'The kids are here!'

Eliza instantly goes stiff. 'Okay, then.' As you'd imagine, the atmosphere between the two of them is roughly sub-zero these days.

I clench my jaw and try as hard as I can not to make fists. I want to punch Bryan in his stupid face until it's turned into raw, red hamburger. But this is Callum's birthday, so I'll do what Eliza is no doubt doing herself – I'll swallow down the disgust and put on a happy face for the poor kid.

Eliza takes Callum's hand. 'Why don't we go and say hello to all of your friends?' she says to him, trying not to look at her ex-husband. Callum doesn't look too sure about all of this, but allows his mother to lead him out towards the front door, closely followed by his shitbag of a father.

My mother watches Bryan go with a look of thinly veiled loathing. 'I think this is a good time for me to make a move,' she says. 'Isobel at A Cut Above is expecting me.' This is probably just as well, to be honest. I could punch Bryan about a bit, but Mum probably has some sort of metal implement stashed about her person thanks to the statue making and could do some real damage to him if she worked up enough of a head of steam.

'Okay, Mum,' I say to her, giving her a kiss. 'I'll call you later in the week.'

'That's great, son.' She turns to Allie. 'Nice to see you again, Alison,' she says.

'You too, Mrs James,' Allie replies.

Mum looks down the hallway at the hordes coming our way. 'I think I'll leave through the back.'

'Good idea,' I reply, grabbing a couple of cans of Coke from the heaving party table. 'Allie and I'll go outside, too. We can see what Mr Chippy is up to.'

The clown may look terrifying, but he is quite easily the preferable choice to twenty screaming, snotty children.

When I say as much to Allie as we're walking across the lawn having watched Mum leave, she rolls her eyes. 'You know, for someone who's earned a living writing music for small children, you don't have much of an affinity with them.'

'I know.'

'It's such a shame. They *love* The Foodies so much.'

My turn to roll my eyes. 'They like whatever's bright and shiny and popular this week.'

She chooses not to respond, but her eyes narrow. Best to let this conversation topic drop now, I feel. 'You want to play a few chords while we wait?' I ask, pointing at the guitar.

She shakes her head. 'I don't think so. Mr Chippy is grumpy enough without having to hear me murdering an open C.'

I turn to look at where the clown is arranging his own equipment on the other side of the enormous green gazebo. He's trying to set up a small golden box on a tripod and is swearing sulphurously under his breath as it fails to cooperate.

'Need a hand?' I ask.

He looks at me in a way that's guaranteed to spark off my night-mares again. 'No. I can do it,' he snaps.

'Fair enough.' I look back at Allie. 'This promises to be a fun afternoon.'

She punches me playfully on the arm. 'You're doing something nice for your cousin.'

'Yes.' I throw Mr Chippy a doubtful look, then turn an ear to the screaming tumult now erupting from the house. 'A cousin with an unwholesomely good memory, it transpires. I should never have gone to bloody Amsterdam,' I say regretfully, as I plonk myself down on my stool – which immediately sinks a good six inches into the grass.

It takes Eliza and the few other parents who have stuck around for the party a good hour to get the children under some semblance of control, giving them food and drink whenever it's asked for and corralling them around the garden like sheepdogs with an unruly, screaming flock.

Allie and I attempt to hide behind my amplifier while all of this goes on. This proves to be a little difficult, as it's only three feet high.

Mr Chippy has buggered off – and who can blame him? As a small boy dressed as Yoda runs into the side of my amplifier, I'm starting to better appreciate why he was being such a touchy bugger earlier. He *knew what was coming.*

I check the amp for damage while Allie tends to the small, crying Yoda impersonator. Bruises heal. Dents in amplifier cabinets do not.

Eliza comes over about five minutes later. Her hair is now a mess and she has a look on her face that suggests much wine will be imbibed before this day is out.

'You about ready to go?' she asks. 'We need to get these fuckers sat down and looking at something.'

I laugh. 'Starting to regret this whole thing, are you?'

'You mean marriage and childbirth? Just pick up the bloody guitar, Nate, before I have to insert it in you somewhere.'

I elect to keep quiet and do as I'm told. This is probably the wisest thing I've done all week.

Eliza goes over to the other harassed parents. They all have a quick conversation and then start to gather the bouncing, E-number-filled children under the gazebo for a little light afternoon entertainment. I have to confess I'm feeling quite nervous as they congregate on the grass in front of me. It's one thing to perform in front of a theatre audience where you can't see them thanks to all the lighting – it's quite another to stare into their eyes as you perform. Children are the fiercest critics in the world. They have no self-control, no filter and no consideration for the artist's ego. They will let you know their completely unvarnished opinion of your talents without a second thought.

Gulp.

The running order for today's performance is simple. I will accompany Mr Chippy while he does his thing for a while. Then after he's left to go and call the HMRC helpline, I will do a few Foodies songs, interspersed with some other children's favourites. The whole thing should only take about half an hour at the absolute most, thanks to the tiny attention spans that children around the ages of five and six suffer from.

Looking at the crowd, I'm a bit dismayed to see Callum sat slightly in front of, and apart from, all the other children. This is his party, but it seems like the other kids are giving him a bit of a wide berth. Being different may sound like a great thing when you're a fully grown adult who wants to be interesting at dinner parties, but it's an awful thing when you're small. I look up to see that Eliza has noticed this as well. The sad look on her face makes me want to cry.

Bryan is right at the back of the garden, drinking a can of beer, and apparently couldn't give a shit. I want to go over there and ram that beer down his throat.

I count to ten under my breath and strum my guitar a couple of times, going straight into the introductory few notes of 'Take Me Out to the Ball Game' once everyone is paying attention. This is supposed to be the cue for Mr Chippy to arrive on the scene.

When he doesn't at the allotted moment, I start to wonder if he hasn't just left the party completely to go and petrol bomb the nearest Inland Revenue office.

I play the notes again. Still no Chippy. Eliza throws me a panicked look. I throw it straight back at her, as I have no idea what to do. I then look over at Allie, as if she might have any answers. 'Too much to hope you've got your Libby costume in the boot of the car, eh?' I say, which earns me a set of very pursed lips and a magnificently irritated frown.

Third time's a charm, I think to myself, and play the introduction again.

This time, Mr Chippy comes cartwheeling and jumping out of the house, displaying the kind of gymnastic prowess you'd normally find buried in the BBC sporting schedule at 3 a.m. Toby might be a miserable bugger when he's not doing a show, but it looks like he turns it on one hundred per cent when he's performing.

His aforementioned grumpy demeanour only shows itself as he comes tumbling past me. I have to step backwards to let him past. As I do, he throws me a look of deep-seated contempt.

Mr Chippy stops tumbling around and stands just off to my right, next to his box of tricks with his legs splayed, a decidedly idiotic expression on his face. 'Hello!' he cries in a happy voice, waving his hands at the crowd. Most of the children respond with much screaming and hand-waving back in his direction. A couple look a bit shell-shocked, but for the most part they seem quite comfortable with the idea of a fully grown man dressed as walking nightmare fuel. Only Callum seems deeply unimpressed by Mr Chippy. He's staring directly at the clown's box on its tripod and is ignoring everything else.

Mr Chippy then goes into an energetic slapstick routine to the accompaniment of my guitar. For the most part, he continues to sound bright, cheerful and happy. The mask only slips when he has difficulty pulling out an enormous comedy handkerchief from his sleeve. The material gets caught for the briefest of moments inside the cloth. When

Mr Chippy turns away from the children to sort it out, I clearly hear him say, 'Come on, you cunt,' under his breath. The handkerchief does eventually come free with a tug, and he's instantly back to the happy, jolly, singing clown again. The kids may not notice the seething anger bubbling just under the surface, but I bloody well can, and it's deeply disconcerting, to say the least.

Mr Chippy moves on to the props he has in his big box, which include balloons for making animals, a large clown horn that makes a satisfying *awwwooooggaaaahhh* noise every time he squeezes the end, a rubber chicken and a big, squeaky hammer. The last one gives me unpleasant flashbacks to hitting Cleethorpes over the head in front of Primark.

As Chippy is getting on with his routine – which mainly seems to involve falling over a lot and making stupid faces as he does so – I notice Callum slowly get up from where he's sat apart from the rest of the group. His mother and Allie are both rapt with attention, watching the clown hit himself repeatedly with the hammer, so neither of them see him rise. I'm still playing the guitar, so there's not much I can do to stop the little boy walking quickly up to Mr Chippy's box of tricks.

Chippy sees him and bends over to speak to the little boy. 'Ho ho! Now what are you up to, then, birthday boy?' he says to Callum in a sing-song voice, his head wobbling about like it's on a spring.

Callum sensibly ignores him completely and stands up on tiptoe next to the box. 'Do you like my magic box?' Mr Chippy asks, doing his best to incorporate this unexpected interloper into the act. 'You mustn't look in it, though!' he continues. There's now a very, very slight edge to his voice. 'It's full of lots of magic and wonder!'

Callum continues to ignore the clown and instead starts poking at the box with one exploratory finger.

'Ho ho! Maybe your mummy should come and get you, my little friend!' Mr Chippy says, looking into the crowd. Eliza is now walking carefully towards her son, as if he's likely to explode at any moment. 'That box is all part of my big, big finale, so make sure not to touch it!'

The edge in Chippy's voice is now sharp enough for me to shave with. Quite clearly there's something in the box he intends to wow the crowd with as the show comes to an end, and he doesn't want the surprise ruined.

Callum couldn't give a shit about that, of course. This is a kid who knows what he wants, and what he apparently wants right now is to get into that box – exciting climax be damned. My hastily repaired volume knob is testament to the boy's curiosity, and I don't think anything the clown says is going to stop him.

Mr Chippy is reaching forward to grab Callum in his arms when the boy evidently finds exactly what he was looking for and gives the box another hard poke. I hear a clicking noise from somewhere deep within, and the box instantly blows open, sending a cloud of glitter and brightly coloured plastic balls into the air.

'Oh, you little bastard!' Chippy snarls, this time barely under his breath. He grabs Callum and picks him up. 'I told you not to do that!' he snaps at the boy in a gruff voice.

This would probably be quite terrifying to the average child, but Callum is not average in the *slightest*. He looks at Mr Chippy with an expression of unholy rage and smartly pokes him in the eye with his index finger. Callum likes a good poke, as Mr Chippy has just discovered to his detriment.

The clown bellows in pain and starts to shake the boy roughly. This instantly makes me see red. I can put up with some prick being rude to me because he's screwed up his tax return, but manhandling Callum like that?

I throw the guitar round on its strap so it's sitting on my back and step forward. 'Put him down!' I order Mr Chippy. The clown's eyes snap round to look at me. One of them is now red and streaming. This makes

---

Mr Chippy look even more terrifying, if such a thing were possible. 'Put Callum down!' I repeat, grabbing Chippy's sleeve.

'Get off!' he shouts, dropping Callum to the grass. The boy immediately starts to scream. Mr Chippy then turns his full attention to me, giving me the stink eye. 'Don't you touch me, you prick!' Audible gasps from the adults. High-pitched giggles from the children.

'What the hell is wrong with you?'

'What the hell is wrong with me?' Chippy screeches. 'What the hell is wrong with *me*??!!'

The watching children are now more invested in this show than at any point previously. This says a lot about the mindset of your average six-year-old.

'I'll tell you what's wrong with me!' Chippy hollers. 'Seventy-five thousand quid down the drain because I have a shitty accountant! That's what's . . . that's what's wrong with me!'

Oh God, now he's crying. I'm standing in front of a crying, enraged clown before a crowd of apparently sociopathic children. There's every chance Stephen King is about to jump over the garden wall and kick me up the arse.

'I'm sorry about all of that, but it's no reason to take it out on Callum!'

Chippy's face distorts into a hateful sneer. 'No. You're right,' he says with a growl. 'Much better to take it out on you.'

And with that, Chippy punches me square in the middle of the forehead.

This knocks me to the ground in a daze, snapping the neck off my poor old Telecaster as I fall on to it.

I figure the clown was probably aiming for lower down on my face, but that puffy onesie he's wearing isn't designed for close-quarters combat – which saves me from a broken jaw.

Instead, I get a nice relaxing nap on top of a broken guitar for my troubles.

As I fade out of consciousness, I can hear the children cheering excitedly. I guess seeing an adult knocked out beats a few plastic balls and a bit of glitter any day of the week. Eliza should have just stuck them all in front of a DVD of *Rocky IV* and saved herself a whole lot of trouble.

To be fair, I think the tumour is as much at fault for the blackout as the punch. Mr Chippy didn't hit me all that hard, but when your brain is already being scrambled by a big, grumpy tumour called Herman, it's not going to withstand even a weak punch from a big, angry clown called Mr Chippy.

I awake to find myself on the single bed in Eliza's spare room. This isn't the first time I've woken up bleary-eyed in this room, but it's the first time it hasn't followed a heavy night of drinking.

'Oh dear,' I mumble, as my hand goes to my head.

'You're awake!' I hear Allie say with some relief from where she's sat on the bed next to me.

'Apparently,' I agree, sitting up.

'Be careful, you idiot,' I hear Eliza remark as she comes into the room carrying a wet towel, which she plonks on my head without much ceremony.

'We were just about to call an ambulance,' Allie tells me. 'Do you remember us bringing you up here? You managed to walk, but you looked completely out of it.'

I shake my head. 'I don't remember any of that. Just him punching me. How long ago was that?'

'About half an hour,' Eliza says.

That's quite scary, actually. Half an hour is a long period of time to lose like that.

'How's your head?' Eliza's eyes flick meaningfully over at Allie as she says this.

Oh God, woman, there's no way I can tell her now!

'It's fine, thanks,' I reply, lying through my teeth yet again.

'Oh, well, that's okay, then,' my cousin says in a flat voice. 'But if it hurts for any reason, *you will tell one of us, won't you? That would be the right thing to do.*'

Subtle, Elsie – very subtle.

'I will,' I respond, in an even flatter voice.

Eliza's lip curls in disgust. 'I'm going back downstairs before the kids destroy my house. You come down when you're ready.' She then storms out of the room, leaving me alone with Allie.

'Why is she so mad all of a sudden?' Allie ponders.

'No idea. Must be all the stress of the party, I guess.'

A sudden, sharp pain courses its way through my head. I can't help but gasp.

'Are you okay?' Allie asks, leaning forward to hold my head.

'Yeah . . . I'm fine, honestly! Just a little . . . a little woozy still. I think I might lie here for a while on my own . . . in the quiet.' I force a smile. 'I don't think I can quite handle the children again yet, and Mr Punchy might still be downstairs.'

'Oh . . . okay.' Allie looks a little sad that I'm apparently dismissing her. 'Well, I'll come back to check on you a bit later.'

'Yeah, that would be great.'

She gives me a swift kiss on the lips. My stomach turns. Not because of the kiss, you understand, but because of my towering cowardice.

When Allie has left the room, I gasp in pain and lie back down, closing my eyes tight shut and willing the headache to pass.

As I take slow, deep breaths for several minutes, I can feel the pain ebbing away somewhat. I relax a little back into the bed, continuing to breathe deeply and not think about what Herman might be doing inside my brain as a reaction to the clown's punch.

Then, I feel something touch my index finger. My eyes fly open and I see Callum looking at me, his hand closed around my finger.

'Hello,' he says in a small voice.

'Hello, Callum,' I reply, sitting up again. 'Er, how are you?'

'Are you hurted?' he asks, ignoring my question.

'Um . . . maybe. Just a little, though.'

His head cocks to one side, a frown on his little face. 'No. Don't lie to me. You hurted really bad.'

I let out an involuntary gasp. How the hell? *What* the hell? What does he mean by that? Kids are supposed to take you at face value, not question your honesty.

'I . . . er . . . um . . .' Oh great. I've been rendered mute by my six-year-old second cousin.

Callum, without asking permission, because that's just for losers, jumps up on to the bed next to me, forcing me to move my legs and swing them round to sit next to him. He grabs my finger again.

'Mummy says not to lie when I'm hurted,' Callum informs me, instantly sending me on the kind of guilt trip that requires a heavy luggage allowance and a stern look from the girl at the check-in counter.

'Do you . . . do you get hurt a lot?' I ask, actually trying to change the subject away from me, because I am a prick of the highest order.

Callum cocks his head again. 'Not ows on me,' he says.

'Not ows on you?' I trust he means bruises, scrapes and the like. They are part and parcel of being a six-year-old.

'No.' His little brow furrows. 'But they don't like me, so I have inside ows.'

Oh good Lord, I could cry.

'Who doesn't like you?'

Callum squeezes my finger. I think it's involuntary, but I can't be sure. 'Other kids. They don't like me. Because I'm not a normal boy.'

Christ almighty.

The kid looks at me with his usual critical expression. 'Mummy says I shouldn't lie when I feel hurted.' His face clouds even further. 'You shouldn't, either.'

'I'm sure . . . I'm sure they *do* like you, Callum . . . the other boys and girls, I mean,' I tell him, doing that thing that all adults do when they think they can convince a child the truth of something just by *sounding like an adult*. He doesn't reply. The boy has the evidence of his own eyes and experience.

I think back to the gap the other kids placed between themselves and Callum out in the garden. Other children can be massive shits to those who are different. The lack of consideration they have for the talents of guitar-playing idiots like me pales against the way they treat their own kind sometimes.

I feel as if I should say something to make the poor little blighter feel better. 'I am hurted really bad, Callum.' I roll my eyes. '*Hurt* really bad. My ow is inside, too.'

'Do the boys and girls not like you, either?' he says.

'It's a bit different than that. There's . . . there's an *ow* inside my head. A really horrible one.'

The little boy looks at me and lets go of my finger. He stands up awkwardly on the bed beside me, wraps his little arms around my head and gives me the softest, most gentle kiss on my forehead.

'Bad ow,' he says. This is the closest Callum and I have ever been, both literally and figuratively, and it fair takes my breath away.

'Yeah, bad ow,' I repeat. My voice is thick with about a thousand different emotions. 'And thank you for the kiss,' I say, and force out a smile.

The smile fades as I look into his eyes. What must it be like to be six years old, have a shithead for a father and know that the kids around you don't like you, just because you're a little different from them? To have people avoid you all the time, just so they don't have to worry about what you—

Oh Jesus Christ.

That's *me*.

I've been doing *exactly that*.

Tears form at the corners of my eyes, and I look at the little boy with a grave and guilty expression on my face. 'I love you, Callum,' I say. This is shamefully the first time I have ever said this to him. It will not be the last. In fact, I'm pretty sure the little bastard is going to get thoroughly sick of hearing me say it from now on.

An epiphany then strikes me so hard that it makes my head swim – it took being diagnosed with a fucking *brain tumour* for me to make a proper connection with this boy.

I lean forward and give Callum a hug. I will *never* avoid being close to this boy *ever* again.

'Awww. Well, isn't that lovely?' I hear a voice say from the doorway. Eliza is standing there, a broad smile on her face. She notices that I have tears in my eyes. 'Are you all right, Nate?'

'He has an inside ow,' Callum tells her in a very serious voice.

His mother gives me a meaningful look before returning her gaze to her son's face again. 'Yes. He does, Callum. And I'm glad he's at least told *somebody* he loves about it.'

I can't think of anything to say in response to that.

Eliza sighs. 'Well, I'd better be getting this one back downstairs. They're about to cut the cake.'

'Fair enough. I'll come down in a minute. Just want to compose myself a bit,' I tell her.

She nods, regards me gravely for a moment and then exits the room with her son in tow, leaving me alone with my thoughts.

I've had countless meetings with Mr Chakraborty. I've tried Cleethorpes' strange therapy methods. I've attempted off-grid living and herbalism. I've even tried giving money away. But nothing has had a more profound impact on me in this whole bloody mess than a small child, who believes he has no friends, giving me a kiss to help take away my pain. Who knew such a small thing could have such a dramatic impact?

Maybe I need to take a leaf out of Callum's book. If I want to leave this world having done something worthwhile, then maybe I need to start being a bit more honest with my affections as well . . .

Mummy says I shouldn't lie when I feel hurted.

You. Shouldn't. Either.

LYRICS TO THE FOODIES SONG 'COME ON, GIVE US A HUG'

Herman the Grumpy Potato sings:

I'm feeling cranky. Nothing is going right,
Got out of bed on the wrong side, it's not a
pretty sight,
I'm tired, I'm slow, I'm stuck in the mud,
Today is looking like a dud,
There's nothing you can do, to make me feel
brand new!

All of The Foodies sing:

Come on, give us a hug, Herman! Come on,
don't be shy,
You might not want to do it, but we think you're
a terrific guy!
Hugging shows we love you, whether you like it or not,
Hugging makes us feel happy, that's why we do
it a lot!

Herman the Grumpy Potato sings:

Leave me alone, hugging doesn't help!
I'm in a really bad mood, if you hug me I'll just yelp!
I'm bored, I'm mad, I'm feeling blue,
There's really nothing you can do,
So just leave me alone, I want to sit in the corner
and moan!

All of The Foodies sing:

Come on, give us a hug, Herman! Come on,
don't be shy,
You might not want to do it, but we think you're
a lovely guy!
Hugging shows we love you, whether you like it
or not,
Hugging makes us feel happy, that's why we do
it a lot!

WITHOUT A CARE HOME

I'm going to tell her. *Today.*

No matter what happens. No matter the consequences.

. . . oh, who am I trying to kid? I *know* what the consequences will be. Allie is going to bugger off as quickly as she possibly can. Not only do I have a tumour that could kill me, I've also covered it up and lied to her consistently about it for our entire short relationship. The idea of losing her terrifies me. It makes my breath catch in my throat – but I can't go on like this any longer. I feel far too much for Allie to keep putting her through this.

The time has come to man up and tell the truth.

. . . now, do I do it by text or email?

It's been a week since my brief but devastating conversation with Callum. A week to ponder his profound words, while also trying my hardest to get rid of the headache that Mr Punchy sparked off.

I stayed in Eliza's spare bedroom for the rest of the party, my head throbbing like a bastard. By the time Allie came to see me again, all I wanted to do was get in a taxi, go home and swallow every single painkiller I possessed. I have to confess I was a bit short with both her and Eliza before leaving, but being civil when white-hot agony is coursing through your grey matter is quite impossible. I promised to call them both the next day, then bundled myself into a cab and went home. I called Eliza first to apologise and arrange a time when I could pick up my guitar and amplifier. I also told her I was going to be honest with Allie when I next saw her, which headed off another argument before it had a chance to surface.

I didn't tell her about the secret bank account I've opened up in Callum's name, however. I opened this account because I just don't trust Bryan to be a decent father to Callum in the coming years. By the time Eliza finds out about the account, I'll be long gone, so she won't be able to shout at me about it. It's a win-win situation. Callum will be taken care of, and I won't have to have my eardrums punctured thanks to having hopefully escaped to another plane of existence.

I called Allie straight after speaking to Eliza and told her I would see her in a few days, once I felt a little better. I suppose I could have just confessed everything to her over the phone, but that didn't seem right. This kind of shit needs to be done face-to-face and when I'm not bleary-eyed and fuzzy-headed from a Herman headache.

Which, friends and neighbours, I'm happy to say is today. The headache has cleared.

. . . only I'm not actually *happy* about it at all, am I?

Part of me secretly wanted the headache to go on and on, just so I never had to have the conversation with Allie. However, when I woke up today, I felt clear-headed for the first time in a week and knew there was no putting it off any longer.

'So you're feeling better now?' Allie says down the phone when I call her just after breakfast.

'Yes. Are you free today?'

'I am. I'd like to see you if I can?'

'Of course, that'd be lovely.'

'Great.' She pauses for a second. 'Actually, I've been meaning to ask you about something . . . about that money you gave away to the lady with the donkey sanctuary?'

'Oh yeah?' I reply with a small shudder, remembering Pipsqueak's excited member.

'Would you be willing to give any more money away, by any chance? To another worthy cause, I mean?'

I'd told Allie all about my visit to Winnifred and her charges, including the incident with Pipsqueak. She laughed so hard I was worried I might have to start administering CPR at some point. I didn't tell her the real reason for giving the cash away, of course – that I'm trying to do something worthwhile before I die. She just thinks I did it out of the goodness of my heart.

I truly am a shameless *worm*.

'Um . . . yeah, sure . . . I'd love to, actually,' I tell her.

'Would you be willing to come and see somewhere with me that could do with your help?'

'Yeah. No problem.' I was planning on visiting the GivingLocal. com website again sometime soon anyway, but it sounds like Allie has someone she'd like me to help out instead, which suits me just fine.

'Great! Can you meet me on the other side of town after lunch, at about one? I can text you the postcode.'

Hmmmm.

That's not ideal, to be honest.

I had hoped to be able to go over to Allie's flat to confess my sins. That way I could have just left quickly once she told me the relationship was over. Now we'll be meeting somewhere strange, which will make the whole thing more awkward.

'Yeah, that's fine,' I reply, keeping the reluctance out of my voice. 'What kind of place are we going to?'

'Um . . . I'd rather you saw it for yourself. I have a good reason for that.'

Cryptic.

'Okay, well . . . I'll see you later, then, I guess.'

'Yes. You will.' Allie pauses. 'Are you all right, Nathan? You sound very low. Are you well enough to do this?'

'Yeah. I'm fine. Honestly,' I tell her, trying to sound a bit more perky.

She pauses for a moment on the other end of the line. 'Nathan . . . does what happened at the party have anything to do with those things you haven't been able to tell me about yet? You know? Like you said in the car that day on the way back from the hospital?'

I blink a couple of times in surprise. Allie hasn't mentioned that conversation again, but it's obviously been preying on her mind.

How the hell do I reply?

'Er . . . it might have. A bit.'

Pathetic.

'Ah. I thought so.' She doesn't say anything else. You can tell she wants to push the issue but doesn't quite know how. It's exquisitely awful.

'Look, I'm fine. Honestly,' I tell her. 'I've just been cooped up in here for a few days and need to get outside.'

. . . and destroy both of our love lives in one fell swoop.

'Why don't we sort out this thing you want to show me and worry about everything else later?'

'Okay!' She actually sounds a little grateful that I've moved the conversation on. 'That's a good idea. I guess I'll see you at one o'clock, then?'

'Yep. You will.'

I end the call and spend a few moments considering my options. Do I just blurt out the truth as soon as I see her? Or wait for the appropriate moment? She obviously has something she wants me to see, so it's probably a good idea to hear her out. I'll just have to pick the right time when I get there.

Feeling some sort of half-hearted resolve, I go upstairs to take an *extremely* long shower. I also pop a few painkillers into my pocket as I leave the house – just in case.

The postcode Allie gave me takes my cab driver to what appears to be a bog-standard suburban street on the east side of town. It's not the most salubrious area, to be honest. There aren't quite any mattresses left out on the front lawns or untaxed cars in the driveways, but I do spot a couple of moth-eaten England flags hanging from windows here and there. The houses are all uniformly from the 1970s and are that special kind of drab that only England in the 1970s could create.

I spot Allie's little Fiat 500 parked up and tell the cabbie to pull up behind it.

'Hiya,' I say as I climb out. I pay the cab driver and walk over to where she's standing beside her car.

'Hey.'

Allie looks a little nervous. This is quite ironic, given that it's me who's here to deliver bad news. I should be the one with the nerves. However, I think I've dropped into something of a fatalistic acceptance of the way things are going to turn out today. Allie is going to break off the relationship, of that there is no doubt. There's nothing to really be that nervous about from my point of view.

'Everything okay?' I ask, as I kiss her on the cheek and give her a small hug. 'You seem a bit tense.'

'Er, well . . . There's something I want to show you, and I don't know what your reaction is going to be.'

'Oh . . . I'm sure it'll be fine.'

'I hope so. They could really do with your help and I don't want to screw it up.'

'I guess you'd better show me why I'm here, then,' I say, affecting what I hope is a positive tone. Let's face it, I'm likely to throw the cash at Allie's good cause no matter what it is, given the circumstances. That way, when she does break up with me for repeatedly lying to her, at least she won't think I was a complete bastard. She could be about to lead me round to see Helena and her dog turd glue company and I'd still probably fork over fifty thousand pounds.

Alison takes my hand and we start to walk down the road a little way.

She leads me around a corner and stops. In front of us, about fifty yards away and across the road, is a massive and ramshackle old building that must have been built a good forty years before the rest of the houses around here were thrown up.

The mansion – there's no better word to describe it – is built of grey stone and has a red-tiled roof. There are some flashes of art deco here and there around the windows and door frame, but other than that, the place is built in a fairly utilitarian style. I can count at least a dozen windows just at the front of the place, suggesting it's a very big building indeed.

It's in a right fucking state, there's no doubting that. I'm reminded of Winnifred's donkey sanctuary, only the decay here is far, far worse. There are roof tiles missing and cracks in a lot of the windows. The large front garden is overgrown, and the driveway is festooned with weeds.

This place must be abandoned.

'Looks awful, doesn't it?' Allie says.

'Yes.'

'What do you think it is?'

'Scheduled for demolition?'

'Not quite.'

Allie leads me closer to the building. As we do so, I see a sign at the entrance to the drive that had been previously hidden by an oak tree in desperate need of a trim. The sign reads 'Helmore Lodge Care Home for the Elderly'.

'You're *kidding me*,' I say in disbelief. 'People can't live in there, *surely?*'

Allie's eyes suddenly get very misty. 'They do. One very special person in particular.'

She leads me across the road and up the care home's overgrown driveway, which I now notice has small signs dotted here and there that say 'Parking for Staff Only'. Most of them are empty.

The front doors of the building are *awful.* Not because they are in a dilapidated state, but because at some point in the past, some genius ripped out what were probably very attractive 1930s-style art deco doors and replaced them with a set of hideous '80s UPVC nastiness. Any self-respecting architect would be throwing up as they examined this travesty.

We go inside and I'm hit with an overpowering smell of mustiness. It's not unpleasant, but it is a strange odour to the nasal cavities of one lucky enough to live in a house built only eight years ago. The entrance lobby is quite large, with huge sets of heavy oak double doors leading away to both the left and right and a broad staircase rising up into a fairly gloomy-looking first floor. The decor can be described as tired at best – and fucking knackered at worst. I would describe the carpet as threadbare, but that would probably be giving it too much credit.

Just to the left as you enter the building, somebody has constructed a small reception out of plasterboard and hope. Sat behind the tiny desk is a young black girl in a blue nurse's outfit, attempting to work at a computer from 1998. Allie goes over to her.

'Hi, Carla,' she says with a smile.

'Hey, Allie! How are you doing?'

'Fine, thank you. This is my friend Nathan,' she says by way of introduction. 'Nathan, this is Carla. She's one of the staff here.'

Carla gets up and proffers a hand. 'Nice to meet you, Nathan.'

I shake it and give her a winning smile. I get the feeling that winning is in short supply around here, so being overtly nice seems like the best thing I can do. 'Nice to meet you, too. Lovely place you have here.'

Carla gives me a disbelieving look. I might as well have just told her that Martians were parked outside on the driveway, offering to trim the hedges for just ten Intergalactic Credits.

'How is he today?' Allie asks Carla as the girl sits back down.

'Oh, the usual.'

Allie's face screws up. 'Oh no.'

Gosh. We're obviously here to see somebody who's not doing very well *at all*.

'Yeah,' Carla looks quite troubled. 'In fact, everyone's having one of *those days*.'

'Oh no,' Allie replies, her hand going to her mouth.

Bloody Nora. One of *those days* can only mean one thing, right? In a care home for the elderly? Someone's *died*, haven't they? Some poor bugger has died and here we are to witness the toe-curling aftermath.

A sudden wave of fear washes over me.

I can't do this! I can't be in this place!

I didn't realise Alison was going to bring me to a care home full of sad, old people, all of whom are probably at death's door. *I'm* at death's door, too! What good is it going to do me to be around people who are only a couple of places ahead of me in the queue?

But I'm here now, aren't I? I should have said something while we were still stood out on the street, but the shock of being told that people were forced to live in a place like this overrode any other considerations until we walked in through the front door. I should have told Allie about the tumour already, then I wouldn't have to go through this!

I open my mouth to say something, but Allie has already snaked her hand back into mine. 'Thanks, Carla, we'll go through and say hello to him.' She gulps. 'I just hope . . . hope they're not *too* bad.'

Carla winces. 'Good luck,' she says, giving us both a look filled with pity.

Allie moves towards the double doors on the left-hand side, pulling me along with her.

I don't want to do this. I don't want to spend any time in a room of people breathing their last. I'm not good around old people. I got fired from a paper round when I was twelve because I couldn't deliver to 36 Clarkwell Street. The old lady who lived there always answered the door to me, and she looked like an ambulatory cadaver. I didn't know whether to hand over the gazette or aim for the head to make sure she wouldn't keep coming for me.

Allie pauses by the doors and looks at me. 'This might be a little . . . *distressing*,' she says, not knowing the half of it. 'They're all lovely people, really.'

Oh, for fuck's sake. Are they going to just start dropping dead at my feet? Will I be corralled into helping Carla put the bodies into bin bags?

'They cope the best they can, bless them,' Allie continues, 'given what this place is like.'

'Okay.' This is *awful*.

She gives me a thin smile. 'Try to keep an open mind, won't you?'

I swallow hard. I'm about to come face-to-face with the Grim Reaper himself, and she wants me to keep an open mind.

I take a deep breath. 'Come on, then,' I say.

Allie gives me that thin smile again and pushes the doors open . . .

Beyond is – well, beyond is *not* what I was expecting *at all*.

There are not a load of immobile, dust-covered pensioners sat in broken chairs, letting out their last death rattles. Neither is the room as silent as the grave, nor as smelly. When Allie said the residents cope the best they can with the dilapidated old building they live in, I didn't quite get what she meant.

I didn't expect quite so much laughter, for instance. Or so much terrible, terrible *acting*.

The room is full of large chairs and a lot of them are indeed in pretty bad shape. Almost every single armchair shows signs of wear and tear. I can even see the white upholstery stuffing coming through a couple of them. The carpet in here could give the one in the hallway a run for its money in the threadbare stakes, and the last time I saw curtains like that I hadn't been born yet. There's Artex on the ceiling. Oh, so much *Artex*. It's yellowed with age and cracking in several places. There's also what was once a grand fireplace in the centre of the far wall, around which the majority of the armchairs are placed.

In front of the fireplace are two old men reciting Shakespeare *very badly*. One is bald, short and holding on to a Zimmer frame. He looks a tiny bit unsteady on his feet. He's still managing to wave his arms around theatrically, though. The other looks more limber – a tall, grey-haired man with a heavy tan, a wicked smile and a very loud mouth.

'Now is the winter of our disco tent! Made glorious summer by this Yorkie bar!' he exclaims, to the general amusement of all gathered.

'And all the clowns that poured water on our house,' says the other old boy, one arm extended out in front of him while the other still grips the frame. 'In the deep bosom of Deidre buried!' He points at one rather large lady in the front row of the audience. She roars with laughter and leans forward to give him a playful slap on the hip.

I turn and give Allie a look.

She cringes. 'I know. I know. Welcome to the madhouse.'

The tall, more ambulatory pensioner is doubled over with laughter, until he notices Allie and me standing there. 'Aha!' he cries happily. 'Our guests have arrived!'

'Hello, Grandad,' Allie replies, waving uncertainly at the crowd of old people.

Well, that explains everything, then. No wonder she would like me to consider putting some money into this place.

'Well met, my favourite granddaughter!' he tells her in ebullient fashion, coming over to join us. His gait is somewhat unsteady as he does so. This is a man still very full of life, but not even enthusiasm can stop the march of time on the human body. He's robust enough for his age, but there's an underlying frailty there, no doubt. He also looks oddly familiar. 'You find us in our weekly sojourn into the works of the bard,' he says, leaning in to give her a kiss on the cheek.

'You mean *murdering* the works of the bard,' Allie replies with a roll of her eyes.

The old man nods. 'I take your constructive criticism on board, my dear.' He points to the other old man he was 'onstage' with. 'Don't say anything to Bernard, though. He has the soul of a poet and the ego to match.' He then looks at me for the first time. 'But enough of this idle Shakespearean discourse – surely this must be your most recent gentleman friend, Nathan?' He looks down his nose at her. 'I do hope he's a better prospect than that nincompoop Zack you were with a few months ago.' He looks back at me. 'Could barely string two words together . . . and had a strange, wispy beard that put me in mind of my dear old auntie Mildred.'

'Grandad!' Alison exclaims in horror.

'Pleased to meet you!' I say, stepping in before this goes any further. I get the impression that Allie's grandfather is not a man who is afraid to speak his mind, whether he should or not. He also appears to like the sound of his own voice, which is fine, as so do I. 'I can string at least five words together if you give me a long enough run-up, and I own a very expensive shaver that takes just five minutes to charge.'

The old man smiles broadly. He claps me on the shoulder and looks at his granddaughter with delight. 'Much better! And wealthy to boot, by all accounts. I look forward to buttering him up as much as possible.'

Allie's head goes into her hand. 'Nathan, this is my grandfather Freddie Stockhouse. I apologise in advance for everything that comes out of his mouth.'

Freddie Stockhouse? I'm sure I've heard that name before . . .

I peer at him closely for a second. Then it hits me. 'Were you . . . were you in a band in the sixties called Reluctant Badger?'

Freddie's eyes light up.

'Oh God, no!' Allie wails.

'Yes!' Freddie confirms with triumph. 'Indeed, I was!'

'You played the crumhorn, didn't you?' I continue, scarcely able to believe it.

'And the hurdy-gurdy!' Freddie reminds me.

'Of course!'

A few years ago, I indulged in a hippy phase, musically speaking. For about three months I immersed myself in the flower power music scene, listening to as many albums of the period as I could. Along with all the classic bands like Jefferson Airplane and Hawkwind, I also dabbled in more obscure fare. Easily the strangest of the bunch was Reluctant Badger, who had three albums out in total, each of which more zany and bizarre than the last.

'I have all of your albums!' I cry excitedly.

'Do you?!' the old man replies in disbelief.

'Yes! *Montezuma's Packet of Peanuts* is great, but I think you guys really peaked with *Chickens Halfway up the Mountain*.'

Freddie throws his arms around me. 'You truly are a wonderful boy! I am usually recognised for my time treading the boards, but it's most welcome to hear that my brief sojourn as a rock musician went down well with at least one person!' Freddie fixes Allie with a meaningful stare. 'Marry this boy immediately, my girl! I demand it!'

'Grandad!' Allie looks mortified.

I'm starting to see why she had a look of dread on her face before we came in here. I thought it was because somebody had died. By the way Allie looks right now, she probably wishes it was her.

Freddie snakes one arm around her as well. 'Why don't you both come and sit down? We have prepared something of a show for Nathan here to help him understand our plight.'

'You have?' Allie replies. 'But I just wanted you to meet Nathan and for him to have a look around the place . . .'

Freddie looks aghast. 'But that would have been so *boring*.' He starts to pull us towards two armchairs that have been hastily vacated by two of the residents. 'No, no. We've been planning this for a few days now. All you have to do, Nathan, my boy, is sit back and let us regale you with our tale. Fear not! It has been written with a comedic bent. We're not the types to wallow in our own misery or inflict it on others!'

I am propelled into the armchair before I have much of a chance to respond to this. I hadn't expected to be an honoured guest ever again. I had quite enough of that over in the West Country. But now I have to sit and watch while a bunch of frail, old people try to convince me I should give them cash for their nursing home, apparently through the medium of stand-up comedy.

'I'm really sorry about all of this,' Allie says from where she's sat beside me in a faded-green armchair. 'Grandad is like this all the time, and he tends to whip the others up.'

'It's fine. I'm rather hoping he'll break out the hurdy-gurdy at some point and do a rendition of "I Once Slapped Buddha on the Backside". That's my favourite Reluctant Badger track.'

Freddie takes centre stage in front of the fireplace again, looking directly at me. 'Our story will begin soon, young Nathan, but first a few introductions are in order. This is my main cohort and brother in the theatrical muse, Bernard Goldberg.'

Bernard bows and gives me a toothy smile. Well, half-toothy, anyway.

'Going around the room,' Freddie continues, 'we have Deidre, Michael, Babs, Patty, Kenneth Not Ken, Harry, Lottie and Grub. Then there's Arthur, Kathy, Kay and Ralph, Sam, Midge and Bob.'

He meant that to rhyme, didn't he? I just *know it*. I wouldn't have put it past the old man to force at least a couple of them to change their names to make the rhyme scan properly. From the expression on Allie's face, she'd agree with me wholeheartedly.

'So now our story shall start!' Freddie exclaims, dropping into oratory mode like the old pro he so evidently is. ''Tis a tale of woe, most egregious! Featuring a cast of misfits and reprobates!'

This makes the assembled pensioners titter. Being referred to as a reprobate obviously becomes less of an insult and more a compliment the older you get.

'For our tale, Bernard will play the part of Alfonse Helmore, proud owner of this care home until the dark days of a decade ago!'

'His name wasn't Alfonse,' Allie whispers out of the corner of her mouth. 'It was George.'

Bernard affects an expression of such beneficent good nature that Mother Theresa would have looked like a member of the Gestapo by comparison.

'I shall play the part of Lord Pinchyface!' Freddie roars. 'Proprietor of the evil corporation Lockard Holdings PLC!'

Allie sighs. 'Lord Pinchyface is Simon Lockard, the man who bought the care home.'

Freddie's face clouds. 'Don't give the plot away, young lady!'

'Sorry, Grandad.'

'Good girl . . . Our tale of woe begins with the kindly Alfonse slipping into his dotage.'

Bernard pretends to slip on some dog poo, because that's the level Freddie is choosing to work at. Still, the rest of the crowd are finding it very funny, so who am I to judge?

Freddie puffs his chest out and addresses Bernard. 'I, Lord Pinchyface, see that you grow old, Alfonse Helmore! You can no longer sustain this fine and elegant home for the old! You should be in it yourself!'

'Aye. I grow weary of this life and its tribulations!' Bernard replies in a voice cracked and wavering. 'I shall see that this fine and elegant place which I have presided over for all these years is sold to you, Lord Pinchyface, safe in the knowledge that you shall take care of its residents – of which I shall become one – from now until the end of days.'

'Yes, yes! I shall do that very thing, my old, old friend.' Freddie puts a comforting hand on Bernard's shoulder. 'Rest now. I will carry your burden from here!'

Bernard groans and goes to sit down in the nearest chair. I can't tell if the groan was genuine or put on for the show.

Freddie's eyebrows knit and he sneers. 'Ha! Now the old fool has gone, I will start to squeeze this place for all the money I can! First off, to sack half of the staff!'

Three of the ladies in the room stand up. It takes a while – they are all very old, after all.

'You!' Freddie intones, pointing at them.

'Who? Us?' the three old women respond together in perfect harmony.

'Yes, you! Begone! You work here no more!'

The three old ladies all start to cry theatrically. They slowly return to their seats with their heads bowed.

'And next, I will cut the maintenance budget by *two-thirds*!' Freddie cries with a flourish, before cackling like a pantomime villain. 'Aha ha ha ha ha!'

'*Aha ha ha ha ha!*' all the other men in the room repeat right after him.

From my left-hand side, I see Deidre of the large bosom rise to her feet. She clasps her hands in front of her and tries her best to look pitiful. 'But, Lord Pinchyface, who will take care of us now? Who will be there for our needs? We pay so much to live here, where does the money now go?'

Lord Pinchyface draws himself melodramatically up to his full height. Freddie wobbles a bit uncertainly for a moment, but otherwise pulls off the towering villain very well. 'Yachts! Many, many wonderful yachts!' He cackles again. This time all of the audience other than Allie and myself boo him loudly. He points an angry finger at them 'Quiet! Quiet, you fools! You cannot do anything to stop me! You are old and nobody cares about you! You cannot afford to move anywhere else! Nobody cares what you think! I will bleed this institution dry, until there is no money left! Aha ha ha ha ha!'

'*Aha ha ha ha ha!*' the men all repeat the evil laughter once more, while all the women do their best horrified swoons.

On the surface this all looks like good fun, but underneath, once you get past the theatricality and look at what's actually going on here, it's bloody *horrifying*. These poor people are forced to live in a crumbling building because some rich arsehole sees it as a way of stuffing his bank account, rather than giving care to those who most need it.

I am suddenly and comprehensively mad as hell at Lord Pinchyface – or whatever his real name is.

'You are an evil, evil man!' Deidre shrieks from beside me in the falsetto voice of a classic damsel in distress.

'Quiet, oh foul, large-bosomed wench!' Freddie replies haughtily. He then does something that shocks the hell out of me. He mimes *motor-boating Deidre*.

A man in his eighties has literally just squeezed an imaginary pair of large breasts between his two hands, pressed his face forward and shaken his head from side to side with his lips loose.

Motor-boating.

And the reaction from his friends and fellow residents is to all collectively shriek with laughter.

How do they *know* what motor-boating is? Old people shouldn't know about things like that, should they? They all stopped having sex in the 1950s when the lights came back on.

The only motor-boating they should know about is the type done on the Thames after the blitz.

Allie shares my horror. Her mouth is hanging agape and her eyes are wide. We youngsters are usually safe and secure in the knowledge that sex is only something that *we* are allowed to do – or even think about. Having this reality shattered completely by one old man's bit of hilarious mime is disturbing to say the least.

What else are these people hiding from us?

I look at them all laughing their heads off and have to sit back in some kind of disbelieving admiration. Here they are, in their autumn years, living in a place that's falling apart, and yet they are not sat around bemoaning their lot – they are making the legendary 'best of it'. There's no one here sliding into depression or wondering at the futility of it all.

I suddenly feel quite ashamed of myself.

Freddie once again affects his high and haughty stance. 'Now, all of you, just be quiet and accept your lot! You will all die here in this foul and pestilent place. There is nothing that can be done to change that! Aha ha ha ha ha!'

'*Aha ha ha ha ha!*' go the men.

Then Bernard rises from his seat. From somewhere he has found a white tea towel, which he has cut two eyeholes in and draped on his head. I assume he's going for ghost rather than clan member.

'*Woooooo* . . . Not so fast, Pinchyface!' he wails with a ghostly tremor.

Freddie recoils. '*Aaaarggh!* 'Tis the ghost of care homes past, come to visit and torment me!'

'Yes, Pinchyface, it is I, Alfonse Helmore, returned to haunt your days! *Wooooooooo* . . . With an important clause written into the buyout contract for this care home that states' – Bernard rifles for a moment in one of his pyjama pockets and pulls out a crumpled piece of paper, which he reads from. He still keeps the ghostly voice as he does it – 'which reads that if the owner of the home does not control at least ninety per cent of all assets linked to the estate of George Helmore, then they will not be allowed to make any pertinent financial decisions regarding the care home and the estate without the permission of fellow asset holders.' Bernard then holds up both hands and wiggles his fingers. '*Wooooooooooooo.*'

Freddie initially looks aghast, but then appears to realise something. 'Aha! But the only other asset holder in this home is Lionel Helmore, your cousin, who resides in Canada and does not care what I do! Your scheming will come to naught, dread ghost! Aha ha ha ha ha!'

'*Aha ha ha ha ha!*'

'*Wooooooooo* . . . That's quite true, Pinchyface, but the residents of the home have been in touch with Lionel, thanks to something called 'the Google', and have discovered that he is willing to sell his stake in the home to them for what is frankly a ridiculous sum of money, the money-grubbing little bastard.'

'Stay in character, Bernard,' Freddie says from the corner of his mouth.

'Sorry. The money-grubbing little bastard . . . *woooooooooo.*' Waggly fingers.

Oh, I see. That's why they need the money. If they can hold a stake in the home, they can stop whatever nefarious plans Pinchyface might have for the place in the future.

Bernard floats closer to my chair. 'If only – sorry, *wooooooooo* – if only there were someone kind enough to help us. Some good, young soul, who may or may not be currently engaged in a relationship with the granddaughter of one of our residents, who would come to our aid at this most trying of times.' Bernard wiggles his fingers over my head. '*Wooooooooooo.*' He then freezes and gives me an expectant look.

I look to my left. The look on Deidre's face is much the same. I look to my right. The whole audience is staring at me – including Allie. She has tears in her eyes and a dismayed look on her face. She knows this is very important to them, but also knows I am being royally put on the spot here.

I look up and see Freddie, frozen at his most high and haughty. The pleading look in his eyes rather ruins the pantomime villain impression, though.

Here we are, then. They've done their pitch to the best of their abilities. I can see them spending days practising to get it right, just so they can put on a show for me . . . instead of just coming right out and asking for money. Who can blame them for that? These people must have a lot of pride and respect for themselves. I'm sure the idea of simply asking for cold, hard cash would be anathema to them.

How the hell can I say no? I'd give them the money just based on what I've seen here today, but throw in the tears in the eyes of the woman I love and am about to lose and what possible other decision could I make? That money has to go somewhere – it might as well go to the man who played the crumhorn on the seminal hit 'My Love Requires Pumping Thrice Weekly'. I want to do something worthwhile with my cash before I go. What better place could I choose to spend it than here?

And what the hell . . . if they can put on a show to ask me, I can sure as hell put on a show to *answer*. It might be one of the last I get to do, so I'd best make a good job of it.

I rise slowly from the threadbare armchair, placing my hands on my hips as I do so. In an instant I go from Nathan James – mild-mannered musician – to *Tumour Man* – the cerebrodondreglioma-powered super-hero, ready and able to throw his cash at any and all good causes! Aha ha ha ha ha!

'I will help you!' I exclaim, in my biggest, butchest superhero voice. I look at Bernard. 'I will give you the money you need, strange, ghostly tea towel man!' I point a thrusting and manly finger at Lord Pinchyface. 'You shall not be allowed to destroy this place any more, oh foul and evil miscreant! The good people here shall receive . . . er . . . *how much do you need, Bernard?*' I say to the old boy out of one corner of my mouth.

251

'Seventy-five thousand quid,' he replies with a gulp. I hear Allie gasp in horror.

'Bloody hell, *really*?' I reply, not able to keep the shock out of my voice. I give Bernard a rather horrified look.

'Yeah. Sorry about that,' he says. 'Can we still have it? Er . . . *wooooooooo*?'

That'll take up the rest of my Brightside cheque and a lot more besides. What with the money I need for Callum, it looks like I'll have to sell some stuff . . . probably starting with my dusty Porsche.

Then I look at Bernard's expectant face again and the tears in Allie's eyes.

Oh, come on, you idiot. What else are you going to do with the money? And that stupid car is just going to waste anyway. This is what you wanted. *This is where you get to make a bloody difference.*

'Yes, yes, of course,' I tell Bernard, trying to keep the wobble out of my voice. 'That's fine. You can have all the money you need.' I shrug, and give them all a winning smile. 'After all, you can't take it with you, can you?'

I puff out my chest and return my attention to Lord Pinchyface. 'These fine people shall have the seventy-five thousand pounds they require, and you shall be defeated, you monster!'

The crowd of old people all start to applaud my terrible acting, for some reason. Freddie gives up his own act and returns from being the villain of the piece to one of its heroes. The smile on his face is a wonderful thing to behold.

He comes over to me and shakes my hand, tears of gratitude in his eyes.

This is all getting a bit much.

'Thank you, my boy,' he says in a voice full of emotion. 'We really are most grateful.'

'My pleasure, Freddie. My absolute pleasure.'

What a *fantastic* feeling! What a *marvellous* thing!

Nothing I have ever bought – not the Porsche, not the red Prada dress, not the Les Paul guitar and certainly not the bloody bifold patio doors – has ever filled me with such a sense of pure pleasure!

'What do you mean, *you can't take it with you?*' I hear Allie say in a small voice from beside me.

I look down at her.

She looks back up at me with a mixture of confusion and doubt.

Oh shit.

Not like this.

It wasn't supposed to happen like *this* . . .

I wave a shaking hand. 'Oh, nothing. Don't worry about it. Just a turn of phrase!' I try to sound light and carefree and fail completely.

Allie rises from her chair and fixes me with a stare that's impossible to break away from. 'What's going on, Nathan? What did you mean by that?'

The room has now gone quiet. Freddie has stepped away, the rest of the residents are watching in silence and Bernard has thankfully taken the tea towel off his head.

'I didn't mean anything, Allie!' I reply, a cold feeling of dread clawing its way up from my belly. 'It was just a . . . just a figure of speech. I didn't . . . I didn't . . .'

Stop.

Just *stop.*

My shoulders slump. I take a long, deep, ragged breath and look into Allie's eyes.

'I'm sick,' I say, heart hammering.

'What?'

I try to clear my throat. 'I'm sick, Alison. There's something wrong with me, and . . .'

Say it.
Say it and have done.

'. . . it's going to kill me.' I clench my jaw for a second. 'I'm going to die.'

Allie's response is just what you'd expect. Her legs go out from under her and she falls back into the chair.

'What is it, son?' I hear Freddie say in a soft voice.

I look at him. 'It's a brain tumour. Something called a cerebrodon-dreglioma – if you can believe that.'

From the back of the assembled residents, a man's voice pipes up. 'I had one of those!'

'Did you, Kenneth Not Ken?' Freddie responds.

'Yep. They whipped that bugger out, though. Still got the scar.' He pokes himself just above the left temple.

All eyes return to me.

Great. Now I have to explain myself. Just what I wanted.

'Mine isn't like that,' I tell them. 'Mine's way down deep in the centre of my brain. It can't be cut out, radiation wouldn't touch it and chemo would just make me worse. It's a very rare version of this type of tumour, named after some Eastern European doctor whose surname I've never been able to pronounce.' I force myself to look back down at Allie. 'It'll keep growing, until one day soon it gets too big and . . . shuts me down.' There are tears in both of our eyes now. 'I'm so sorry, Allie.'

'Why . . . why didn't you *tell me*, Nathan?' There's sympathy in her voice, no doubting that. But there's something else there, too.

The thing I knew would be there, but would have loved to have been wrong about. There's *anger*. It's a small thing at the moment. But it'll grow. Just like this damn tumour, it'll grow until it gets too big and shuts me down.

I shake my head. 'I don't know . . . I guess I was just afraid that if you knew the truth, you wouldn't want to see me any more, and I really didn't want that.'

'So instead you *lied* to me?' She looks hurt. She has every right to.

'I'm sorry,' I repeat, lost for anything more constructive to say.

The faces on the crowd of pensioners around me all show hastily arranged sympathy. I have to look away from all of them and down at the rotting, shagpile carpet.

'When were you diagnosed?'

I can't breathe. 'Over five months ago.'

'Oh Christ.' Allie's hand goes to her mouth in shock. She seems to draw in on herself.

Freddie and the rest of the gang simply don't know where to put themselves. Mere moments ago they were celebrating the fact that they might have a chance to save their care home from annihilation, and now they find out the bloke giving them the money is about to drop dead. These people are quite frail and I don't know if they can handle that amount of whiplash.

'So the headaches . . .' Allie says, trailing off.

'Yeah. The tumour's fault,' I tell her.

Her eyes widen. 'That's what that business at the hospital was about after you had that reaction to the herbs!'

I nod. I guess it's nice to get it all out in the open. 'I was taking the stupid things in the first place due to what Herman was doing to my head.'

'*Herman?*'

How embarrassing. I really should learn to think about what I say before I blurt it out. 'I, er, I've given the tumour a name. It's really hard to keep saying cerebrodondreglioma all the time.'

Allie looks aghast. 'And you thought it would be a better idea to name it after your grumpy potato? A bloody *children's character*?'

Well, when you put it like that, it sounds *silly*.

'Look, Allie, I am so, so sorry for lying to you like this.'

She stands up.

Here we go. That anger is starting to assert itself a little bit more now. '*Why*, Nathan? Why did you have to lie to me all this time? I thought we had . . . had something.'

'We do!' *Did*, you moron. It's now definitely *did*. 'I couldn't say anything because I couldn't bear to lose you!'

'So you thought keeping me in the dark about an illness that's going to kill you was a better idea?' She throws her hands up. 'Again, *why*, Nathan?'

'Because . . . because . . .'

'Because he's in love with you, my dear,' Deidre says from beside me. I feel her comforting hand on my arm. 'Isn't that right, Nathan?'

I can't nod or say anything, but I guess the tear rolling down my cheek says everything I need to.

Allie can't respond, either. Getting told your new boyfriend is both dying and in love with you in the space of two minutes is not something that's easy to process. Not without extensive amounts of time and hard spirits anyway.

'Perhaps the two of you would like to be alone?' Freddie says, breaking the awkward silence. He puts an arm around Allie's shoulder. 'I'm sure there's a way you two can get through this.'

Nice try, Freddie. But take a look in her eyes, will you? She's already running away in her head. It's only a matter of time until her body catches up.

'I . . . I have to go,' Allie says. 'I need time to . . . I . . .' She can't even look at me.

The girl who I would very much have liked to grow old with – if I'd been given half a chance – backs away from me, her grandfather and the rest of the residents and hurries towards the double doors.

I watch her go with bone-chilling acceptance.

'I'm sorry, my boy,' Freddie says. 'If I'd have known our little show would bring all of this up, I would have postponed.'

'No need to apologise, Freddie,' I tell him. 'Shakespeare liked to mix comedy with tragedy, didn't he?' I wipe the tears out of my eyes. 'I think I'd better see if I can catch up with her. Don't worry about the money. You'll get it as soon as I can send it over to you.'

Freddie nods. 'Go get her, my lad.'

I give him a look of such gross self-pity it makes my face ache. 'I don't think there's any way of getting her now, Freddie.'

Deidre squeezes my arm. 'Don't give up, Nathan. Not yet.'

'Why not?'

'Because you didn't see the way she was looking at you when you offered to help us. Now *go*.'

I catch up to Allie just as she's climbing into her car.

'Alison! Please! I need to talk to you.'

She looks at me as I come trotting up the road towards her. 'Nathan . . . I can't . . . can't talk right now. I just need to go home and . . .'

'Drink a lot?'

She smiles in spite of herself. 'Probably.' She gives me a disbelieving look. 'Was Deidre right?'

'Yes. Absolutely. I'm in love with you and it's completely unfair of me.'

She shakes her head. 'It's not unfair! It's just that . . . I can't . . .'

I smile softly at her. 'It's *okay*. Really, it is. You don't need to say it. Just go. I'll be fine.'

She lets out a gasp. 'I'm sorry, Nathan, I just . . .'

'Go.'

She tries to say something else, but stops herself. What the hell else is there really *left* to say?

Allie closes her car door, fires up the engine, gives me one last look and drives hastily away from the kerb, not looking back as she does so. This leaves me staring down the road, watching her go, the first sensations of a headache forming deep in the darkest depths of my brain.

Show's over, folks – well and truly, this time. Nothing to see here.

HAVE A LITTLE FAITH

23 SEPTEMBER

Amplifier on.
> Microphone on.
> Guitar tuned.
> Plectrum in hand.

And . . . *play.*

I begin a simple three-chord harmony into the emptiness of my studio. It's an upbeat little number that came to me while I was in the shower this morning.

As I play, I also sing a little song.

'*Oh, Allie, I'm so sorry . . . I should have been more honest with you, by golly.*'

'*Oh, Allie, I'm a dipshit . . . I don't blame you for leaving my life, the second you heard it.*'

'*Oh, Allie, I hate this tumour . . . It's ruined my life good and proper, that's no rumour.*'

'Oh, Allie, but without it . . . I'd never have got to be with you, no doubt about it.'

'Oh, Allie, I'm so confused . . . I need some answers about all this, to lift my mood.'

'Oh, Allie, I'd like to keep singing . . . but I have to go now, as I can hear the doorbell ringing.'

I stop playing my strange little ditty and put the guitar to one side. For a moment, I find it hard to get off the stool. The unfairness of everything that's happened to me has temporarily rendered me immobile.

Allie knowing about the tumour is absolutely the right thing – and I should have told her a long time ago – but *my good fucking God* it still *hurts* that I've probably lost her. I've had to give up the best thing in my life because of the *worst* thing in my life, and I resent that with every fibre of my being.

I hear the muffled sound of the doorbell ringing again from beyond the studio, sigh deeply and go to answer it.

I open the front door to find my mother standing there with a rather perturbed look on her face. 'Hello, son. I got your text.' She looks at me incredulously. 'You want to go to *church*?'

I've always had a problem with God – mainly because he probably doesn't exist, and nothing that non-existent should cause so much trouble on such a regular basis.

These days, I'm fully prepared to be proved wrong about this, of course. Nothing would give me greater pleasure than the safe and secure knowledge that there is a God and, by extension, an afterlife.

Also, if God does exist, I would ask the bastard to explain to me how it's possible for a man so permanently close to death to fall head over heels in love.

Surely this is a design flaw that he needs to address as quickly as possible. It's like embarking on an extensive road trip when your head gasket's about to blow. There should be some kind of mechanism in place to stop that kind of thing happening.

I kind of figured it might be a good idea to go and have a word with him . . . if he's actually up there, of course.

'And you really want me to come to this church with you?' Mum says doubtfully, as she sips her coffee.

'Yes.'

'I'm not sure it would be a very good idea, Nathan.'

'Why not?'

Mum looks uncomfortable. 'Religion has always been something I've tried to steer you away from. My mother was a wonderful woman in some ways, but her religion sometimes made her intolerant of others. It wasn't pleasant to be around.'

'She was Catholic, wasn't she?'

'Yes. A very *old-school* Catholic. If you weren't feeling guilty about something, then you weren't trying hard enough.'

'Well, this'll be different. It's a newer church than that. Came over from America a few years ago.'

Mum puts down the coffee mug and fixes me with a knowing stare. 'You've never once considered religion in your life, Nathan. Not even after your diagnosis. What's changed now? Why this sudden need to—' Realisation dawns on her face. 'Oh. This is because of Alison, isn't it?'

'No!' I look away from her. 'Yes . . . probably . . . I don't know.'

It's been three weeks since Allie found out about my illness, and she hasn't been in contact since. I have to admit that for a couple of days I held on to the hope that my phone might ring, but that didn't last much past forty-eight hours. I knew damn well that telling her the truth would end the relationship, and that's exactly what happened.

I did hear from Freddie at Helmore, though. Apparently, the plan to stymie Lord Pinchyface is already going very well indeed and the future of the home is looking far more secure, thanks to my contribution. The residents are going to name a new stairlift after me, to show their gratitude. This seems completely appropriate, for some reason.

Freddie also asked me if I'd spoken to his granddaughter. It hurt me down to my core to admit that I hadn't.

I'm not sure if I'd have picked up the call even if Allie had rung, though. Far better for her to move on and find someone else. Any other decision would be stupid, and Allie has never struck me as the stupid type. Splitting up was definitely the right thing to do.

So, here I am, single again. And still sporting a killer brain tumour.

'How did you find out about this church?' Mum asks, breaking me out of this morose train of thought.

'When I got diagnosed, they handed me a leaflet about the church at the hospital,' I tell her. 'I looked them up online the other day. It's one of those new types of evangelical church. They're happy for anyone to come along, and they seem to do some interesting sermons about dealing with the kind of . . . problem I've got. I thought it'd be worth checking out, and I guess I'd like a little company when I go.'

'Those kinds of churches are a bit *strange*, Nathan.'

'I had a look at their website. It all seems quite normal. No weirder than the Church of England stuff I've seen in the past.'

'Hmmm.'

'Look, if nothing else, it won't be *boring*. These evangelical churches are less about the pews, the quiet praying and the smell of old cloth and more about the tambourines and raucous singing. It could be quite good fun – musically speaking, if nothing else.'

'All right, son,' she says with a sigh. 'But don't expect me to join in with any *singing*. Your father always said I have a voice that could strip paint at forty paces. I don't want to be arrested for criminal damage.'

What I'm not telling my mother is that I've planned this trip for her benefit as much as I have for mine. The sermon we're going to see is by the fabulously named Carmichael Renfro and is all about how to deal with serious illness – up to and including the terminal kind.

Mum hasn't come to terms with what's happening to me yet. I know that because she *still* hasn't looked through the will I sent her.

She obviously thinks there's hope I might survive all of this, and there's nothing I've been able to do to convince her otherwise thus far. Maybe she might hear something in Carmichael Renfro's sermon that could do the job for me . . .

***

'Well, that's not a church,' I remark as we pull up into the car park the next day.

'I don't see any steeples,' Mum points out as she switches her car engine off. 'And there's a distinct lack of stained-glass windows.'

'It looks like an industrial warehouse.'

'That's because it's an industrial warehouse, Nathan.'

I give my mother a look and climb out of the car.

She's not wrong, though, is she?

This doesn't so much look like a place of worship. It looks like somewhere you'd come to pick out your new window fittings. The building is a single-storey brick and metal box, stretching off to the left and right for a good hundred feet in both directions. I would double-check the address on the satnav were it not for the fact that nailed to the wall next to the glass entrance is a sign saying, 'Heavenly Outlook Evangelical Church – Come One, Come All!'

'Well, it looks warmer than St Peters down the road,' Mum remarks. 'And it probably won't smell funny.'

'Here's hoping,' I reply, and wander across the car park, noting that a steady stream of people is making its way into the building as I do so. Today's service looks to be quite popular. I glance at my watch. It's coming up to 11 a.m. I was always under the impression that religious observance on a Sunday had to happen at stupid o'clock in the morning, and yet here we are. Perhaps the evangelicals believe that part of praising Jesus is having a nice lie-in beforehand. This is something I could definitely get behind.

Mum and I join the steady trickle of bodies piling into the church/ ex-branch of B&Q. The congregants all look like perfectly normal human beings to me. Not a loony among them. I don't quite know what I was expecting, but when I hear the word 'evangelical' I tend to picture socially maladjusted folk who enjoy corduroy trousers, leather sandals with socks, acrylic sweaters and a permanent look of good-natured insanity.

We go through two sets of double doors and into a massive open auditorium – one that continues the industrial theme with exposed steel girders and white ceiling panels above my head, interspersed with large skylights that let in the sunlight, bathing the whole place in a pleasant glow. The walls and floor are both spartan white. The place looks as clean as several whistles. There's not a statue or picture of Jesus anywhere to be seen – but there is a large stage constructed at one end of the hall, with rows of comfortable-looking chairs laid out in front of it, towards which all of the people are heading. The stage is bare except for a few microphone stands – though there are speakers on both sides.

'I suppose we should go and sit down,' I say to Mum.

'All right. At the back, please.'

I nod. At the back sounds like a sensible decision to me.

As we take our seats, a few of the people say hello to us in a very friendly manner. The atmosphere here feels homely and pleasant, despite the size and austerity of the building. As the seats fill up, I feel a small smile creep across my face. There's a real sense of *belonging* here. It pretty much radiates off these people in waves.

When everyone seems seated and ready to go, a hush descends over the hall. Then out on to the stage comes . . . a rock band.

I was expecting someone in corduroy trousers, but no, instead we have a band composed of three people – a lead guitarist, a bassist and a singer. There's no drum kit, which would have given the game away before I'd sat down, but I can see a fourth person crouched down off to one side of the stage with a laptop.

The singer – a woman in her mid-thirties – grabs a microphone off the central stand and waves at us. 'Good morning!' she says into the mic in an excited voice.

'Good morning!' the vast majority of the crowd repeat in equally happy tones.

'Are we all here to praise the good Lord and his son Jesus Christ?'

'Yes!' the exultant cry goes up. Not from me and Mum, I hasten to add – we're sat like a couple of silent plums, awaiting developments.

'Then get up out of your seats and sing with us! Praise the Lord!'

The audience members pretty much all stand at once. It's like the general has just walked in on his troops.

The two guitarists start to play. While they are a little amateurish to my professional ear, they can carry a tune well enough for this crowd, it appears. It's not a song I'm familiar with, but the congregation know it extremely well, singing along with the woman onstage like their lives depend on it.

As a musician, it's a little hard for me not to get caught up in the moment. I love a good sing-along as much as the next person, so while I don't get up and start dancing, I do stamp my feet and bob my head back and forth in time to the music.

Mum sits there with her hands held firmly in her lap and a suspicious look on her face.

The song itself is all about how great Jesus is. This should come as no surprise to anyone. The lyrics are universally about how wonderful it is to love Jesus and how wonderful it is that he loves you right back.

The world is full of people who love Jesus, you understand – and all the joy in the world quite obviously stems from this.

It's not going to win any awards any time soon, but it's catchy as fuck – and is quite frankly the sort of thing I'd write, only I'd focus on talking fruit instead of our Lord and saviour.

When the song ends and the rapturous applause dies down, the singer steps forward to address the crowd. 'Hello, everyone. What a wonderful way to start today's service that was. For the newcomers amongst us, my name is Lindsay and I am the church's community outreach officer.'

Community outreach officer sounds like a job at the local council, rather than a member of a church, but we'll let it slide, as she has a pretty good singing voice.

'I'd like to welcome up onstage someone I know you've all been looking forward to hearing speak. To give our sermon for the day, please welcome – all the way from the Heavenly Outlook central church in Wisconsin, USA – Elder Carmichael Renfro!'

The thunderous applause that follows would be enough to wake up God if he were having a quick mid-morning nap. On to the stage comes the most tanned and luxurious human being I have ever seen in my life. Carmichael Renfro is dressed in a sharp light-grey suit and has the kind of quaffed hair that most daytime TV game show hosts can only dream about. He is so tanned that there's every chance he's been dipped in gravy browning. He also has a set of teeth so bright that I'm considering putting on my sunglasses, even here in the back row.

'Praise Jesus! Praise Jesus!' Carmichael screams into the microphone in a thick American accent.

'Praise Jesus!' the crowd cries back at him.

'Oh Jesus,' my mother says in a low voice, shrinking into her chair.

'How are you fine folk today?' Renfro asks his adoring crowd – as if he didn't know. The audience cheers and jumps up and down a bit, indicating that they are doing quite all right actually, thank you very much.

'That's good . . . that's so, so *good*,' Renfro says in a voice you could make expensive ladies' gloves out of. 'I'm so pleased to be here in the UK, touring our wonderful ministries. We're a young church, but we are *growing* – praise the Lord!'

'Praise him!' several of the crowd members crow right back at Carmichael Renfro. There seems to be some kind of competition going on to see who can praise Jesus the most. So far, there's a fat bloke in a red T-shirt down at the front who appears to be in the lead, though the skinny woman in her fifties parked about three rows in front of Mum and me is giving him a run for his money.

'Today, my good, good people, I want to talk to you about *sickness*,' Renfro says. 'I want to talk to you about sickness and how the ministrations and love of our good Lord can help you cope with it, no matter how bad it is – how the love of Jesus Christ can help you change the things you cannot accept and accept the things you cannot change.'

Sounds good to me. I hope Mum is paying attention. Acceptance is what I'm after from her, and hopefully this will help her find it. Even if she doesn't have the kind of faith Renfro and his flock possess, I'm hoping that the message he's preaching will at least hit home with her.

Carmichael Renfro then launches into what can only be described as the most animated religious sermon I've ever witnessed. I vaguely remember tired, old men in cassocks from my childhood delivering sonorous and dull speeches from ornate pulpits at Christmas. This is nothing like that.

Renfro is a whirling dervish, a conflagration of pinwheeling arms and convulsive legs. He runs across the stage like Sebastian Coe. He twirls and whirls like a gymnast on amphetamines. He roars at the crowd like Brian Blessed on a mountain. It's quite something to behold.

And what he says about sickness speaks to me. Oh my, yes, it speaks to me *good* and *proper*. This is largely because Renfro does not simply quote from Bible passages. If he were up there saying things like, 'God viewest thou suffering and shall taketh thee up into heaven once thou hast carked it, where thou shalt sit beside his mighty graciousness, eating of the plums and other fruits,' I would have switched off immediately. But he's not doing that. Instead, Renfro is talking like a normal human being, even though he's doing it at a decibel level outlawed by most aviation authorities.

'I know that your pain is *bad*,' he says, exuding passion, 'and that the sickness never seems to *end*. I know you feel like there is no *hope*, that nobody is there for you. You feel left behind, you feel out of place, you feel closed in, you feel *alone*!'

Yes, Carmichael – all of those things and more!

'But, my friends, believe me, trust me, be in no doubt when I say that you are *not* alone. That you are *not* left behind. That the suffering and pain you endure *will* come to an end.' Renfro's voice now drops. 'Because, my friends, our Lord is with you. With you for all your days, both good and bad. He sees your pain and suffers it with you. He knows what it's like to be a person alone and without hope. And let me tell you, my friends, that he will see an end to your pain, through his grace and love. He will take away that suffering! He will remove that sense of hopelessness! He will make you feel whole again! You will have peace and you will have rest! Praise Jesus!'

'Praise Jesus!'

Compelling stuff, isn't it? Carmichael Renfro sounds utterly convincing. Chances are you're perfectly healthy and still like the sound of what he's saying.

Now put yourself in my shoes.

I am, and always have been, a man without faith, but here I am, standing on a precipice, and Renfro's words sound pretty *marvellous* to me.

If I can just make that leap and accept God into my heart, then all of this worry, all of this suffering will be far, far easier to deal with. I will not go into that dark night alone and scared!

I've completely forgotten about Mum by this stage, to be honest. Hell, I've even forgotten about Allie as well. This guy has caught my full attention in a way I never expected. I came here hoping to break Mum out of her cycle of denial and get some answers about why I had to fall in love at the worst possible time, but instead I'm apparently cycling my way fast towards a religious conversion . . .

I'm sat forward in my chair now, hanging on Renfro's every word. I want to believe, *damn it*, and this man is *making me*.

The look of cynical boredom on my mother's face suggests she won't be leaving here today any more convinced of my impending demise, but at the rate I'm going, I'll be leaving convinced that it's a demise that might not be as permanent as I'd feared, if God has anything to do with it.

The flamboyant American's sermon comes to a close after about half an hour, but that is not the end of today's performance – not by a long shot.

'If you are in pain, my friends, if you feel suffering as our Lord did, then come to me now, come to me and I will help you! By the grace of our Lord, Jesus Christ, I will cast that pain from you in this place!'

Two people get to their feet. One does it quite slowly and looks in a dreadful amount of pain as he does so.

'Come up, sister! Come up, my brother!' Renfro bids them.

The two churchgoers – a gaunt middle-aged woman and an old boy with obvious arthritis in his arms and legs – go up on to the stage. Renfro asks the woman her name, which is Valerie, asks her if she is a member of the church, which she is, and then asks her what her ailment is. She suffers from inflammatory bowel disease, which has obviously taken a heavy toll on her, from the looks of things. Quite what the good Lord can do about it I am keen to discover.

Renfro places a hand on the woman's belly and starts to pray. As he does, the crowd all start to clap, cheer and wave exultantly. After a few moments, Renfro starts to scream at the top of his voice. 'Begone, pain! Begone, foul illness, from this woman's body! In the name of Jesus Christ, I demand you give this woman surcease!' And with that, he jumps away from her like she's just given him an electric shock.

Valerie then turns and beams at the crowd. I've never seen someone look so *happy*. She then bounds back to her chair like a springing gazelle. It's an *amazing* transformation.

Then it's the turn of the old boy, who just about manages to walk forward to greet Renfro, his every movement accompanied by a wince on his face.

Renfro lays one hand on his shoulder. 'You are in great pain, aren't you, my friend?'

'Yes, Carmichael.'

'What ails you?'

'My arthritis, Carmichael. I'm riddled with it.'

'And what is your name?'

'Alistair, Carmichael.'

'And are you a member of our wonderful church?'

'I am, Carmichael.'

Renfro places his hands on the old man's shoulders. 'Then let us cast this pain from your body, Alistair! Let us raise the roof of this house to the Lord so that he might answer your prayers and give you peace!'

For a second time, Renfro prays, and now the audience is even more animated, even more excited. They cry and shout, they scream and stamp their feet. They pray hard and stand on their seats.

And the man they are watching is clearly building up to something big. He is now shaking on the spot, hands still clamped on poor old Alistair's shoulders. The prayers fly from his mouth, accompanied by a fair amount of spittle. I don't know if Alistair's arthritis is going to be cured, but he's certainly going home plastered in another man's phlegm.

Renfro climaxes with his entreaty to God to end this man's suffering. When he does his electric shock thing this time, though, something odd happens. Alistair also flies backwards, as if some force has erupted between the two men. For a moment it looks like the old boy is going to lose his footing and collapse, which will surely do his arthritic limbs no good whatsoever, but instead of falling, he sticks one leg out as fast as you please and steadies himself on the stage like a ninja after a particularly cool backflip.

'How do you feel, Alistair?!' Renfro shouts at the man, a broad grin on his face.

Alistair does a little jig. A man who could barely walk a couple of minutes ago does a little jig right there on the stage. 'I feel wonderful!' he exults.

The crowd goes fucking bonkers.

Even I start applauding.

The results are quite *incredible.*

Alistair pretty much cartwheels back to his seat, with people clapping him on the back and shaking his hand as he goes.

The praising now goes on for what feels like a fortnight, until Renfro eventually calms the herd with a few gentle hand gestures. 'Now, my friends, is there anyone else who needs my ministrations? Anyone else who needs their pain to be taken away?'

I feel myself rise from my seat, almost involuntarily.

'Nathan?! What are you doing?!' Mum exclaims from beside me, but I ignore her.

There's a hush from the crowd as I get to my feet. Renfro gives me a knowing look and bids me to come onstage with him. 'Come up, my friend. Come up and receive the grace of our Lord.'

What have I got to lose, eh? I've already lost my future and my girlfriend. There's not much more that can be taken away from me, is there?

I walk up on to the stage, several hundred eyes following me as I do so.

Renfro holds out a hand for me to shake. 'Hello, my friend, and welcome. What is your name?'

'I'm Nathan,' I reply.

'Are you a member of our church?'

'Er, no. Not at the moment.'

This earns me an indulgent and somewhat speculative smile. 'Then what brings you here today, Nathan? Are you sick? Do you suffer with an illness?'

I swallow hard. 'Yes.'

'What ails you, my friend? What test has the Lord sent your way?'

I look out into the crowd. I'm a little reluctant to be so open in front of a bunch of strangers. 'I have a brain tumour. A bad one.'

Renfro nods solemnly. 'A mighty test for any man, Nathan. Has it left you feeling scared and out in the cold? In need of the good Lord's warmth?'

'I . . . I suppose?'

He places a hand on my head. It's quite sweaty. 'Then let me fill you with that warmth! Let me fill you up!'

In no other circumstance would I allow a sweaty American man with a spray tan to place a hand on my head and tell me he's about to fill me up with something.

Renfro begins to pray. This time he starts off lower and deeper than ever before. Similarly, the crowd stays hushed to begin with, echoing the tone and timbre of his chanting with their own low prayers.

Then the build begins. The prayers become louder. Renfro's hand takes a firmer grip on my head and starts to shake.

I feel absolutely nothing, other than a mild headache coming on thanks to having my bonce squeezed like an overripe melon.

Now I'm getting the Renfro shower treatment as his praying starts to get louder and louder, heading towards its theatrical crescendo. The crowd is frantically arm-waving and praising Jesus like their lives depend on it.

I am absurdly reminded in that instant of the moment in *Indiana Jones and the Temple of Doom* when the bloke in the big hat rips out the boy's heart and shows it to his followers.

One of my hands involuntarily covers my chest. I don't know if Renfro has the capacity to reach a hand into my ribcage and pull out my ticker, but I'm taking no chances.

And then Carmichael Renfro arrives at his destination, eyes wide and goggling. He jumps away from me as if hit by that divine electric spark once again.

I feel about as electrified as a hand whisk.

'Praise Jesus!' exclaims the crowd, looking forward to seeing me bounce around the stage, no doubt.

Unfortunately, I can't oblige them, as I feel no different. In fact, the headache is just getting worse thanks to a combination of harsh lighting and Renfro's melon-squeezing grip.

Speaking of whom, the religious leader is looking at me with curiosity, and not a little sadness.

'Friends, friends! Please! If you could all calm yourselves for a moment.' They do so, though it takes a good half minute. 'It seems our new friend Nathan's illness truly is a strong test. I must say to you now that my ministrations here today have failed him.'

A collective sigh of disappointment goes up from the crowd. I have to say I'm feeling just a tad disappointed, too. I wanted to leap off the stage like the old boy just did, but it appears I may be a tougher nut to crack.

'It's my fault, my friends,' Renfro says, head bowed. 'I have failed our friend Nathan.' Cue lots of shaking of heads. 'Yes, yes, my friends. The Lord has not seen fit to grant me the strength to cure him today.' He clenches his fist and looks up. 'But God's love is strong, my friends!'

'Yes!'

'God's love is great!'

'Yes!'

'God's love will not desert Nathan! It will lift him up! It will see him whole again!'

'Yes! Yes! Yes!'

Renfro claps that familiar, comforting hand on my shoulder. 'Nathan, you must join our church, for it is the only way for you to receive God's grace and be fully healed.'

'Really?' I respond, eyes narrowing slightly.

'Yes. And your healing can only come if you surrender to God's grace . . . and make your contribution.'

'What?' My eyes narrow even *further*.

'Contribute, Nathan! For does not the Bible say in Proverbs 3:9 that you should "Honour the Lord with your wealth and with the first fruits of all your produce; then your barns will be filled with plenty, and your vats will be bursting with wine"?'

'I don't know, does it?'

'Yes, of course!' He squeezes my shoulder gently. '*Give*, Nathan. Give and it will be given to *you*.' He pokes me with a finger right where my heart is. He's not yanking it out and shouting '*kali maa! kali maa!*' while he does it, but I get the distinct feeling that he's after something else – my bloody wallet.

My eyes are now so narrow I can barely see out of them. 'So let me get this straight. You can't cure me today, like you did the other two, because I'm not a full member of the church. And to become a full member and get cured, I have to give you money?'

Carmichael Renfro actually contrives to look sincere. 'Yes indeed, Nathan! God's love, grace and healing are *so close!*'

'And how much money will I need to give you to receive God's love, grace and healing?'

He attempts to look spiritual. 'Who can say, Nathan? God's will is not ours to define!'

My expression now resembles that of somebody who has just sucked on a large, fresh lemon. 'Take a stab at it.'

Renfro appears to think for a moment. 'Oh, if I were to be presumptuous,' he says, 'I'd say a tithe of ten per cent of your earnings over the past three years would be a good start. For did Abram not give a tithe to our good Lord, as it is written in Genesis 14:20?'

'Are you asking me or telling me?' I reply, keeping a lid on my emotions for the time being.

'I'm telling you, Nathan.' Renfro squeezes my shoulder once again. 'The good *Lord* is telling you, Nathan! Praise Jesus!'

I do a quick bit of mental calculation. Ten per cent of my annual earnings for the past three years is about forty grand.

Forty fucking *grand* to have a walking suntan squeeze my head while spitting on me.

Realisation instantly dawns.

I've been taken for a right fool here, haven't I? I got hooked by Renfro's clever sermon because of my fragile state of mind and found myself on the receiving end of a good, old-fashioned religious con.

I'm wasting my time here.

Time I just *don't* have. Time I should be spending doing something *constructive*.

'Nathan?' Renfro says to me. 'You look lost in thought. Is the good Lord working on you? Are you ready to join us?'

I turn calmly and look at Renfro with a beaming smile on my face that doesn't reach my eyes.

'Yes! Yes, my friend! I can see his grace filling you even as I speak!' Carmichael crows.

I look at Renfro's hand, still squeezing my shoulder. 'The only thing filling me, Carmichael, is the overwhelming desire to kick you up the backside.'

Renfro's face falls. 'I'm sorry?'

'You heard. Please let go of me, or I will insert my foot into your bottom with extreme prejudice.'

'My *bottom*?' His look of complete confusion warms my soul.

'Yes, Carmichael. That's right. *My* foot' – I point down at the extremity in question and give it a waggle – 'will be inserted into *your* bottom' – I then point at Renfro's ample posterior and continue – 'in a manner that will have you praying for a hot bath and powerful painkillers faster than you can scream "Jesus saves".'

'Jesus saves!' I hear a lone voice cry from somewhere in the audience. Apparently, somebody isn't paying as much attention to the proceedings as they probably should.

Carmichael Renfro *is* paying attention however, given that I can see one hand snake protectively around to his backside.

The other hand flies off my shoulder at the same time, proving that the message has finally gotten through. Praise the lord.

Renfro then gives me a dark look. 'You must have the *devil* in you, Nathan, to threaten such a horrible act to someone who wants to heal you.'

'Possibly,' I reply with a smile. 'But the devil has all the best tunes, so I'm fine with that if you are.'

Carmichael doesn't have a response to this. Which is probably a first for him.

I lightly push the suited idiot out of my way, jumping off the stage to a rising chorus of angry comments and harsh looks from a crowd that have finally realised I'm probably the bad guy here. I am more than happy to play the part for them, given that I've just dodged a very large and manipulative bullet.

'Come to your senses, my son?' Mum says to me as I reach the back row.

'Yes. And I'm sorry we ever came here. Let's beat a hasty retreat, shall we?'

I can feel the eyes of the congregation boring their way into my back as Mum and I hurry out of the auditorium. As we reach the exit doors, I turn and give them all a large and thrusting middle finger. It's an extremely immature and childish thing to do, but it also feels *entirely* appropriate.

Outside, the righteous indignation dribbles out of my body as soon as I've walked back to Mum's car.

It's quite obvious that the church has no answers for me and never did.

'Are you okay, son?' Mum asks me as she opens her car door.

'Not really, no!' I burst out with an anger I didn't know was there until this moment. 'I'm going to get killed by a brain tumour and nobody can help me!'

'Nathan! You're not going to get killed by your tumour!' my mother replies adamantly. 'You're sick, but it doesn't mean that you're going to die!'

I put my head in my hands for a moment, take a few deep breaths and then look back up at her. 'Yes, I am, Mum. *Yes, I am.*' I point back at the stupid church. 'Why do you think we're *here*? I brought you here to listen to a sermon about dealing with serious illness so that you'd finally come to terms with what's happening to me . . . and all I do is nearly fall for a bloody con because I'm so terrified that I'm going to die having lived a worthless life and that I have no time left to make amends for it!' I lean forward against the car, deflated. 'I have *no* time left. It could happen any time. I could just . . . *go.*'

'No, Nathan. I *refuse* to believe that.'

I give her a pleading look. 'Please, Mum. I *need* you to believe it. I need you to believe *me*. Because if you don't . . . and I die . . . you won't be . . . you won't be *prepared.*'

And there's the rub.

Mum *has* to accept that I could die any time, otherwise it'll just be so much *worse* for her when it inevitably happens. I know it and, by the looks of her changing expression, she's finally starting to accept it, too. Maybe this trip wasn't such a waste of time, after all.

She looks skywards for a moment, an agony of indecision on her face.

This is what it looks like when someone you love is coming to terms with something awful. It's the most terrible thing I think I've ever had to witness.

'Oh, Nathan!' she eventually cries, and hurries around the car to grab me in a firm embrace. 'It's so, so unfair!'

'Yeah, it is,' I agree, voice choked with emotion.

We stand there for a few minutes – a mother coming to terms with a horrible truth and a son wishing it were all a lie – until the congregation starts to pile out of the church.

'I think . . . I think we'd better get out of here before they try to stone us to death,' I say, reluctantly breaking the embrace.

My mother's eyes are full of tears, but she manages a small smile. 'Okay, son.' She pulls me close to her again. 'I love you, Nathan. I love you so much.'

'I love you, too,' I reply, feeling a bit better about everything thanks to that parental hug.

Who needs the love of a god when you have the love of a mother, eh?

In the car on the way home, I conclude to myself that there is definitely no such thing as God.

If he were real, I probably wouldn't have a tumour in my head, Justin Bieber wouldn't have a career and Allie wouldn't have left me.

If God did exist, then he'd surely want to cut me some slack right about now. After all, I've saved a load of donkeys and a care home, haven't I?

Yeah, I'm sure that if God were knocking around up there somewhere, he'd want to *reward* me. He'd do something *nice* for me.

For instance, when we turn into my driveway in a minute, Allie would be standing there waiting for me, having had a change of heart.

But that's just *not* going to happen, is it? Because there is no God.

I scowl and make a small involuntary noise of disgust.

'You okay?' Mum asks.

'Yeah, I just need a couple of painkillers, that's all. All that religion has given me a headache.'

'That's what tends to happen if you hang around it long enough,' Mum replies sagely.

I smile grimly and stare out of the window, pondering on Carmichael Renfro and his merry band of followers. I wish I could share in their happy delusion, but I just don't think my heart, my head or my bank balance could countenance it.

When Mum turns into my driveway a few minutes later, I nearly suffer a coronary, because Allie is standing at the far end of it, waiting for me.

Er . . . praise Jesus?

'What . . . what are you doing here?' I ask her as I walk over, having climbed unsteadily out of the car.

Mum scuttles past us both. 'I think I'll pop inside and make a cup of tea,' she says, pulling out her key. 'Hello, Alison.'

'Hi, Tamsin,' Allie replies, giving her a shaky smile.

'Why are you here?' I repeat, still not able to believe what I'm seeing – and also comprehensively worried that God does indeed exist and has been watching me masturbate all these years.

'I, er . . . I just wanted to come and see you,' she replies in a small voice. 'Something's happened and I wanted to tell you. I wanted to see you.'

'What's happened?'

'My grandfather . . . my grandfather . . .' She's struggling to get her words out.

I step forward. 'What about him?'

Allie starts to cry softly. 'He died, Nathan. He died yesterday.'

And with that, she's in my arms.

I have no idea whether it's a good thing or not, but she's there, and God knows I have no intention of letting her go for as long as it's within my power to hold on.

NO TIME

27 September

Look at her.

Just look at her, will you?

I mean, you should probably ignore the thin line of spittle coming from her mouth that's gently soaking the pillow, and that crust around her eyes looks like it'll need a good going at with a warm flannel, but other than that, isn't she just *perfect*?

She's everything Sienna *wasn't*.

I'll get up and make her a cup of tea in a moment, but I'll let her lie in a while longer, I think.

Today promises to be difficult for Allie. Burying someone you love usually is.

Freddie died of a massive and sudden heart attack during the night. Bernard found him when he went to see why his friend was late for breakfast. He was quite amazed that the old man had gone in such a quiet manner. 'You'd have expected some kind of speech, at least,' Bernard had told Allie. 'Something florid and obtuse about travelling into the great beyond.'

Allie got the call from her mother the morning of his death. Twenty-four hours later she was standing on my driveway.

'You were the first person I thought of,' she told me as we sat in my kitchen together after my mother had left. 'After my family. I just . . . wanted to see you. To let you know he was gone.'

'He was a unique person, Allie,' I replied, not yet willing to think about why I'd be the person she'd want to see after such news. 'I only met him once, but I can see why you loved him so much.'

'He was the one that got me into the theatre,' she said. 'He used to take me to see so many shows when I was a child. I always knew I wanted to be on the stage, right from then. To follow in his footsteps.'

'Ah . . . so without him there'd be no Libby the Happy Lemon,' I said, trying to lighten the mood a little.

Allie gave me a look. 'She's all *your* fault, mister.'

'Well, regardless, I wouldn't have met you if he hadn't made you interested in the theatre, so that's something I definitely have to thank him for.' I closed a hand over hers. 'Are you sure you want to be here, Allie? With me? After what I told you, and now with Freddie's death . . . I'm probably going the same way as him at some—'

Allie leant forward and placed a finger over my mouth. 'Enough. Enough talk about death,' she said, and shifted closer to me, leaning forward to kiss me with a ferocity that quite took my breath away. 'Take me upstairs and show me life instead.'

And upstairs is pretty much where we've been ever since. We've barely left my bedroom.

My bedroom is a magic place when Allie is with me. In there, you forget about everything that hurts.

But now we have to leave it, as today is the day Allie has to bury her grandfather – and I have a cup of tea to make.

As I potter around the kitchen, I start to consider my own feelings about the upcoming service. The idea of attending someone else's funeral doesn't appeal in the slightest. It's like watching somebody get a root canal when you're next in the dentist's chair.

Today isn't about me, though. Today is about *Allie*, and I will stand there and watch Freddie being put in the ground, even though it'll be like pulling teeth for me every single moment.

Allie smiles when I wake her gently, placing the tea down beside her. Then she remembers what's going to happen and has a little cry in my arms.

Yes, today is not a day to be concerned about what's going on in my stupid head. Today I am just a pair of arms and a soothing voice. This suits me just fine.

'Bloody hell, he was popular, wasn't he?' I say, dumbfounded, as we pull up at the graveyard and get out of the car. The place is *packed*. I've never seen so many people at a funeral in all of my life. There must be *four hundred* people here. No wonder the whole service was scheduled to take place out here in the open air. You'd never have fitted even half the people gathered into that small church.

Allie smiles and takes my hand. 'Yes. People loved him. He was a very special man.'

I look up and squint at the early autumnal sunshine. 'Good weather for it.' It's an asinine thing to say, but I'm still quite blown away by the amount of people who have turned out to see Freddie buried, so my mind's drifting a little.

'Yes, I suppose,' Allie replies. She then turns to give her mother, Jennifer, a weak smile, who returns it in kind. I would have liked to have met Jennifer and Allie's father, David, in better circumstances than at a funeral.

I just hope I get the chance to see them again before mine comes around.

Stop it. Arms and a soothing voice, remember!

I breathe deeply, give Allie's hand a comforting squeeze and start to walk with her towards the gathered mourners.

The ground where Freddie will be buried is close to the back of the graveyard. His casket sits by the side of the open grave, ready to be hoisted in by several black-clad pall-bearers, who are loitering discreetly off to one side. There's a fair bit of grass surrounding the grave, where the majority of the mourners are tightly packed. A space has been cleared right in front, into which Allie's family and I slot ourselves. To my left and right I can see Freddie's fellow Helmore Care Home residents, all decked out in funereal black like the rest of us. Most are sat down on foldaway chairs, as you'd expect due to their age and infirmity. Bernard looks close to tears, as does Deidre. Who can blame them?

The vicar looks reassuringly boring. There are no expensive suits or tans here. This man is all about the cassock, dog collar and soft voice, which is only right and proper.

It is with a soft voice that the vicar starts to tell Freddie's life story to us – and I have never heard anything so incredible in all of my life.

I knew Freddie Stockhouse was both an actor and a musician, but the extent of his career comes as a complete surprise.

'He knew *Laurence Olivier*?' I whisper to Allie from one side of my mouth.

'Yes,' Allie replies in an equally hushed voice. 'They used to get drunk on port and play cards badly. Olivier cheated a lot, apparently.'

It appears Freddie Stockhouse had done pretty much everything in his time on earth.

Other than curing cancer and climbing Mount Everest, the old bastard had accomplished practically every good thing there was to do in this life – and he travelled extensively across the planet to do it. His passport must have been as thick as a telephone directory.

From sailing around the Cape of Good Hope, to performing in front of the Japanese emperor's family, to starting a successful youth theatre in a deprived Indonesian village, this man had achieved so much it's a wonder he made it to eighty-seven without dropping dead years ago from overexertion.

The fact he did it all with barely two pennies to rub together half the time makes it all the more incredible. It seems Freddie was the living epitome of the phrase 'money can't buy you happiness'. It's a lesson I only started to learn myself a few months ago.

'*Lion taming?!*' I exclaim, my whisper so loud this time that Bernard looks up from his sad reverie for a moment to see what the noise is.

By the time the vicar is telling us about how Freddie gave up six months of his life to build toilets in Africa, I'm reeling.

So much *life*! So much *experience*! So much *time*!

No wonder there are so many people at this bloody funeral. Freddie Stockhouse must have met *thousands* of them during his life.

And here I am . . . barely into my thirties and I'm probably already *finished*.

Christ on a bike.

The open-air service takes a good half an hour to wrap up, such is the length of Freddie's obituary. Eventually, though, the vicar stands aside to allow the pall-bearers to do their job, and Freddie Stockhouse is slowly lowered into place, to the accompaniment of Frank Sinatra's 'That's Life'. This couldn't be more appropriate – especially given the fact that Sinatra apparently once spilled his drink over Freddie in a Las Vegas bar and offered him one of the showgirls as compensation.

While Ol' Blue Eyes sings, I do my job as a pair of arms and a soothing voice as Allie cries softly into my shoulder. Her mother, Jennifer, gives me a thankful look. I also think I see a little pity in there as well, which tells me Allie has very probably told her about my condition.

As the crowd starts to disperse on its way to the wake being held at Helmore Care Home, Allie and I linger by Freddie's grave for a while, letting the silence eventually wash over us as the graveyard empties.

'What a life,' I say softly, watching the wind pick up a few leaves from the grass in front of the grave.

'It was. The stories he used to tell me were quite amazing.'

'I wish . . . I wish . . .'

'That you'd got to know him better?'

'Er . . . yes, that's right.'

That wasn't what I was going to say.

What I want to say is that I wish I had the time afforded to me that Freddie had. But I can't say anything of the sort – because I'm a pair of arms and soothing voice today, and *nothing else.*

'Shall we go?' I say, turning to Allie to look at her. 'It's getting cold, and people will be expecting us.'

'In a while, please,' she replies. 'I'm just enjoying the peace and quiet at the moment.'

Allie might be enjoying the peace and quiet, but for me, it's *torture.* I need people around me. I need noise and distraction so my thoughts don't keep coming back to the fact that, compared to Freddie Stockhouse, I've had no life at all.

I manage to maintain my role as comforting arms and a soothing voice until about 7 p.m. By then I've had a couple of drinks and I'm tired from being on my feet all day. That bastard headache is back again as well, of course. Its presence is almost an inevitability now.

My resolve breaks as Allie and I are walking towards her flat, having been dropped off just up the road by her parents.

Checking Out

'Are you okay, Nathan?' Allie asks me as we amble along the road. 'You've been quiet for most of the day.'

'Have I?'

'Yes. When Bernard was talking to you about Freddie's time in Reluctant Badger, you didn't look like you were paying that much attention. I thought that's something you'd be really interested in.'

Damn it. I thought I'd done better at hiding how I was feeling throughout the day.

'Sorry. I . . . I had something on my mind.'

Allie pauses for a moment. 'Your illness?'

We haven't really talked about the tumour since she told me about Freddie's death. It's been better that way. 'Yeah, I guess,' I reply reluctantly.

Allie stops. 'Are you feeling all right? Is it hurting you? Oh, I'm so sorry, Nathan. I should have thought about it!'

'No! Please! Don't worry! I didn't want you to have to think about it, not with what's happened to you in the past few days. And I'm not feeling poorly, honestly! It's just that your grandad led such an amazing life and I've done nothing with mine . . . and now I'm not going to get the chance to change that, and I . . . I . . .'

Allie looks incredulous. 'What are you talking about? You *have* done things with your life! I've only known you a few months and I can see that as plain as day.'

I shake my head. 'You *say* that, but I don't *feel* it. There's so much I wanted to *do*, Allie . . . so much I wanted to *accomplish*, and now I won't, because I have no time.'

Oh great, now I'm getting tearful again. The dam that I'd rather effectively raised throughout the day in order to help Allie is crumbling away – and the problem with damming your emotions up is that when it breaks, those feelings come bursting through without any control.

Allie grabs my hand. 'You don't know that, Nathan! You don't know how long you have. You might have plenty of time!'

Nick Spalding

I pull away from her. I shouldn't, but it's a reflex action.

She doesn't understand!

'No, Allie. I *don't have time*!' I'm sounding angry now, and I don't want to – not today, not when I made a promise. 'I can't do anything! I can't go anywhere!' I look to the darkened skies. 'I'm frozen! Any second now it could end and I'm *terrified*! I've done nothing worthwhile and now I'm never going to get the chance to!' The look I give Allie is so full of self-pity that a part of me just wants to curl up and die. 'Your grandfather had eighty-seven years. He had a *life*. But you can't go dancing with royalty or tame any lions when you know you could drop dead at any moment!'

Allie steps forward. 'Nathan, I—'

I thrust out both hands. 'No! Please, Allie! I don't want to talk about it any more.' I stumble backwards. For some reason I have the overwhelming urge to get away from her – to get away from *everything*. I just need to be alone.

I look around for a cab and see one parked up at the top of the road. 'I'm going to go now.'

'No, Nathan, please stay with me!' Allie begs.

'I can't! I can't stay with you! I want to more than anything else in this world, but I CAN'T!'

And with that, I'm running away.

The tears blur my vision as I close in on the cab. I don't look back at Allie standing there on the street corner alone, because if I do I might just turn around and go back. And that would be a bad idea – because sooner or later, I'm going to have to go away *permanently* and there will be no turning back then.

I jump in the cab, wiping my eyes.

'Where to, mate?' the cabbie asks.

I think for a moment, trying desperately to marshal my thoughts. I need to get to somewhere alcoholic and quickly.

'The Elysium Bar . . . take me to the Elysium Bar,' I tell the cabbie, and slouch back into the seat, nibbling on one finger and staring into space at nothing.

***

Two hours later and I'm still staring into space, but for *vastly* different reasons. It's amazing how six double vodka and Cokes can change your perspective on life – largely from a vertical one to something more horizontal.

I'm about to order a very ill-advised shot of tequila from the barman when I feel a hand on my shoulder.

'Nathan!' a female voice says from behind me. I look around to see a brunette in a small black dress. It's testament to the power of vodka that it takes me a good ten seconds to realise that the voice belongs to someone I was sleeping with until fairly recently.

''llo, Sienna,' I tell her, affecting a smile. The last time I saw this woman I was throwing her out of my house, so I figure I can at least try to look pleased to see her to make up for it. Mind you, I'm so drunk, I probably just look like I've suffered a head injury.

. . . another head injury, I mean.

'How are you?' she asks, which is a loaded question, if ever there was one.

''nestly, Sienna? Been better.'

She affects a sympathetic look. 'That tumour thing again?' she says, like I have a nasty case of irritable bowel syndrome and not a life-threatening cerebrodondregliwhatshisface.

I stare at her for a second, trying to think of a response that doesn't involve too many swear words or spittle. 'Yeah. Still that tumour thing,' I eventually say.

'Aw man, that sucks.' Sienna says, which is probably the best I'm going to get out of her, sympathy-wise. She looks around for a second. 'Are you with anyone tonight?'

''scuse me?'

'Are you with anyone?' she asks again, curling an arm around my neck. 'Only I am. And I don't like it.' Her eyes have gone smoky. 'How about you and me go back to my flat and relive some good times?'

I look at her for a second in disbelief . . . and then burst out laughing, nearly falling off my bar stool as I'm consumed by maniacal giggles.

'What's so funny?' she asks, recoiling a little as I basically fall apart in front of her.

It takes a good few moments for me to get control of myself. I have no idea why her request is so hilarious . . . but it just *is*. 'I don't . . . I don't think that'd be a very good idea, Sienna,' I say, wiping my mouth. 'I might . . . I might drop dead b'fore you get my cock out.'

This makes me laugh so hard that I do indeed topple off the stool for a moment, one unsteady hand the only thing between my head and another concussion courtesy of the bar's edge.

Sienna's eyebrow arches as I sit back down carefully. 'Well, if you change your mind any time, then give me a call.' She runs a hand down my chest. 'I miss you, Nathan. We had a fun time together . . . we can again, if you like.'

This just sends me off into another huge gale of hysterics. For some reason, seeing Sienna and being offered sex with her so bluntly is possibly the most *ludicrous* thing I've ever experienced.

'Sure thing, Sienna!' I cry, tears of laughter in my eyes. 'Why not? After all . . . we've got all the time in the world, haven't we?'

'Yeah! Of course!' she replies, completely missing the point of both this conversation and my entire life.

A young black woman in an equally small blue dress approaches us. 'Sienna! We're going back to Sasha's place. She's got blow and a new hot tub!'

Sienna's eyes go wide. 'Wow, Nevaeh! That sounds great!' She turns and looks back at me. 'How about it, Nathan? You want to come back to Sasha's with us? You'll have a great time with all of us, I promise!' She holds out one hand towards me, an expectant look on her face.

I give Sienna and her extremely attractive friend a long, hard look and can instantly feel the axis of my world shifting beneath me.

This time it has nothing to do with the drink, though.

It would be so *easy*, wouldn't it?

. . . so easy to just get up, take Sienna's hand and follow her back to a flat I've never been to before, where drugs, sex and a hot tub await me.

I can take the path of least resistance. I can just fucking escape *everything*.

It's certainly something the old Nathan would have been well and truly up for – the Nathan that effectively stopped existing the second I walked out of Mr Chakraborty's office nearly six months ago.

But here and now, I can *be that Nathan again*. Tonight, I can *live that life again*.

No tumour. No death sentence. No time limit.

Wouldn't that just be *so* wonderful? To be *him* again? If only for a short while?

After all, what's really stopping me?

I'm half off the stool and reaching out to take Sienna's hand when Allie's face flashes through my mind. Not as it was the last time I saw her, in the street earlier tonight, but as it was the first time I ever saw her – red, blotchy and sweaty in that stupid Libby the Happy Lemon costume.

My hand, within touching distance of Sienna's, freezes in mid-air.

I'm going to die and nothing I do matters any more.

Except this.

Except *Allie*.

I slump back down on to the stool, feeling the world shift on its axis again.

'You go,' I tell Sienna with a smile. 'Go and have fun in the hot tub. I'm going to stay here and order another drink.'

'Okay,' Sienna replies, looking disappointed. 'But I'll see you again soon, yeah?' she says, as her friend grabs her arm and tries to lead her away.

I give Sienna a grave look. 'Yeah, sure,' I tell her – knowing full well that I'll probably never lay eyes on her again.

And with that, Sienna is pulled away from me, back into the crowd and out of my sight.

I turn back to the bar and order that tequila I'd promised myself.

'Don't you think you've had enough?' the barman asks, watching me sway back and forth on the stool.

I fix him with a drunken stare. 'Oh, good grief, *yes*,' I reply, with a smile on my face that doesn't reach my eyes.

This is the last coherent thought I have that evening.

. . . or for the *next two days*, for that matter.

WORTHWHILE

30 September

Somehow, I end up in Wales.

I remember rejecting Sienna's advances and necking the shot of tequila I eventually persuaded the barman to serve me, but after that things gets a bit, well, *hazy*.

At some point, my drink-addled brain decided it would be a good idea to take me on a magical mystery tour that eventually ended over forty-eight hours later in a place called Mumbles, just outside Swansea. Maybe it figured I could do with cheering up a bit and decided that no one can be truly that depressed in a place called Mumbles.

And it was absolutely right – up until the point the alcohol left my body.

This happened about fifteen minutes ago in a stream of vomit behind a wheelie bin parked outside a beach cafe that enjoys splendid views of the extremely picturesque Swansea Bay. It's just gone 10 a.m. on a brisk Saturday morning and I feel ugly as all sin.

I think I spent most of last night in a beach hut belonging to a hippy named Jeff T. You can ask me how I came to meet Jeff T and I'm sure I could make something up for you, but I doubt it would be close to the truth. I have a horrible feeling that the 'T' in Jeff T might stand for 'trafficker of narcotics', but I'm going to try my hardest not to pay attention to that fact . . . and hope that the local police don't, either.

Yes, Nathan James is in a sorry, sorry state as he orders a cup of very strong and very black coffee from the cafe owner, who has been giving me a strange look for the past ten minutes as I've sat huddled on one of his benches.

I've managed to retain all of my clothes, which is a saving grace, but I've been dressed in them for three days, which is not. If I go rummaging in my pockets I can find such wonderful souvenirs as a broken ballpoint pen from somewhere called Maple Heights Country Club, three small metal bolts, a torn set of instructions for an IKEA bed frame and a small, mouldy potato on which someone has scrawled in permanent black marker pen the legend 'Herman is bastard'. I'm assuming it was me.

The coffee warms me somewhat as I sit back on the bench and contemplate my next move. That starts with looking at my mobile phone properly for the first time in forty-eight hours.

Apparently, the heroic amount of alcohol I've consumed wasn't enough to stop me from sending text messages – unfortunately.

It appears I sent a text to Mum at some point in the early hours of the morning after Freddie's funeral, when she'd messaged me to find out where the hell I was. The text I sent said, 'Im fine mam. Just neededed som time on myy own. Will be back soone. Love u. And I need tim. I don't have tim. I love u but I donn have tim.'

My mother's reply was simply, 'Stay safe, and say hi to Tim if you find him.'

There's nothing from Allie, though.

Why should there be? I've put that poor girl through the bloody wringer, haven't I?

I currently have zero idea what the state of play is between us after my disappearing act, but I'd better call her and find out what it is. If this is the straw that breaks the camel's back and she wants to have nothing more to do with me, then I'll have to accept it. I've probably used up all of her goodwill at this point . . . and then some.

I am a stupid, selfish idiot – one who should apologise as quickly as possible. Not for the first time in my life, my thumb hovers over Allie's number. I press 'Dial', thumb shaking from a combination of cold and fear.

'Nathan?' she answers on the second ring.

'Hi,' I reply, wincing at the loudness of her voice.

'Where are you?'

'Mumbles.'

'Pardon?'

'I'm in Mumbles.'

There's a pause. 'The little town near Swansea?' She sounds amazed.

'Yes. How did you know that?'

'The coastguard dropped Grandad off there in 1965 after his raft sank. He was doing a charity race out from Weston-super-Mare and got a bit lost. Are you coming home?'

'Hopefully. Once I work out where the nearest public transport is.' I pause. 'You don't sound angry with me . . . Aren't you angry with me? After I left like that?'

She sighs. 'I was a little at first, and I was worried about you, too – but then I spoke to your mum, who told me she'd heard from you and that you'd probably be all right and would come home when you wanted to.'

That's my mother. She knows her ridiculous son so well.

'I'm sorry I ran away from you like that,' I say. 'I'm sorry I haven't been around to help you.'

'Don't be. It's actually given me the time I needed to do something. To arrange some stuff with you out of the way.'

Well, that's disconcerting. I thought Allie might be mad at me for buggering off on a two-day bender, but it appears she's quite happy about it, as it's given her time to catch up on some important admin. 'Um . . . okay. That's *good* . . . I guess?'

'Come home, Nathan. Come home *now*. I need to see you today, and I'm not taking no for an answer.'

'Yes, Allie.' I reply, sounding for all the world like a scolded little boy, which in many ways I am.

'Good. Call me when you're about an hour away from your house.'

'Okay, Allie, I will.'

'I'll see you later, then.'

Allie hangs up, leaving me sat on my cold stone bench, looking out to sea, with the wind whipping around my head and a headache clanging behind my eyes. I put up with this for about three minutes, before getting up and staggering over to the cafe owner to ask him where the nearest train station is.

It's in Swansea, so my next stop is the nearest taxi rank – but not before I divert into Boots to buy some painkillers, a bottle of Lucozade and a travel-sized can of deodorant.

I make it home – more or less in one piece – about five hours later. They are five hours spent mostly sleeping and dribbling in a pool of my own stink. I'm basically one of those train passengers you always do your best to avoid when you're choosing which carriage to sit in.

An hour away, I call Allie as I promised I would. She is quite curt with me, which I would feel more hurt about were it not for the fact that my head is pounding so hard I have to take another three painkillers just to get it to calm down enough to see straight.

Eventually, the taxi carrying me to my door from the train station turns into my road. I've consumed three bottles of Evian, which has helped with the headache and the dry mouth, but this has also woken up my digestive system. I am in dire need of a bacon sandwich.

Instead of bacon, though, I get a lemon.

And a toffee.

And an orange, a sausage and a block of cheese.

The taxi bumps up on to my driveway – and standing there are The Foodies.

. . . minus Herman the Grumpy Potato.

Quite clearly I'm suffering from some kind of alcohol poisoning that's causing hallucinations.

'Um . . . can you see that?' I ask the cabbie.

'The five idiots at the end of your drive dressed as The Foodies?' he replies.

'Yes.'

'Yes.'

'Thank you.'

'My two youngest love The Foodies,' he remarks, taking the cash from my hand. 'Can't get enough of 'em.'

'Good for them,' I tell him.

As the cab backs out of the drive, I slowly walk towards the living, breathing embodiments of my overactive imagination with severe trepidation. Libby the Happy Lemon steps forward and lifts up the top part of her head.

'Hello, Nathan,' Allie says to me.

'Hi,' I reply. 'What's . . . what's going on?'

Allie thinks for a moment. 'Let's call it a wake-up call, if you like.'

'A what?'

She gives me a look and takes my arm. 'Come on, Nathan James. I have something to show you that you really need to see.' She looks over at her fellow Foodies. 'Okay, guys, in you go. I doubt they'll wait for much longer.'

The Foodies all give Allie a thumbs up.

'Um . . . where's Herman?' I ask, as she leads me up towards my front door.

'He's not invited,' Allie tells me. 'Not here. Not today.'

For some reason, this makes me *unaccountably* happy.

As we approach the front door, I see my mother standing there, her expression a mixture of happiness and apprehension. 'Hi, sweetheart,' she says with a smile, before it slips off her face. 'This was all Allie's idea. Just in case, you know . . .'

'Know what?' I try to say to Mum, but Allie is now propelling me through the doorway and into the hall, before I get the chance to learn more.

'Right. Stand there,' she orders. 'I've gone to a lot of trouble to set this up and I want it to all go to plan.' She looks at her fellow Foodies again, who are now lined up in front of the closed kitchen door. 'Okay, you lot. Are you ready?'

There's a chorus of agreement from the costumed actors. I swear I can hear Jonathan and Hamish's voices amongst them, which must mean they've managed to patch things up. I do hope Hamish can keep his anger management issues under control. I'm in no fit state to break up a fight today.

'Great, guys. Let's do it like we practised, then,' she tells them, and flips the top of her Libby head back down again. She then looks at me. 'It's time for you to see what you've accomplished, Nathan James. To see what you've done that's *worthwhile*,' Libby says, in her muffled, lemony voice. She then fumbles open the kitchen door and parades into the kitchen, the rest of The Foodies in her wake. There is a roar of approval as they do this.

Children.

There are *children* in my house.

I'm suddenly frozen to the spot.

'You'd better go in there,' Mum says from beside me. 'She's put a lot of effort into this over the past couple of days. That girl is one of a kind, my son.'

I give her a wild-eyed look, but do as I'm told.

I hesitantly go through into the open-plan space that comprises my kitchen, dining room and lounge. Through the now legendary expensive bifold patio doors at the end, I can see that my well-manicured garden is chock-a-block with children – a good *thirty* of them. 'Oh my good fucking Christ,' I moan quietly.

I take a few steps forward, my legs a bit shaky. Looking to my right, I can see Eliza crouched down in front of my stereo system. She gives me a wave. 'Hello, Nate,' she says with a grin. 'Nice to see you made it back in one piece! Stand by for some fun!'

'Fun?' I say in a shocked voice, which elicits a high-pitched bray of laughter from my cousin.

Looking ahead again, I can see that Allie and the rest of the crew have now lined up at the bifold doors. I walk forward to get a better (worse?) view of proceedings. Eliza presses 'Play' on the stereo and I hear the soundtrack to the song 'Come on, Give Us a Hug' fire up.

The Foodies then launch into the dance routine for the song, which involves much hugging of one another and the children gathered. The kids are having a bloody good time with it, as they always seem to.

Among the throng of kids is one I instantly recognise. Callum is haring around the garden like a thing possessed. He's dressed in his customary Foodies T-shirt and is being chased by another boy wearing one, too. The other boy catches up with Callum and grabs hold of him, sending both boys tumbling to the ground. For a moment, my heart races, wondering how Callum will react to this, but then he's back on his feet, giggling his head off and hugging the other boy. I've never seen him look so *happy*.

The Foodies have now reached the chorus of the song. This is normally when Herman is supposed to give in and allow himself to be hugged by his Foodie pals.

To my horror, though, Allie has changed the lyrics somewhat. It's been accomplished quite awkwardly on the audio track that's belching out from the stereo. All she's done is record over one existing lyric with her own voice . . . but it's a profound change that makes me groan out loud.

'Come on, give us a hug, *Nathan*! Come on, don't be shy!' the audio track now goes.

Actually, it's 'Come on, give us a hug, Her-*Nathan*,' as Allie hasn't quite got the timing right, but we'll let her off, as she's done all this in two days.

All The Foodies now start to beckon me over into the garden. It is quite apparent that I am now supposed to take the place of Herman the Grumpy Potato in the dance routine.

I quite literally want to die.

No, I *don't*.

Yes, I *do*.

I can't move my legs. My head shakes back and forth slowly as I realise that I am meant to be the centre of attention here and there's very little I can do about it. Allie obviously has a point to prove, and she's not going to let me go until it's well and truly made.

The chorus plays once more and now the children have joined in. Still I can't bring myself to move into the garden. I know I should just do what I'm told, but I'm paralysed by an overwhelming fear that I neither understand nor can do anything about.

The chorus plays for a *third* time and still they beckon me forward. Callum in particular is wildly gesturing for me to come forward. It doesn't make any difference, though. My feet are still firmly rooted to the spot.

Then I feel a comforting hand close around my arm.

'Come on, sweetheart, let's go out there,' Mum says.

I look down at her. 'I . . . don't think I can,' I tell her in a small voice.

I feel a hand on my other arm. 'Of course you can, Nate.' It's Eliza. 'We're with you. And we love you.'

'Let's go, Nathan,' Mum says again. 'Your girlfriend is waiting for you.'

'Why is all this happening, Mum?' I plead, still not quite sure why I have a house full of people.

Mum smiles. 'Let her explain, Nathan. Let her explain.'

And with that, Mum and Eliza gently propel me into the garden and into the large foam rubber arms of Libby the Happy Lemon.

As soon as she takes me in a tight embrace, I am instantly surrounded by the children, who all go in for a mass hug. Tiny arms close themselves around both Libby and me, and I find myself wrapped in a warm cocoon of giggles and shrieks.

I look down to see Callum squeezing my leg the tightest. He is looking up and, for what feels like the first time in my life, he's smiling at me.

It is, I have to say, a rather *wonderful* thing to experience.

The chorus of 'Come on, Give Us a Hug' repeats a few more times until it fades. It's only when Eliza switches the music off completely that the hug ends and the children break away to go and be with their parents at the rear of the garden. Callum is the last to leave me, giving my leg an extra-tight squeeze before he goes to join Eliza.

'What's all of this about, Allie?' I ask as she flips up the top half of her Libby head so I can see her properly again. She looks just as sweaty and red as the first time we met. For a split second, I think back to almost taking Sienna's hand at the Elysium Bar and instantly feel *very* grateful that I didn't.

'It's simple, Nathan. You told me you didn't think you'd accomplished anything. You said you'd never done anything worthwhile.' She holds out a hand, indicating the crowd of people. 'Well, here you go. Here's how wrong you are.'

'I don't . . . I don't understand.'

She turns and fixes me with a firm gaze. 'These *children*, Nathan. These children *love you.*'

I shake my head. 'No, they don't. They love *you*. They love The Foodies.'

She punches me lightly on the arm. 'You *are* The Foodies, you idiot! Don't you think they *know* that? Look at them. Look at them *properly* for once in your life!'

I do as I'm told and see the faces of thirty happy children beaming right back at me. Not at Libby or Smedley or Chewy, but *at me*. I spot Callum and his new friend, now with their arms around one another. Eliza's son is smiling at me with what feels like the ferocity of a thousand suns.

And this is the moment that it hits me. It *finally* hits me.

That maybe – just maybe – The Foodies *do* mean something. That they aren't just a pay cheque and an embarrassment. That the strange and bizarre singing foodstuffs that I made up in a hurry all those years ago aren't just a load of throwaway rubbish. Not to these kids, anyway.

I've been searching for a way to leave my mark on the world ever since I was diagnosed with that stupid tumour – and it's been staring me in the face this entire time. I've *already done it*.

Gosh.

'You make them happy, Nathan. *You*,' Allie tells me. 'And thousands more like them, out there in the world. Do you know how *valuable* that is? To make a child *happy*?'

I stand there slack-jawed for a moment, before gathering my thoughts. 'No. I didn't. Not until now, anyway, I guess,' I tell her in a husky voice.

Allie looks up at me, a hopeful expression on her face. 'Do you get it *now*, Nathan? Do you finally understand what you've *done*? What makes you *worthwhile*?'

A tear gently courses its way down my cheek. 'Yes. I suppose I do.' I look at all of the children gathered in front of me. 'How could I not?'

When I turn back to Allie, though, there's confusion in my eyes. 'But why have you gone to all the trouble to show me this, Allie? After all, you've only known me a short time and, well . . . you know what's going to happen to me. You know what's coming.' I can barely say the words. 'I probably don't have . . . have much time.'

She looks to the sky for a moment, before gazing back at me again. 'I know, Nathan, I know. And don't think I don't realise that. Don't think I haven't thought *long* and *hard* about all of this. About what might happen to you, and what that might mean for me . . .'

'And?'

She smiles, tears in her eyes. 'And it's *okay*. I can accept it. I *do* accept it. I don't know how much time we have, but I know I want to spend that time with *you*.'

I'm dumbfounded. 'Why? Why would you *do* that?'

Allie rolls her eyes. 'Because I'm *in love with you*, you bloody idiot. And love doesn't care about time.'

Then she's kissing me.

I'm crying, she's crying, and she's kissing me.

My time is short and my life hangs in the balance – but none of that matters right now, because I *have* left my mark, I *have* done something worthwhile, but most of all . . . because *she is kissing me.*

And my headache is gone.

MOMENTS

20 JANUARY

. . . still here.

Surprised?

I know I am.

I bet you were expecting a different ending to this story, weren't you? Especially after that last bit.

You knew what was coming. It's been there ever since that first fateful meeting with Mr Chakraborty, when my pronunciation of cere-brodondreglioma was unconvincing, to say the least. All through this, my death has loomed large over proceedings – the final and inevitable denouement to this sad little tale. It had to be the way things ended, didn't it? *Surely?* With poor old Nathan Michael James breathing his last?

Maybe you thought Allie would take over for this last bit, just to wrap things up after my departure. A final chapter written by her about my funeral, possibly. It would certainly have served more narrative sense and would have been the predictable note to end things on.

My life, though, as has hopefully been made quite obvious by now, is not *predictable*. Not in the slightest.

. . . nor is yours, for that matter.

I should be dead. I should have done the decent bloody thing and popped my clogs at the correct moment, just to give this story the ending you've been expecting.

And yet here I still am. Still kicking and screaming.

Chakraborty is amazed.

But not half as amazed as I am!

I'm still sick, don't misunderstand me. I haven't been visited by a magical tumour-curing fairy. Herman is still there, biding his time and waiting for the moment to strike.

I still have headaches – sometimes they are debilitating, sometimes they're not so bad. When Allie's by my side they never seem quite so dreadful, that's for certain. The tremor in my left hand comes and goes more often as well, so I don't get to play the guitar as much as I'd like – but when it's not there I make sure I pick up my guitar and play, just like yesterday, and windmill my arm around until it's too sore to lift.

I don't get the bad dreams any more – that's certainly a saving grace. My nights are peaceful with Allie by my side, breathing softly and dribbling a bit into the pillow.

Allie is with me pretty much *all* of the time now, actually. After all, we have a lot of love to share and not much time to do it in.

We've started a new kid's music club at the local community centre together. Callum was the first to sign up. He can already play the C and G chords on his tiny new guitar.

I'm still scared, I won't lie to you. But these days, I have Allie to kiss the fear away, which is just about the best thing in the universe.

. . . and I'm *learning*.

Learning what's really important.

I've stopped worrying so much about what's *going* to happen or what has *already* happened and I'm thinking more and more about what *is*. Right *now*. In front of me.

And what's in front of me is *life*.

Glorious, glorious *life* – with all its frailties, frustrations and strife. With all its passion, brilliance and excitement.

There's nothing quite like it, you know.

You should have a go at it sometime. It really is quite worth it.

I may have only a small amount of time left to me, but that doesn't mean I have *no* time. It doesn't mean I can't *enjoy* my life.

Because what a waste that would be, eh?

What a huge waste of effort on the part of the universe it would have been to have created something as *wonderful* as Nathan James – only for me not to have any fun with it. To not cherish each and every moment afforded to me on this strange and confusing planet we all live on.

Because that's all I have. That's all *any* of us have.

Moments.

Moments captured between a void.

I fully intend to celebrate every one of those moments the best way I can, no matter what they are.

The soothing sound of my mother's voice. The giggle of a happy child with a new best friend. The sound of a clear, crisp guitar chord. The kiss from the woman I love first thing in the morning and the lovely cup of tea I make for us both right after.

So, it's time for me to say goodbye now, my friend, and to wish you well.

I'm quite busy, you see.

There are moments to be had.

ABOUT THE AUTHOR

Photo © 2017 Chloe Waters

Nick Spalding is the bestselling author of ten novels, two novellas and two semi-fictional memoirs. Nick worked in media and communications for most of his life before turning his energy to genre-spanning humorous writing. He lives in the south of England with his wife.